Somebody's

Knocking

at My Door

FRANCIS RAY

Somebody's

Knocking

at My Door

 ST. MARTIN'S GRIFFIN NEW YORK

www.stmartins.com

Library of Congress Cataloging-in-Publication Data

Ray, Francis.
    Somebody's knocking at my door / Francis Ray.—1st ed.
        p.   cm.
    ISBN 0-312-30734-9
    1. Adult child abuse victims—Fiction.   2. Parent and adult child—Fiction.
3. Terminally ill parents—Fiction.   4. African American men—Fiction.   5.
Fathers and sons—Fiction.   6. Family violence—Fiction.   I. Title: Somebody's
knocking at my door.   II. Title.

PS3568.A9214S66   2003
813'.54—dc21
                                                                          2002045249

First Edition: May 2003

10   9   8   7   6   5   4   3   2   1

This book is dedicated to my mother, Mrs. Venora Radford,
who always believed I could do or be anything I wanted to be,
and who refused to let me think otherwise.
I love you, Mama.

acknowledgments

As always I want to thank God. Without His blessings this book would not have been written.

My gratitude also goes to the following:

Alvena B. McNeil of New Orleans, Louisiana. You never tired of answering my questions about your wonderful city and the fascinating people who live there. I appreciate you so very much.

Adolphus Green, Career Education Instructor at South Oak Cliff High School in the Dallas Independent School District in Dallas, Texas. You were gracious enough to invite me into your woodshop and patiently explain the equipment and procedures involved with cabinetry. Your students are fortunate to have you.

The sensational staff at my library branch, Polk Wisdom, in Dallas, Texas. Dorothy Dozier, Sharon McCollins, Carole Bonner, Kronda Rolfe, and Anita Tolbert, you guys are the best. Your continued help with research throughout my career has been immeasurable.

And again to my husband, William H. Ray, and my daughter, Carolyn Michelle Ray. I am blessed by your love and thankful for your support.

Somebody's
Knocking
at My Door

one

"Kristen, sorry to keep you waiting."

Kristen Wakefield turned from studying the oil-on-canvas painting in the antebellum home of Claudette Laurent to see Claudette's husband, Maurice, striding confidently across the drawing room toward her. Gossip had flowed like a river when he had married the wealthy and middle-aged socialite four months ago. Not only was he a junior salesman with the insurance brokerage firm she'd inherited from her father, he was ten years younger. Many thought Maurice had used his charm and good looks to take unfair advantage of Claudette's grief over her father's death several months ago. Kristen hadn't been one of the gossipers.

When her widowed mother had unexpectedly fallen in love with Kristen's godfather, Jonathan Delacroix, Kristen had almost ruined their relationship because of her own recent disaster with love. If Claudette had found happiness, Kristen wished her all the best.

"Hello, Maurice, I was just enjoying looking at the paintings." Kristen extended her hand. "I think Claudette has the finest collection of nineteenth-century art by people of color in the country."

Fit and trim in a tailored, gray pinstriped suit, Maurice smiled graciously as he took her hand into his. She was amazed to find his hand surprisingly soft. "Thank you. Claudette will be happy to hear that. She respects you and your opinion highly."

"I feel the same way about her." Kristen caught a whiff of expensive cologne as she glanced around the spacious room with its high ceilings, meticulously restored eighteenth-century furnishings, and gleaming Waterford chandeliers. "You have a magnificent home. I wish it was daylight so I could see the grounds."

"Thank you," he said, obviously delighted. "You'll have to come back and we can give you a tour. We love it here. It's close enough to New Orleans for business, but far enough away for us to have our privacy."

"You certainly have the best of two worlds." Kristen gently tugged her hand free when he gave no indication of releasing it. "Will Claudette be joining us soon?"

Maurice shook his head of neatly trimmed black hair, the expression on his amber-hued face saddened. "I'm afraid not."

Dismay surged within Kristen, who was acting on behalf of the Haywood Museum in New Orleans. It had taken months to coordinate their schedules.

"Claudette's plane has been delayed in Baton Rouge. She won't be back until much later tonight," Maurice told her.

Kristen groaned silently in disappointment. But this wouldn't be the first time a potential donor to the museum had cancelled on her. The very fact that they could donate money or loan valuable pieces for exhibition meant they were wealthy and the demands on them usually high. Claudette wasn't a figurehead; she worked in the firm, just as her father had done before his death.

The important thing Kristen had to remember was that Claudette was interested in helping the museum increase its collection of nineteenth-century African-American art by placing her extensive collection on permanent loan and influencing her friends in the art circle of New Orleans to do the same.

"I understand. Please let Claudette know that I'll call in a couple of days and make another appointment." Kristen extended her hand again. "If you'll call your driver to take me back to the city, I'll say good night."

"Nonsense." Maurice caught her hand, then deftly stepped beside her, his other hand going around her slim waist. Kristen couldn't help her start of surprise. He didn't appear to notice. "I just got off the phone with Claudette. She feels terrible that she couldn't meet with you. She made me promise to go on with dinner as planned."

"That's really not necessary," Kristen told him, trying to move away.

"Claudette and I disagree," he said, steering her smoothly out of the drawing room and into a garden room down the wide hallway. A cozy table for three waited. A bottle of vintage wine peeked from a silver ice bucket. Flickering white candles surrounded by creamy orchids provided the centerpiece. The heavy scent of flowers hung in the air. Through the curved, multipaned windows behind them, light reflected off the Mediterranean-blue water in the rectangular-shaped swimming pool.

Releasing her arm, Maurice stepped behind a chair and pulled it out. "While we eat, you and I can become better acquainted and you can tell me about how you want Claudette's help. I'd like to offer my assistance as well."

Kristen stared at the gracious smile on her host's face and sank into the cream-and-blue silk padded armchair. Perhaps the evening wouldn't be a waste after all. "Thank you."

"The pleasure is mine." His fingertips grazed her bare shoulders as he removed his right hand from her chair.

Kristen flinched in surprise, but Maurice was already taking his seat. Her frown disappeared as quickly as it had come. It had been an accident. She'd dressed for dinner and worn an off-the-shoulder black dress. If her hair had been down as usual, it wouldn't have happened.

Taking his seat across from her, Maurice pulled the bottle of Dom Perignon from the antique ice bucket and filled her glass. "This is one of my favorites. I visited their vineyards when I was in France last year. You've been to Paris, of course."

"Several times," Kristen replied, trying to get over the inexplicable need to rub the spot where he'd touched. "The last time was three years ago. Dr. Robertson was kind enough to give me an extended leave from the museum to obtain my master's. I traveled extensively for a year, doing a work-study program with the top museums in the world before returning here two years ago."

He replaced the bottle, his gaze holding hers. "The Parisians have a unique way of looking at love and sex. If it feels good, do it. They aren't bothered by inhibitions."

"I suppose," Kristen replied, a bit surprised by the shift in topics. "But as I said, I went there to study and learn about art."

"But making love is an art." He picked up his glass. "To art and nineteenth-century paintings by people of color."

Kristen reached for her glass. After living in New Orleans off and on for seven years, she'd discovered many people here were more casual in their conversations about sex. While she had yet to get used to such frankness, she realized dealing with Orleans required an open mind. "To nineteenth-century paintings by people of color."

Over the rim of his glass, Maurice watched her as he drank. Moistening her lips, she twisted uneasily in her seat, set the wine down, then reached for her water goblet.

His dark eyes narrowed. "The wine isn't to your liking?"

"It's fine." She set the crystal glass on the linen tablecloth with a hand that wasn't quite steady. "What time is Claudette's flight getting in?"

He smiled, showing perfect teeth, and rang a small, silver bell on the table. "Hours yet."

The words were barely out of his mouth before a young woman in a black uniform with a white organza apron pushed in a serving cart. Lifting the silver domes, she placed a bowl of lobster bisque in front of each of them, removed the third place setting, then discreetly withdrew.

Maurice picked up his soup spoon. "Now, tell me how Claudette and I can help your project."

Relaxing, Kristen placed her damask napkin in her lap, picked up her spoon, and tried to comply. "In the 1850s people of color helped shape New Orleans into the city it is today. They dominated the craft-related trades. Perhaps in no other city in America did they express themselves in the arts so eloquently."

"There is no other city like Orleans," Maurice said, sipping his wine.

"I agree," Kristen said. "The French Quarter lures millions each year but how many are aware that the black iron grillwork surrounding the courtyards and on the many balconies was designed and made by people of color?"

"I certainly wasn't."

Kristen couldn't hide her astonishment. "One of Claudette's ancestors was an ironsmith. Didn't she tell you?"

He smiled charmingly. "She might have mentioned it, but we're still newlyweds."

"Of course," Kristen said, but she remained puzzled. Her mother and Jonathan shared everything. So did her brother, Adam, and his wife, Lilly.

"Please continue," Maurice said as the maid removed their soup bowls and placed artichoke salads in front of them.

"I want to make sure the contributions of the painters of that era are not forgotten. Artists such as Johnson and Tanner. Tanner, like many of his white contemporaries, had to go to Paris to study, to fulfill his dream of becoming an artist. He and other artists like him painted what was in vogue at that time—portraits, landscapes, and religious pieces. Although many artists of color were successful, a large number of their works was lost as time and neglect took its toll."

Maurice's fork poised over his salad. "And you want to change that? How commendable."

Kristen smiled, pleased that he understood. "I admire the courage and grit of Tanner and artists of color who pursued their dreams regardless of the fact that in 1891 people of color were thought of as inferior in America. However, too little of their work is on permanent exhibition in major museums where they can be seen and appreciated on a daily basis. Even less is noted in art textbooks."

"How many are there on permanent exhibition in the Haywood Museum?" he asked.

Kristen sighed and leaned back in her chair. "Three. Two from Claudette and one from a friend of my stepfather's."

Disbelief crossed Maurice's face. "That's disgraceful! Something has to be done."

"I'm so glad you understand," she told him, her meal forgotten. "It's important to bridge the gap between modern African-American artists and the forerunners of centuries ago, men and women who by their dedication and hard work paved the way for today's artists to be able to express themselves any way they choose.

"They didn't paint about the 'black experience' but from the heart. Their struggles and triumphs are not in the art textbooks, but they deserve to be told," Kristen said with absolute conviction as the maid removed her untouched salad and placed grilled swordfish with lemon and herbs in its place. "The ability to create and appreciate art comes from within and not from the pigment of one's skin."

Ignoring his food also, Maurice propped his elbows on the table and linked his fingers. "This is very important to you, isn't it?"

"Yes, it's something I've wanted to do since I read Dr. Driskell's book, *Two Centuries of Black Art*, when I was in grade school," she told him. "My mother paints as a hobby and I grew up surrounded by art. I was fortunate to learn early about their contributions."

"Is your mother as beautiful as you, *chérie*?" he asked, his gaze steady, his voice husky.

Kristen blinked. "What?"

He laughed playfully and picked up his wineglass. "Forgive me. My Creole ancestry is showing. Claudette is forever after me. Please continue."

Kristen felt gauche. She'd never been able to accept a compliment with aplomb. "Too much of their contribution has been lost or ignored. If Claudette were to make an indefinite loan of perhaps four more of her paintings, I feel sure, because of her reputation in the art community, others would follow. Gradually I could build a permanent collection at the museum and do a definitive background search on the artist and the work itself. Perhaps publish a paper."

"Then there might be a way for me to help you." His intense gaze locked on her, he drained his glass for the second time. "I have a great deal of influence on my wife. I might be persuaded to use it on your behalf."

Kristen simply stared. The uneasiness that had been circling her crouched down in front of her like a waiting tiger with teeth bared. "What are you talking about?"

Calmly, Maurice refilled his glass. "I can be very discreet."

Stunned with disbelief, Kristen continued to stare across the table at Maurice. He sipped his wine and acted as if he'd asked her to pass the salt.

But what burned her was that he had the colossal audacity to think she'd accept his crude offer. Just like Eric, a man she'd foolishly thought she loved. He'd loved only himself.

She shot to her feet. She wasn't twenty and starry-eyed with love as she had been seven years ago. "Please tell your driver I'm ready to leave."

Maurice leaned back casually in his chair. "Oh, I don't think so."

Her anger almost choked her. "You can't possibly think I'll agree to anything so coarse and demeaning."

"I have a lot of influence on Claudette. Her love and devotion to me is unquestionable. I can use my influence to help you or crush you. You have something you want, and I can help you get it." His eyes roamed over her, lingering hungrily at her breasts. "But in exchange you have something I want."

"I'm going home if I have to walk." She tossed her napkin down and started for the door.

"If you leave, you can kiss your job at the museum good-bye," he threatened as he came to his feet.

She whirled back. "Just try it!"

"I'll do more than try," he warned, then rounded the table, blocking her path to the door. "I've done some checking on you since Claudette introduced us at the opera several weeks ago. Dr. Robertson might think highly of you, but Smithe, the chief curator, isn't so keen on having an assistant who wants to have her own program instead of helping him with his. He personally told me he'd like to get rid of you at the first opportunity."

She wanted to deny Maurice's words, but couldn't. Dr. Smithe had been hired six months ago and Kristen could do nothing to please him. He was a petty art snob who thought she had acquired her job because of her family connections, not because she'd rightly earned it.

"Smithe needn't distress you, Kristen," Maurice placated as he watched her closely. "With my help you can have his job in a couple of years. You and I will make your vision a reality, then *your* name will be *in* textbooks." His voice filled with seductive charm, he moved closer. "If you're worried about the servants there is no need. I instructed them to leave after the entrée was served. Claudette will never know." He took another step. "I'm an excellent lover. Let's go upstairs where I can show you."

All too clearly, Kristen remembered Eric in his hotel room in New York taunting and jeering, baiting her with his depravity the same way. Her stomach churned just as it had done then. "I'm going to be sick."

Maurice jumped back in distaste, all lazy seduction gone. "The powder room is down the hall. Second door on the left."

She took off running, her heels clicking on the hardwood floor, then muted on priceless Persian rugs. Her heart beating wildly, she burst into the half-bath, locking the door behind her.

Trembling violently, she leaned her head back against the door and closed her eyes. She thought she had grown up since her disaster with Eric. But apparently she was still as naive as she had been then. This time she'd let ambition blind her. Opening her eyes, she glanced around the elegantly appointed, windowless room.

A knock on the door snapped her head around. "Are you all right?" Maurice inquired.

Telling Maurice to go straight to hell might be satisfying, but it wouldn't give her the time she needed to think of a way out of this mess. Replicating gagging sounds, she repeatedly flushed the commode. "Eh, I'll come back."

Hearing him move away, Kristen plopped down on the padded commode seat. She was safe for the moment, but she was also ten miles from New Orleans' city limit and seventeen miles from her apartment. How could she get out of this sticky situation? A taxi wasn't about to come this far out of the city for a fare, and even if one did, she'd have to deal with Maurice before she reached the front door.

Propping her elbow on her thigh, she rested her chin on the top of her hand and cursed Maurice's deceitfulness. Having grown up where having a driver was the norm, she'd thought nothing of his offer to send a car for her when he'd called her office that afternoon to confirm her dinner appointment with Claudette. It had made perfect sense to Kristen, since she was unfamiliar with the location of the estate, that he didn't want her traveling the winding, narrow road at night alone. She'd believed he was being thoughtful.

He had set her up and she'd fallen for it. She bit her lower lip. What was she going to do? Despite Dr. Smithe's animosity, she enjoyed her job and didn't want to lose it because of a loathsome man like Maurice. Besides, there wasn't another museum or institution in the city where she would have an opportunity to increase awareness of nineteenth-century African-American art . . . if she were fortunate enough to be hired after they learned she'd been fired.

She didn't have any doubt in her mind that Smithe would fire her on the spot if there were even a hint of scandal or the possibility of her upsetting a major benefactor of the museum. The director, Dr. Robertson, was a fair man, but he had the reputation of the museum to think about. Maurice had obviously taken that into consideration when he set his plan in motion.

Kristen had to think of a solution that would get her safely out of this situation without causing herself, Claudette, or the museum any embarrassment. Besides, she genuinely admired and liked Claudette. Apparently she wasn't aware of the type of man she'd married. And Kristen wasn't going to tell her.

Claudette was a gracious, courteous woman, but she struck Kristen as the kind who protected what was hers. Maurice was right about one thing: Claudette was madly in love with him. Kristen had no experience with a mutual loving relationship, but she'd seen how her mother, first with Kristen's father and then with Jonathan, and her brother with his wife, stood behind their spouses. So would Claudette. There was no way Kristen would come out on top if word of this got out.

So . . . what to do?

Her gaze fell on the bronze bust of David beside the mauve embroidered hand towels on the marble vanity. Picking it up, she hefted it in her hand. The fantasy of hitting Maurice over the head lasted less than five seconds before she replaced the bust. Giving the husband of one of the largest benefactors of the museum a concussion, no matter how deserved, seemed a sure way to create a scandal that neither Claudette nor the museum would appreciate.

Frowning, she cut a glance at the closed door. With all the rumors flying around about Maurice marrying Claudette for her money and his lack of personal funds, Kristen hadn't heard anything about him being a womanizer. She wasn't going to be the one to spread that tale. The only person she'd confide in would be Angelique.

Angelique.

Kristen straightened, her fingers fumbling in excitement to open her purse. Grabbing her cell phone, she punched "speed dial" for her best friend and next-door neighbor, Angelique Fleming. In both her professional and her private life, Angelique handled men with ease. She would know what to do. After the tenth ring, Kristen slumped against the back of the commode. Angelique didn't believe in cell phones or answering machines.

Disconnecting, she dialed information, then punched in another number. A deep, gravelly voice answered on the third ring. "The Inferno."

In the background Kristen could hear loud music and the louder, rambunctious voices of men. "May I speak to Angel, please? It's an emergency."

"Angel's not here." The line went dead.

Kristen stared at the phone. What did she do now?

"Kristen. Kristen."

Kristen jerked upright and stood.

"Come on out so we can talk."

"Not until I know the driver is with you," she told him flatly.

The doorknob rattled. "This is ridiculous. Open this door!"

She jumped at what sounded like the flat of his hand banging against the door.

"Open up or you'll be sorry!" he yelled, his voice rising.

"You're going to be the sorry one when my friend gets here," she said, hoping she was convincing and forever thankful that the oak door was solid.

"Whom did you call?" he asked, sounding worried.

Wishing she could take a small amount of satisfaction in the sudden fear in his voice, she said, "You'll see when he gets here."

Maurice pounded on the door again. "You're lying. You wouldn't dare call anyone and risk your job or having Claudette find out. Now open this damn door!"

"If I were you I'd leave. He's built like a Mack truck and crazy about me."

"Now I *know* you're lying," he chuckled nastily. "You aren't dating anyone. Smithe thinks you're frigid, but all it takes is the right man."

"You both can go to hell!" she yelled, infuriated with them because they had discussed her, and with herself that she let it matter. She wasn't frigid, she was selective. "I'm going to enjoy seeing him beat you to a pulp."

The doorknob rattled. "I'm going to find the key and when I get back I'll take you right there on the floor."

Fear made her tremble. She had to get out of here. But how? Maurice was right. There was no man in her life.

two

Rafe Crawford was a solitary man. It was not the life he would have chosen, but he had been given little choice in the matter.

He'd come to New Orleans twelve years ago with little more than the clothes on his back. At first he'd just wanted to wake up without fear, but in trying to blot out the past by working long hours as a cabinetmaker's helper, Rafe had discovered he had a talent for making furniture reproductions. He had an eye for detail and the patience it took to duplicate furniture the way it had been crafted a hundred years ago.

Rafe heard the phone ring and dismissed it. That's what he had the answering machine for. He had few friends, and it wasn't likely a client would call after nine at night. Besides, he didn't like to stop in the middle of a cut. He prided himself on his workmanship.

His work was all he had. The only legacy he would leave behind, and he intended it to be the best. The Crawford name would mean something beside hate and cruelty. His hands clenched, but they remained steady. He'd had plenty of practice controlling his anger.

He heard the distinctive click of the answering machine and prepared to duplicate the straight cut on the other side of the walnut board in his large hands. The thirty-six-inch length of wood would be one of five shelves in a highboy he was making for an exacting and very wealthy client in Natchez.

"Rafe! Rafe? Please be there. This is Kristen. I need you."

Rafe's head came up, and he quickly drew the wood toward him out of harm's way.

"Rafe, please be there."

Flipping off the switch, he set the wood aside. Fear as he had known it few times in his life propelled him across the large room. The only reason he could think of for Kristen calling was because something had happened to his stepmother, Lilly, or her son and Rafe's little brother, Adam Jr. He'd seen Kristen over the years. They'd been polite strangers, drawn together because her brother had married Rafe's stepmother after she'd divorced Rafe's father.

He snatched the receiver from the wall. "This is Rafe. What's the matter?"

"Oh, Rafe, thank goodness!"

"What is it? Is it Lilly or Adam Jr.?"

"No, it's me! I couldn't think of anyone else to call."

His brows bunched as he heard a muffled noise. "What's that sound?"

"Maurice Laurent. He's beating on the door. That's why I'm calling." She paused. "This is rather embarrassing, but he has me trapped in the bathroom."

"Trapped?"

"He's a married man and he's made some unwanted advances."

"Son of a bitch! Hang up and call the police!"

"I can't do that."

"Why not?" Rafe asked, a forgotten anger surging though him as he remembered how helpless he had felt when his father used his strength to abuse Lilly.

"He's being obnoxious, but so far nothing more. The police will ask a lot of questions and I'd rather this not get out if at all possible. His driver picked me up. If you can come get me, I'd appreciate it."

Reaching behind him, Rafe lifted his truck keys from the metal hook. "Where are you?"

She quickly gave him the address. "I really appreciate this."

He heard the relief in her voice and clenched his fist against his own helplessness. "I've delivered furniture out that way. I'll be there in twenty minutes." He gave her his cell phone number. "Call me back in one minute. I want you to stay on the line with me until I get there."

"Thank you."

"I'm on my way."

He ran for his truck. Jumping inside, he backed out of the driveway and sped off.

He bumped stop signs and ran signal lights when he could. He did his best to keep Kristen talking about her family. He knew they were close. He'd long since stopped regretting that his wasn't.

Having grown up in a small town in east Texas, he was used to driving narrow, winding roads. He made better time than he thought, but whenever he heard the noise of the man beating on the door, his insides would clench and he'd remember his father, his face hard, hate spilling from him.

"I see the lights of the house, Kristen. I'm almost there."

"Please, hurry!"

Rafe took the next curve without slowing down. The Silverado hugged the road. Then he was speeding up the long driveway. Lights shone from every window in the antebellum home. Screeching to a halt, Rafe slammed out of the truck. "I'm here. But don't come out until I tell you."

"He may not let you in."

"He'll let me in."

Bounding up the steps, Rafe transferred the phone to his left hand, then pounded the door with his right fist. "Police! Open up!"

As expected, it didn't take long to get a response. The double lock disengaged. The door swung open to reveal a tall, trim man who out-weighed Kristen by thirty pounds. Rafe's anger escalated.

"Officer—you're not the police!" Maurice started to close the door.

Rafe shouldered the door open and entered the house. "You'll wish I were if Kristen isn't all right. Kristen, you can come out!"

Maurice ran after Rafe as he strode down the wide hallway. "You can't just barge into my house. Get out!"

"If you know what's good for you, you'll stay out of my face," Rafe said, his voice as hard and cold as ice.

"Rafe!" Kristen cried as she came out of a door off the hallway. By the third step she was running. "Rafe, you came!"

He thought she'd stop. She didn't until her arms were wrapped tightly around his waist. His initial reaction was shock. He automatically reached to push her away, then felt her trembling. His arms closed around her protectively. This time he'd been able to help.

"It's all right. It's all right. I'm here." Awkwardly, his hand brushed down her slim back. "I'm here."

"Please, let's go," Kristen said, her voice unsteady.

His arm around her waist, Rafe turned to leave. The man who'd answered the door blocked their path. "Move!" Rafe ordered.

Moistening his lips, Maurice held up both hands. His worried gaze flickered from Kristen to Rafe's hard visage. "Now, wait a minute. I don't know what she's told you, but she came on to me. She was trying to get me to influence my wife. When I rebuffed her, she locked herself in the bathroom and started making threats."

Kristen gasped. "That's a lie!"

Maurice kept his gaze on Rafe. "I'm a married man. She came on to me."

"Rafe, he's lying!"

"I'm not. The bitc—"

Rafe's fist cut off the foul word Maurice had been about to say. He went down like a puppet whose strings had been cut. Unmoving, he lay sprawled on the Oriental rug.

"Come on." Rafe's hand clamped tightly around Kristen's upper arm as he led her outside to his truck. Opening the door, he helped her in, then slammed the door. Kristen jumped and Rafe cursed under his breath.

Rounding the truck, he worked to get his anger under control. He tried, he really tried, but after five miles he couldn't contain it any longer. "Why the hell did you go out there?"

Kristen flinched at the whiplash in his deep voice.

He shoved his hand over his head, knocking his baseball cap off onto the seat. He didn't appear to notice.

Kristen glanced at the hard profile, the clenched jaw, and swallowed. She didn't think she'd ever seen anyone so angry. "His wife was supposed to be there."

"When you saw she wasn't there, why didn't you leave?" he asked, taking a turn with only a marginal decrease in speed.

Kristen braced her hand on the dashboard. She thought about telling him to slow down, then just as quickly dismissed the idea. He didn't appear to be in the mood to listen. "He said Claudette, his wife, wanted me to stay and talk about my project for acquiring nineteenth-century artwork by people of color. Since he's never shown the slightest interest in me the couple of times we've met, I believed him."

Rafe snorted and took another turn. "Talk about naive."

Kristen took exception to the statement. It wasn't easy growing up the baby in a family of overachievers. She'd been working hard to develop her independence and a backbone long before the fiasco with Eric. "Anyone can make a mistake in judgment. And as satisfactory as it was to see Maurice's prone figure, he struck me as a man with a big ego. I was trying to avoid a scandal. He'll want retribution when he wakes up."

Rafe jammed on the brakes. Tires screeched. The truck fishtailed, then stopped. Kristen rocked forward until the seat belt jerked her back.

"Do you want me to take you back?" he snapped.

Realizing he was angry on her behalf, she didn't take offense. "Of course not. Please take me home."

Shifting the truck into gear, he pulled off. Looking at his stern profile, she didn't think he planned to break the heavy silence. She wrapped her arms around herself. After his help, she owed him an explanation.

"I've worked hard to secure my position with the museum. It's my own special project to build the African-American permanent art exhibition into one of the finest in the country. It's something I can do and that I love doing. I'd hate to lose my job before I'm finished."

"Men like that are cowards," Rafe told her. "Your job is safe."

"I hope you're right."

Maurice was ready; the stage was set. Reclining in the middle of the king-sized canopy bed he shared with Claudette, he gingerly positioned the ice pack over his throbbing nose and listened to her hurried steps coming down the hall. She was surprisingly fit and trim for a fifty-five-year-old woman, but she was too inhibited to satisfy him sexually. All she had going for her was her endless bank account. While that satisfied one craving, it left his carnal desires needing a discreet outlet.

He thought he had found it in Kristen Wakefield.

He scowled, then winced as pain shot through the middle of his face. He'd miscalculated. The couple of times he'd seen her she'd shown herself to be easily intimidated by Dr. Smithe, eager to keep her job and establish her own program, and naive despite her wealthy background. He'd been wrong, but so had she.

No one got the best of him.

Claudette Laurent, slim and elegantly beautiful, entered her bedroom, then came to an abrupt halt, her dark eyes widening. She rushed across the room to her husband. Hitching the slim, plum-colored skirt over her shapely knees, she climbed on the bed. "Maurice, what happened? Simon said you'd been attacked."

Maurice groaned and slowly removed the ice pack. The chauffeur had told Claudette exactly what Maurice had instructed him to say. "Kristen's friend hit me."

"Kristen?" Claudette's black eyes rounded in bewilderment. "Why? I don't understand."

His hand closed over hers. Gently he replaced the ice pack on his face. "I-I wish I didn't have to tell you this," he said, regret heavy in his halting voice.

"Maurice, I want to know who hurt you and why." Tender fingers touched his cheek. "Please, what happened?" she demanded, but her hand was gentle as she touched his cheek.

The ice bag lowered, he brought her left hand to his lips and kissed the five-carat, flawless white diamond wedding ring that had been her mother's. A heavy sigh drifted from his lips. "Since you insist. I warn you it isn't pretty. Kristen Wakefield tried to seduce me to gain my assistance in getting you to help with her acquisition of nineteenth-century paintings. When I refused, she locked herself in the bathroom and called some guy. I think she told him that I had tried to attack her. As if I'd ever be interested in any woman but you." Maurice snorted in disgust, then groaned in pain.

"Are you all right?" Claudette inquired anxiously. "Maybe we should call a doctor."

"No, I'll be fine now that you're here." He squeezed her hand. "It's best you know what happened next. When the man she'd called arrived, he forced his way into the house. Coward that he was, he hit me when I was trying to explain what had happened." The look in his black eyes went cold. "A woman like that shouldn't be allowed to work at the museum."

"Kristen always impressed me as a shy but trustworthy young woman," Claudette said slowly, a frown wrinkling her brow.

"My nose didn't get this way by itself," he snapped, then tried to leave the bed. "Obviously you're more concerned about Kristen than me!"

"No. I'm just surprised." She placed both hands on his shoulders and applied gentle pressure. "Please lie back down."

He complied, but he kept his unrelenting gaze on Claudette. "I won't let this go unpunished. In the morning we're going to see Dr. Robertson. I won't have your name associated with any institution that has unprincipled people working for it. If your father were alive, he'd be outraged at what happened tonight. He wouldn't let that woman get away with what she tried to pull. He'd see that she paid for her duplicity."

"And so will I," Claudette replied, her voice taut with anger.

He had pushed the right button. Claude François Thibodeaux. Claudette idolized the old fart.

Maurice relaxed back against the mound of down pillows and placed the ice pack over his face to hide his little smile of satisfaction.

No one got the best of him. Ever.

"Kristen, you're wanted in Dr. Robertson's office."

Kristen froze at her desk in her tiny office in the museum. The smirk on Dr. Smithe's thin face caused her stomach to churn. A picture of Maurice out cold last night flashed before her. Trembling fingers clenched around the pen in her hand.

"Well, hurry up," the chief curator snapped with undisguised disapproval.

Swallowing, Kristen rose slowly. She wanted to ask what the director wanted, but couldn't. If Smithe's satisfied expression was any indication, it wasn't good.

Leaving her office, she quickly went two doors down and entered Dr. Robertson's outer office. His secretary, Mary Edmondson, glanced up from talking on the phone. Instead of her usual warm greeting, she said nothing.

Kristen rubbed her damp palms on her slacks. "Dr. Robertson wanted to see me."

"Go on in—they're waiting."

They. Kristen didn't need to ask who *they* were. Her feet felt like lead. Her stomach churning, she crossed the room and opened the door. The three people in the small office filled with diplomas, awards, and African art turned immediately. Dr. Robertson's mocha-hued face was full of concern. But the expressions of the other two made Kristen want to run.

Claudette Laurent's beautiful face was as cold and as hard as the large diamond on her finger. Her black eyes matched their glitter. She turned away, her body rigid and unforgiving.

Maurice's entire being emanated hatred. In his set features she saw the promise of retribution that she had feared. She couldn't even take pleasure in his swollen, and probably painful, nose.

"Kristen," Dr. Robertson said. "Please come in and have a seat."

Kristen noted that a third chair had been pulled up in front of the desk, but separated by at least four feet from Maurice. Claudette sat on the other side of him. Kristen perched on the edge of the straight-backed chair and clasped her shaking hands in her lap.

Dr. Robertson, a small man with horn-rimmed glasses, salt-and-pepper beard, and gray hair, propped his arms on his desk. "Kristen, Mr. Laurent has come here with a serious accusation against you. He says you tried to use sex to persuade him to influence his wife to support your acquisition of nineteenth-century art. When he refused, he was beaten."

"He's lying, Dr. Robertson," Kristen denied angrily. "He's the one who tried to coerce me to have sex with him. I refused and locked myself in the bathroom." She cut a glance at Maurice. "He sent a car for me so I wouldn't have a way home if I refused. He was hit by the person who came to pick me up because Maurice called me a foul name."

"Oh, come on," Maurice said, with a dismissive wave of his hand.

"This woman is obviously lying. I called her yesterday to tell her Claudette wouldn't be available, but she insisted on coming and asked that I send a car for her."

"You said no such thing!" Kristen said, wishing Rafe had hit him harder. "You set me up. You had a cozy little dinner all planned."

Maurice turned up his bruised nose. "That dinner was for my wife and me to share on our four-month anniversary."

Kristen's mouth dropped open. What kind of man cheated on his anniversary? Her gaze went to Claudette, but the other woman stared straight ahead. "Claudette, I'm sorry, but Maurice is lying. I went to your house last night because I thought you were there and I wanted to discuss the paintings."

"Surely you don't expect my wife to take your word over mine," Maurice sneered, placing his manicured hand over his wife's.

Kristen watched the loving gesture with a sinking heart: then she recalled the answering machine. "I've got proof."

This time Claudette's gaze swung to her.

"She's lying, darling," Maurice said, his voice a bit unsteady.

Kristen ignored him and spoke to Claudette. "When I called a friend for help his answering machine was on. Part or all of our conversation should be recorded. It'll prove what I said is true."

"If there's a tape, she faked it," Maurice accused, his gaze locked on his wife's.

"In the interest of fairness, I feel we should listen to the tape," Dr. Robertson said.

"Are you saying you believe her over me?" Maurice asked with obvious indignation.

The director didn't back down. "In the seven years I've known Kristen, I've never known her to act in any way that would bring discredit to her or this museum. If the tape would clear up the matter, then I see no reason not to listen to it."

Kristen sent Dr. Robertson a look of gratitude. "If Rafe is home, he can bring the tape over."

Dr. Robertson picked up the phone on his desk. "Call him."

• • •

This was all his fault, Rafe thought as he entered Dr. Robertson's office and saw the look of desperation on Kristen's face, the hatred on Maurice's. If he'd controlled his temper she wouldn't be in this position. He wanted to reassure her, but couldn't. His father's prophecy that he'd ruin everything he touched was coming true.

"Thank you for coming, Rafe," Kristen said, then introduced him to Dr. Robertson. From the way Maurice was hovering over the woman seated by him, Rafe knew she must be his wife.

"Haven't you done enough to Kristen? I'm the one who hit you, not her," Rafe said, his voice filled with contempt.

Maurice jerked back in his seat as if he expected Rafe to attack him again. "As I told you last night, she fabricated the entire thing. Did you actually see me try to force myself on Kristen?"

"I heard you banging on the door," Rafe answered, his black eyes narrowed.

"You heard a banging, but it wasn't me." Maurice glared at Kristen. "She did it to try and get back at me for rejecting her. Well, it won't work. I love my wife."

"Perhaps we should listen to the tape," the director said.

Rafe connected his answering machine to the phone and pushed "play." Kristen's voice came on. The fear and desperation in her voice was easily distinguishable. So was the banging.

The museum's director stared at Maurice. Claudette leaned forward and stared at the answering machine. Maurice stopped glaring at Kristen and tightened his arm around his wife's shoulders.

Kristen was sure Maurice was going to get his until she heard herself refuse to call the police and say he was only being obnoxious.

"See! See!" Maurice cried in his defense. "If she had been afraid, she would have called the police."

Kristen said nothing. The disappointment on the director's face said it all. When the tape ended with Rafe giving her his cell phone number, she realized how badly she'd handled the situation.

"That proves she lied," Maurice declared, his face wreathed in a satisfied smile. "What frightened woman wouldn't call the police if she thought she was in danger?"

"I was trying not to cause a scandal," Kristen explained. "I didn't want the museum or Claudette embarrassed by what happened. I just wanted to leave."

"You lied! My wife and everyone in this room knows that, don't you, dear?" His other hand closed over Claudette's.

Everyone's attention centered on Claudette. She stood, rigid and regal and self-assured, aware of her wealth and her power. She knew how to wield both.

"Harold, I will not support any institution that employs people who pander, lie, inflict pain, or defame others to cover up their misdealing," she said. "I have a great deal of influence in the art circles and in this city. I won't hesitate to use it if this matter is not dealt with quickly. The decision is yours." She walked briskly from the room, Maurice following closely behind.

"Kristen, I—"

"Please, Dr. Robertson," she interrupted the director, her voice and face resigned. "You don't have to say it. You'll have my resignation as soon as I can clear out my desk."

"No," Rafe said, his hands clenched at his sides. "This is all my fault. You did nothing wrong."

"It doesn't matter. Claudette believes I did." Kristen's fingers raked through her straight, black hair. "This museum can't survive without private donations. Claudette's threat is real. If I stay, the museum will suffer. I can't allow that to happen. You have to see that."

Rafe caught her arms and stared down into her troubled face. "You're just going to walk away and let him win?"

"I don't have a choice." She looked at the director. "And neither does he. Do you?"

The older man slumped back in his chair. "With regret, I accept your resignation."

three

❧

Claudette Marie Estelle Thibodeaux Laurent had been taught since the cradle to adhere to her family's strict code: honor above all else. Her ancestors had been free people of color and had lived and prospered in New Orleans since 1803. Thibodeaux was a name that was synonymous with integrity. Having recently celebrated her fifty-fifth birthday, she had no intention of abandoning the code.

"Claudette, I can't begin to tell you how much your faith and devotion means to me," Maurice said, cupping her elbow as they left the museum and walked down the stone steps toward the waiting white Rolls.

"You're my husband," she answered, trying to recall the breathless rush of joy that knowledge had brought just four short months ago. She'd been so lost and alone after her father's death—then Maurice had come into her life. He'd been charming and so solicitous, catering to her every need, making her feel loved and cherished. The world had ceased to be so desolate and bleak.

His hand slipped around her still-trim waist, drawing her closer. His lips brushed her black hair. "Why don't we go home and let me show you how much you mean to me?"

"I'm sorry, Maurice, but I have an appointment with Barrett to discuss the prospectus for a couple of businesses we want to sell insurance to." She nodded to Simon, the elderly driver holding the door of her car open, then slipped gracefully inside.

Maurice placed one hand on the top of the car and leaned down to place the other one on her thigh. "I'd like to get my hands on you," he said suggestively.

"Maurice!" Claudette's gaze flickered to the uniformed driver who had been with her family for the past thirty years.

Maurice laughed roguishly, then removed his hand to take hers and kiss her palm. "My sweet. I do love you so."

Or do you love my money? The thought leaped out of nowhere, but it had been nagging her for the past month as Maurice's attentiveness to her waned, and he took more and more time off from work. He'd been scrupulously conscientious before their marriage, but now he had changed. Although her father's company . . . her company . . . had over a hundred employees, she, like her father, knew everyone.

Maurice had been one of the many employees to offer their condolences after her father's death. He'd found her crying in her office one afternoon when he had brought a contract for her to sign. Day after day he'd returned, cheering her up with his teasing banter and endless charm.

Soon she became aware of him as a man and herself as a woman. He'd proposed on bended knee in a room full of yellow roses, her favorite flower, barely a month after they'd met. For the second time in her life she'd followed her heart. She prayed nightly that she would not regret it as much as she had the first time, when she was sixteen.

Maurice's work habits were deplorable. He went to work late, had long lunches, and left early. The only way she knew his whereabouts was from the bills that poured in. He spent lavishly and worked little.

"Barrett said you were behind on the policies for the Evans firm. Perhaps you could go in with me," she said, studying him.

His smile vanished. He straightened. "Barrett may be the vice president of sales, but I'm my own man. I won't be treated like a child or tattled on." He spun on the polished wingtips Claudette had paid for and walked away.

She sprang out of the car and hurried after him. "Maurice!"

He turned, his face rigid. "Yes?"

"I didn't mean to offend you. I'm sorry," she said, trying to make peace, to find her way in a marriage that she knew was in desperate trouble. She wasn't blind to the gossip that was going on about them. The general consensus was that she had "bought" herself a husband.

She had little experience with romance. After that one youthful indiscretion, she'd worked hard to restore the faith and trust her parents had lost in her. When her mother died a year later, Claudette had become her father's hostess, his confidante. His passion was Thibodeaux International, and it became hers.

After graduating from private Catholic high school, she'd enrolled in a university in New Orleans to remain close to him. Rather than pursue her own desire to become an artist and major in art, she'd taken business courses to please him. He reasoned that, as his daughter, she was destined to marry a man of wealth and prestige and raise a family. She was not going to be a painter if he had anything to say about it.

She'd listened to him, and tried to enjoy her life and not see it as settling or repentance. She'd always thought her time would come.

She'd like to think she hadn't waited too long.

"Maurice, I don't want us to have an argument," she said when he remained silent. "Please try to understand."

"You know how this business is," he said angrily. "It takes time for a company to decide to spend millions on an insurance plan for their employees."

"Of course," she said, trying to placate him, realizing she'd been doing that a great deal lately. "I have to be going. I'll see you later. What are your plans?"

His mouth tightened for a brief instant; then he shrugged and said, "I'm going to Antoine's to see if the shirts I ordered are ready."

More money. Antoine had made her father's shirts. A cotton shirt with French cuffs, the kind Maurice wore, cost upward of $375. She'd taken him there after they returned from their honeymoon in the south of France. He'd ordered twenty shirts. "I'll see you later then. Good-bye." She started for the car.

"You forgot something," he said, catching up with her. Before she could ask what, his lips, warm and persuasive, pressed against hers. Lifting his head, he tenderly cupped her cheek. "I love you, Claudette. Skip the meeting."

She stared up into his mesmerizing black eyes, wanting to believe that she hadn't made a mistake, needing to believe that last night had happened just the way he had said. He *was* a handsome man. Kristen had been very insistent about her art project. Maurice wouldn't try to seduce a woman in *their* home. Of that she was sure.

"Let's go home," she said.

He kissed her cheek, "You're the only woman I love."

Leaning against him, Claudette walked back to the car, determined to do whatever was necessary to save her marriage. Maurice loved her. Only her.

Fighting tears, Kristen packed her possessions in a cardboard box she'd found in the copy room. Each article she placed inside made the knot in her throat grow. The Seth Thomas desk clock from Adam. The day planner from Lilly. The engraved, black-and-gold pen set from her mother. The desk set from Jonathan.

Her family had been so proud of her. She'd accepted the museum position after graduating from Stanford, determined to get on with her life and forget about Eric, who had used her as a shield to hide his own perversion. She'd been gullible enough to believe every lie he'd told her.

Just as she'd been naive and gullible enough to believe Maurice Laurent.

"Kristen, I'm sorry," Rafe said.

"It's not your fault." She picked up the English ivy from the windowsill and placed it on top of the box, then looked around. Nothing of hers remained. It was as if she hadn't spent the past seven years carving a niche for herself. She felt an emptiness inside.

Despite Smithe, she'd enjoyed her work. She could have made a difference. She blinked back tears. What was she going to do now, and how was she going to tell her family?

"I'll get that for you." Rafe picked up the box.

Not sure she could speak without bursting into tears, she nodded. After one last look, she opened her office door. Praying she wouldn't see anyone, especially Smithe, she hurried out the back door to the parking lot.

"I'll put this in my truck out front and follow you home."

Kristen shook her head, then activated the trunk on her BMW coupe. "I can manage."

Rafe put the box inside, then closed the trunk. Watching Kristen swipe her eyes with the heel of an unsteady hand, his insides twisted. "You shouldn't drive."

"I'll be fine. Good-bye, Rafe." Opening the door, she got inside and started the motor. Putting the car into gear, she backed up and drove off.

Rafe's fists clenched—then he sprinted around to the front of the building to his truck. No way was he letting her drive home without making sure she reached there safely.

He caught up with her two blocks away and stayed a couple of car lengths behind until she pulled into her apartment complex, a twelve-story, glass-and-rose-stone structure that screamed wealth and luxury living. When she parked, he drove up beside her.

He felt utterly helpless when he saw her press her forehead on top of her hands resting against the steering wheel. He'd caused that. She'd called him to help and instead, he'd caused her to lose a job she loved.

His father had always told him that he'd ruin anything he touched.

"You got book sense, but no common sense," Myron Crawford had taunted his oldest child and only son too many times to count. And, if he felt like it, he'd pull out his belt or grab the extension cord or anything handy to drive home his point.

His mother had been able to shield him at times, but his temper often ran ahead of good sense and he'd get another beating. After his mother died when he was sixteen and his sister, Shayla, was fourteen, the beatings grew worse. Then his father married Lilly and Rafe thought he'd change. He hadn't. Now he had two targets.

Rafe had stayed to graduate from high school because Lilly had begged him to do so, but after receiving his diploma, he hadn't gone back to the house—too many bad memories. If he had, the next time his father hit him, one of them would have ended up dead. So, he'd hitchhiked to New Orleans and only returned to see Lilly and his grandmother when he was sure Shayla, his father's favorite, or his father weren't there.

One night he'd awakened from a sound sleep and known his beloved grandmother had passed. He'd mourned her and known she'd understood that he couldn't have gone home for her funeral, just as he'd known Lilly would understand. She was only six years older and he'd never thought of her as his stepmother, but as a loving big sister. By then he and Shayla had drifted farther and farther apart.

She thought nothing of asking for new clothes, which she usually got, while Rafe's were threadbare. She seemed oblivious to their father's harsh treatment of Rafe. He'd tried to reason that maybe she was afraid to speak up or try to help because she didn't want to be on the receiving end of their father's wrath. Sometimes he was more successful than others.

His love and respect for Lilly, who tried so hard to stand between him and his cruel father, enabled Rafe to put aside his hatred and return to Little Elm for her divorce hearing. Despite all her good work in the church and in the community, people were ready to believe the worst of her. Rafe's testimony and the scars on his back changed their minds and that of the judge. Myron Crawford might be a deacon in the church and a pillar of the community, but he also abused his wife and son.

Rafe rolled his shoulders, almost hearing the whish of the lash, the biting sting. His hands knotted. No matter how hard he tried to run from the truth or to make things different, his father had been right. He was worthless to anyone. It was best for everyone if he stayed to himself.

Putting the truck into gear, he backed up and sped off. He'd done enough to hurt Kristen. She was home safely. The least he could do was honor her wish to be left alone.

Arriving at his carpentry shop a short while later, Rafe went straight to his workshop on the bottom floor of the warehouse he'd scrimped and saved to buy. His small apartment was on the second floor upstairs.

Pulling on his goggles, he set about cutting the legs for the highboy. This was the only thing he was good at. The only thing that he didn't mess up. He'd learned that in his father's house.

He wouldn't forget again.

four

"I'd like to tie Maurice's thing into a knot—perhaps then he'd think twice about trying to use it indiscriminately."

Kristen sat on the sofa and watched Angelique Fleming, her best friend and next-door neighbor for the past two years, pace in front of her. They'd met the day Kristen moved into the high-rise building. Angelique, a fabulous cook and deplorable housekeeper, had brought over a fish stew and lemon cake, then pitched in to help.

She'd amused Kristen's family with colorful stories about the city and about how she'd come to live in the upscale apartment. The original owners had divorced and both refused to sell. The solution was to lease it out. They were in their late sixties and each was hellbent on outliving the other and moving back in.

Angelique and Kristen's friendship had started that day and had grown to a solid bond. She'd been the only person Kristen had been able to tell the truth to about losing her job.

"Perhaps I should have called the police last night."

Angelique, five-feet-nine, voluptuous, and exquisite, spun around on tennis shoes. Hazel eyes flashed. "Don't you dare blame yourself! You wouldn't have had to make a decision if Maurice hadn't made the proposition. You're the wronged party here."

Kristen's hands flexed on the mug of Angelique's hot chocolate heavily laced with whipping cream. "I still lost my job."

"That's what steams me." Hands on her shapely hips, Angelique shook her head of thick, curly, auburn hair that reached almost to her tiny waist. "Men have been getting away with this crap since the beginning of time. I see them all the time at The Inferno. Pillars of the community, frothing at the mouth over the women working there, willing to slip them a little money under the table for a private get-together. Well, when my dissertation is published, their little 'fun' will be exposed."

"You still plan to use their real names?" Kristen asked, her feet tucked under her as she sipped the hot chocolate, wanting to feel warm again.

Angelique grinned. "I certainly do. I've checked with a lawyer friend of mine. There's nothing they can do because I'm only telling the truth. I've got names, dates, everything I need to nail their sorry hides to the wall."

Kristen's shoulders slumped inside the fluffy, white terry cloth robe. "Wish I had something on Maurice."

"Me, too." With a scowl, Angelique plopped down beside Kristen on the camelback sofa covered in a soft floral print. "I bet you dollars to beignets, you aren't the first woman he's pulled that on and you won't be the last."

"I was so gullible," Kristen mumbled.

"You're naive," Angelique said. "Men like that have a sixth sense about women they can come on to."

"Women without a backbone." Kristen slid down on the plump sofa, her misery increasing.

"Trusting women or women who have nowhere to turn or who have something to lose." Angelique patted Kristen's knee beneath the cashmere throw. "You fit all three. He didn't count on you getting the best of him." Her white teeth flashed in her exquisite face. "I'd like to have seen the look on his face when Rafe punched him."

"He never knew what hit him," Kristen said, perking up a bit at the memory. "His nose was still puffy today."

"Good. He won't underestimate you again."

Kristen set the mug on the polished cherry end table next to her. "I don't ever want to see him again."

"If you do, look the bastard in the eye and do this," Angelique said, making a balled fist then twisting it. "He won't bother you again."

Kristen pulled her bottom lip between her teeth. "I'm thinking of going home to Shreveport."

Angelique reared up. "This is your home! Don't let him win!"

"That's what Rafe said," she admitted softly.

"He's right. Wish I had met him the day you moved in. Too bad he'd already left when I came over. Sounds like a nice guy." Angelique settled back in the sofa. "Why haven't you two gotten together before?"

Kristen shrugged. "I don't know. I called a couple of times and left messages on his machine. He called back and got my machine. We just got tired of playing phone tag, I guess."

"Well, it's a good thing he was home last night."

"Yes, I didn't know what to do after I couldn't find you."

Angelique made a face. "Pete was just in one of his antisocial moods. I was at the club. I'll wise him up on that. If he doesn't tell me when I have a phone call again, I'll pluck his eyebrows the next time he gets drunk and passes out."

Kristen was amazed as always by Angelique's courage and her ability to handle any situation, especially the ones involving men, with ease. She would have made mincemeat out of Maurice. "You're going to the club tonight?" A couple of nights a week Angelique went to The Inferno to interview the dancers.

"Nope." She toed off her spotless white tennis shoes, then pulled her purple-sock-covered feet under her jean-clad hips. "I'm staying here with you and we're going to think of a thousand ways to punish Maurice—then you're going to forget him and move on with your life."

"It's not going to be that easy. The museum was more than a job—it was my chance to make my mark," Kristen said quietly.

"All the more reason to grieve for the loss, then go on. Take control of your life."

"I'm not like you, Angelique," Kristen said, aware that while she was tiptoeing through life, Angelique was living hers to the fullest. She held down a full-time job as a counselor at a rehab center while writing her dissertation.

Angelique smiled impishly. "Like Mama Howard said, there's only one of me. I'd been through five foster homes before she and Papa Howard got me when I was eight. They had to nail the windows shut to keep me from running away."

"Now you're twenty-seven, and weeks away from graduating with your doctor's in psychology."

"Yeah. I thank God for my foster parents every day." She elbowed Kristen in the side. "How do you feel about pouring syrup over Maurice and staking him to a bed of fire ants?"

"I know the first place I'd pour the syrup," Kristen said, her eyes like shards of glass.

Angelique whooped. "That's my girl! I knew you had it in you. Tell me more."

Kristen obliged, but soon the novelty wore off and when Angelique left an hour later, Kristen was back to fighting tears and questioning her judgment. Dragging herself to bed, she huddled beneath the down comforter, knowing the worst was yet to come when her mother and stepfather returned from his medical conference in Hawaii. How was she going to explain to them that she'd lost her job?

The moment Kristen had dreaded for the past three days finally happened Sunday night at 7:10. Her answering machine clicked on on the fourth ring.

"Kristen, Jonathan and I just got back from his conference. We had a wonderful time. Wait until you see the video of us doing the hula." Her mother's bright laughter filled the line. "But there is something else. I met a woman, one of the other doctors' wives, who has two paintings by Tanner and one by Johnson that she'll consider placing on permanent loan at your museum. I told her all about your plans. I'm so proud of you and what you're doing."

Arms wrapped around her waist, Kristen listened to her mother with a sinking heart. She'd worked so hard, waited so long, to hear her mother say those words and feel she deserved the praise. She'd wanted to accomplish so much. Now that was impossible.

"When we talk I'll give you her telephone number. I love you. Jonathan sends his love. Good-bye."

Kristen went out on the balcony in the living room. Spread out before her was New Orleans, a city of endless possibilities and delights. To her left was the French Quarter. In the distance was the tower of the Saint Louis Cathedral. At night the complexion of the city changed completely. Sedate and easygoing by day, the city became untamed, mysterious, and seductive once the sun went down, luring you with the feeling that anything could happen.

In New Orleans, it usually did.

She'd come to Orleans during her junior year in college and fallen in love with the city, the history, and the rich heritage of the people of color. Despite the obstacles in their path, they had accomplished so much. She'd felt a kinship with them, felt she could do the same.

Maurice's accusation had made that impossible. Her eyes briefly clamped shut.

How could she tell her mother and stepfather that she'd failed? She braced her hands on the balustrade. If they were aware of the accusations against her, they'd instantly leap to her defense. Her mother would be on the next plane. Eleanor Wakefield Delacroix was a lioness when it came to her children. She'd proven it time and time again. Kristen remembered when Adam lost his sight after a severe beating by car thieves. Her mother had never backed away from making tough decisions or lost faith that he'd regain his sight.

She'd been right. He had regained his sight and his neurosurgery practice was thriving. But he'd regained more than his sight; he'd gained a new outlook on life. These days he was happier, less driven. He took time out to enjoy his life with Lilly and their son. Life had knocked him down, but he'd be the first to say it was worth it because it was during his blindness that Lilly had come into his life. What he'd thought was the worst thing that could happen to him had turned out to be the best.

Kristen wished she could look past today and see that for herself. She gazed back at the phone. If she didn't call her mother, Eleanor would try to reach Kristen tomorrow. The last thing she wanted was for her mother to call the museum and learn she didn't work there. But she hated lying. She shoved her hand through her hair and went to the phone, praying she'd think of something.

"Hello," said a deep, male voice that sounded breathless.

Kristen bit her lip. Apparently she'd caught her mother and stepfather in one of their frequent romantic moments. For some reason she always felt embarrassed. Perhaps because it always reminded her of the shameless way she'd acted when she'd seen them kissing for the first time. "I'll call back."

"Kristen, don't you dare hang up this phone," Jonathan said. "We were just unpacking."

She laughed in spite of herself. That wasn't all they were doing. "Mother said you had a great time. Welcome back."

"We did. Your mother is tapping me on the shoulder. Here she is."

Kristen's hand flexed on the phone as she waited for her mother to come on the line.

"Kristen—hello, sweetheart. How are you doing?"

Kristen forced brightness into her voice. "Just fine, but I wanted you to know I'll be out of the museum on another project for the next couple of weeks so call here if you need me."

"You're going to be searching for paintings and donors to the museum?" asked her mother.

"Yes." She could certainly keep that from being a lie. "You mentioned a woman you met who might want to help."

"Paulette Banks. She lives in Virginia. I'll find her address and phone number and fax it to you tomorrow at home."

"Thanks, Mother. I'm glad you're back and that you had a good time." Kristen shifted the conversation to a surefire topic, her mother's first grandchild. "I spoke with Adam and Lilly earlier in the week and they're fine. So is Adam Jr."

"He is such a precious little angel. I bought him all kinds of souvenirs," her mother practically cooed. "I hope he has cousins to play with one day."

"Take your time, Kristen," Jonathan spoke into the receiver. "You deserve the best."

"Of course she does," her mother said. "I just want her to start weeding though the frogs to find her prince."

"Don't mind your mother, Kristen. She loves too much, but that's why I love her."

"And I, you," Eleanor said softly.

Kristen didn't have to be there to know they were sharing a kiss.

They were a loving couple. So were Adam and Lilly. "I'm happy you two have each other," she said, meaning it.

"You'll find the one for you one day. It took me fifty-nine years. You have a long time to go," Jonathan told her with a laugh.

At the moment a man in her life was the last thing Kristen wanted. "Welcome home and good night." After her mother came on the line to say good-bye, Kristen hung up.

Just as she stepped away from the phone, a knock sounded on the door. Glad for a distraction, she went to answer it. Angelique stood in the doorway, dressed in a fitted black top and slacks.

Gazing at Kristen's somber face, the other woman shook her head. "Thought so. Grab your purse and let's go."

"Angelique—"

"It's Angel tonight. Come on or you'll make me late."

Angel was the name Angelique had used when she worked at The Inferno to put herself through undergrad school, and now when she did research for her dissertation. "I can't go to a man's club."

"Why not? You don't have the excuse that being there might be a bad reflection on the museum."

"You're right." Angelique never tiptoed around anything.

"Get your purse. I want to show you women who'd give their souls—hell, they probably already have—to be in your shoes for one day."

"I know I have a lot to be thankful for, but it's just that . . ." Frustrated, Kristen shoved her hand through her hair.

Angelique brushed by her and went to the bedroom. She came back with Kristen's purse. "Come on, I've seen your world. Let me show you mine."

five

The Inferno was just off Bourbon Street. After passing gentlemen's clubs in the French Quarter with pictures of women with their hands coyly covering their bare breasts clearly proclaiming the type of entertainment inside, Kristen was surprised when Angelique stepped into a recessed doorway next to a courtyard and rang the bell beneath a small brass sign that read PRIVATE.

She heard a lock click, then the red door opened. She stared at a mountain of a man dressed in a black tee shirt and slacks. His bald head was as slick as an egg.

"Hi, Angel. Didn't expect you tonight," he said, his gaze running briefly over Kristen.

Smiling, Angelique looped her arm through Kristen's and stepped onto the polished hardwood floor. "You should remember that I like to surprise people, Mack."

"Guess I should," he said and closed the door. "You know the way."

Angelique tugged Kristen to get her to move down the short entryway to a set of dark oak sliding doors. When Angelique opened them, Kristen heard the pulsating beat of a current pop song, the hum of conversation, the clink of glasses, but all she saw was another wall . . . until they turned. She came to an abrupt stop.

She hadn't known what to expect, raunchy or tacky, sleazy or tasteless. The Inferno was neither.

The gentlemen's club was spacious, made to look even more so by the abundance of floor-to-ceiling mirrors around the room that caught and reflected your every move. Not one man in the forty or so seated either at the thirty-foot rosewood bar or the tables in the dimly lit room seemed to notice their arrival. Their eyes were trained on the voluptuous brunette with her long, golden legs wrapped around one of four shiny poles on the raised stage.

The dancer wore a gold sequined thong and a demi-bra. Sparkling gold fringes hung from her nipples. She arched gracefully backwards to land in a perfectly executed split. The provocative smile on her lush, red lips beckoned as she reached behind her back and unclasped her bra.

Kristen gaped.

Seeing a stripper in person was nothing like watching one on television. The volume of the men's voices reached a feverish pitch as the garment fell away. Kristen turned away in embarrassment and bumped into a table.

"Move," ordered a man who was trying to see the dancer.

"Sorry," she mumbled.

Angelique tugged her to a booth in the back of the room. The moment they sat, a waitress in a revealing, skintight, red-leather bustier appeared and placed a small bowl of beer nuts on the round table. "Hi, Angel. Your usual?"

"Hello, Ambrosia. Make it two."

"Be right back."

The blond-haired woman pranced away on four-inch heels. As she passed the tables, more than one hand reached out to give her a friendly pat on her swaying hips. She tossed the men a grin and they almost always tossed her a bill.

"Isn't touching against the law?" Kristen asked.

"Like I said, welcome to my world where there's a thin line between the law and a 'good old boy' just blowing off some steam." Angelique popped a handful of nuts into her mouth.

Kristen understood immediately. It was another case of men being in power and being able to push the rules when it came to women.

With each whistle, each bill pushed down a woman's cleavage or inserted into a thong, Kristen recalled Maurice, his lies, how he'd ruined her life. There probably weren't too many men at the club who'd want their families or business associates to be aware of where they were tonight.

"Men actually try to delude themselves that they're just having some harmless fun, bringing a little excitement into their sex lives. For some it might be the truth, but for others it's all about power and control of a woman," Angelique said, her voice tight.

"Your dissertation deserves to be published," Kristen said with absolute conviction as she glanced around the room.

Angelique nodded toward a balding man two tables over. He was getting a lap dance from a giggling redhead. "Judge Henry Randolph. A criminal judge. What do you want to bet, if she came before him, he'd act as if he didn't know her and show no mercy?"

"You'd lose," a woman said, sliding into the booth beside them. Statuesque, she wore a beaded blue gown that looked as if her breasts were about to spill out. "All he's looking at are t and a. One of the dancers made the mistake of hinting in court that she knew him. He threw the book at her. It was a warning to the rest of us." Her blue eyes flashed. "He's a vindictive bastard. Not one of us will make that mistake again."

"Cinnamon, meet Starlight," Angelique said.

It took Kristen a few seconds to realize she was Cinnamon. She almost lifted her hand in greeting, but caught Angelique's shake of her head. "Hello."

"Here you are." The waitress placed napkins and drinks on the table.

Kristen looked at the clear liquid with a cherry in a tall, slender glass, then picked it up and took a tentative sip. She smiled. Club soda and lime.

"You're a dancer, too?" Starlight asked.

Kristen was flattered. "I'm not that agile or talented, I'm afraid."

Starlight gave Kristen a thorough once-over. "You've got what it takes. Strip you down to the bare essentials and men would be standing in line to put money in your G-string."

"Ah, I think I'll pass," Kristen said and watched Angelique cover her mouth to hold back a laugh.

"Just as well. There's enough competition here already," Starlight said, her gaze going to the judge now contentedly sipping his drink. "Wish we could reverse our roles. Teach men like him a lesson. They are such users."

"Not *all* men," Kristen said quickly.

Angelique lifted an arched brow and popped more nuts into her mouth.

Starlight leaned closer to Kristen and jabbed a finger at her cheek. Beneath the heavy make-up a faint bruise could be seen. "Enough of the creeps are. My old man didn't like it when tips were down this week and he didn't have money to score or make his car payment."

Angelique sat forward. "Starlight, back off."

Oddly, Kristen wasn't intimidated. "Neither my brother nor my stepfather would hit their wives."

"Well, whoop-de-do," Starlight sneered and stood up. "Time for my number."

"Sorry, I didn't mean to make her angry," Kristen said, watching the woman walk away.

"Not your fault. Starlight wants to believe all men are scum," Angelique said. "It helps her accept she's living with scum. If she ever lets herself believe differently, she'll have to deal with why she lets him beat on her and she takes it."

Kristen lifted a brow. "You're going to make a wonderful psychologist."

"I will, won't I?"

They both laughed. Neither Angel nor Angelique lacked self-confidence.

"You lovely ladies look like you're having fun. Mind if I join you?" a well-dressed man asked with a lurid smile. In his hand was a tumbler filled with dark liquid.

"Yes," Angelique and Kristen said in unison, then looked at each other and laughed again.

The man, already bending to sit, slowly straightened. The smile slid from his narrow face. "You two aren't the only women in here." Tight-lipped, he strode off.

"That felt good," Kristen said, leaning back against the booth. "Wish I had told Maurice off."

"If you stay in New Orleans you might get the opportunity." Angelique picked up her glass and took a healthy swallow.

"At least I know what a cheat he is. Claudette still believes in him."

Kristen shook her head. "I feel sorry for her. She loves a man who is using her for his own gain."

"Sounds as if you've been there," Angelique commented.

Once Kristen might have lied, but in the past few days she was beginning to see things differently. "I have. He was charming, of average intelligence, and into sadomasochism. I wanted to surprise him and ended up being surprised myself."

"Mine was my history professor when I was a sophomore in undergrad school. It wasn't until I was in a relationship with him that another student wised me up. Seems that each semester he chose a student from his class to warm his bed."

Kristen gazed at Angelique with new eyes. "I always thought you were too smart to fall for the wrong guy."

"With the right man, no woman is that smart." She scrunched up her face. "Or should I say the wrong man."

Thoughtful, Kristen played with the moisture condensing on her glass. "I guess you're right. I've always admired Claudette. Since her father's death she runs a multimillion dollar company, yet she can't see through Maurice."

"Scary, isn't it? You can't tell what's inside until you unwrap the package and then it's too late," Angelique said, sipping her drink. "That's why I'm going to wait until I've established my practice before I even think about becoming involved with a man again. I can't afford to have my focus blurred."

"At least you have a future," Kristen responded, misery sweeping over her again.

"So do you. You just have to decide how badly you want it and what you'll do to get it."

"Before I lost my job I was so certain. Now I'm not so sure."

"You might not like hearing this, but if all it took was one setback for you to give up, maybe you didn't want it as bad as you thought."

Kristen thought about what Angelique had said the next day and the next. How badly did she want to increase awareness and appreciation of African-American art? Was it something she had lightly chosen or did she feel a real kinship with the artists and their struggles?

Staring at a reproduction of Tanner's *Two Disciples at the Tomb* on the wall in her living room, she tried to decide. He hadn't given up. How hard must his struggle have been?

An example closer to home was her brother, Adam. There had been a dark, tragic period in his life when he had been blind and unsure he'd ever see again. But even before his vision returned, he had refused to let the loss of his sight define his manhood. He'd been down, but he hadn't stayed down.

Her mother certainly wouldn't have let anyone destroy her future. She was a brilliant, gifted woman who was in medical school at nineteen. Before Kristen's father's death when she was fifteen, he'd been one of the leading cardiologists in the country.

Success ran in her family, but at twenty-seven she had yet to achieve her own. Her family's love and praise couldn't erase the recurring fear of failure she felt at times.

Her family fought for what they wanted. They jumped in with both feet. Even Jonathan had put everything on the line for her mother's love. They didn't look at the odds; they kept their eyes on the goal. They were so self-assured and she had never been.

Perhaps because as she grew up people never let her forget how brilliant, how athletic, how popular Adam was. The more her instructors, family friends, and associates praised him, the more insecure she became. The fact that her family loved her unconditionally somehow made it worse. She'd grown up wanting to prove to her family that their unshakable faith in her was justified.

She was still trying.

She wandered back into her bedroom and stared at the open suitcase on her bed and the clothes beside it. Deep in thought, she picked up a pair of cranberry slacks and simply held them.

If she left, Maurice would go on to his next victim, carefree and happy, while she was still jobless and miserable. And what would happen the next time there was another roadblock in her career path? Would she run?

The unexpected death of the father she adored, Adam's blindness, her own failure at love, and now this had taught her that there were no guarantees in life. All you could do was live it, and do your best to be able to look at yourself in the mirror without shame or regrets.

If she left Orleans she could do neither. Her hand clenched on the linen, wrinkling the cloth. "No. I won't run!"

The words burst from her mouth, and hearing them, she knew she was staying. Walking to the closet, she hung up her pants, then the rest of her clothes. Finished, she put the empty suitcase back in her closet.

If Maurice crossed her path again, he'd better watch out. She'd run once from a man. Never again.

First thing, she needed a job. Refusing to think her lack of a reference from the museum might hinder her, she went to the utility room and gathered the newspapers she hadn't bothered to open for the past five days. In the kitchen, she grabbed a red pen and started going through the classifieds.

Museums were out, but she had her master's in art history in a city full of private institutions, collectors, and art galleries. She'd start with them first and if nothing materialized, she'd broaden her scope. She wasn't giving up.

By nine the next morning Kristen, wearing a Carolina Herrera black pantsuit, her hair swept up in a sophisticated chignon, was filling out an application at The Art Institute, a private foundation for endowment of the arts. The human resource manager, Mr. Dockett, appeared very impressed by her alma mater, her honors thesis, and her extensive traveling to museums across the country. He regretted that he only had a position open for a research assistant.

Feeling good, Kristen took the application and sat at a small desk in his secretary's outer office to fill it out. She was zipping along until she reached the space where she had to disclose the reason for leaving her last employer. The Montblanc gold fountain pen her mother had given her wavered. She kept remembering the dire warning printed on the application that all information had to be true.

The institute would call the museum. They weren't about to allow anyone to be around priceless paintings without checking their references. Since Dr. Smithe was her immediate supervisor, he'd be the one they'd ask.

"Is there a problem, Ms. Wakefield?"

Kristen glanced up at Mrs. Carruthers, Dockett's secretary, watching her closely. "No," she said, then quickly wrote in the blank that she left her last position to broaden her artistic horizon, then handed in the application.

Mrs. Carruthers, a practiced smile on her narrow face, laid the tri-fold sheets aside without looking at them. "Thank you. You'll be hearing from us."

Kristen left and went directly to the next prospect on her list. Each time she wrote the reason for leaving her employee, her anger at Maurice grew hotter. Because of him she had to lie. Then fear would take over that, because of him, she might not get a job.

Three days later she was at the computer in her home office continuing her job search when the phone rang. She pounced on it in the middle of the second ring. She'd filled out ten applications in person and sent out fifteen resumes via e-mail.

"Hello."

"This is Dr. Smithe. Stop listing the museum as your last employer and save me the time and bother of telling prospective employees how badly you performed your duties," he sniped. "Dr. Robertson isn't talking about the reason for your abrupt departure, but I know there's more to your resignation than what's being said. I'm just delighted you're gone. You've already been replaced."

Kristen hung up on him, too angry to do anything else. Propping her elbows on the desk, she placed her forehead in her open palms. Maurice wanted to ruin her, and so did Smithe. Both were mean-spirited, selfish men, but she'd be double-damned if she'd let them run her out of town. She'd prefer a job in the arts, but they'd made that impossible. This time their pettiness only made her more determined.

Picking up the newspaper on the desk, she flipped to the classified business section. She had excellent computer skills. Somewhere in here was a job.

At the sound of the doorbell, she hunched over further, concentrating on the ads. But by the sixth ring she gave in and went to answer the door. Only Angelique would be that persistent.

Kristen was already prepared to ask for Angelique's help when she opened the door. Her eyes rounded in surprise as she stared at her unexpected visitor. "Rafe."

"Hi, Kristen," Rafe managed, shifting from one foot to the other. It had taken him most of the day to work up his nerve to come, then another fifteen minutes of standing in the hall before ringing the doorbell. He didn't blame her because she'd stopped smiling when she saw him. He'd ruined her career.

"I . . . er . . . bought you some food." It was the only way he could think of to help. His grandmother had always tried to feed him after he and his father had gone a couple of rounds.

"Thank you."

He shoved the two white paper sacks atop a large pizza box toward her awkwardly. "I didn't know what you like so I bought more than one thing."

Looking a bit stunned by the offering, Kristen peeked into the sacks that held a po' boy sandwich in one and cartons of Chinese take-out in the other. "I like all three."

He nodded. At least he'd gotten something right. Reaching into the pocket of his denim shirt, he pulled out several folded sheets of white paper. "This is for you. I called Lilly—"

"No!" Dark brown eyes widened in alarm. "You told her!"

"No. No," he rushed to reassure Kristen. "I just asked what your degree was in. I wanted to go on the Internet and look for another job for you." He shifted again. "I think several sound promising. A couple of the colleges are looking for instructors—so is the school system."

"You did that for me?" she asked, amazed.

"After causing you to lose your job, it's the least I can do." He stuffed his hands into the front pockets of his worn jeans. "I went to Mrs. Laurent's office, but she wouldn't see me. I'm sorry for the way things turned out."

"The one who should be sorry is Maurice. I finally figured that out," she told him, her voice hardening.

"Good." He liked the determined look in her eyes. She was on her way to being all right. "I won't keep you then."

"Wait," she called when he turned to go. "You can't leave me with all this food. Have you eaten?"

"No, but I don't want to be in the way."

"Come on in." She stepped back.

He frowned. His hands came out of his pockets. "You're sure?"

"Positive. Close the door, then join me in the kitchen." Not giving him a chance to decline, she walked away.

Rafe entered cautiously and shut the door behind him. His booted feet sank into the plush white carpet. The room was as sleek and elegant as the woman living there. White on white with splashes of red and yellow dominated the color scheme. The fine wood furniture was of antique quality. White sheers leading to a balcony were drawn to display a breathtaking view of the city by night.

"Rafe?"

"Coming," he said, then followed the direction she had gone through the living room, down a short hall. He found her setting the round, wooden table for two.

She looked up at him and wiped her hands on her black slacks. This time she was the one who appeared nervous. "Won't you have a seat?"

Her nervousness bothered him. She'd never been that way before. Then the reason hit him. His temper had frightened her the other night. He was his father's son. His hands went into his pockets again. "I don't want to bother you."

She smiled and it lit up her beautiful face. Maybe, just maybe he hadn't ruined her life.

"I can't eat all this and I detest food going to waste." Opening the po' boy sandwich piled three inches high with fried shrimp, lettuce, tomatoes, and red onions, she placed half on each plate, then sat down. "Thanks for the ads, but it won't do any good. Dr. Smithe, my ex-boss, called just before you came. He made it very clear that I was doing myself more harm by putting the museum down as my last place of employment."

He studied her. "What are you going to do?"

"Find work," she said with resolve.

Taking a seat, he said grace. "You remind me of your mother."

"I do?" She paused with her sandwich in her hands. "How?"

"You're both gracious women. She never made me feel as if I was intruding on your family holidays in her home."

Kristen heard the wistfulness in his voice. Another person trying to find where he belonged. "You weren't. We were happy to have you. Adam Jr. loves his big brother. I didn't think he'd ever get off that rocking horse you made him last Christmas."

A slow smile blossomed on Rafe's handsome face. The day Adam Jr. was born, Lilly had called and told him his little brother wanted to see him and they expected him within the week. Lilly and Adam had always considered him Adam Jr.'s big brother. It was a position of responsibility he took pride in. Adam Jr. was the only one he ever let get close. "I'm making him a sleigh and a wooden train set for Christmas."

"Your work is beautiful."

Pleasure spread through him. "Thank you. I like working with my hands." He placed his sandwich on the sunshine-yellow plate. "I know what it is to find enjoyment in what you do. I took that from you."

She folded her arms across her chest and stared across the small, round dining table at him. "Rafe, do you want us to be friends?"

Uncertainty entered his eyes. "Y-yes."

"Then don't ever let me hear you say that losing my job was your fault again." Unfolding her arms, her voice gentled. "If you hadn't helped me, I don't know what I would have done. Maurice would have found a way to get back at me in any case. He told me so up front."

Rafe's gaze went flat and hard. "I wish I had hit him harder."

Kristen laughed. "Exactly. I'm rid of Maurice. Poor Claudette is married to the scheming rat."

"You sound as if you feel sorry for her," he said.

"I do. She's a gracious and wonderful lady." Kristen picked up the box of fried noodles. "Sooner or later she'll find out, and Maurice will get his. She'll be hurt, but she'll survive. Claudette is nobody's pushover. At least not for long."

"You also have your mother's toughness." He bit into his sandwich.

"I'm working on it." Setting the noodles aside, she picked up the list Rafe had brought her and started going down the names. "I'll have to broaden my range of employment places. I'd hoped to be able to stay in the art field and keep an eye out for possible acquisitions for the museum, but that's impossible now."

He set his empty plate aside. "You still plan to help?"

"It's not the museum's fault. Dr. Robertson had no other choice."

"You might still be able to help. There's a listing for a gallery manager on the last page. Maybe the owner will take knowledge over an employer's recommendation. It's in a high-dollar area in the historic section of Royal Street." Getting up, he shifted the papers to find the listing. "Here it is."

Her face lit up. "St. Clair Gallery. I know the owner, Jacques Broussard. He's a wonderful man. You're right, his gallery has the work of some of the best artists in the country." She smiled up at Rafe. "I got the distinct impression at the last gala the museum gave during the Christmas holidays that he didn't care for Dr. Smithe's snobbish ways."

"In that case, looks like your luck has turned. You better jump on it and call tonight." Rafe's blunt-tipped finger poked the sheet of drafting paper in her hand. "It's only a little after seven."

Kristen went to the phone and punched in the number. Closing her eyes, she crossed her fingers as the phone rang. After the third ring the answering machine picked up. Disappointed, she hung up. "Answering machine."

"Did the recording say what his hours were?" Rafe asked. "A lot of stores stay open late on Thursday. Plus it's summer and the tourist season is in full swing. If he's busy, maybe he let the machine pick up."

"You think?"

"Grab your purse and let's go find out."

Kristen ran to her bedroom closet for the black, double-breasted jacket that went with her pants, then draped an animal-print scarf under the collar. If Jacques was at the gallery, she wanted to look her best. The museum had hired her on the basis of her finishing with honors from Stanford in the top one percent of her graduating class. Her credentials were excellent.

Rafe was right. She knew art. Checking her purse for her comb and lipstick, she hurried back out.

"Ready."

"You look great. You always do," he said, then briefly bent his head as if embarrassed by the admission.

"Thank you." She wondered if he knew how much she needed that boost.

Opening the door, he stepped back. "Got your key?"

"Yes." She took a deep breath. "I'm ready."

He nodded. "I can see it in your eyes. You're going to get this job."

She smiled up at him. "I'm certainly going to give it my best shot. Mr. Broussard won't know what hit him."

six

New Orleans hadn't gotten the name The Big Easy for nothing. Summertime meant a sea of moving humanity in the French Quarter. People meandered down sidewalks, jaywalked across streets, laughing and having a good time, and more often than not sipping cool drinks of the alcoholic variety.

No one seemed in a particular hurry to reach his or her destination. Street musicians and dancers happily entertained those passing by and those patiently standing in long lines to get into restaurants. Parking spaces were as scarce as an honest politician.

Rafe had moved fifteen feet in ten minutes and didn't hold out much hope of getting further. Tourists, the locals, and teenagers, out of school with nothing to do, swelled the number of people on the sidewalks and in the streets. "I'll find a place to park and wait at Café Du Monde."

About to get out, Kristen's hand stilled on the door handle. "I thought you were going to stay with me."

Rafe glanced down at his denim shirt and jeans. "Not dressed for it and it may take a while to find a place to park. You can't take the chance and wait. Good luck."

Her big words came back to nip her on the backside. Kristen's stomach rolled. She didn't want to go in there by herself.

"Just remember you're your mother's daughter and you'll be fine."

The fear left as quickly as it had come. She smiled. "Mr. Broussard will be lucky to have me."

Rafe chuckled. "Get going before someone gets there ahead of you."

She hopped out of the truck, then waved as Rafe finally got the chance to go through the traffic light. Straightening her scarf, she hurried down the street, then turned onto the cobbled sidewalk of Royal Street. It was lined with art galleries, antique shops, and restaurants, many of which had been handed down from generation to generation and were registered with the historical society.

The man she sought, Jacques Broussard, was an exception. He had purchased the gallery from the owner when none of his family wanted to run the business. Jacques might have the same problem. His only child and son, Damien, was a successful corporate lawyer. But for now, Jacques was a vibrant part of the art scene in Orleans and well respected.

Seeing a man come out of St. Clair Gallery, Kristen breathed a sigh of relief and quickened her strides. She threw a quick glance though the plate glass window at the spacious gallery as she passed, then entered.

She spotted the owner immediately. Even from twenty feet away, she could tell the smile he usually wore was a bit strained. The reason was obvious. In the two years she'd been acquainted with Mr. Broussard, he'd always prided himself in the way he conducted his business. Customer service and satisfaction were of prime importance. With only him in the shop and five people milling about, he couldn't do that.

True, browsing in the varied shops in the Quarter was as much a part of the tourist attraction as strolling through Jackson Brewery. Owners usually left customers to browse freely, but obviously the people in the shop were serious.

Excusing himself, Jacques left a young couple in front of a seascape by Kent, then hurried across the room to a man in front of a painting by Ralph Brown of three black children playing in the rain. The couple he'd just left frowned at him. The well-dressed, slender man in a tailored suit checked his watch. The fashionable woman by his side folded her arms across her chest. A black Prada bag hung from her shoulder.

Kristen took her courage in her hand and seized the opportunity. Placing her purse in the seat behind the ornate desk near the entrance to the gallery, she approached the couple. "Hello, my name is Kristen. Can I be of service?"

Relief swept across their faces. "Please. We know the price, but not very much about the artist."

"Were you interested in the painting as an investment or appreciation or both?" Kristen asked, trying to decide where to start.

"Both," the woman answered, glancing back at the forty-by-forty painting in a heavily carved and ornate gold frame. It portrayed a turbaned woman in African clothes walking down a dusty road with a small child a few steps behind.

"A painting by Robert Goddins will appreciate in value *and* please the eye," Kristen said, thanking God she was familiar with the work. "Goddins was born in Chicago and raised in Dallas by his widowed mother. He is self-taught. His paintings have hung in the Smithsonian and The Dallas Museum of Art. His works in many media include acrylic, pastel, and mixed media, as you see in this painting, *Woman and Child*."

"I don't know," the woman said, studying the painting from different angles.

Kristen, who had never sold anything in her life, went on instinct. "If you want to keep looking, I think you should. A painting should draw you out of yourself and into it. Goddins's paintings always make you think."

The woman smiled. "He does, doesn't he?" She held out her hand. "Thank you."

The handshake was brief, but firm. "Please. Let me get you one of our cards." Kristen turned and almost bumped into Jacques. "I—I . . ."

Silently he handed her a business card. Taking it, she gave it to the woman because she had appeared the more interested of the two. "Please call if we can be of any further service, even if it is not about a painting from here. Art is to be appreciated wherever you find it."

"That's the same way I feel. Thank you, Kristen."

Kristen waited until they left, then turned to try and explain to Mr. Broussard, but he had gone to assist another couple. The door opened and a woman came in. Deciding she had nothing to lose, Kristen went to help.

Thirty minutes passed before the shop was clear. Kristen squared her shoulders as Jacques approached her. At least he was smiling.

"Thank you, Kristen. I appreciate you pitching in," Jacques said, still smiling as he folded his arms. "Now, is there something I can help you with?"

"A job."

He frowned. His arms slowly dropped to his sides. "The gallery is open the same hours as the museum."

With an effort, she kept her face emotionless. "I no longer work for the museum."

He studied her for a long time, then refolded his arms across his chest. "You mind telling me why?"

She'd expected the request, but she had one of her own. "On one condition. That the conversation goes no further."

He didn't hesitate. "All right."

She didn't hesitate, either. Jacques Broussard was highly respected in New Orleans. He might not have the money that Claudette Thibodeaux Laurent had, but his clout was just as formidable. "An individual unjustly accused me of trying to coerce him with sexual favors to help with a project for the museum. If I hadn't resigned, certain individuals would have used their influence to see that private donations would be cut off from the museum."

"Only a handful of people have that kind of influence in this city," he said, his eyes narrowed.

"It wasn't a bluff," she told him, her anger escalating all over again. "You might as well know that although Dr. Smithe is unaware of the reason for my resignation, he refuses to give me a good recommendation for another job."

"He's a snob. I wish Dr. Robertson hadn't hired him," Jacques said with obvious distaste. "Smithe's displeasure is a point in your favor."

Her lips twitched. "Yes, sir."

"What did Dr. Robertson say?"

Her chin lifted. "That he'd accept my resignation with regret."

Jacques nodded his balding head. "I admire Harold a great deal. He's smart and he knows people. He's worked thirty years to build the museum into what it is today."

"He's a wonderful man." The tension in her shoulders eased. "That's why I resigned. I didn't want the museum or him to suffer because of me."

"You have courage as well as intelligence and beauty," Jacques said, studying her closely. "It would take a saint or a fool to resist. Since I know all the people powerful enough to exert such pressure on the museum, I'd have to say I've met more saints than fools, but I'd trust Harold with the key to Fort Knox. Can you start tomorrow?"

"Yes!" she burst out, excitement flowing through her.

Chuckling, he extended his hand. "You didn't ask about salary, days off, benefits."

"You trusted me, I have to trust you," she said.

"Still," he said, quoting a salary figure. "We open at ten sharp Monday through Saturday and close at five except on Thursday when we extend the time an hour. Sunday it's one to five." He smiled. "Or as you saw today, whenever the last customer leaves. Be here at nine in the morning and we can go over your duties."

"I'll be here—and thanks, Mr. Broussard."

"Thank you. I need a manager who is knowledgeable, competent, and reliable. You're the one helping me."

The door opened behind them. The couple she had helped earlier entered.

"Kristen, we decided to get that painting."

She gasped, then faced Jacques with a wide grin. "They want to buy *Woman and Child*."

"Welcome aboard."

Café Du Monde, the original French Market coffee stand, was famous for its *café au lait*, strong chicory coffee laced with thick cream, and beignets. The mouth-watering aromas filled the air. People were lined up to get inside the tented eatery. Despite being in New Orleans for years, Rafe had never developed a taste for the strong coffee. Instead he sipped his soft drink and kept an eye out for Kristen. The more time passed, the more anxious he became.

What if she didn't get the job? Then he saw Kristen and she was grinning. He stood without being aware of the smile on his face. Waving, she quickly weaved her way through the ever-present crowd and narrow spaces between the small tables. "I got the job," she told him, her arms going around his neck.

He stiffened before he could stop himself. He'd had the same reaction the first time she'd hugged him, but she'd been too upset to notice. This time she wasn't.

She froze, then slowly withdrew her arms from around his neck and stepped back. Her lower lip tucked between her teeth. "I didn't mean to embarrass you."

"You didn't." A half-lie was better than seeing the hurt expression on her face again and knowing he was the cause. "I didn't want to get your suit dirty," he continued, brushing at the faint traces of powdered sugar on his shirt from a beignet he'd eaten while waiting.

Her smile returned. "Don't worry about it. If it hadn't been for you, I wouldn't have this job."

He shook his head. "You're the reason you got the job. It's kind of noisy in here. Why don't we leave and you can tell me all about it on the way to your place." Lightly taking her arm, he left the restaurant, aware that he was lying again, even more aware that he was reverting to the same defensive mechanism he'd used as a teenager so people wouldn't get too close. He felt just as lonely and ashamed now as he did then.

Kristen took to the managerial position at St. Clair's like the proverbial duck to water. She loved art, and she quickly learned to relish the chance to share her feelings with people who came into the shop, whether they were browsing or seriously considering a purchase.

In her job as the assistant to the curator at the museum, she'd often been stuck with paperwork, fund-raising, event planning or some other task that kept her off the floor where she could interact and mingle with the patrons. That was a thing of the past at St. Clair's.

Her antique Chippendale desk was positioned a few steps from the door. If she wasn't with a customer, she was able to greet everyone who entered. She always did it with a friendly smile.

"I'm delighted that I was wrong about you," Jacques said with a good-natured laugh after closing the door for a customer.

Since he was smiling, her hands continued to hover over the computer keyboard instead of clenching. "In what way?"

"Selling *Woman and Child* could have been because the Franklins were ready to buy anyway." He waved his hand toward the receipt book on the desk. "In this business it's extremely important that the buyer has confidence that the seller knows what they're talking about and believes in their integrity. You exemplify both."

Kristen placed hands that had started to tremble in her lap. "You thought there might be some validity in the accusation?"

He waved her words aside. "If I thought that, I never would have hired you. This is more than a business, it's my passion. It was you I wasn't sure about."

Twin lines furrowed her brow. "I don't understand."

The door behind him opened. "Excuse me." Kristen stood and went to greet a group of teenagers.

Despite her uneasiness about the conversation with Jacques, her smile didn't show it. "Welcome to St. Clair's. If you have any question you have only to ask." Her hand extended toward the T-shaped gallery. "Enjoy."

Too nervous to return to her seat, she went to stand by Jacques. "You were saying."

He nodded toward the five laughing teenagers who wore bagging jeans and sported tattoos and multiple piercings. "Do you think they're potential buyers?"

"No."

"Why?"

She didn't like to judge people. She'd done too much of that in the past with horrendous results. "The pictures here are for the serious buyer or art lover. From the way they're laughing and playing, I don't think they're either."

"Yet you treated them as if they were."

The twin furrows returned. "How else was I to treat them? Just because they may not have the money to buy or aren't interested in buying doesn't mean they don't have the mental capability to appreciate art."

"That's what I meant," he said, catching her by the arms. "I wasn't sure you'd be able to relate to the customers, to make them feel at home.

The few times I'd met you, you seemed rather withdrawn or—" he paused briefly "unsure of yourself."

She didn't take offense. He'd described the old Kristen perfectly. "And now?"

"I'm thinking about giving you a raise so you won't leave."

Her face blossomed into a smile. "Jacques, thank you."

"Later," the teenagers chorused as they left the shop.

"Later," Jacques and Kristen said, then grinned at each other.

Almost immediately, the door opened. In walked Angelique dressed in black, her thick auburn hair in a single braid down her slim back.

"You came," Kristen said, going to greet her friend. Angelique could take art or leave it. Usually she left it.

"I had an appointment later at the club so I was in the area." Angelique closed the door, then glanced around the gallery, lifting her oversized shades to peer closer at the discreet price tag on a painting near the entrance of the gallery. "*Disbelief* is right."

Unsure if she meant the outlandish price or the abstract painting itself, Kristen drew Angelique to Jacques. "Angelique, neighbor and best friend, meet Jacques Broussard, my boss."

"And friend," Jacques added, taking Angelique's hand and kissing the air just above it. "It's always a pleasure to meet a beautiful, intelligent woman."

Angelique lifted a naturally arched brow. "I'll bite. How do you know I'm intelligent?"

"Because you're Kristen's friend and you're intelligent enough to know that at five thousand dollars, Rene's painting is overpriced," he told her.

"Then why have it on display?" Angelique asked with her usual straightforwardness.

"Angelique, didn't you come to see me?" Kristen asked, although she had wondered the same thing.

"And outspoken," Jacques said not unkindly. "Rene is a wonderful artist, but not in abstract. He wanted a chance to display the new direction of his work and, as a friend and gallery owner, I gave it to him. Hopefully, he will soon come to realize where his talent lies and return to portraits."

"If not?" Kristen asked, finally understanding Rene's daily call to see if the work had sold.

"He will," Jacques stated emphatically. "Above all else, Rene is practical. He enjoys the praise his works garnish and the money that goes with it too much to do otherwise."

Kristen studied the painting with its sharp angles and bold slashes of garish purple and orange, and felt a distinct kinship with the artist. "Too bad he couldn't have both."

"Very few can," Angelique said from beside her. "It takes a special person to stick to their dreams when confronted with stark reality. You're one of them."

Surprise had Kristen turning sharply toward her friend. "Me?"

"You. You stayed instead of leaving." Angelique glanced at Jacques, her dark lashes swept down flirtatiously over her light brown eyes. "But considering you have such a charming boss, I don't blame you. Perhaps I should have majored in art instead of psychology."

"Should I make an appointment for your couch?" Jacques bantered.

Angelique grinned. "I'll hold you to that in about a year."

The door opened. A man in a gray chauffeur's uniform held it open for a silver-haired woman with a polished teak, heavily carved walking stick. "I'll take care of Mrs. Moreau," Jacques said, quickly moving to assist the matronly woman inside.

"Your boss is great," Angelique said, bracing her hips against the desk.

"He is, isn't he?" Kristen glanced over her shoulder at Jacques as he stopped with Mrs. Moreau in front of a painting by Paul Goodnight. "I took this job out of desperation, but I've quickly come to enjoy working here. I couldn't truthfully say that when I was at the museum."

"Considering the fringe benefits, I don't blame you." Angelique came off the desk and pointed outside. "Now, *that's* what I call a man's man. Built *and* good-looking, in an earthy sort of way."

Kristen followed the direction of Angelique's gaze and couldn't believe her eyes. Rafe, looking lost and uncertain, stood on the sidewalk, clutching a package wrapped in bubble wrap beneath his right arm.

She hadn't seen or spoken with him since the night she got the job. She'd called twice, but always got his machine. He'd called, but always when she was at work. She didn't think the timing of his calls had been an accident.

Their gazes met, he clutched the package, then started to walk away. *Oh, no, you don't.*

"I'll be back."

Rushing out the door, Kristen called to him. "Rafe, wait!" Afraid he wouldn't comply, she caught him by the arm, felt the flex of his muscles, and agreed with Angelique's estimation of his physique. He was in excellent condition. "You were leaving without coming in?"

He shifted uneasily. "You were busy." The excuse was weak at best. He was a coward, plain and simple.

"Angelique just dropped by to say hi." Kristen took his arm and started back inside. "She's been dying to meet you."

He balked, the uncertainty on his face growing. "I don't want to be in the way. I just brought you this." He shoved the wrapped bundle toward her.

Her hands automatically closed around the bubble wrap, then tightened at its weight. "It's too heavy for food unless you plan to feed the customers as well," she teased.

He smiled before he could help himself. "It's something I made for you."

Her dark eyes lit with delight. "I'm worse than Adam Jr. when it comes to presents." She gave it back to him. "I'll get the door."

Aware that it was her way of getting him inside the gallery, but unable to think of a reasonable excuse, he went in and placed the package on the desk.

"Angelique Fleming, meet Rafe Crawford, my sister-in-law's stepson, and if he tries to leave, sit on him. Rafe. Angelique." Kristen began opening her drawers, looking for her scissors.

Rafe, who had begun edging back, stopped. He hadn't thought she'd pay any more attention to him.

"Hello, Rafe," Angelique said, placing herself in his direct path to the door. "I'd hate to sit on you after such short acquaintance, but good friends are hard to find. Besides, she feeds me when I forget to buy groceries so I'd like to keep her happy."

"Eureka." Brandishing the scissors, Kristen cut the clear wrapping tape, then began to peel the bubble wrap away.

Rafe had meant to give her the gift, then leave. Now he discovered he couldn't. It had nothing to do with the woman who was half his size who had positioned herself in front of the door, and everything to do with Kristen carefully unwrapping the package as if it were the most precious thing in the world.

He had designed and made it to make up for the inexcusable way he had acted after she got the job. She'd obviously wanted to celebrate, but old fears had kept him from joining her. He just hoped it wasn't too late for her to realize he was happy for her. But once he'd finished, he had started second-guessing himself. Kristen had enough money to buy anything she wanted. Perhaps he'd overstepped, yet the pounding of his heart told him how much her approval meant.

She gasped when she finally pulled away the final sheet of tissue paper. Her gaze immediately lifted to Rafe's.

She didn't have to say a word. The pleasure on her beautiful face said it all. Strangely, the wild beating of his heart increased.

Kristen's trembling fingers grazed the burled walnut of the museum-quality domed writing box, the brass hinges. She lifted the circular ring to reveal the red velvet lining. "It's beautiful," she finally said. "It looks authentic."

"I should hope so," Rafe said, pride in his voice. Picking up the fourteen-by-six-inch box, Rafe carefully turned it over and pointed to the discreet initials in a corner. RBC.

"There's a lot of old wood in buildings around here, plus furniture that is too badly damaged to be restored. I buy it." The pad of his scarred thumb swept across the brass hinges. "I get the hardware and the fabric from an antiques dealer." He set the box back on Kristen's desk. "After seeing this, she asked me to make a tea caddy for her."

"Could you make me one?" Kristen asked, her hand resting on the burled top. "Mother's birthday is in a few months and she loves tea."

Before Rafe could speak, a woman from behind him said, "Young man, could I order one, too?"

Rafe turned to see who had spoken and saw an elderly woman, her gaze direct, her bearing regal despite the wooden cane she leaned on. She wore diamonds and pearls. Her white suit was tailored. He'd been around the Wakefields and his wealthier clients enough to recognize affluence and authority when he saw it. This woman oozed both. Her patronage could do a lot for his business, but he found himself tongue-tied. He wasn't used to being around this many people or being the center of attention.

"I'm sure he could," Kristen interjected. "As you can see, he is meticulous about every piece he creates."

His head jerked toward Kristen. He saw the smile, but more so the almost imperceptible working of her mouth. *Say yes.*

He gave his attention back to the woman. "I don't have any cards with me, but I could call you after I've made some sketches for you to look at."

"Excellent. Jacques has my number." The matron started toward the door Jacques held open. She paused, leaning heavily on her cane. "Do you have other reproductions?"

"Yes, ma'am, but this is the first box I've made," he confessed. "I make reproductions of furniture from the eighteenth and nineteenth centuries."

"I'd like to see what you have. Call me." It was an order.

"Yes, ma'am."

She had barely set her tiny foot on the crowded sidewalk before the chauffeur was there to take her slim arm and lead her to a black Bentley a short distance away.

"Well, now," Jacques said, going to the desk and gazing briefly at the writing box. "Considering you picked up customers in my shop, I think it's only fair that I charge you a commission."

seven

Before Rafe could answer, Jacques extended his hand. "A poor joke. Jacques Broussard."

"Rafe Crawford." The handshake was firm. "But I wouldn't have had the possibility of a sale if I hadn't been in your shop. You're entitled to a cut."

Jacques eyed him closer. "A fair and honest man. Qualities our young people need to learn."

"Old ones, too," Angelique quipped.

Jacques nodded. "My sentiments exactly. You're a wise woman."

"Thank you," she said. "I get the feeling you're no slouch yourself."

"Thank *you*," he said, then, "I'm having a soirée Saturday night at my home for an art critic friend of mine who's just moved from Charleston. I'd like all of you to come."

Rafe's mouth had opened to decline when Kristen said, "I think it's best for your sake if I don't come."

"Why?" Jacques asked, genuinely puzzled.

Kristen's hand clenched atop the box. "You probably have a lot of friends in the art world who will be there. The person who made the accusation against me may be in attendance. It would be awkward."

"You can't let him rule your life," Rafe said, getting angry all over again.

"I agree," Angelique said. "Remember what I said." Her hand lifted, clenched, twisted.

Jacques winced. "I never want to make you angry."

"Most men don't," Angelique retorted.

Rafe kept his gaze on Kristen.

"I'm not going." Kristen took her seat. She'd never been the brave type. "Rafe, thank you for the box. It's beautiful. Angelique, you said you have an appointment."

Angelique nudged Rafe with her elbow. "I think she's trying to throw us out. You going?"

Rafe hadn't known what to expect of the woman Kristen called *friend*. He'd never had a close friend who'd stick up for him no matter what. Lilly had tried and suffered because of it. The scar from his father's belt would be on her leg until she died. Perhaps it was best that he was alone: Yet . . . "No. You?"

Angelique sat on the corner of the desk and crossed her long legs. "Not until she says yes."

Kristen straightened papers on her already-neat desk. "Jacques might have an objection to you two keeping me from working."

The owner gave a Gallic shrug. "I want you there. People in the art world can become rather insular and boring. You three would liven things up."

"I'm not going," Rafe said, looking shell-shocked and shaking his head.

"Why not?" Kristen stopped shifting papers.

"I—I—don't do well in crowds," he finally said, his gaze faltering, his hands fisting by his side.

Without thought, Kristen rose and placed her hand on his arm, felt the muscles bunch. In his eyes she saw the loneliness that had stared back at her so many times in the past. And, yes, the same insecurity. She'd missed it before. Perhaps she had been too self-absorbed, too busy trying to conquer her own fears and insecurities. Suddenly it was important that he conquer his as well.

"I'll go if you will," she said quietly. If Rafe was a loner by choice or by chance, she couldn't say. She simply knew she wanted to change that.

"Kristen . . ." he began, faltered, then tried again. "You'll have more fun without me."

"No, I won't, because I won't be there." She folded her arms stubbornly across her chest. "What do you say we go and support each other?"

His hand raked over his hair. She couldn't realize what she was asking of him. He didn't want people in his life. People he'd eventually miss. Besides, he wasn't all that sure what to do with himself around all the important people that were bound to be there. He'd probably embarrass her.

"I need you there with me," she said softly, her beautiful, dark eyes imploring.

Need. He'd never wanted anyone to need him again, yet inexplicably he had made a promise to himself long ago that he'd never again let anyone else down who did. He'd given up a lot, but never his integrity. "All right."

"Great!" She lifted her arms to hug him, then saw him stiffen. She brought her hands together and clapped. She'd forgotten public displays of warmth made him uncomfortable. Her family showed affection openly. For the first time, she wondered what kind of childhood he'd had. "It will be fun."

Doubt lingered on his face. "I guess I better get going."

Jacques stuck out his hand. "Kristen has my address. You can come over anytime after eight. It's black tie."

"Black tie," Rafe repeated, the panic vivid on his face.

Kristen came around the desk. "It won't be any problem to rent a tux in time," she told him, wanting to touch him to reassure him, but afraid it would do the opposite. He didn't look convinced. "Isn't that right, Angelique?"

"No problem," Angelique agreed, her practiced gaze going over him. "Forty-two long. Right?"

He gulped. Nodded.

"I'll call this friend and he'll put one back for you," she said. "I'll give the number to Kristen so you can go by there and pick it up."

He swallowed again, then looked at Jacques as if expecting him to say he was joking about the party being formal. It was not to be.

Jacques smiled knowingly. "Henri likes to dress, but the caterer is excellent so the food and drink will make up for having to wear a tux. There will also be dancing."

Rafe's eyes went wide again.

Kristen didn't think; she simply took Rafe's arm and led him out the door. If he heard any more she'd never get him to go, and it was important to her that he did.

On the sidewalk she pulled him into the recessed doorway of a vacant storefront. "It won't be that bad. I'll help you pick out a tux and I won't leave your side the entire time we're there."

"I guess you think I'm overreacting," he said slowly, staring out at the passing crowd.

"Actually, you remind me of my father," she told him.

His attention whipped back to her, his expression incredulous.

Folding her arms, Kristen leaned against the door frame behind her. "He was a wonderful father, husband, and doctor. His practice kept him extremely busy and when he was home he liked to relax and enjoy his family. In his profession, a fair amount of socialization was necessary." A wistful smile stole over her face.

"He'd complain about Mother dragging him to another party, about her never being ready on time, but that night or the next day, when I saw him, he'd always be happy."

Rafe tried to remember if his father had ever smiled at him and couldn't. "You're lucky to have had him in your life."

"Yes, I was. We were very close. I didn't think I'd ever get over his death, but time and my family helped. So did Jonathan."

He thought of his grandmother and her death. She had hoped and prayed so hard for them to become a family, for her son's hatred of his own son to end. It hadn't, and with her death Rafe no longer cared. He hadn't heard from his father or sister since he had testified in Lilly's divorce case seven years ago. "Tell Angelique I'll take care of the tux. What time should I pick you up?"

"Eight-fifteen."

"I better get you back to work." He started back toward the gallery and she fell into step beside him. They were both silent until they reached the door and Rafe opened it and stood aside. "By the way, should I expect you to be ready?"

She smiled. "Probably not."

He smiled, then walked away.

Humming, Kristen entered the gallery. "He said to tell you he'd take care of the tux himself."

"Looks like you can add three to the guest list, Jacques." Angelique grinned, her arm slipping casually though Jacques's "We'll certainly try to keep it live for you."

"Of that I have no doubt." He patted her long, slender fingers on the sleeve of his fine, black wool suit jacket.

Behind them the door opened and in strode a tall, well-dressed man in a tailored gray suit, carrying a briefcase. He had a self-assured air about him. "Art galleries should be added to the list of places to meet good-looking men," Angelique quipped.

"Thank you," Jacques said. "Hello, Damien."

"Hello, Dad."

Surprised, Angelique glanced between the two men. They shared little in physical appearance except their six-foot height. Damien's build was athletic, his father's cuddly. While Damien's face was classically handsome with close-cropped, wavy hair, his father was simply good-looking, his hairline receding.

Damien appeared to be studying Angelique as much as she was studying him. While she was used to men looking at her, she hadn't felt the prickle of awareness from such a look in a long, long time. She didn't like it one bit.

Looking at his son, Jacques's lips twitched. Despite Damien being thirty-seven, Jacques could still read him. Damien obviously didn't know whether to be interested in Angelique for himself or worried about his father. Since Damien had given Jacques most of the gray hairs in his head while he was a teenager, Jacques decided to let him wonder.

"Damien, you met Kristen Wakefield when she worked at the Haywood Museum. As I told you, she's my new manager." His gaze went to Angelique. "This is Angelique Fleming. My son, Damien Broussard."

Hands were shaken, greetings exchanged, but it was obvious Damien was more interested in Angelique. "I don't believe I've seen you in the gallery before, Ms. Fleming."

"This is my first time," she confessed, annoyed that her voice sounded breathless, almost giddy. She cleared her throat. "I'm not much of an art connoisseur. I came to visit Kristen."

"But you'll come again, and I will personally teach you to appreciate art," Jacques said.

Angelique gratefully turned to him, away from the disturbing attraction of his son. "You may have your work cut out for you."

"Then it will give me more time to spend with you," he said graciously.

"You're a charmer, Jacques." She glanced at her watch, giving her an excuse not to stare at Damien. She'd seen handsome men before, but this one drew her like a homing beacon. Dangerous. "Time to go to work."

"My car is a short distance away—perhaps I can drop you off," Damien said.

Angelique looked at the worsening traffic outside. "I can be at The Inferno by the time you get one block."

"The Inferno?" Damien repeated, his lean, hard body stiffening. "You work at a men's club?"

"She's just—"

"You object to a woman making a living?" Angelique snapped, interrupting Kristen.

"I object to a woman stripping and the other things she does to make money that way, yes." Damien didn't back down.

"Have you ever been a customer or a recipient of those 'other things'?" Angelique asked silkily.

Damien's well-shaped head snapped back in shocked anger. "Of course not!"

"Then all this is based on hearsay," she said in a conversational tone, although she was simmering. Another self-righteous prick. Just like the men she planned to expose.

"I interned at the district attorney's office before I went into corporate law." A muscle leaped in his strong jaw. "I've helped prepare cases against those women."

"How many men in the clubs did you prosecute?" she asked, already knowing the answer.

"The men weren't an issue," he said.

"Horse apples! You let the men slide because it's easier to prosecute the women. That way you don't show the men up for the creeps they are." She whirled toward Jacques, "You know what? Make that two for your party."

"My father invited *you*?" There was pure horror in Damien's voice.

"Damien, I think you've said enough," Jacques said, then turned to Angelique. "The party is at my home, not my son's. My guests are my own. I expect to see you."

Angelique cut a glance at the silently fuming Damien. "I'll be sure not to wear my G-string." Still fuming, she turned to Kristen. "Leave it alone. Got it?"

Kristen nodded reluctantly. You took Angelique as she was. If people didn't like her association with The Inferno that was their problem, not hers. She wasn't ashamed of her past nor should she have been. "Got it."

The glass on the door rattled as Angelique shut it behind her. All three watched her stalk away.

"Looks like I was right," Jacques said into the strained silence. "The party will be far from dull."

"I apologize if I upset you, Kristen," Damien said, still smarting. It wasn't often that a woman or anyone else got the best of him. They certainly didn't have the last word.

"Angelique is the one you owe the apology to, Damien," Kristen said tightly. "She's a wonderful person and a very good friend."

Damien inclined his dark head slightly. "If I have erred, I will apologize."

Kristen's gaze narrowed. "Did you learn to dance around like that during your tenure with the district attorney or as a corporate lawyer?" she asked. Not waiting for an answer, she turned to speak to Jacques. "Thank you for being so gracious to Angelique. I consider it an honor to be her friend. Now, if you'll excuse me, I need to get a painting ready to ship."

Jacques shook his head as Kristen stalked off as well. "It takes a special talent for a man to be so self-righteous that he needlessly angers two beautiful women in the course of a few minutes. Didn't know you had it in you." Jacques started toward his desk at the other end of the gallery.

His father's words stung Damien as he knew they were meant to. He'd always admired his father. His grip on his leather attaché case tightened as he followed. "That's not the kind of woman you or

Kristen—at least from what I've heard about her background—should associate with."

His father abruptly turned. "Exactly what kind of woman is she?"

Damien blinked. He couldn't remember the last time his father had used that sharp tone with him. "She means that much to you?"

Instead of answering, Jacques rapped Damien on the head with his knuckles, the same way he had when he was growing up and his father had thought he'd done or said something particularly stupid. "Is there any gray matter in there?"

It usually annoyed Damien for his father to do that, but under the circumstances he couldn't have been more pleased. "So you're not serious about her?"

Jacques lifted his hand to rap him again, but Damien quickly stepped out of harm's way.

"Stand still when I'm trying to discipline you," Jacques instructed.

Since there was no heat in his father's voice, Damien said, "I love you and I worry about you. So sue me."

"I used to know this fantastic lawyer. Maybe I can get him to take my case," Jacques answered. "Sharp as they come, if a little stiff these days. Takes after his mother's side of the family."

Damien relaxed. "Is this the same family where the youngest daughter ran off with an earnest but poor shoe salesman and her father came after them with a preacher and a shotgun?"

"Your mother loved telling that story. We were married in a church with both our families there." Jacques took his seat behind his desk. "And not a gun in sight."

Damien placed his attaché case on an uncluttered corner of the desk. "Only because you were already married when Grandpapa caught up with you in Baton Rouge."

Jacques lifted a framed photograph from his desk, his face softening. "I'd never met anyone like her. She was the sun and the moon and the stars all wrapped up in one. I didn't think I'd be able to live without her."

Damien didn't have to look at the photograph. In his mind's eye, he saw the picture of his parents, young and so in love, on their first anniversary. What the picture didn't show was his mother's bulging stomach. With Damien.

Damien's hand gripped his father's shoulder. His mother's death from pneumonia ten years ago had been hard on them both. "You made her happy."

Jacques set the picture aside. "We made each other happy. Any chance you're ready to settle down? At thirty-seven, you're not getting any younger."

It was an old topic of conversation. Damien loosened his silk tie and sprawled in the burgundy leather chair across from his father. "Women have changed since the day you met Mother. They're more interested in your bank account than in you."

"Not all of them."

"Enough. Frankly, I don't have time for it. Thibodeaux International didn't slacken when Claude passed." He laced his fingers across his hard, flat abdomen. "Business is booming. Claudette is as shrewd as her father, at least in some things."

Jacques's mouth twisted with distaste. "Is that husband of hers giving her a hard time?"

"He's not around the office enough to do that," Damien answered simply. His father and Claudette had been friends for as long as Damien could remember. His father was rightly worried about her. Claudette had made the worst mistake of her life by marrying Maurice.

"I've invited her to the party," Jacques said, drumming his fingers on a stack of order forms.

"You're going to have quite an eclectic group there," Damien said, switching his thoughts back to Angelique.

Yes, I will." Jacques leaned back in his executive chair. "Too bad you had other plans. Should be a night to remember. I'm rather looking forward to it."

Damien gazed at his father, trying to read his expression. Nothing. His poker face was firmly in place. Was he thinking about Angelique or merely making a statement?

The woman could mean nothing to his father, but even as the thought ran through Damien's mind, he dismissed the idea. He had wanted her the second he'd laid eyes on her. Sleek, trim, and exotic. At the club, she probably drew men like bees to honey.

He recalled her last taunting words about not wearing a G-string and his body hardened. His father would be no match for her. Obviously she used Kristen for entry into a world of money and power to meet wealthy men, then fleece them for all they were worth. She was probably as greedy and as grasping as they came.

Just like Maurice Laurent.

He'd walk through hell before he'd let that woman hurt his father.

"If the invitation is still open, Dad, I think I'll come after all."

"What changed your mind?"

I won't let the same thing happen to you that happened to Claudette. "As you said, it will be fun."

eight

※

Rafe Crawford was shaking in his new shoes. On each arm was a beautiful, poised and elegantly dressed woman, Kristen in siren red and Angelique in chic black, and he had absolutely no idea what to do with them now that they were in the high-ceilinged drawing room inside Jacques Broussard's house in the Garden District.

He swallowed the knot of fear in his throat that had been growing since he'd arrived at Kristen's place. She'd answered the door with a cheerful greeting, and for a moment, he'd been speechless.

In the past he'd always tried to keep his distance from her. Since she'd called him he hadn't been able to do that. Until that moment he hadn't realized why. Her quiet beauty and shy smiles appealed to the dark, lonely part of him. The realization increased his nervousness. Learning that Angelique was riding with them hadn't helped. Escorting them to the Lincoln Continental, all he could think of was being grateful that he had had the foresight to rent a car.

Despite the animated conversation of the two women that he was sure was meant to put him at ease, he hadn't said five words during the fifteen-minute drive. He felt strangled by his black bow tie, ill at ease in the confines of the tuxedo and pleated shirt.

He'd never worn either before tonight. At least his shoes didn't pinch. He just wished he weren't shaking in them. He glanced around the elegant room and swallowed.

People were everywhere. On the parquet dance floor, surrounding the three white-linen-draped buffet tables, on the terrace, or simply milling about the beautifully decorated room with food or a flute in their hand. He didn't belong here.

Then he felt Kristen stiffen. Seeing her staring straight ahead, he followed the direction of her gaze. Rage built within him as he located the cause of her sudden discomfort.

Across the room, Maurice was talking to a young woman, their heads close together. It could have been innocent, but the voluptuous brunette's over-bright laughter and the flirtatious way she occasionally flipped her straight hair said otherwise.

"You don't have to be afraid of him, Kristen," Rafe said, unconsciously stepping closer.

Kristen shook her head. "His arrogance is simply beyond belief. Claudette might be blindly in love, but the rest of us see him for what he is."

Angelique quickly caught on and watched the tableau being acted out in an alcove near the terrace. "Unfortunately, the only one that counts in this scenario is his wife. For whatever reason, love or keeping face, some women choose to look the other way."

"Perhaps not any longer." Kristen directed their attention to a tall, elegant woman in a long, white gown working her way through the crowd toward Maurice. "Claudette Laurent. Maurice's wife."

"Looks likes there might be trouble in paradise and it couldn't happen to a more deserving prick," Angelique said.

Claudette joined her husband and the young woman he'd been chatting with for the past ten minutes with the social smile she'd cultivated for thirty-eight years. No matter what, appearances must be maintained. "Hello, I don't think we've met. I'm Claudette Laurent."

Maurice's dark head jerked up. His eyes widened as his gaze bounced between his wife and the other woman.

Still wearing a seductive smile, the brunette glanced from Maurice to Claudette. "Are you related?"

Claudette looked at Maurice and waited for him to make the announcement. Saying she was Maurice's wife would have been too obvious. But had his smile become more of a grimace? Seconds later, Claudette was sure it was her imagination when Maurice slipped his arm around her waist.

"I thought everyone at the party knew that Claudette is my beautiful wife," he said, admiration ringing in his voice. He kissed her cheek.

Claudette couldn't prevent the little shiver that raced over her body as Maurice's lips brushed across her skin, just as she couldn't keep her gaze from the woman he'd been so cozily ensconced with.

Shock, then anger, radiated across the younger woman's face. She walked off without a word.

"How rude," he said, his tone sounding genuinely baffled: then he turned the full wattage of his adoring smile on Claudette. "Thanks for rescuing me. Trying to be cordial to that woman was a strain—all she wanted to talk about was herself. Another starving artist wanting a handout. Shall I get you another glass of wine or some canapés from the buffet?"

The apprehension Claudette had experienced on seeing Maurice and the other woman so close together receded. She'd obviously been trying to influence Maurice into helping her career. Just as Kristen had. *He loved her.*

It wouldn't be the first time some self-serving person had tried to use her for his or her own gain in the art community. She mustn't let Kristen's unfounded accusations and her own insecurities about her age destroy her marriage. She'd caused enough gossip by marrying Maurice: she wouldn't cause any more by giving even a hint that all wasn't well between them.

Claudette lifted the nearly full flute of white wine. "I'm fine."

"When you're near me all I can see is you." Maurice kissed the fine-boned fingers holding the delicate stem, then lifted hooded eyes. "How soon do you think we can get out of here and go home?"

"Not much longer," she said, her voice breathless. Another unfounded worry laid to rest. She did satisfy her husband sexually. She shouldn't have worried because he hadn't approached her in several days. Perhaps she should have approached him, as one of the women's magazines suggested, but that wasn't in her character.

"Since there are people here you'll want to see before we leave, why don't we circulate?" he asked. "I promise not to leave your side until we do," he said.

Pleasure swept through her. He was so considerate. She'd never doubt him again. Caught up in basking in her husband's love, she didn't notice the three stern-faced people approaching until it was too late.

"Hello, Claudette," Kristen greeted, ignoring Maurice. She couldn't believe he'd apparently managed to pull the wool over Claudette's usually shrewd eyes again. But hadn't Kristen had the same blind faith in Eric?

Seeing Maurice's smug smile moments after the woman he'd been talking to had angrily walked away, Kristen remembered that she had run, too, rather than expose him for the immoral man he was. No more. She wanted to face him and show him that she had survived in spite of him. "Lovely party, isn't it?"

Maurice's jaw clenched. His hand moved from his wife's waist to close around her bare forearm just as their host joined them.

"Hello," said Jacques, looking like the successful man he was in his tailored black tuxedo. He stopped beside Angelique and glanced around the small group. "Glad to see you got here. Has everyone met?"

Silence reigned.

Jacques continued as if his question had been answered. "Then I guess you know that Angelique and Rafe are friends of Kristen, the new manager of St. Clair's."

Claudette, who had been staring straight ahead, finally looked at Jacques. Her eyes widened in astonishment.

"I'm lucky to have her," Jacques said, speaking directly to Claudette. "I trust her implicitly and she has wonderful work ethics." His gaze flickered to Maurice. "You can't say that about everyone."

"Excuse us." Tight-lipped, Maurice pulled his wife away.

Kristen's hand clenched around her red beaded bag, but she was beaming at Jacques. "You'll never realize how much that meant to me."

"It's no more than the truth." Jacques looked at a stern-faced Rafe by her side. "How are you holding up?"

"About as well as I expected," Rafe answered slowly. "I thought I'd take Kristen and Angelique to the buffet table."

"Excellent idea."

"You two go on," Angelique withdrew her arm from Rafe's. "I'll be with you in a minute."

As they moved away, Angelique studied Jacques's tense features closely. "You make me want to reassess my opinion of men."

He frowned. "Have they treated you so badly?"

"A few, but I was talking more about men in general."

"But it's been my experience that lumping any group is unfair. You struck me as a fair and very perceptive young woman."

"That's why I've got their number." Angelique watched Jacques's gaze search the room for the second time since they'd been talking. It was more than a host assuring himself his guests were having a good time because his gaze always stopped on Claudette Laurent, and when it did, a sweet longing would come over his face. "How long have you cared about her?"

Jacques casually brought his attention back to Angelique. "What if I said I don't know what you're talking about?"

It might have been years since Angelique had loved a man who hadn't loved her back, but she still remembered the aching pain. Seeing her history professor in class or on campus always sent her into a tailspin. It hadn't mattered that she had been the one to end their five-week affair. Pride couldn't comfort her heart. It continued to yearn, to grieve.

She'd gotten a well-deserved A in the class. If he had tried to give her anything less, she'd already warned him that she would go to the president of the university. He may have taken her for gullible once, but he had known she wasn't bluffing about her grade. Her degree was too important to her.

Months passed before she fully accepted the loss and moved on. She recognized the "look" on Jacques's face immediately.

Sympathetic, she looped her arm though Jacques's and briefly leaned her head on his shoulder. "I've been where you are."

"He was stupid."

"Yes, he was." Angelique laughed softly, grateful that she could. "I guess you know she's married to a user."

"I know." As if they were connected even in a crowd of people, Jacques's gaze easily found Claudette on the dance floor with Maurice. She seemed completely enthralled by him as they moved to a soulful ballad made famous by the legendary Billie Holiday, another woman who'd had man problems of her own. "Would it make sense if I said I hate that for her just as much as it makes me happy that's he a worm?"

"Very much. Your conflicted emotions are to be expected," Angelique told him. "And although she's not demonstrating it at the moment, if she's as smart as Kristen says she is, Claudette will wise up and toss Maurice out before much longer and you'll have your chance."

The heart-wrenching last note of the singer's voice that sounded unerringly like Holiday faded with the long wail of a sax. Maurice kissed Claudette's hand. Jacques finally looked away.

Even if Claudette divorced Maurice, that didn't mean she would suddenly fall in love with Jacques. On the contrary, she'd probably be even more leery of a relationship. They were friends, good friends. She had no idea that his devotion to her had matured into love, and she never would. "What was that little scene I interrupted?"

"What scene?" Angelique asked with wide-eyed innocence.

Jacques wasn't fooled. "When I came up, Rafe looked as if he wanted to tear Maurice's head off, you looked like you'd help, and Kristen looked angry and determined." His gaze suddenly narrowed. "He's the one, isn't he?"

"You'll have to ask Kristen that."

Jacques muttered a French expletive that needed no translation. "Sorry."

"I've heard worse."

Now he was the one studying her. "Once again I get the feeling that there is more to you than meets the eye."

"You mean more than bump and grind?" she tried to say it flippantly, but it fell flat. She wanted Jacques's respect.

He waited patiently.

"Can you keep a secret?"

"Damien won't hear it from me," he told her.

So much for not being obvious. "My dancing days at The Inferno are long gone. I worked there the last two years of undergrad school to help with tuition and pay off the loan my foster parents had taken on their house to get me into school. I go there now to gather data for my dissertation in psychology titled 'Exposing the Double Society.' I'm tired of men's sanctimonious double standards."

Jacques nodded as if he weren't surprised by her revelation. "A woman of indeterminate measure and grit. Now, I'd better circulate and I expect to see you at the gallery. You could start by coming in tomorrow afternoon. The last Sunday of the month I always have a private get-together for area artists."

"Will the artist who painted *Disbelief* be there?"

"Yes, and I just found out tonight that so will my friend, Henri, the art critic." Jacques looked pained. "He savaged *Disbelief*."

Angelique patted his shoulder in sympathy. "I'll try to be there."

"Thank you."

She started across the floor to join Kristen and Rafe at the buffet table. Halfway there, she stopped. Her skin prickled. She glanced around the room, half-expecting to see Maurice. What she saw was almost as bad.

Across the crowded dance floor, Damien stared at her, his mouth pinched in disapproval. Just like a man, dancing with a woman who was wrapped around him like wet tissue paper and his attention was on another . . . even if it was with distaste.

He didn't want her here. That much was obvious. Thought she shouldn't be around "decent" people.

Tough.

Pushing away the little pang of hurt she felt, Angelique lifted her chin in a direct challenge. She went where she pleased and at the moment that was to the buffet table. She'd seen a plate of scallops earlier and they were calling her name.

Damien's dark eyes narrowed on the graceful curve of Angelique's slim, bare back. The floor-length gown flowed over her body like liquid darkness, making a man want to pull the material away slowly in brilliant light so he could see, then devour, what lay beneath.

For Angelique, that man would apparently have to be able to pay a price, a very high one. Damien knew clothes. Her gown wasn't cheap. He didn't have to guess how she'd gotten the money to pay for it.

His black eyes narrowed in determination. He couldn't understand why Kristen and his father didn't see Angelique for the opportunist she was. But one thing he knew for sure, she wasn't adding his father's name to her list of sugar daddies. Before tonight was over, he'd make sure she'd moved on.

By the time Kristen and Rafe had worked their way to the head buffet table, her anger had disappeared, helped by the frequent worried look Rafe kept throwing at her. She'd been aware of his anxiety when he'd picked them up, anxiety that had increased when they'd entered the drawing room. But after seeing Maurice, Rafe's concern had been solely for her.

Strangely, his unselfish actions made her want to put him at ease and see that he had a good time. "What do you want to try first?" she asked as they neared the first table, laden with bite-sized delicacies.

"I'll think I'll pass." Rafe frowned down at the table.

Kristen smiled at him over her shoulder. "We both eat or no one eats." She picked up two plates trimmed in 14-carat gold, handed them to him, then proceeded to fill both as they moved down the buffet line laden with imported cheese, fruits, shrimp and lobster canapes, and smoked salmon.

"Hello, Kristen. How are you doing?"

Kristen momentarily faltered as she recognized Mary Oliphant, a museum patron and art collector, ahead of her in line. "F-Fine. And you?"

"Wonderful. We're leaving for Italy on Friday," Mrs. Oliphant said, taking some crabmeat and placing it on her plate. "Since you work for Jacques, are you still interested in acquiring nineteenth-century African-American art?"

Luckily, Kristen had just placed a cube of cheese on one of the plates Rafe held because she almost dropped the silver tongs in her hand. "Yes, but how did you know I work for Jacques?"

The woman laughed, full and throaty. "He was singing your praises last night at an art council meeting. Dr. Robertson was there and said he'd hated to see you leave the museum, but understood you wanted to broaden your horizons."

Kristen worked hard to keep her mouth from dropping open. Bless Dr. Robertson's sweet heart. First thing Monday morning she was calling the museum director and thanking him. "Having a permanent collection of nineteenth-century African-American art on display at the Haywood is a personal goal, not just because I worked there. As I recall, you have a couple of paintings from that period. I'd appreciate any help or suggestions you might give me."

The woman's long face became thoughtful. "Why don't you come and sit with us and we'll talk about it?"

She started to say yes, then looked back at Rafe. "Is it all right?"

"You lead. I'll follow."

The decision, Kristen acknowledged less than fifteen minutes later, had been a wise one. People at the Oliphants' table, as well as those who dropped by, were interested in Kristen's idea. And best of all, Mrs. Oliphant and her husband agreed to loan *Landscape with Brook* by Robert S. Duncanson if Kristen could get a firm commitment for a total of fifteen paintings.

"Thank you," Kristen said, shaking both of their hands.

Mrs. Oliphant looked at Rafe, sitting patiently and quietly by Kristen. "I imagine you must want to get to the dance floor."

"I'm not much of a dancer." He almost smiled. "You're saving Kristen's feet."

People sitting around the table laughed. Kristen thought of the many times he'd saved her. Perhaps she could pay him back.

"Rafe is an artist himself. He reproduces exquisite eighteenth- and nineteenth-century furniture. You should see the writing box he made for my desk. It's magnificent." She sent him a smile. "I can't tell you the number of people who have seen it and wanted to purchase it."

Fingering the emerald-and-diamond necklace encircling her throat, Mrs. Oliphant leaned forward, her interest obviously piqued. "Do you have others at your shop?"

"Kristen's is the first and only one I've ever made," Rafe told them.

Kristen observed the interested faces of the women seated around them. Having an exclusive on any item was a coup. "But he's going to make tea caddies. Each one is unique since they're fashioned by hand and fitted with antique hardware. I've ordered one for my mother's birthday. After seeing Rafe's sketches, Mrs. Moreau ordered one as well," Kristen finished, smoothly throwing out the elderly woman's name. Mrs. Moreau loved antiques, had a house full of them, and had strong ties to the New Orleans Historical Society.

Women and men looked at Rafe with new interest. It only took one person to ask for his card before they all wanted one.

To Rafe's chagrin, he didn't have any. Kristen came to his rescue. "I'm sure you're all in Jacques's address book. I'll drop a few of Rafe's cards in the mail Monday." Like Mrs. Moreau, the people sitting around them were used to being catered to. However, once Rafe's work was accepted, as Kristen was positive it would be, the women would shamelessly seek him out just as they did their favorite designer or decorator.

He wouldn't be pleased by the attention. Oddly, she, too, wasn't pleased by the prospect of women running after him.

Kristen stood. "Now, if you'll excuse us, I think I'll see if my feet are in as much danger as Rafe claims."

Laughter followed them as they made their way to the edge of the dance floor. The five-piece band was playing a heavenly melody by Duke Ellington. Rafe glanced around the room as if looking for the nearest exit. Kristen took charge again by putting her left hand on his broad shoulder and extending her right.

He stared down at her and gulped. "Thank you for what you did back there, but I wasn't kidding about my dancing."

"I'll chance it." She laced her fingers with his strong, calloused hand. Her brow puckered at the unexpected spiraling of heat that radiated from their joined palms. Rafe's hand jerked in hers and she wondered if he felt it, too, or if he was just nervous. *Probably nervous.*

"The song will be over before we take one step," she teased.

Rafe stared down at her. She had a smile on her winsome face that said she could conquer the world. He liked it, liked to think he had helped put it there.

"I'm not sitting down until we dance," she warned him.

Slowly he drew her closer. He tried not to notice how good she felt or how the exotic fragrance she wore teased and stimulated his senses. He couldn't. He was the little boy with empty pockets staring through the plate glass window into the candy shop, wishing and dreaming. "This is not exactly my kind of music."

"Stop stalling," she told him. "Dance."

He cautiously took a step, then another, and miraculously discovered that his size twelves kept missing her small feet. He hadn't forgotten. He hadn't danced since a junior high sock hop. His mother had given him permission to remain at school, but his father had met him at the door with his belt when he'd gotten home.

"Why the frown?" Kristen asked.

Once again, her perception caught him off guard. "Just concentrating on missing your feet," he told her. More lies, but as far back as he could remember, lies and secrets had been a part of his life.

"I think you can stop worrying." She moved closer and laid her head on his shoulder. "You dance beautifully."

He waited for his body to tense. And waited. It never happened.

Instead he felt a curious unfurling of warmth and protectiveness as Kristen's soft, warm body snuggled against his. They fit flawlessly. With her cheek against his chest, they moved in perfect harmony.

He searched his memory and couldn't recall feeling this way before. With her so close to him, she made him feel as if a candle had been lit in the dark places of his soul.

He'd ceased thinking his life would ever be normal, that he could have friends or a loving relationship with a woman. His unruly temper and his father's bad blood made that impossible, but tonight . . . just for a little while . . . perhaps he could get a little glimpse of what that kind of wonderful life would be like.

His body relaxed. As he drew her closer, he let himself dream.

Damien was a patient man and it was finally paying off. Angelique had just stepped onto the terrace, and for the first time in the past hour, there wasn't a slack-jawed, drooling man by her side.

Disgusted with the men panting after her and more than irked with Angelique, he checked to see that his father was on the other side of the room, busy with his guests: then he slipped through the folding glass doors. Luckily, there was no one else outside. When he was a few feet away, she turned. Even in the half-shadows, he saw the anger glinting in her eyes.

"So you finally stopped skulking around and worked up enough nerve to face me." She stood there, beautiful and seductive and bathed in moonlight, a trailing bougainvillea loaded with dark red blossoms behind her.

He'd expected her anger, had been prepared for it, but not the sudden, strong sexual pull she exuded. He stopped in his tracks.

"You have something on that bigoted, self-righteous mind you want to say to me, so here I am." She lifted her hands and held them wide in challenge. "Take your best shot."

Her attack on his character effectively got him back on track. "You know nothing about me."

"Ha! So you can dish it out but you can't take it." She folded her arms. "Your knowing nothing about me didn't seem to stop you from declaring me unfit to be around your father."

That she was partially right fanned the flames of his aggravation. "My father is a wonderful man."

"I bet he wonders where he picked you up from."

Her taunt hit home. His father had often said similar words to Damien when he had tested his parents' love and patience to the limits as a wild teenager. "I want you to leave my father alone."

She shook her head in disbelief. "Jacques is old enough to make his own decisions about his friends."

"His age is the factor here," Damien pointed out.

"If your father heard you say that, he'd bean you over the head."

Damien vividly recalled the last time his father had rapped him over the head—it had been about her—and though she was right, that was beside the point. "Leave him alone."

Her arms came to her sides and she started toward him. She didn't stop until they were toe-to-toe. "And who's going to make me?"

Damien had never reacted well to threats, and he didn't now. He leaned down until they were nose to nose. "I will."

"Better men than you have tried." She stepped back, her eyes challenging. "See you around, sonny boy."

Damien watched her reenter the house. He heard the music, then silence closed around him when the terrace door shut. Slowly he un-clenched his fists and clamped his hands around the balustrade. He wanted to feel animosity, but all he felt was the need to drag Angelique back out into the moonlight and down onto the grass beneath him. She wouldn't bend easily to him, but she would bend.

Heaven help him. He wanted Angelique Fleming.

Angelique was shaking. She desperately wanted to claim it was because she was furious. She couldn't. She never lied to herself or backed away from the truth.

Damn Damien Broussard for threatening her. She should have wanted to slug him, but when he put his face in hers all she had wanted to do was yank him by the tie, put her mouth on his, and go from there.

"Wine?"

She glanced up at the smiling young waiter and the tray of drinks he offered and shook her head. Another thing she never did was drink alcohol when she was deeply troubled. Too many of the clients she counseled at the rehab center had turned to drugs for solace and ended up spiraling out of control.

The same thing could happen to her if she were around Damien. Damn him most of all for making her want him.

Jacques never considered himself a masochist. He found no pleasure in pain. So why did he continue to torture himself by sneaking glances at Claudette every chance he got?

The answer was simple. He loved her. No matter how great the pain, the pain of not seeing her was far worse. Despite Angelique guessing his secret, he felt no fear that his other friends would. Since her sudden marriage, Claudette often drew polite and not-so-polite stares. Despite it all, she'd always held her head high.

She was a Thibodeaux. She could hold her own in an unenviable situation that would shatter a lesser woman. Never Claudette.

She could be near her breaking point, but the outside world would never know. Her father had accepted nothing less than perfection and a strict code of conduct from the daughter who adored him. Thibodeaux honor was more highly prized than their hefty bank account. To his credit, her father had loved her as well. If he were alive he would have seen through Maurice, just as so many of their friends had.

Love was truly blind.

Standing with a group of his associates, Jacques nodded at the appropriate times to the conversation around him and sipped his Chaute le Fette. Henri, the guest of honor, was having a wonderful time shredding the merits of a nationally known artist with his rapier tongue. He'd be just as vocal tomorrow afternoon in his appraisal of *Disbelief*. Since Jacques agreed with the art critic's assessment, if not the way he expressed his opinion, he let his mind drift back to Claudette.

At his age, he should have had better sense than to fall in love. However, technically, this hadn't been his fault. Nothing in his past had prepared him for this eventuality.

He'd always been a decisive man and acted accordingly. He'd seen his precious Jeanne strolling down Canal Street with her parents and immediately wanted her for his wife. It hadn't mattered that they were wealthy, and he barely got by selling shoes. Not for one second had he doubted the eventual outcome.

Her family had eventually accepted him because they were married, and because he had discovered his true destiny lay in discovering hidden talent and being able to foresee trends in art. Too bad he hadn't seen the disaster with Claudette coming.

With Claudette, his affection for her had snuck up on him. They had started out as friends with a common interest—art. She had been a guest in his home and he in hers. After Jeanne's death, he attended social functions by himself. Since Claudette was often by herself, they seemed to gravitate to each other. He enjoyed her no-nonsense attitude, her sharp mind, her deep sense of purpose.

It wasn't until after her father's death and she was mourning that he began to realize how his feelings for her had grown into something deeper. For the first time in his life, he didn't act. By the time he'd sorted through his new emotions, it was too late. She was married. Worse, married to a man who was without scruples.

Jacques's fingers clenched dangerously on the wine stem when he saw Claudette and Maurice start toward him. They were probably coming to say good night, then they'd leave and go home.

To bed.

Afraid he'd snap the delicate stem, he handed the glass to a passing waiter and prepared to be a good host. He forced cheer into his voice. "I hope you aren't calling it a night already."

"I'm afraid so, I have an early appointment in the morning," Claudette told him. "It was a wonderful party." As she had been doing for the past twenty years, Claudette touched her smooth cheek to his.

Jacques's heart thundered. He clasped her fragile hands in his and wished he could keep holding them, wished he had the right to hold *her*. "Good night. Thank you for coming."

Maurice gave a brisk nod. "Good night."

Good manners and courtesy dictated that Jacques return the gesture, but he did it in the same manner in which it was given. He and Maurice hated each other and they both knew it. "Good night."

Jacques watched them leave. It disturbed him that he wanted another man's wife, but what distressed him more was the eventual pain Claudette would have to endure when she finally accepted the truth about the kind of man Maurice really was.

nine

Angelique was madder than a wet hen when they left Jacques's house, and Kristen was determined to find out why. After Rafe had seen them both to their doors, she'd gone inside her apartment, changed into sweats, and gone next door. Angelique answered the chime, still wearing the Dior gown she'd gotten for fifty dollars at a resale shop, the anger just as vivid in her hazel eyes.

"What happened?" Kristen asked, closing the door behind her.

Angelique stalked to the living room done in the eclectic mix of garage and resale finds that suited her volatile personality. "I want to throw something. Preferably Damien Broussard! But with all the hot air in his big head, he'd float instead of smashing against a wall!"

Understanding dawned. Kristen shoved the stack of medical journals and textbooks aside on the cushions of the overstuffed sofa covered with the fringed paisley shawl Angelique had discovered in a trunk she'd purchased at a garage sale, and then sat down. The trunk was a catchall at the other end of the sofa. Papers were stacked on the floor beside it. Angelique never seemed to remember to put things away. Since she'd started working on her dissertation, her place was more cluttered than usual. "You spoke with Damien at the party?"

"That's putting it mildly." Angelique pulled the pins out of her hair. Glossy auburn curls tumbled past her shoulders. "He warned me to stay away from his father."

"Why don't you just tell him the truth?" Kristen asked softly.

Angelique stopped pacing. "He has no right to pass judgment on me or anyone else! He's so sanctimonious!"

"Damien thinks he's protecting his father," Kristen pointed out. "If I didn't know you, I might be concerned for Jacques as well."

Angelique flung her hand up in disagreement. "You'd never act that way."

"I might have," Kristen admitted honestly. "But by the time you told me about The Inferno, I had come to know you. Just tell him."

"No!"

"Why, for goodness sake?"

Angelique started to repeat what she had said about his being so self-righteous, but couldn't. She pushed the stack further aside on the sofa and plopped down beside Kristen. "He gets to me."

"I already know . . ." Kristen's voice trailed off. Rearing up, she stared at Angelique as her meaning sank in. "Oh!"

Angelique let out a disgusted breath. She thought she had more sense. "How can I be attracted to a man I despise?"

"I can't answer your question any more than I can answer the one I've been asking myself most of the evening." Kristen pulled the blue silk pillow from behind her back and hugged it to her chest. "How could I have been around Rafe these past seven years and never really looked at him, never noticed how gentle and caring he was?"

"Uh-oh." Angelique's eyes rounded. "You, too?"

Kristen bit her lip. "I'm not sure what I'm feeling. I had to threaten him to get him to take me to his workshop tomorrow."

Angelique's head plopped against the back of the sofa. "We can certainly pick 'em."

"Maybe it'll wear off," Kristen offered, her brow puckered. "When I used to dream about falling in love, it was with a man who would sweep me off my feet. I don't think that's Rafe's style."

"So get him so hot and bothered it becomes his style," Angelique suggested.

Kristen flushed and drew the pillow closer. "Is that how you plan to win Damien over after you tell him the truth?"

Without answering, Angelique got up and went to the bar and poured two glasses of white wine. She gave one to Kristen as she reclaimed her seat. "All my life I've been trying to get people to accept me as I am, to like me *in spite of.*" She sipped her wine. "A TV psychiatrist would tell you I'm seeking approval because my parents abandoned me when I was three and I haven't gotten over their rejection. That's why I acted out so badly in all the foster homes I was placed in, why I continue to try and shock people."

"What would Dr. Angelique Fleming, soon to be known far and wide on the talk show circuit, say?" Kristen asked softly.

Angelique's glass clinked on the round coffee table in front of her. "That he's right."

"Wouldn't that same TV psychiatrist and Dr. Fleming agree that the first step toward healing is admitting the problem?"

Angelique looked at Kristen with such a strange expression that Kristen laughed in spite of the serious situation. "You have been my best friend for the past two years. It's understandable that I should have picked up some of your wisdom by now."

"Wish I felt wise now." Angelique picked up her glass, more to have something in her hand than wanting the drink. "I'm attracted to a man who thinks I'm for sale to the highest bidder."

"I'm attracted to one who is a confirmed loner."

"Like I said. We sure can pick 'em."

"What do you think we should do?" Kristen asked, tucking her lower lip between her teeth.

Angelique twirled the delicate stem in her hand. "We've both been hurt badly in the past, and, the way things look, we might be on that same road again."

"Personally, once was more than enough." Kristen stared down into her glass.

"So, it comes down to a basic psychological principle, fight or flight." Kristen's head came up. "Which?"

Angelique considered. "We'll skip the physical attributes because that would make us shallow. I mean just because they're both six-feet plus of mouth-watering muscles, washboard abs, and wide shoulders is no reason to forgo common sense."

"Don't forget great hands. Rafe's are wide-palmed and calloused, but when he touches me . . ." Kristen shivered and took a quick sip of wine.

"Damien's mouth was created for sin, and I bet he knows just how to use it." Angelique took two sips.

"Rafe's chest is broad and hard, yet comforting."

"I didn't get a chance to scope it out, but I bet Damien has a tight butt."

"Rafe probably does, too."

Morosely, Angelique lifted her glass and said, "I don't think we have any choice."

Resigned, Kristen raised hers. "I don't, either."

"Flight—and pray it's not too late."

The glasses clinked, the women drank, both lost in their own thoughts. When they went to bed that night it was a long time before either went to sleep.

Claudette stood on the balcony of her bedroom later that same night and stared blindly at the city lights in the distance. The summer breeze was soft and fragrant from the many flower gardens surrounding her home.

In her lifetime she'd stood in this very spot, daydreaming, despite the pragmatism that had been taught to her as a child, that somewhere out there was a man who would love her, make her laugh, and hold her when she cried.

Such a simple dream. For a moment, the city lights in the distance blurred. She blinked and they reappeared.

Perhaps that was why she had believed James Cassell so readily. Just looking at his strikingly handsome face had caused her sixteen-year-old heart to ache. What did it matter that he was twenty-one, with a reputation for drinking and drugs that his wealthy family unsuccessfully tried to keep quiet?

From the moment they'd met at Regina Brown's eighteenth birthday party, they were drawn to each other. Her parents had seen them dancing too close and forbade her from seeing or talking with him again. She'd moped and cried for two weeks until James called her one night when her parents were at the theater. Overjoyed that he still thought of her, she quickly put on her prettiest dress and slipped out of the house to meet him at the gazebo.

Her heart pounded when she glimpsed him in the moonlight. He had stepped from the iron structure and pulled her into his arms to kiss her. His tongue in her mouth had frightened her at first, then excited her. She thought she'd melt in a little puddle at his feet. Her legs shook so badly she could hardly stand.

"You're too young and innocent for me, but I won't let you go," he said fiercely, his gaze burning hotly into hers. "You're the best thing that has ever happened in my crummy life. I won't lose you. I can't."

So many emotions swirled through her mind, but the one that was uppermost was that she loved him. Her parents and everyone who thought him beyond redemption were wrong. He just needed love. *Her* love.

He kissed her again. She put the full measure of her love into returning the hungry kiss. She would have done anything for him. She was so sure things would work out for them. James only had to show her parents what a wonderful man he was—then they wouldn't object to their seeing each other. In the meantime, they'd continue to meet secretly.

She was so sure—and so dead wrong. She shivered, her hands rubbing the chill away from her arms.

Less than three weeks later, James was dead and he had taken her secret shame with him. It had taken months for her to show her parents that she was truly repentant before they had finally forgiven her. There had been no more dreams.

Until she'd met Maurice. The lights blurred again. Tears rolled down her cheeks, but there were no arms to hold her, no lips to kiss the tears away.

After they arrived home from the party, they'd gone directly to bed. Their lovemaking had been rushed and unsatisfying. Almost immediately, Maurice had left their bed.

"I'm too restless to sleep. I'll take one of the guest bedrooms tonight." Then he was gone.

An hour ago she'd heard him pass her door. A call to the chauffeur confirmed her suspicion. He'd taken the Porsche she'd given him as a wedding present and left.

Was she wrong again about the man she loved?

The door behind her opened. She whirled around.

Maurice stood there with a bouquet of flowers in his hand. "I went for a drive and couldn't stop thinking about you."

With love shining in her eyes, she flew across the room. She didn't reach for the flowers, she reached for him. Roses, carnations, and daisies scattered at their feet.

Maurice roughly pulled her down on the Persian rug that had been in the Thibodeaux family for a hundred years. Claudette went willingly. He needed her. Just her. Her dream had come true.

Maurice needed release and at least his wife was good for that. Besides, it was her fault that Beverly wouldn't let him into her apartment. If Claudette hadn't interrupted them at Jacques's party, he would be in her bed now, driving into her. The thought excited him and made him harder.

He'd even thought to take her flowers. They might not have gotten him what he wanted from her, but they sure worked now.

What did they say about all cats in the dark? With a snide grin, he pushed up Claudette's nightgown.

Angelique came to the St. Clair Gallery Sunday afternoon to prove a point. She'd decided after a restless night that sooner would be better when it came to confronting Damien. Sipping her mineral water, she moved around the crowd of artists deep in discussion about their work or that of their contemporaries, and kept her eye on the door. Kristen had left thirty minutes ago for her date with Rafe, but Angelique wasn't ready to give up.

If she had read Damien correctly, he thought she was a party girl. He'd be at the gallery to see if his threats had worked. He might be opinionated, but he loved his father.

"Excuse me. Have we met?"

She glanced at the thin, gray-haired man in a red sports jacket and snowy white ascot. "No. Excuse me."

"But I'm sure of it," he said, stepping around in front of her. "I'd never forget so beautiful a face."

Something about the lurid grin on his face had her studying him more closely. She'd run into men she'd met while working at The Inferno before, but not in a long time. When she had, they usually looked the other way. "And where, exactly, would we have met?" she asked, not even trying to hide the impatience in her voice.

His hand closed around her arm. "Perhaps we could discuss it someplace more private."

She fought the impulse to wipe the grin off his face with a right hook. "Take your hand off me," she hissed.

The smile slid away at the coldness of her voice. His bony fingers uncurled. "There's no need for that kind of attitude."

She faced him squarely. "If you want to see attitude, touch me again without my permission."

His lips curled in anger. "Why, you—"

"Is there a problem, Henri?"

Angelique would know that deep, resonant voice anywhere. So much for catching Damien unaware.

She glanced up and groaned. He was all lethal male, ready to rip the head off of anyone who dared get in his way. Despite the handmade suit and wingtips, he was no joke. Unfortunately, she didn't know whose head he was after.

"No. No problem, Damien," Henri quickly said. "I was about to join a group and give my opinion of *Disbelief*."

Damien bought his gaze back to her and Angelique well understood why Henri had hurried away. She liked her head just where it was. "Thank you."

"I didn't do it for you."

She'd deal with that hurt later. "I'm aware of that. Your love for your father is admirable."

He stepped closer. "Stay away from him."

"I go where I please," she said, acting instinctively to his threat and not counting the cost.

His narrowed gaze bore into her. "Push this and you'll regret it."

She already did. Her pulse beat out an erratic staccato.

Fortunately, he straightened. "Don't make me tell you again."

When he walked off, Angelique made her escape. She had the answer she'd come for. She'd stay away from Jacques because if she didn't and Damien came near her again, she might do something very, very stupid.

Kristen was ready when Rafe picked her up. She was polite and friendly. She fully planned to keep it that way until Rafe stepped in front of her to open the passenger door of his truck.

Her gaze unerringly went to his butt encased in faded, form-fitting denims before she could stop herself. *Tight.* Just as she'd thought.

"Kristen?"

Flushing, she scrambled into the cab. What had gotten into her? She never did things like that!

"You all right?" Rafe asked, a frown on his face as he continued to hold her door.

Ducking her head, she opened her handbag and began rummaging inside. "Of course. I can never find my lipstick."

After a long moment, he shut the door, then went around the back of the truck and climbed in. "If you'd rather not go to the shop, I understand."

The flat inflection in his voice caused her head to snap upward. The voice might have been flat, but the eyes weren't. They held a certain wariness. "Surely I can't be the only person who's ever seen your shop."

His long fingers flexed on the steering wheel. "Prospective clients have been out there."

"Friends?"

He faced forward, his body rigid. "I work all the time."

Her heart turned over. That could have been the truth, but she didn't think that was all there was to it. For some reason, Rafe chose to be by himself. Again, she wondered about his childhood before Lilly had become his stepmother when he was sixteen.

Her sister-in-law had said little about her five-year marriage to Rafe's father. When they had met Lilly for the first time, she hadn't mentioned it, and by the time Kristen had learned about the marriage, Lilly's divorce was final. So much was happening in Kristen's own life at that time that she hadn't asked. Adam was recovering from his eye surgery, their mother, Eleanor, and Jonathan were planning a wedding, and Kristen was trying to get over a painful breakup and move to New Orleans.

"Did you and your father build things together when you were growing up?" she probed.

His head came around. His eyes, dark and tortured, were hot with rage. The change was so unexpected, Kristen gasped, cowering against the seat.

"The tour is off." Rafe bit out each word. "Please get out."

"But—"

"No," he interrupted. "It's off. I mean it."

"But—"

"Now!" he snapped.

Kristen's hand fumbled for the doorknob, her eyes searching Rafe's tightly controlled features. Finally the door opened and she almost fell out. As soon as she was standing, he reached across and jerked the door closed, then spun off.

Kristen was still trembling when she let herself inside her apartment. Rafe's rage, controlled though it was, was upsetting and confusing. What had happened? She'd never been that afraid before. Not even with Maurice. And Rafe had helped her. But who would help him?

The question popped into her thoughts so clearly she jerked around, half-expecting to see someone in the room with her. Closing her eyes, she massaged her temple. "That's what a restless night will do for you," she mumbled, but the question refused to go away. *Who would help Rafe?*

Pushing away from the door, she crossed the room and picked up the phone. There was only one person who might be able to give her the answers she needed.

"Hello." Lilly answered on the third ring, the east Texas twang gone from her voice after living in California for the past seven years.

"Hi, Lilly." Kristen perched a hip on the corner of the sofa. "How are you and the men in your life?"

Laughter drifted through the line. "We're all fine. They've gone sailing with a neighbor and his son."

"So you get a moment of quiet," Kristen remarked, trying to decide if it would be rude to come out and ask point-blank about Rafe's childhood.

"Exactly. My pie business has really started booming since a couple of the airlines have begun ordering. I've even had a few companies trying to buy the recipe, but I told them it's not for sale."

Kristen's fingers flexed on the phone. This was the opening she needed. "Rafe's grandmother gave you the recipe for the pineapple-pecan praline pie, didn't she?"

The brief silence on the phone told her she hadn't asked the question as subtly as she might have. Lilly always referred to her ex-husband's mother as Mother Crawford. "You've been talking to Rafe?"

She plunged ahead. "Yes. He made me a writing box."

"Oh, Kristen. I'm so happy. He needs a friend so badly. You won't let him be alone. I prayed so hard for this. Thank you!"

Kristen was caught off guard by the exuberance in Lilly's voice. When Kristen had first moved to New Orleans, her sister-in-law had often mentioned Rafe, but after a while she'd left it alone. Now Kristen felt ashamed. She hadn't given Rafe more than a passing thought until she was in trouble.

She squirmed on the arm of the sofa. "Don't read too much into it, Lilly. Rafe's not easy to get to know."

"Neither was your brother when I first met him, but then neither was I," Lilly admitted quietly.

Adam had been angry and defiant during his blindness. He wanted nothing to do with his family. "He was hurting. He didn't mean it."

"I realized that the moment I stopped being so concerned about myself. He needed me just as much as I needed him."

Again Kristen felt the sting of Lilly's words. Lilly had arrived at Adam's estate with all her possessions in a broken-down car, but she'd stayed and helped Adam believe in himself. It hadn't been easy. Adam had slammed more than one object against the wall when he was upset.

"Did his anger ever frighten you?" Kristen asked, unaware that her voice had dropped to a whisper.

Once again there was a telling pause. "Daily in the beginning, but I soon realized he wasn't angry with me, but at his own helplessness."

"You were aware of Adam's situation from the beginning. I haven't a clue with Rafe. I asked a simple question about his father a little while ago and he got so angry—"

"Oh, Kristen."

"What?" She came unsteadily to her feet at the anxiety in Lilly's voice. "What is it?"

"Rafe's father is a hard, cruel man who took every opportunity to denigrate him. Mentioning his father brought back all that pain."

"I'm sorry. I didn't know," she said, realizing the great depth of the anguish she had caused Rafe.

"We both try to forget it," Lilly said quietly.

Rage swept though Kristen. Lilly had been a target of Rafe's father as well. "You were running from him when your car broke down near Adam's estate in Shreveport, weren't you?"

"Yes, but I found Adam. Your brother is wonderful."

Now. But when Lilly had first met him he had been difficult to be around. "So are you."

"Thank you." Again a slight pause. "Kristen?"

"Yes."

"Please give Rafe another chance. He has a quick temper, but he'd never hurt you. He needs someone . . ." A long sigh drifted through the phone. "I'm sorry. This isn't your responsibility. I'll fly down there tomorrow and surprise him. Adam Jr. would love seeing his big brother."

"You have your business to run. I'm not walking away, Lilly. I just need to regroup," Kristen said, hoping that she was right.

"Be sure, Kristen. I don't mean to be unkind, but if you can't see this through, then it's best that you stay away."

Her grip on the phone tightened. "Meaning I'm not as strong as you or Adam or Jonathan?"

"You've never had to fight for what you wanted in life. The rest of us have. It gives us an edge," Lilly said. "But you're a Wakefield. You have the tenacity and the intelligence to reach any goal. You just have to decide how badly you want it."

Rafe had told her the same thing and made the same comparison. He'd believed in her when she was struggling to believe in herself. Despite his obvious reservations, he had gone to the party last night because, again, he wanted to help her. But could she help him?

"What's the address of his shop?"

ten

❧

Rafe's warehouse was just inside the city limits. The prefabricated, gray building had an office in the front and two other structures of different heights attached at the back. Rosebushes loaded with lush, red blooms climbed white trellises on either side of the front door. A sign in bold letters read REPRODUCTION & DESIGN BY RBC. Two twelve-foot, galvanized sliding doors were to the right.

Kristen stared at the sign and recalled the same initials on the bottom of her writing box. Initially, she hadn't thought anything about it—now she understood. Seeing "Crawford" on his sign would have been a constant reminder of the man he wanted most to forget.

And she had made him remember.

Despite the temperature being in the upper eighties, Kristen shivered. Nerves. Plain and simple. And she had yet to face him. Removing the keys from the ignition, she dropped them into her handbag and got out of the car. Not giving herself a chance to change her mind, she went directly to a door marked OFFICE.

When ringing the doorbell and knocking didn't elicit any response, she twisted the brass knob and opened the door.

Immediately she was assaulted by a loud noise that sounded like a buzz saw. *Rafe.* She hadn't seen his truck, but there was a paved road that went around to the back of the building where it could be parked or it could be behind one of those huge doors she'd seen earlier. Closing the door behind her, she took a cursory glance around the large office.

Framed drawings of furniture he'd sketched with a smaller insert of the actual finished piece covered the spotless white walls. The maple desk had nicks and scrapes, but was polished to a high gloss. A gray file cabinet squatted in the corner.

A gurgling sound spun her around. The water cooler. She stuffed her hands into the pockets of her white linen slacks. She wasn't sure she could do this.

Bravery for her was trying a new dish at a restaurant. She did her best to avoid confrontation. Then Lilly's words came back to her. *If you can't see this through, it's best you stay away.*

The sound coming from beyond the door in front of her stopped, then after a few moments started again. He was working. If she left now he'd never know she'd come.

But *she* would. She'd always remember that he had come without a moment's hesitation to help her, but she'd been afraid to open a door to help him. Her hand closed around the knob, twisted.

Although the man working had on protective glasses and his head was bent as he stared down at a piece of wood in his hand, she recognized Rafe immediately. She closed the door and took another step, then another, and didn't stop until she was less than fifteen feet away.

He flipped a switch and the noise stopped. Picking up the foot-long length of wood, he turned it over in his large hands, then went still. Slowly his head lifted. Gloved fingers clamped around the unfinished pine. Never taking his eyes from her, he removed his earplugs.

"Hello, Rafe. I came to visit." She nodded toward the wood he gripped in his hand. "I can tell that's a leg, but what is it to?"

"You shouldn't be here." His voice was tightly controlled.

"You promised to show me around. Remember?" Casually, she walked closer. "I saw your drawings in the outer office. Impressive. Did you make one of my writing box?"

"Kristen, go home."

She stepped around the big piece of machinery. "A promise is a promise."

He lifted the goggles. His eyes were like chips of black ice. "I don't want you here."

Her step nearly faltered. She couldn't keep her gaze from going to the wood in his hand, then she looked directly at him.

Air hissed through his teeth at his sudden intake of breath. Her eyes widened as he lifted the wood, then sent it clattering and skidding across the gray concrete floor. "Leave!" Rage emanated from him in waves. His chest heaved.

"I thought we were friends."

"I don't have time for friends."

But you want friends. She turned and walked back around the table toward the door. Reaching the discarded piece of wood, she picked it up, then started to brush her hand across the surface.

"No!" Rafe quickly strode around the bench and took it from her.

She couldn't keep the hurt from her face. "You hate me so much that I can't even touch it?"

"You don't belong here," he said.

"Then where do I belong?" she asked. "I've been trying to find the answer to that since I was in college. No matter how hard I try, I can't find what matters in my life. I thought it was art, but at the first bump, I was thinking of giving up, would have given up if not for you and Angelique. I haven't found anything to center me. I guess I can't blame you for not wanting me around."

He caught her when she went to turn away. "Kristen, don't." His gut clenched. He wanted her gone, but he'd cut his hand off before he hurt her. "Please don't cry."

She sniffed and he couldn't hold out. "I took the wood away because I didn't want you to get splinters in your hand. I've got gloves on. See?" He stuck the unfinished wood under her nose. "It's a leg. It goes on a highboy."

Kristen brushed the moisture away from her eyes. "Sorry. I don't like winning by being underhanded."

"What do you think you've won?" he asked, trying to sound stern but failing. She looked so pleased with herself.

"The chance to be your friend." She smiled tentatively up at him.

Misery knotted his stomach. Friendship was impossible.

"Do you have time to show me around the shop or do you need to finish that? If you don't mind, I'd love to watch."

He worked in solitude. Always had. Always thought he would. "Only if we settle something first."

Grinning, she held up both hands, palms out. "I won't touch anything."

He shook his head, his expression serious. "The work you're doing with the paintings is important. A legacy is important." He looked around the room. "A man likes to think he's leaving something important behind. You're going to see that that happens. I don't ever want to hear you sell yourself short again."

"Got it, and thank you," she said quietly.

He shifted awkwardly. She could cause him a lot of trouble if he wasn't careful. "It's the truth. Come on. I'll show you around."

Rafe tried to keep it simple. Kristen probably wouldn't remember a band saw from a radial saw, a router from a portable sander. Recalling that her cocktail table had cabriole legs, he tried to make up for his rude behavior by showing her how the leg was constructed and the tools he used to shape the leg by hand as it turned in the lathe.

"Between the World Wars, cabriole legs were quantity-produced on profile lathes and the individuality of a hard-carved piece was lost. They used glue and screws instead of stagger dowel."

"I'm checking mine out as soon as I get home," she said, her face scrunched up in concentration.

He didn't doubt her for a minute. "From what I saw, it's high quality. Come on, I'll show you out back where I dry lumber."

"I thought you got your lumber from houses and damaged furniture," she said, following him out back and toward a crop of trees.

"When I can, but that's not always possible. Beautiful lumber is very expensive. FAS cherry, first and second quality, costs seven dollars a board foot. Walnut is even more expensive. If I can buy green lumber and dry it myself, I can cut the cost in half or less."

A hundred feet from the main building were three six-foot piles of lumber on three stacks of concrete blocks in two parallels of three. On top of each pile was a tarp weighted down with scraps of wood and bricks.

"Not very pretty, but it will be," he said.

Kristen heard the pride in his voice, the assurance that she hadn't heard before. "Your work is beautiful."

"Thank you," he said quietly.

Not wanting to embarrass him, she nodded toward the line of trees. "Is that a creek back there?"

"Yeah. One day I came out here and there was a gator sunning himself by the drying pile."

Kristen grabbed his arms and pulled him back. "An alligator!"

Rafe saw the fear in her huge eyes and cursed his stupidity. "You're safe, Kristen."

"Me?" She stared up at him. "I'm worried about you. I saw a documentary once. They're vicious, silent, and fast. You're out here by yourself. If you were to get hurt, there'd be no one to help you."

He didn't know what to say. His mother, grandmother, then Lilly, were the only ones who had ever cared about him.

"Don't they have alligator repellent or something? You should call the zoo tomorrow and ask."

Thinking only to calm her fears, he rested his large hands on her shoulders. "I'm safe. I left him alone and he left me alone."

She glanced uneasily toward the trees. "He could have just eaten."

Rafe caught back a laugh. "The creek is almost dry, so I'm safe."

Her worried gaze came back to him. "Really?"

"Really." He didn't even think as his hand slid down her arm to reassure her. They started back inside. "That's it."

"Not quite. You haven't shown me where you stay." She spotted the curved wooden stairs in the back of the elongated room leading to the second floor and started toward them. "Where did you find this? It's exquisite."

Rafe watched her hand with rapt attention as it ran reverently over the gleaming mahogany balustrade. He tried not to think of her doing the same thing to him. He cleared his throat. "A house being demolished. I couldn't bring myself to cut it up. The newel posts are new."

She continued up the stairs. With a sinking heart, Rafe followed. He was finding a headstrong streak in Kristen that he hadn't expected.

Kristen opened a half-leaded glass door and stepped into a sparsely furnished room. The area was spotless and lifeless, the furniture at a bare minimum. Sofa, chair, table, two bookshelves crammed full of books.

The small kitchen was the same. Two crudely made chairs bracketed a table.

"My first efforts," he said from behind her. "I keep them to remind me to stay humble. You might as well see the rest."

Kristen followed him. He opened a door and stepped back. She stepped around him and into his bedroom. She felt an unexpected tingle of something and resolutely shook it off. This was too important for her to let her emotions mess it up. Rafe was sharing, and she wanted to weep for him.

The walls and four windows were bare, the room as lifeless as the others. But at least the dark cherry, king-sized headboard and double dresser were of good quality. A single chair sat in the corner near a portable TV on an unfinished wooden table. Rafe had a place to live, but he hadn't bothered to create a home.

Somehow she'd see that that changed. She faced him. "Thanks for the tour. Now, I need to ask one more thing."

His eyebrows bunched. "What?"

She grinned despite the caution in his face. "Please, let's go out to eat. I'm starving."

Kristen arrived at work thirty minutes early Monday morning. Opening the door to the gallery, she went directly to Jacques's Rolodex and began to write down the names of the people at his party who'd wanted Rafe's card. Her nose wrinkled. Rafe admittedly had purchased the cheapest cards he could find. They were plain and ordinary. His work wasn't.

His finished products were spectacular, worthy of being in the finest homes in the country. She planned on helping that to happen.

The gallery door opened. She got up from Jacques's desk and walked around the partition to see who had entered. "Morning, Jacques."

"Morning, Kristen. I see you're at it already."

"Yes." She returned to the desk and picked up the Rolodex. "Thanks for letting me use this. I'll have it back in a jiffy."

"Take your time and get all the names you need." He took a seat behind his desk. "I like Rafe and his work."

"You should see some of his bigger pieces," Kristen said with enthusiasm. "I went to his shop yesterday. I was tempted to ask him to let me purchase a writing desk he had just finished and make another for his customer."

Jacques leaned back in his chair with an indulgent smile. "Looks like you're about to add another area to your sales list."

She couldn't deny it. "A talent like Rafe's deserves to be seen."

"If he has you on his side, it will be."

Her eyes widened in pleasure. "Thank you."

"It's no more than the truth." He opened his locked desk and drew out a receipt book. "This speaks for itself. You're an asset to St. Clair's."

"Then would it be all right if I kept a few of Rafe's business cards on my desk? After I've had them remade, of course," she said. "I promise not to mention his business unless asked."

Leaning forward, Jacques propped his elbows on his desk. "I don't have a problem with that."

"Thank you."

"Wait," Jacques called when she turned to leave. "You say you've been to his shop? Is it in the city?"

"Yes. It's in a huge, old warehouse. He lives upstairs." She frowned. Like the cobbler whose children needed shoes, Rafe needed furniture. The place was spartan, with only the bare essentials. He said he'd been shopping once, but had been put off by the high prices and poor quality. "He needs curtains."

Jacques wrinkled his nose and Kristen was sure he was trying to keep from laughing. Angelique had laughed last night when she told her the same thing. She was a good enough friend that she hadn't mentioned their toast. Kristen was definitely leaning toward a fight mode.

"I'm a mentor with an at-risk program for a high school. School is out, but I've kept in touch with three of the young men who I think have real potential, if I can get them to finish high school and keep up their grades." His fingers drummed on the desk. "It's a well-known fact that students involved not with just sports, but cultural programs like art, excel academically. I agree, but the boys thinks art is for girls and wimps."

Kristen took the seat in front of his desk. "I was involved in a mentoring program my junior year at Stanford. We had the same problem. If I can help in any way, you only have to ask."

"As a matter of fact, you can."

"Just name it."

"Get Rafe to let them come out to his shop."

Her and her big mouth, Kristen thought later that evening as she drove to Rafe's place. How was she going to get Rafe to work with the three teenagers she'd met shortly after lunch? They'd been loud and defiant, but they had responded to Jacques's stern tone immediately. They wore the official costumes of teenagers these days—baggy pants, long-sleeved shirts, and do-rags. At least they had the right shoes. Steel-toed brogans.

Parking, she reached into the back seat for the two packages. She was nervous enough about how Rafe would react to the curtains without also asking him to mentor. Men tended to be territorial about their spaces. Lilly had thought it was a wonderful idea. Kristen hadn't asked Angelique her opinion.

This time she didn't bother ringing the bell, just opened the door and went inside. She certainly hoped Rafe didn't leave his door open all the time. Entering his shop, she saw him sanding the legs he'd cut the day before. He glanced up and her heart did a little flutter.

"Hi. You're working on the highboy?"

Laying the wood aside, he came around the front of the workbench. "Yes."

She almost sighed. The wariness was still there. "Just go ahead. I bought you a present."

"A present?" He stared at the packages in her hand.

"Actually, it's for your windows. Curtains. The rods are already up so this won't take long. Don't come up until I call."

She rushed toward the steps leading to the second floor before he could stop her. Once again, she marveled at the curved mahogany stairwell. In his apartment, she went straight to his bedroom, the largest of the three rooms. Although he hadn't expected her, it was as neat as it had been the day before. And just as before, the sterile room tore at her heart.

Opening the package, she unfolded the lightweight, gauzy blue material, then pulled over a chair to stand on. Slipping off her heels, she climbed on top. The tips of her fingers almost reached the round rod. If she could just stretch a little bit more . . .

She lost her balance and pitched forward. A scream tore from her before she could stop it. Automatically, her arms windmilled as she tried to fling herself backwards away from the window. She succeeded, but she overcompensated and the chair tipped. She was still screaming when she felt herself falling.

She heard a grunt. It took a fraction of a second to register that the sound had come from the solid body beneath her. Rafe. Sprawled across his wide chest, she pushed her hair out of her face, then wished she hadn't. He was furious.

"I ought to shake you until your teeth rattle!" He sat up with her in his arms. "You could have been killed!"

Although the same thought had flashed through her mind, she tried to reassure him. "Now, Rafe, it—"

"Just shut up."

Kristen shut up. She realized she wasn't the only one trembling. "I didn't mean to frighten you."

His hands flexed around her arms. "I heard you drag something across the floor and guessed what you were going to try and do." A muscle leaped in his jaw. "The window is thirty feet up."

"I thought about that when I started to fall. That's why I tried to throw myself backward." Pure terror flashed in his eyes. Pushing aside her lingering fear, she palmed his face. "I'm all right. The next time, I'll be more careful."

"There'll be no next time." He came to his feet, bringing her with him as if she weighed nothing. His calloused hands manacled her upper arms as he set her on her feet. "If I need curtains, I'll buy and hang them. Got it?"

"But—"

He gave her a shake that reminded her of his earlier threat. "No buts!"

Fear never crossed her mind and backing down wasn't an option. Rafe needed soft, pretty things around him and she was going to see that he had them. "I accepted the writing box from you."

"I didn't have to endanger myself to give it to you." He swallowed. "If you had fallen through that glass . . . your beautiful face . . ." He swallowed again.

"You think I'm beautiful?" she asked, her voice filled with undeniable pleasure.

He snatched his hands away and glared at her. "I'll help you put the curtains back in the package so you can return them."

"They were on clearance. I can't take them back." She picked up one of the panels. She'd mull over Rafe thinking she was beautiful later. "They'll look wonderful on the window. They're light enough for the sun to shine through and at the same time give the room a little lift. Lilly thought it was a great idea."

His brows bunched. "When did you talk to Lilly?"

"During my lunch break, when I was looking for these." She set the chair upright and walked back to the window. "She said you liked blue."

"When did you get so pigheaded?"

She shrugged. "I'm a Wakefield."

Rafe stalked over and took down the straight rods from the four windows. "I'm only helping you do this because I know I'll never hear the end of it."

Kristen wisely said nothing, just threaded the curtains when he handed her the rods. Twenty minutes later they were finished. Hands on her hips, Kristen stepped back to admire their handiwork.

"I knew it, Rafe. Don't they look wonderful?"

To Rafe, what looked wonderful was Kristen. She shone like a star out of reach. He could admire the brilliance, but never hope to touch it. It had been crazy to let her keep coming back into his life. She made him want things he couldn't have.

Kristen walked over and straightened the curtains for the second, then the third time. "A decorative rod would be even better."

"No way," he said, vehemently shaking his head.

"What were you doing when I arrived?" Ignoring him, she picked up the packing paper and the sacks.

He frowned. "Sanding the legs."

"Could anyone do it?" She put the paper into a dented brass trashcan.

"The paper is too rough for your soft hands."

Her face softened, and his stomach dipped as if he were on a roller coaster.

"I didn't mean me." She sighed and took a deep breath. "Look, I'm not good at subterfuge so I'll just ask. Jacques is mentoring three students and he wants you to let them come out and visit your shop. I think it's an excellent idea."

"No, and I mean it," he told her flatly.

He turned and went back down the stairs. Kristen was on his heels.

"I met them today. They're loud and boisterous, but they responded to Jacques. They respect male authority," she said, crossing to him. "I want them to see the talent and patience it takes to design, then create furniture. To see the pride you have in your work."

He sat down behind his workbench. "You and Jacques must know a lot of artists."

"These kids have no talent or interest in paintings."

He paused on reaching for the sandpaper. "They have any in carpentry?"

"No, but they could if they saw you at work." She took his calloused hands and ignored the leap in her pulse, the jerk of his hand. "Not many people can do what you've done. You've made a success of your life with these hands and grit and intelligence. They need to see that it can be done."

He pulled his hands free and picked up the sandpaper, but his strokes against the wood were slow and deliberate as if he were thinking. "I'd like to help, but I'm not very good with people. I'm not patient."

"Now who's selling himself short? Jacques and Angelique like you. People responded to you at the party. You can do this." She pointed to the furniture piece in his hand. "How much patience does it take to complete a piece of furniture?"

His hand paused, then continued the long, even strokes. "I can't. Don't ask me."

"Are you at a place where you can stop?"

His head came up abruptly. She didn't usually jump from one subject to the other. Maybe she'd hurt herself in the fall. Before the thought had clearly formed, he came to his feet, studying her upturned face closely. "You sure you feel all right? Maybe we should go to the hospital and have you checked."

"If anyone should be checked, it's you. You were on the floor. I was on top. Remember?"

He remembered too well. So did his traitorous body. He'd been caught between wanting to keep holding her and needing to chastise her for endangering herself. "You landed pretty hard."

She waved his words aside. "There's nothing wrong with me that food won't cure. Let's go grab a bite to eat and you can tell me all about the customer for the highboy."

Surely, if she were hurt, she wouldn't be hungry. Besides, if they went out to eat he could keep an eye on her a little longer. "Let me wash up and I'll get my keys." He laid the wood on the bench.

Pulling her keys out of the pockets of her slacks, she jingled them in her hand. "I'll drive. Unless you're one of those men who doesn't like to be in the car with a woman driver?"

He almost smiled. "I never thought about it very much."

"Well?"

"I'll chance it."

eleven

❧

The Catfish Shack was aptly named. The restaurant's roof was tin, the walls weathered a dull gray. The four entrees were printed neatly on a small child's writing slate. Plastic marine life attached to a fisherman's net stretched around the room, serving as the decoration.

"You sure you want to eat here?" Rafe asked, once the waitress had taken their order.

Kristen picked up her large, red plastic glass of unsweetened tea. "Angelique introduced me to some great little places. The true way to judge if a restaurant is good is to see if the parking lot is full."

"That wouldn't be hard for this place." Unimpressed thus far, he glanced around. There were two booths and four tables besides their own.

"Give it a chance. The linoleum floor is clean and the odor of fish didn't slap me in the face when I walked in." She propped her elbow on the scarred wooden table. "Now tell me about the highboy."

Instead of doing as she requested, he leaned back in his chair and looked at her. As usual, she looked as if she'd just stepped off the cover of a fashion magazine. Her long black hair was pulled away from her arresting face in a ponytail. She wore a tangerine-colored blouse that tied in a knot at her tiny waist with matching cropped pants. Gold hoop earrings twisted in her ears each time her head moved. Several gold bracelets jingled on her left wrist. On the other was an expensive watch that cost more than any car in the graveled parking lot.

"What?"

She should seem totally out of place in the cramped little restaurant, but somehow she didn't. "I just never thought you'd be comfortable in a place like this."

She lifted a delicate brow. "You mean because of my background?"

He tried to back pedal. "I didn't mean to offend you."

"You haven't, and you're right. Before Angelique and I became friends, I wouldn't have come in here." she told him. "I'd like to think it wouldn't have been because of snobbishness, but because I just never thought to. This is near your place—why haven't you been in here?"

"I keep busy and seldom eat out. I have a helper to do minor work, the rest I do myself. The furniture takes weeks to construct."

"Here you are," said the waitress as she set their plates down. "If I can get you anything else just holler."

"A doggie bag," Kristen joked, looking at the four-inch-high pile of golden fried catfish and French fries on her plate.

The robust waitress gave a deep belly laugh. "I bet he can eat it 'iffin you don't. Carolyn's bringin' th' rest."

"Rest?" Kristen parroted.

A bubbly teenager with a spotless, white, oversized apron over a black tee shirt and blue jeans approached. She had five tiny gold hoops in her right ear. Her henna hair was spiked five inches over her head. "Corn on the cob, slaw, red beans and rice. Enjoy."

When she had gone, Kristen looked at Rafe smugly. "Told you."

"But how does it taste?" he challenged, not willing to concede she was right.

"Bless the food and we'll find out."

He did and after several bites conceded that she could indeed pick a restaurant. The food was spicy and delicious, the service good. His tea glass was never more than half empty. Watching Kristen's little pink tongue dart out while she ate, he needed it. "You have catsup on your cheek."

"Where?" Her tongue flicked out ineffectually, missing it by a whisker. "Did I get it?"

If Rafe told her no, her tongue would dart out again and he'd probably lose it right there. His hand touched her cheek just as her tongue tried again and licked the side of his finger.

He stilled as a hot shiver of desire raced from his hand through his body.

Their gazes clung. For Kristen, everything narrowed down to Rafe and the need in his dark eyes. She began to tremble. "Rafe . . ."

He snatched his hand back. Beneath the cover of the table, he rubbed his hand on his jeans. It didn't help. "I-I was supposed to call a client tonight. While you finish I'll go see if they have a phone."

Even if Kristen could have found her voice, she wouldn't have tried to stop him. She was just as confused by the attraction as he was. The difference was, he resented it. His response wasn't very flattering, but at least it wasn't personal.

He didn't want anyone in his life.

His father had done that to him. The thought that any father could inflict such misery on his child enraged her. Rafe was going to have some happiness in his life. If that meant putting a halt to whatever was happening between them, so be it.

"I took care of the bill. You ready?"

Kristen knew she would see the wariness in his face before she looked at him. Just as she knew she couldn't let him retreat from her. There was one sure way to prevent it. "Ready." She stood as he held her chair.

"Lilly asked me to check a few estate sales for a sleigh bed for Adam Jr. Do you think you have time to help?" she asked as they reached her car.

The majority of the time Rafe spent at their family gatherings, he was with Adam Jr. The two were almost inseparable when they got together. He'd walk through hell for his little brother. "Adam Jr. will be so excited to learn you helped find his bed."

"I probably could make one," he evaded.

She stared at him across the hood of her black BMW. "Lilly figured you'd say that. But it would cause you to fall behind on your orders. Plus, you have the sleigh and train to complete before Christmas. Have you started them?"

"Not yet," he admitted reluctantly.

Perfect. Tucking her head to hide her smile, she dug in her purse for her keys. "You're in demand and if Mrs. Oliphant and her friends start ordering, you're going to be swamped."

"I'll always have time for Adam Jr.," he said without a moment's hesitation.

"I knew you'd help. We can start looking Saturday." She almost felt guilty that he'd fallen into her trap so easily.

Lines of confusion were etched on his forehead as if he wasn't exactly sure what had happened.

"We'll start out early before all the good stuff is gone." Getting in, she put her seat belt on, started the car, then backed out of the crowded parking lot. "I don't have to go in until twelve. The ones farther out from the city are probably the best. Who knows? I might even see a painting or two."

"I suppose I could spare a few hours," he finally said.

On the two-lane highway, she sped around a car as if it were sitting still. "I'll pick you up."

Rafe pressed his hand on the dashboard when she came to an abrupt stop at a signal light. "I'll drive. If we find anything, we couldn't put it in your small trunk."

"Is that the only reason?" She smiled over at him.

"Let's just say I'm beginning to see what you meant about women drivers."

She laughed and he laughed with her.

"Jacques, I'm sorry, but Rafe said no," Kristen told her boss as she flipped St. Clair's "open" sign to "closed." They'd had a steady stream of customers all day and she hadn't had the opportunity to give him the bad news before.

Jacques paused in straightening *Memory*, a haunting painting of a sunset on water that replaced *Disbelief* early that day. The artist who had painted both had come in that morning with a new attitude. "If he said no to you, I don't think anyone else could get him to change his mind. He really could have helped them."

"Rafe wants to help—he's just not sure if he has the patience," she told him, not wanting him to think badly of Rafe. "I haven't given up. I just have to go slow."

"Then I won't worry about it another second," he told her.

Kristen took her black bag from her desk and draped the long strap over her shoulder. "Don't be so sure. Rafe doesn't change his mind very easily."

Jacques set the alarm, then followed Kristen out the door. "For you, I think he will."

Kristen blushed. "We'll see."

As soon as they stepped outside, thunder rumbled. Lightning flashed. Kristen grimaced at the sky. "Good night. I'd better run before I get soaked."

"I'll see you tomorrow. Drive carefully."

"I will. You do the same." Kristen dashed down the street, her heels clicking on the cobbled street as she tried to dodge people on the crowded sidewalks. A few were trying to make it to shelter, but most were still enjoying themselves.

Just as she pulled onto the street, the sky opened up. Traffic quickly became a snarled nightmare. Her usual ten-minute drive took thirty minutes. The good news was that her parking space was vacant. The bad news was that it wasn't underground. Berating herself for not putting her umbrella back in the car after the last unexpected rain shower, she put her purse over her head and made a dash for it.

She shrieked, then laughed as the cool rain quickly soaked her jersey knit dress. At least it wasn't silk. She entered her condo to the ringing phone. Ignoring it, she went to the bathroom. Undressing, she heard the ringing stop. Slipping on a robe, she began towel-drying her hair on the way to the kitchen for a cup of tea.

The phone on the end table in the living room rang just as she passed. "Hello."

"I was beginning to worry."

Rafe. The deep voice took away the chill she'd felt from getting wet. "Did you call a few minutes ago?"

"Yes. I just wanted to make sure you got home all right." The worry was evident in his voice. "I was out when it started and could barely see the car in front of me."

"Sorry I didn't answer." She sat down on the sofa. "I didn't have my umbrella. I got wet and had to change."

"Oh."

The little word seemed to send a spiral of heat through her. She pulled the collar of the terry cloth robe away from her throat and searched her mind for a way to get the conversation going again. Friendship, and nothing more. "Traffic was crazy."

"You need a bigger car." There was a slight pause. He was trying, too. "And a lighter foot on the gas pedal."

She drew her slippered feet under her and curled up in a corner of the sofa. "I grew up driving in San Francisco. If you didn't get out of the way on the freeways, you were run over. This is child's play."

"Just be careful."

"I will. Don't worry. Since we're leaving so early Saturday, why don't we plan on eating breakfast on the road? I'm sure we'll find a place."

"Rustic with a crowded parking lot."

She heard the smile in his voice, wished she could see it on his face. "You got it."

"I'd better get back to work."

Was there reluctance in his voice or was it wishful thinking on her part? "Thanks for calling."

"You just take care of yourself."

"You do the same."

" 'Bye."

" 'Bye." Kristen slowly hung up the phone and scooted down further on the sofa. She didn't need tea to warm her up or mellow her out. Rafe had taken care of that quite nicely. With an impish smile she wondered what else he could do.

He shouldn't have come.

Damien stared at the recessed red door of The Inferno, trying to crystallize the reason for seeking Angelique out here instead of at her apartment. He knew Kristen's address, knew Angelique lived next door. There was only one reason. Not even the torrential downpour earlier had kept him away.

He hoped that once he saw her dancing, he'd be able to put her out of his mind. Certainly nothing else had worked. He'd close his eyes and she'd be there. He'd turn a corner and see her. The notions were idiotic and romantic. He'd never been either. Or jealous. But that hadn't kept him from wanting to tear Henri apart for putting his hand on her.

Damien could kick himself for wanting to do that and much more. He jabbed the bell.

The door opened and the business transaction was quickly conducted. There was no secret password or handshake, just cold, hard cash. Less than fifteen seconds and a hundred dollars later—credit cards weren't accepted—Damien entered the club. The music was surprisingly loud, considering the cover charge, but then so were the men. A few had the same rabid look he'd seen on the faces of the men panting after Angelique at his father's party.

"Would you like me to show you to a table near the stage? Starlight is a favorite."

Damien barely glanced at the waitress, who had a smile on her face and a tray in her hand. "I'm fine back here."

"What would you like to drink?"

"Scotch and water." He pulled out a chair at a small, round table near the back of the club. The few tables around him were vacant. Apparently most men liked being up front where the action was.

The noise increased and he realized he'd hadn't looked at the dancer. If Angelique were up there, he didn't want to see her wearing bits of cloth, then taking even those off for men to salivate over her. His hand raked over his head. Was he trying to save his father or save himself?

"Here you are, sir." The redhead set the glass on the table along with a little bowl of beer nuts. "Shall I start you a tab?"

"No." He reached into his pocket and gave her a twenty.

"Do you need change?"

He shook his head.

"Thank you, sir. If there's anything else you want, just let me know." She strutted off, her hips swaying.

Had she just sent him an invitation or was he imagining things because of where he was? He was about to take a sip when he heard a woman's laughter. Angelique's laugh. He had absolutely no idea how he knew it was she, then realized it was because of the sudden shiver that had raced through him at the sound.

He jerked around, straining to see in the shadows behind him. He was on his feet when he heard her laughter again. It had come from behind a seven-foot arched wall. He hadn't noticed the area before. It was obscured from the entrance and the dance floor. There was only one reason he could think of why she would be behind that wall.

He rounded the partition, rage pulsating through him and saw . . . Angelique sitting with another woman.

Angelique's eyes widened, something flickered in them. "The stage is the other way."

She was dressed in black, her hair in a single braid as it had been the first time he'd seen her. She was stunning in whatever she wore. "What time do you go on?"

"You just missed my act," Angelique said with a derisive twist of her mouth. The look on her face said he was just like the other men.

Fury pulsed though his veins. His fists clenched.

"Angel, don't tease the man. You know you don't dance anymore. But I do," the tiny blonde beside Angelique said. With a practiced shrug, the red silk wrap slid off her smooth, tanned shoulder.

Damien's attention on Angelique never wavered. "What does she mean, you don't dance anymore?"

"Disappointed?" Angelique sat back in the booth and folded her arms. To think she had wasted precious sleep over him. He was just like all the other men she despised.

"I dance," the blonde said, leaning over to give Damien a better look at the ample breasts spilling from her demi-bra.

Once again she was ignored. "I asked you a question."

"Which I am under no obligation to answer," Angelique replied.

"Trouble here, Angel?" asked a gravelly male voice.

Damien turned to see the baldheaded and burly man from the front door. "Only if you make it."

The man grinned. "I live for trouble."

Seeing Damien wasn't going to back off, Angelique said, "It's all right, Mack. I can handle it." She told herself she was keeping Damien from major bodily injury for his father's sake, not because, despite everything, he made her yearn.

"Just remember you have to pass me before you leave." With that ominous threat, he walked away.

"I hate to miss how this turns out, but my number is next." The little blonde scooted out of the booth and approached Damien. She moistened her red lips with a pink tongue. "My name's Honey. I get off at midnight."

"I won't be here," he said, then slid into the seat in the booth she had vacated, already forgetting her. "I'm waiting for my answer."

Angelique didn't want him near her, tempting her to act foolishly. After Sunday's fiasco it had occurred to her that she was almost afraid to tell him the truth. Somewhere in the back of her mind, she'd wanted to believe that once he knew the truth, his opinion of her would change. But what if it didn't?

"Angelique?" he snapped out her name.

Screw it. "I danced here the last two years of undergrad school."

"Why are you here now?" he asked, his voice heavy with accusation.

The way he was behaving, he didn't deserve an answer, but she had finally decided to take the advice she dished out to her patients: never try to circumvent the truth—it always came back to nip you on the rear. "I'm gathering information for my dissertation."

She had the satisfaction of seeing the surprise on his face. "You're working on your doctorate?"

"That's right," she answered and waited for his apology. It didn't come. If anything, he looked even angrier.

"Why didn't you tell me?"

She couldn't believe her ears. "You were the one who jumped to conclusions and got all sanctimonious."

"You could have explained."

Her temper blew. "Why? I don't need yours or any other person's validation. I'm who I am, and I've worked hard to get where I am. It wasn't easy taking a full load and dancing here."

He glanced around the little alcove, trying not to envision her here with a customer or what they might have done. He gritted his teeth. "You could have found another way."

Her hazel eyes flashed. "It's so easy for you, sitting there in your tailored suit with money in your pocket, an expensive car to drive, a luxurious place to live, spouting all that garbage. We weren't all born so lucky."

Damien didn't back down. "I'm aware that I've led a privileged life, but there *are* student loans, social services, scholarships."

"They don't give scholarships to non-athletic, average students. As for loans and social services, you ever tried to work through the system? Of course not." Her finger jabbed him in the chest. "I have, and unless you're assigned to the right caseworker who doesn't act as if the little money you might receive is going to come out of his or her check, you're up Goose Creek."

Damien opened his mouth, but she cut him off. "You had parents growing up. My father left me at a bus station when I was three. Heaven only knows where my mother was. I used to dream he'd come back or my mother would find me. I was in six foster homes by the time I was eight. At eighteen the money from the state stopped. Without my foster parents scrimping and doing without to put me in Xavier, I probably would have ended up back on the street, homeless."

Remorse and regret went through him. "I didn't know."

"And you didn't ask. You just accused. You think it's easy having men leer at you and think you're for sale? It's not. Women have always survived the best way they know how. You won't make me feel ashamed for surviving." She stood, unbowed and unbending. "You should try dancing in five-inch heels for hours, then tell me I took the easy way out."

She stalked off again, her long, auburn plait swinging down her back like a beacon. This time he didn't blame her. He slumped against the booth. He was usually more fair-minded. As a lawyer, he'd been taught to be analytical. However, his objectivity had flown out the door when she mentioned The Inferno. Right or wrong, he'd always been possessive.

Perhaps because he was an only child of a favorite child. He'd been pampered since birth by a large, gregarious family. He might have ended up sitting on the right of the judge instead of the left if his father hadn't locked him out of the house when he stayed out past curfew one too many times.

He'd slept in the car. He'd thought he'd apologize the next morning and it would be over. He wasn't particularly worried when his parents had knocked on the car window, waking him up, but he began to be when his father calmly asked for the car keys and handed him a suitcase.

"Since you like the streets so much perhaps you'd like to live on them," he had said.

His mother, the woman he could always get around, had stood stoically by his father. "If you ever decide you can follow the rules, the door is open. Otherwise, have a wonderful life," she said.

Being no fool, he'd straightened up. But even in his "bad days," he hadn't shared his girlfriends. As an adult he liked fast cars, but not fast women. So where did that leave him and Angelique?

Damien got up and was about to step into the aisle when Maurice Laurent and another man he didn't recognize passed by him. They worked their way to the front and sat down on the right side of the rectangular stage just as the announcer finished introducing a new dancer.

The spotlight zeroed in on the heavy gold velvet curtain and out came the woman who had been with Angelique. Honey. Small and agile, her skimpy costume left little to the imagination. Maurice waved a bill and she danced over and leaned down. He stuck the money into her red G-string, then whispered something into her ear that made her grin widen.

Disgusted, Damien left. Angelique might have had a different agenda dancing there, but all women didn't.

"Dad, we need to talk," Damien said when his father answered the door at his house. He'd come straight from The Inferno. He saw no reason to put off what was going to be a difficult and embarrassing conversation.

"Business or personal?" Jacques asked.

"Personal."

"Then we better go into the study so I can fortify myself with a Scotch." Going back down the hall, Jacques entered the first room and went to a built-in bar on the far side of the high-ceilinged room paneled in dark oak. Behind the bar, he lifted a crystal decanter. "Want one?"

"Please." Damien rubbed the back of his neck.

Jacques's eyes narrowed. "Must be pretty important. The last time we did this you were considering dropping out of law school."

"It is." He'd wanted to join the Peace Corps. His father had convinced him that he could help the world more if he had an education. "You know I love you, don't you, Dad?

The decanter in Jacques's hand hit the mahogany counter with a loud thud. He came around the bar and took his son's arms, staring hard at him. "Are you in some kind of trouble? Whatever it is, you know I'm with you."

"Not this time." He paused. "I betrayed you."

"What?" Jacques's hands fell away.

Damien's hand shoved over his hair. "I didn't mean it. You have to believe me."

"Son, what is it?" Jacques's hand came back to rest firmly on his son's shoulder.

"I'm interested in the same woman you are."

Jacques snatched his hand away. Shocked horror flashed across his face. "You care about Claudette, too?"

Now Damien was the one shocked. "Claudette? No. I'm talking about Angelique."

Jacques rapped him on the head, then drew his son into his arms for a bear hug. "Don't you ever scare me like that again."

Damien's mind eased in one area, but he felt regretful for his father. "I'm sorry, Dad."

Returning behind the bar, his father poured himself a drink. "What is it the kids say? You snooze, you lose."

"Does she know?" Damien splashed Scotch, then added water in his own glass.

"No, and she never will."

Damien weighed client confidentiality against loyalty and love for a parent. "I don't think the marriage will last."

"And when it's over, Claudette will suffer."

There was nothing Damien could say to that.

"So you have decided to stop judging Angelique?" Jacques asked, tired of his own thoughts.

"She doesn't work at The Inferno. The reason she goes there is to gather information for her dissertation," Damien said, still trying to decide how he felt about that.

"She told me." Jacques took a seat in his easy chair by the white stone fireplace. "You all right with her working there before?"

Damien stared down into his glass. "She had to help put herself through school."

"That's not what I asked," his father said quietly.

Damien's head came up. "If you want to know if I think about those two years she danced there and the men she danced for, the answer is yes. I try not to, but it just creeps up on me and when it does . . ." His hand closed tighter around the glass.

"If you can't handle it, it's always going to be a thorn in your side that's going to grow more worrisome each day." Jacques leaned forward. "You're also the chief counsel for a very old, very prestigious insurance brokerage firm and Claudette is a stickler for high moral principles."

Damien almost snapped out that in that case she shouldn't have married Maurice, but caught himself just in time. "I thought you liked Angelique."

"I do. The question is, how much will *you* still like her if her past becomes a topic of conversation at the club or in the men's room?"

"I'd better not hear it." There was steel in his voice.

Jacques lifted his glass. "Now, that's the son I raised."

"Please take the place setting away, Mia," Claudette told the maid.

"Yes, Mrs. Laurent." The young maid quickly gathered the china, crystal, and sterling, then left Claudette to her own thoughts.

Picking up the candlesnuffer, Claudette extinguished the twin flames. Maurice wasn't coming. She'd told him specifically that morning that they'd have dinner at eight. He'd said he'd be there, then had gone off in his car when the chauffeur had driven her to work. Instead of her surprising him with a romantic dinner, he'd been the one to surprise her.

"Shall I serve you now?" the maid asked.

"Please." Claudette wasn't hungry, but there would be enough talk among the staff about her waiting over an hour for her husband who had never come. But at least Claudette didn't think it would spread further. With the exception of the recently hired maid, Mia, the staff had been with them for years and was extremely loyal. Bridget, the cook, had been with them since Claudette was in grade school. The older woman mothered Claudette every chance she got.

Mia reentered and placed lobster bisque on the table, then withdrew.

Claudette picked up her soup spoon, dipped, but was unable to carry it to her mouth. With the help of Bridget, Claudette had tried to re-create the romantic dinner Maurice had planned for her the night he'd been injured by the man with Kristen. Claudette had thought it might help. Lately he'd been different.

She placed a hand on her thigh. Beneath the blue silk lounger were a vivid bruise and nail prints. He'd been rough with her when he'd returned from his drive the night of Jacques's party, almost angry. She hadn't mentioned the bruise. Nor had he tried to make love to her again. And she didn't want him to.

"Is there a problem, Miss Thibodeaux?" Bridget asked, her brow knitted in concern. Thin as a rail, she was a culinary genius. "It's been a half an hour and you haven't rung for your salad."

"Laurent," Claudette corrected. The older staff members had a more difficult time remembering her married name.

"You haven't made a dent in your soup. You want something else?" Bridget asked, not bothering to restate the name. "There's turkey salad or an omelet."

"This is fine." Picking up her spoon, she began to eat. Propriety must be maintained.

He would not do this to her.

Angelique sat in the second bedroom she'd turned into an office, her notes and research books spilling off the table and onto the floor, and stared at a blank computer screen. She had designated this week as the one to begin writing her dissertation. She'd dropped by the club to thank the women working there. If she were to complete the dissertation in time for summer graduation, she had less than two months.

She placed her hands over the keyboard. Nothing happened. The blank screen stared mockingly back at her. Pushing against the desk, the chair slid backwards across the hardwood floor. Maybe some caffeine would jump-start her brain. In the kitchen she pulled the tab on a Pepsi, then wandered outside to the balcony instead of back to her office.

The night was beautiful, the rain-washed air fresh. Not a living soul was in sight. But she wasn't alone. New Orleans teemed with people, the good, the bad, the ugly. She'd been all three. No one had to tell her she was one of the lucky ones.

She propped her arms on the top rail and stared thoughtfully out into the night. She'd gotten few breaks in life. The most important one had been loving foster parents. Bette and Elmore Howard had fought just as hard for her as she'd fought against them. But no matter how hard she'd pushed them away, they always stood there with open arms and unconditional love.

They were at her elementary school so much for Angelique's misbehavior that people probably thought they worked there. Neither of them became discouraged when she got into a fight, talked back to the teachers, or any of the dozens of other ways she managed to get into trouble. The Howards refused to believe that she couldn't be redeemed. They fought Angelique and anyone else who stood in the way of her succeeding.

She had been in their home about six months before it began to sink in that they genuinely cared about *her*, and not the pitiful check they received from the state. More importantly, they weren't going anyplace no matter what she did.

Going back inside, she picked up the phone in the living room and dialed. It was almost eleven, but she knew they'd be up.

"Hello," answered a bright, cheery voice.

"Mama Howard, I just called to say I love you."

"I love you, too, child. How's that paper going?" her foster mother asked, her voice rich with Cajun flavor.

"It's not," Angelique admitted, scrunching up her face.

"It'll come. 'Member when you had that paper in the tenth grade, you were up all night?"

Angelique chuckled. "That's because I put it off until the last minute."

"You still got a C-plus," her foster mother reminded her. She never forgot a thing when it came to her "children." Then your paper for your master's got an A. Stop looking at the forest and just get through the trees."

Angelique sighed and rolled the cool can against her forehead. "Sometimes it's hard to focus."

"Since when has life been easy for you? You cut your teeth on hard. Now go on back in there and write that paper. I got my hat and suit all picked out. Papa is gonna wear that suit you got him for Christmas. You'll be the first doctor in the family. Everybody's coming."

There it was again. The unshakable belief that had bolstered her again and again. Tears stung Angelique's throat. The Howards had natural children, but considered the fifteen children who had gone through their foster home theirs as well. "Can you send me some fudge?" Her mother's fudge was decadently delicious and loaded with pecans and calories.

"I'll put some in the mail tomorrow. Here's Papa."

"Hello, Angelique. How's it going? You need anything?"

Elmore Howard always thought of his family first. He'd finally retired from the post office last year when their last "daughter" had graduated from college. "I'm fine, Papa Howard. Just called to say I love you."

"Well."

Papa Howard expressed his love in many ways, but he could never say the words. "I'll talk to you soon. 'Bye."

Hanging up the phone, she went to her office and pulled up her chair. Her family loved her unreservedly—that was important. Not Damien Broussard. She didn't need his approval or that of any man. Her hands began to move over the keys.

Man, by nature, is a dominant species. He is bred from birth to rule, to conquer. Whether in times of war or in the sports arena, man will fight to defeat his opponent. If there are no wars, no sports arena, he seeks out another adversary to subjugate to his authority. He turns to woman.

twelve

❧

He should have been working. He didn't have time for this.

Rafe kept telling himself that, but he couldn't get his feet to leave the department store and get back in his truck. He'd passed the mall on the way back into town after a delivery and stopped. They'd forecast rain for the end of next week.

"May I help you, sir?" asked a young saleslady in accessories.

Rafe stuffed his hands into the front pockets of his jeans. "I want to buy an umbrella."

"What kind?" she asked.

He stared at her blankly, then thought about heading for the nearest exit at full speed.

"Umbrellas come in different shapes, lengths, and widths," she explained. "Is it for you or someone else?"

"Someone else," he said. "A woman." He didn't know why saying those two words made him want to duck his head in embarrassment.

"Young, matronly, fashionable, sensible?" the saleswoman ventured, her dark head tilted to one side.

"She's beautiful, elegant like polished teak," he burst out, then flushed.

"I'd say she's also very lucky," the saleslady said with a small smile. "Let me show you what we have."

A short while later, with no more humiliating outbursts, Rafe was in his truck with a black, compact umbrella that Kristen could carry in that big purse of hers so she'd always have it with her. Now, he'd just have to give it to her. He could wait until Saturday, but what if the weatherman was wrong? They certainly hadn't forecast rain for yesterday.

Flipping on his signal, he changed lanes and took the downtown exit. Parking near Jackson Square, he set off for the shop. He had it all planned. He'd pop in, hand her the umbrella, then be on his way. Two minutes max.

He opened the door to St. Clair's, searching for Kristen. He found her, surrounded by three slimly built men in baggy, oversized clothes. He closed the door and quickly crossed the room to them. He had no idea his fists were balled. "You all right, Kristen?"

Surprise, then delight, crossed her beautiful face. "Rafe. It's good to see you. I was just telling the boys about you."

His gaze finally went to the three and he saw they were just kids. They gave him a thorough once-over.

"Rafe, these are the young men I was telling you about," Kristen said. "Rafe Crawford, meet Lee Langley, Pierre Fountain, and Michael Harris. They're juniors in high school."

Rafe nodded, wishing he had followed his first instinct and passed the mall without stopping. His fingers tightened around the umbrella.

"You're the one who made that writing box?" Lee asked, a small, gold hoop earring in his left ear.

"Yes," Rafe answered, unable to keep from looking at Kristen.

"Cool," said Michael Harris, who was lanky with long, curly hair tied at the nape. "We saw one like it next door and the price is unreal. The cheapest one was two hundred bucks."

"Those are antique pieces and took hours to make by hand and are over a hundred years old," Rafe said. "They deserve that price."

Lee nodded. "That's what Ms. Wakefield told us. The dude next door didn't want us touching his."

"Because they're old and fragile," Kristen explained, trying to spare the teenagers' feelings, "You're welcome to examine mine."

"Cool."

Kristen went to the desk and picked up the writing box and held it out. "I know you'll be careful with it."

The young man's hand was already reaching for the box. He paused. "I can examine it better on the desk."

Kristen put it back on the desk and stepped away. The three young men gathered around. They lifted the lid, pulled out the tiny drawers, marveled.

"I don't see any nails," Lee said, after picking it up and turning it over.

"I used pegs and dovetails just as they did a century ago. I use the same techniques for my reproductions whenever possible," Rafe told them.

"How much could you sell this for?" Michael asked, but all three boys looked at Rafe for the answer.

Rafe recognized hope when he saw it. After his grandmother's death, hope and prayer were all that had kept him going at times. "I'm not sure. I made it for Kristen as a gift."

"My boo would probably go for this, too," Pierre, the other young teenager said, finally entering the conversation. He was the slimmest of the three and had a black nylon scarf tied around his head.

"Boo?" Kristen and Rafe echoed.

The young boy sent them a cocky grin. "My girlfriend, Gina. She's tight. Me and her are just like you and Ms. Wakefield."

Rafe stepped away from Kristen. He wasn't about to ask what *tight* meant. Kristen moistened her lips. "Rafe and I are just friends."

"No sweat, Ms. Wakefield," Lee, who appeared to be the leader, said. His look said he could be trusted to keep a secret. "Whatever you say."

"I'd better go." Rafe took another step toward the door. "Good-bye."

"Thanks for stopping by." Kristen waved good-bye as Rafe hurried down the sidewalk without looking back.

Rafe was almost to the freeway before he realized he hadn't given Kristen the umbrella.

Rafe had come to see her for a reason—Kristen was sure of that. He wasn't the type to just drop by for a casual chat, which led her to do a little dropping-in herself to see if he was all right.

The motion detector came on when she pulled up in front of his shop that night and got out. Light spilled from the twin windows in his office. Around her, she heard the soft cadence of insects. She didn't think there were any wild animals out here, but she hurried to the door just the same.

Rafe's head came up when the door opened. Uneasiness entered his eyes. "Kristen."

"Hello, Rafe," she said as if her visit was the most natural thing in the world. "I came to thank you for being so nice to the young boys and answering their questions."

His shoulders hunched beneath his blue plaid shirt. The sleeves were rolled up to above his elbows. "It's all right."

Determined that he realize that what he'd done was more than what many people would do, she took a seat in a comfortable cushioned chair in front of his desk. "You came just at the right moment. I wouldn't have been able to answer any of their questions. They left soon after you did on a foray to find other boxes and compare. I just hope people in the shops are as receptive as you were."

"I have a couple of books I found at garage sales if they want to look at them," he offered.

"I'll tell them." She leaned forward in her chair. "What are you doing?"

A grimace crossed his face. "Record keeping."

"Maybe I can help." She came around the desk and placed one hand on the back of his chair to keep him in place, then placed the other hand beside the ledger. "What seems to be the problem?"

The problem was he couldn't breathe. She was too close. "That's all right."

"Don't be macho, Rafe," she chided. "I had to keep a budget at the museum. What's the problem?"

The problem was that her hand was small and delicate next to his large, calloused one. The problem was they had nothing in common. The problem was he kept forgetting she wasn't for him. He closed the book, and then blinked when she just as quickly opened it again.

Her beautiful face was inches from his. Her soft lips even closer. "I was thinking this morning that slipcovers would do wonders for your sofa."

"Don't you dare," he told her and watched her smile widen. She wasn't the least bit intimidated by him and she scared him to death.

"Stripes or plaid? Or we could do both in the same color scheme of robin's egg blue."

"The figures don't match," he said, flipping back to the column of numbers he'd been wrestling with for the past thirty minutes. "It's time for me to pay my quarterly taxes."

"Let's check to make sure all the entries are entered in the right column and then go from there," she suggested, leaning over to slide the book closer to her.

Her long, silky hair brushed across his cheek. Her shoulder gently bumped his. She was too close and too tempting. Rafe came out of his chair awkwardly. "You sit here."

Concentrating on the ledger, Kristen took his seat. "Pull up the other chair and let's get started."

Rafe pulled up the chair and sat.

Ten minutes later, Kristen discovered the problem and corrected it. Extremely pleased with herself that she'd been able to help, she closed the ledger triumphantly. "Now you can go to bed and sleep peacefully."

Something hot flared in Rafe's eyes, then it was gone. Kristen felt the lingering effect. Her body heated. She was aware of Rafe, inches away from her, as she had been aware of no other man. She gripped the book to keep from reaching out to him.

"If you want, I can check it every couple of weeks for you," she told him a bit breathlessly.

He came unsteadily to his feet. "I can probably manage. It's late. You better start home."

Since she could think of nothing to prolong her visit, she stood as well. "I'll see you Saturday morning at eight."

He stuffed his hands in his pockets. "I'll walk you to your car." The sudden sadness in her face tore at him. He always seemed to make her sad. She picked up her purse hanging on the back of the chair. "Wait. I almost forgot again. It's in the truck. I'll be right back."

Puzzled, Kristen watched him leave, then waited anxiously for his return. He came back shortly, carrying the same small, handled shopping bag with the name of an upscale department store he'd brought into the gallery with him that afternoon. Without a word, he held it out to her.

Accepting the bag, she looked inside. Puzzlement turned to undisguised delight. "Rafe!"

"It'll fit in your purse so you can always have it with you," he told her, his handsome face a mixture of embarrassment and pride.

Setting her large, black tote on the table, she removed the black umbrella from the heavy plastic container and slipped it into her bag. "I won't get soaking wet again."

His expression changed abruptly. He gulped. "Yeah."

The room that had been comfortable suddenly became very hot. "I guess I'd better go."

He almost ran to the door and opened it. Kristen didn't waste time going through it, then getting in her car and driving off. Despite how hard both of them were trying, sexual awareness was growing between them. So far they were both resisting, for different reasons.

As she pulled onto the highway and headed home, she couldn't help but think about what might happen if they stopped resisting.

"Damien, are we keeping you from an appointment?"

Damien raised his head to see Claudette peering over her half-glasses at him from the other side of her desk. "No."

"You keep looking at your watch," she said, her face concerned rather than annoyed. "We are working a bit late."

Three and a half hours was more than a bit, but neither Damien nor Floyd Barrett, vice president of sales who was sitting next to him, would point that out. They were both salaried, not hourly, employees. It wasn't usual for them to be at the office long hours after the rest of the employees went home.

Since Claudette's marriage, she'd left with the office staff at five. But ever since Monday she had reverted to her old schedule. Office gossip was running high as to the reason.

"It's important we get the kinks worked out of these health contracts," Damien said, aware that it would be too late to put his plan to see Angelique tonight into action. "There are several other firms bidding."

"I'd hate to lose this one," Floyd said, his craggy face lined with worry. "Tetaco has over twenty thousand employees."

"We won't," Claudette said, studying the papers spread out over her desk. "We'll be ready next week. Where are the bids from Whitmore Insurance?"

Damien shared a look with Floyd. They'd both hoped she'd end the meeting before she realized the firm's data was missing.

When there was no answer, Claudette glanced up. "Floyd?"

He cleared his throat, then shifted his considerable bulk in the chair. "Maurice hasn't gotten the paperwork back to me."

Claudette adjusted the glasses on her nose, then glanced down at the contracts. "My husband has been busy with other projects. Perhaps you should have considered this and assigned another agent."

Floyd bristled at the reprimand. "I suggested that to your husband and his response was that he didn't need a sitter." There was just enough distaste in Floyd's voice to bring Claudette's gaze back to him. "I left several messages with his secretary and at your home, and they were not returned."

"Where is the file folder? I'll take care of it myself." Claudette adjusted her glasses again.

"Another agent has it," Damien said quietly. No one was going to cover for Maurice. He was hurting Claudette and jeopardizing the company. "I was going over the contracts this afternoon with Floyd in preparation for this meeting and learned of the situation. When it became apparent that we were not going to be able to locate Maurice, the Tetaco file was given to Stevens. He left shortly thereafter for Connecticut. The people at Tetaco want to be in on the bids just as much as we want them to be."

"You took the file off Maurice's desk without his permission?" There was censure in her voice.

"I would have if his secretary knew where it was." Damien said, meeting her gaze squarely. "We loaded the backup files on a disk. Stevens will go over them on the flight out there. He's sharp. He'll be ready."

Suddenly, Claudette felt every bit of her fifty-five years and then some. Whatever happened to her personally, she couldn't allow Thibodeaux International to suffer. Gathering the folders, she stacked them neatly. "Please call Stevens and ask him to convey my personal apology to the Tetaco executives, and my assurance that his company will receive my personal attention in the future."

"I'll call as soon as I get back to my office." Floyd picked up the folders. "I have the president's personal number."

Claudette nodded stiffly. "Good job as usual, gentlemen. Good night." She wasn't sure how much longer she could hold it together.

"Good night." Floyd closed the door behind him.

Damien remained, feeling utterly helpless. Her eyes were too bright. "Claude left the company in good hands, Claudette."

She blinked rapidly. "Thank you. Good night."

It was difficult seeing a woman he'd admired all his adult life so near to shattering. He sensed she wanted to be alone, wondered if telling his father would help either one of them. "Good night," Damien murmured and left.

Claudette held herself perfectly still: then, with an iron will that would have made her father proud, composed herself and removed her glasses. *Honor above all else.* Going into her bathroom, she freshened her make-up, straightened her long, green linen jacket, then picked up her shawl and briefcase on the way out the door.

The Rolls waited at the curb of the five-story downtown office building. Whenever she or her father had worked past six, the car always waited at the curb. Tradition was something you could hold on to, be proud of.

"Evening, Ms. Thibodeaux."

She didn't bother correcting him. "Good evening, Simon, Thank you."

The door closed and she was cocooned in luxury and loneliness. She sat without moving during the twenty-five-minute drive to her home. Getting out, she walked up the white, wooden steps to the veranda. Three proud generations of her family had walked these same steps. In all that time there had never been a hint of a scandal connected to the name . . . until she was born.

The door opened. "Good evening, Mrs. Laurent," the maid greeted. "Would you like dinner now?"

"No. Thank you. Good night." She continued toward the wide, spiraling staircase, her hand resting heavily on the mahogany balustrade as she climbed to the second floor.

Honor above all else.

She opened the door to her bedroom, closed it behind her, then sank to her knees. Sobs racked her slim body. She cried for herself, for the loss of her dream.

Damien sat in the living room of his high-rise apartment with his fingers steepled beneath his chin and stared at the phone as he had been doing for the past thirty minutes. He wanted so badly to call his father and tell him what had happened at the office tonight. Damien had never seen Claudette so shaky. She hadn't been able to ignore— or make excuses any longer for—Maurice's deplorable work habits which, if not corrected, could seriously damage the company's reputation.

Claudette, like her father and his father before him, put the family business first. They also kept their personal business private. So it was anybody's guess what she'd do next. If Damien called his father and hinted that it might be a good idea to call her, would it help or make matters worse for him? If he were in his father's place, he'd want to know if the woman he cared about was in trouble, but it would eat at his gut if he couldn't do anything to help.

Hell, Angelique had needed money years ago, yet hearing it the other night, he'd ached for her and he was only sexually attracted to her. How much worse would it be for his father, who cared deeply for Claudette?

Yanking at his tie, he came to his feet and to a decision. He'd say nothing for the time being. His father was supposed to attend an art council fund-raising meeting at Claudette's house on Wednesday night. Knowing the deteriorating situation of her marriage would only make the meeting more difficult for him. He'd want to help, but Claudette had to help herself. It was rough enough for his father not to be able to tell Claudette how he felt. Damien understood that as well.

But unlike his father, he had no intention of snoozing. Angelique would be his.

Tomorrow, come hell or high water or late meetings, he was going to see her.

thirteen

❧

Unpleasantries were often unavoidable. Unfortunately, they were a part of life. The best one could hope for was that they ended quickly.

Claudette was sitting at the breakfast table sipping *café au lait* when Maurice entered. From the sudden widening of his eyes, she knew he hadn't expected to see her. It was almost ten. She might leave the office with the hourly employees in the afternoon, but she had always followed her father's example by arriving no later than eight each morning.

"Good morning, sweetheart." He kissed her on the cheek, then took his seat across from her and spread his napkin.

"Good morning, Maurice." Despite coming home shortly after two that morning, he looked refreshed and handsome in a single-button, tobacco-brown suit she didn't remember seeing before.

She waited until the maid filled Maurice's coffee cup, took his order for breakfast, then left. "The Tetaco account was reassigned."

His reaction was instant and expected. "That's my account!" he raged.

Claudette set the delicate china cup in the saucer. "Bids are due to Hughes on Monday, two business days from now. When had you planned on meeting with the Tetaco representatives?"

He didn't even blink before he said, "Floyd must have given me the wrong date. I've never missed a deadline."

"Unfortunately, you've missed several in the past couple of months."

He picked up his cup and drank. He liked his coffee strong and hot. "I told you I don't like you checking up on me."

A week ago, even two days ago, she would have tried to soothe. But her father had taught her something else: clean up your own house. "It's not my habit to check up on employees."

The mark hit home. The cup clinked against the saucer. "I'm more than an employee! I'm your husband."

She clasped her surprisingly steady hands, then propped them on the edge of the Chippendale dining table and waited until the maid set down his breakfast of oysters Benedict, then withdrew. "And because of that, Floyd was more lenient with you than any other employee."

"Like he's going to fire me," Maurice sneered, picking up a fork that had been part of the place setting given to her parents as a wedding present from her father's parents.

"He has the authority if he so chooses," Claudette informed him.

Maurice's head snapped back up. He stared at her in stunned amazement.

Placing her ecru napkin on the table, Claudette stood. "Thibodeaux International must come first. I thought you understood that. I thought we could run the company together."

"Together." His eyes widened. "Are you saying you'd make me a full partner?"

Claudette chose to see his enthusiasm as ambition, not greed. "I always wanted us to work together."

He quickly went to her, holding her just as tenderly as he had when they first began going out. "Please forgive me, my precious darling. All I ever wanted was your love, for you to need me. Hearing that you do makes me the happiest man in the world." His knuckles caressed her cheek. "I love you, and I'll do whatever it takes to keep your love."

She didn't want to hope, but found she was unable to help herself. "You mean that?"

"Of course I do." He pulled out her chair. "Eat your breakfast, then we'll go to the office. We have a company to run."

Claudette sat and then picked up her coffee cup, trying to remember if Maurice had had the same bright light in his eyes when he talked of their running the company together as he had when he said he loved her. She was terribly afraid he hadn't.

Maurice could hardly contain his glee as he rode beside Claudette in the Rolls. A full partnership. He'd be rich. Independently rich. Richer, if he were able to stick it out until she died—then the company would be his. Just his.

He could live, travel, and do as he pleased. He'd finally be able to put Atlanta and that sniveling Ann Young behind him forever. He wasn't screwing this up. If Claudette wanted the dutiful, loving husband back, that's what she'd get.

At least for the time being.

"Ms. Fleming, you have a visitor."

With the phone in one hand and a ballpoint pen in the other, Angelique made a notation on the chart of the twenty-year-old woman who'd just left. An addict since the age of twelve, she was seven months pregnant, and saying all the right things to get out of rehab early. Angelique wasn't buying it. She'd make sure her baby would have a chance.

"Ms. Fleming?" prompted the receptionist, who, after working with Angelique for over a year, knew she often became caught up in what she was doing and needed a nudge. "He's waiting. You haven't taken your lunch break yet, and your next appointment is in an hour, at 1:15."

"Sorry. Please send him in." Angelique wrote faster, trying to keep it legible. Relatives often stopped by to ask about the progress of family members. Unless the patient had signed a release, she couldn't divulge the information, but that never stopped them from trying.

The door opened at the exact moment she finished. With a smile, she lifted her head. The smile vanished. "Leave."

"Aren't you interested in why I'm here?" Damien asked, carrying a large, red shopping bag as he crossed to her.

"No." Feeling at a decided disadvantage, she came to her feet. He made her small office shrink.

He stopped when he could go no further. "Not even if I came to apologize?"

She couldn't help her start of surprise. She'd be a fool to miss the voice dipped in moonlight, and the seduction in those dark eyes of his. "I still think you're overly opinionated."

"I think you're exquisite."

Her heart actually thumped. Time to retreat—and fast. She placed her hand on the phone. "Leave or I'm calling security."

The mouth that she'd lost precious sleep over curved enticingly. "I don't think you want to do that."

She put her hands on her hips. It was better than putting them around his stiff neck and dragging him closer. "Threatening me will get you tossed out of here."

"There are many things I want to do to you—threatening you isn't one of them," he said, his eyes dark and hot.

Her knees decided to join her thumping heart. She had to get him out of there. "Seeing me at the club got you worked up, huh?"

His eyes went flat and hard.

"Leave, Damien." She wouldn't feel bad if she'd wounded him.

He almost smiled. "Since you finally called me by my name, I'll forgive you and show you why I came."

She was about to tell him she couldn't care less when he pulled out the largest and by far the most hideous pair of five-inch heels she'd ever seen. The red sequins didn't help.

"I agree, they're gaudy. But beggars can't be choosy. You mind?" he asked, pulling out the chair in front of her desk and sitting without her permission. Removing his shoes and socks, he rolled up his pant legs.

His face pained, he glanced up at her. "You can stop me anytime, you know."

She stuck her tongue in her cheek and tried to compose herself. "Since you went to all that trouble it would be a shame not to at least try them on."

"I didn't think you'd let me off," he said, but there was no rancor in his voice as he bent down.

Angelique peered over her desk to see what he was doing. All she saw was broad shoulders. She rounded the desk and burst out laughing. Damien had one long, wide foot in the open-toed shoe.

"The things a man has to do to get a date," he said.

Her laughter abruptly stopped. Her heart and knees started their symphony again. "That's a poor joke."

"Do I impress you as the type of guy who'd go to this extent to pull a joke?" he asked, his gaze boring into her.

She swallowed. "No."

Nodding emphatically, he put on the other shoe, then started to rise and promptly toppled back into the chair.

"Damien!" Angelique squeaked, rushing to him.

"How about it? Can you forgive an obnoxious, overbearing, and opinionated man and go out with him?"

"You forgot *bigoted*."

His hand swept her hair away from her face. "Go out with me."

Straightening, she moved behind her desk and took her seat. "Why?"

"I'm attracted to you," he told her without hesitation. Then he added, "You're attracted to me, too."

"I was attracted to poison ivy as a kid. The doctor said it was the worst case he'd ever seen. I've got scars to prove it," Angelique told him. "Attraction doesn't always turn out for the best."

Removing the heels, he came around the desk and placed his hands on the arms of her chair. "From what I can see, your skin is beautiful. Of course, if you want to show me a scar or two to prove your point, I'd be willing to look."

"I bet you would." She pushed against his wide chest.

Chuckling, he straightened. "Just trying to present my case."

"What kind of lawyer are you, anyway?" she asked, wishing he were sitting in the chair instead of on the corner of her desk.

"Corporate. I'm chief counsel for Thibodeaux International."

Angelique's dark brow shot up. "Small world."

Damien's body went taut. "What's that supposed to mean?"

"Nothing." She reached for the papers on her desk. Damien's large hand landed on top of hers.

"Do you know Maurice Laurent?" he asked.

Angelique had seen rage before, but she didn't think she'd ever seen it so tightly controlled. "By reputation, and that's more than enough."

"What kind of reputation?" Damien asked.

"You figure it out." She jerked her papers from beneath his hand. "Now if you don't mind, please leave so I can get back to work. My next patient is due shortly."

Lazily, he stood. "The receptionist mentioned you haven't had lunch. Where would you like to go?"

"I'm eating a tuna fish sandwich I brought from home. Alone."

"Speckled Trout Amandine tastes better."

Her salivary glands agreed with him. "You can waste your own time, but not mine. Leave."

"I will once we decide where we're going tonight. Dinner, dancing, theater or all three?"

Temptation, thy name is Damien. "I'll be at home doing my nails. Good-bye. I'm two seconds away from calling security."

He stared down at her a long time, then replaced the heels in the bag and put on his shoes and socks. "Is that your final answer?"

"Yes," she said without hesitation. So what if something inside her protested.

He tipped his head. "Then I guess you leave me with no choice. Good-bye." The door closed softly behind him.

Angelique slumped back in her seat. That was the last she'd see of Damien. She should be happy instead of miserable. So why wasn't she?

Damien arrived back at his office building, after being out all morning with appointments and his visit to Angelique, to find the place buzzing. Claudette had called a meeting of all the executives. Entering the conference room with portraits of members of the illustrious Thibodeaux family mounted on the wall staring solemnly down at them, Damien saw Maurice sitting next to Claudette and grinning like he'd just won the lottery. So much for him getting the boot. Any other man would be knee-deep in dung, but Maurice always managed to come out smelling like a rose.

"Gentlemen, please be seated." Claudette stood at the head of the long, oval table. Maurice sat confidently to her right. "Thank you for coming. I know this meeting is on short notice, but I felt it was important."

Her hands splayed on the polished cherry tabletop. "This company has been in business for eighty years, growing from two employees and a payroll of one hundred dollars a week to over a hundred employees with a payroll in the millions. This was not accomplished without hard work. Your hard work and those who came before you. Many of you worked beside my father to build this company into the nationally known insurance brokerage firm it is today. I thank you."

Claudette paused as the men and women seated around the table acknowledged her thanks with a nod of their heads. "With the passing of my father, I'm sure many of you wondered about the direction and leadership of Thibodeaux."

Damien saw Maurice's grin widen. *Please, no!* Damien thought. *Don't give that asshole any power.*

"Thibodeaux will continue as my father would have wished, with honor and integrity." She placed her hand on Maurice's shoulder. "My husband and I ask your cooperation and diligence in this matter. We pledge to work tirelessly to assist you in any way possible."

Damien put his hand over his mouth to keep from laughing out loud at the perplexed look on Maurice's face. Whatever he'd been expecting Claudette to say, it wasn't a pledge for him to work hard.

Claudette smiled serenely down at Maurice. All eyes centered on him.

"Of course," he finally said.

Claudette patted Maurice's shoulder as if he were a little boy who'd just said his Easter speech all the way through without faltering. "That's all, ladies and gentlemen, and remember, my door is always open to listen to any concerns you might have."

The executives left much happier than when they had arrived. As soon as the door closed, Maurice turned to Claudette, his face mottled with anger. "I thought you were going to tell them that we were going to work together."

"But I just did," Claudette said, her brow puckered in puzzlement.

"Not as your partner!" he almost yelled. Damn it, he wanted that partnership.

"That will come later. If I made you a full partner when all the executives are aware that you've been less than energetic with your accounts, it would not have gone over well." She placed a hand on his tense shoulder.

"Thibodeaux was founded and has grown because of a strong work ethic and the principle of employees being rewarded for their dedication.

Unfortunately, your actions in the past weeks have tied my hands. But once you show them how hard you're going to work, they'll accept your partnership and, more importantly, your leadership. Don't you agree?"

"I guess," he said reluctantly, his expression belligerent.

She continued to smile at him. "Simon will pick us up at six. I'll make reservations at Brennan's, if that's agreeable."

"All right, I'll see you then." Maurice left with a vague sense of unease, which he quickly shook off. The woman hadn't been born who could outsmart him.

fourteen

❧

No matter how much her mind wanted to wander, how badly she wanted to get up, Angelique stayed glued to her chair. She was getting two pages done tonight if she had to sit at her computer until morning.

She twisted in the padded seat, her fingers poised over the keyboard, ready when her brain decided to gift her with some eloquent words that would make Dr. Jones, her advisor, nod his gray head in approval and marvel at her wisdom.

Nothing came. As for wisdom, as she'd told Kristen, she didn't feel very wise. And again, it was all Damien's fault.

What she was feeling was antsy, restless, and very annoyed. It had been building all afternoon. He could have tried harder. What kind of man looked at a woman like he wanted to make a feast out of her, then calmly accepted her not going out with him?

Her hazel eyes narrowed. He probably did it on purpose. He knew she was attracted to him; he'd faked her out. "The bastard!"

Too angry to sit any longer, she came to her feet. She'd fallen for it, hook, line, and sinker. He was probably laughing with some scatter-brained bimbo who'd been born with a platinum spoon between her perfectly capped teeth. Well, Angelique didn't need him. She could forget him like that! she thought, with a snap of her fingers.

Sighing, she stuffed her hands into the pockets of her frayed cut-off jeans. It wasn't working. Positive thinking only went so far. What she needed to do was focus. Nothing had ever stopped her from doing so before.

Pulling out her chair, she was about to sit down when she heard the doorbell. She didn't have to look at the computer clock to know it was a little after nine. She'd been watching it like an anxious mother hen waiting for her chick to hatch. The chime came again.

Could be another grad student or Kristen. They hadn't seen each other that day. Angelique started toward the door. Hopefully, Kristen was having better luck with Rafe. One of them deserved to be happy.

Reaching for the lock, she put her eye to the peephole. She frowned on seeing a young, blond woman in a white uniform with a train case. Angelique's hand paused on the lock. "Yes?"

"Miss Fleming, I'm here for your appointment," said the young woman.

"You have the wrong apartment," Angelique said.

The woman referred to a three-by-five-inch card in her hand. "Angelique Fleming. River Place, apartment number 267. Isn't that you?"

Angelique didn't know whether to be concerned or not. Was this some type of scam? "What was the appointment for?"

"A manicure and pedicure," came the reply.

Damien. Fumbling with the locks, Angelique jerked open the door. "Who set up the appointment?"

"I did."

Angelique whirled to see Damien, arms folded, lounging against the wall, looking positively mouth-watering in a black suit. And she looked like crap. Her cut-off jeans were frayed and faded; her black Xavier sweatshirt had bleach stains splattered all over it from an unfortunate laundry debacle months ago; her hair was piled on top of her head like a schizophrenic bird's nest.

He came upright. Casually, he picked up her hand and studied the oval shape of her short, unvarnished nails. "What color did you have in mind?"

Angelique came out of her stupor and snatched her hand away. These days she didn't have time to get her nails done. "What are you doing here?"

"Seeing that you get a manicure." His mouth twitched. "I thought of a pedicure after my experience in your office. You wear heels all day."

She would not be swayed by his thoughtfulness. "I can do my own nails."

"But why not indulge in some pampering?" he coaxed. "My gift to you."

"Because I pay my own way," she said. It was extremely important that he understood that.

He reached in his pocket and handed the silent, watchful woman several bills. "It seems your services aren't needed, after all. Thank you."

She stuffed the money in her pocket without looking at it. "Thank you, Mr. Broussard."

"Aren't you going with her?" Angelique asked as the woman walked away.

"What do you think?" he asked, his gaze searing her.

She could be incensed or sensible. "Well, come on in. We've given the neighbors enough to talk about."

He stepped over the threshold, stopped, and stared at the books and periodicals scattered over the room.

"Sorry." She closed the door. "Since I started working on my dissertation, they seem to multiply."

"Don't apologize. Reminds me of my law school days. I work best in chaos."

She nodded, folding her arms across her chest. "Would you like something to drink?"

He shook his head, his hand lifting toward her face. She stilled, but his hand went to the clamp on the top of her head and released it. Hair tumbled down her back. He caught the lustrous strands in his hand, then threaded his fingers through them.

She shivered. "Uh . . . you want to sit down?"

His hand massaged her scalp. "No room."

She moaned, feeling her eyes drift closed. "I can . . . I can . . ."

"Yes." His mouth touched hers, heat and hardness, demand and patience. She felt herself tumbling, whirling in the storm of his kiss as it swept her up.

His hand closed over her bare breast beneath her sweatshirt. Her body quivered. She moaned. "Damien."

"Yes."

He bowed her over, his mouth kissing her harder. Her hand clutched his head, pulling him closer even as her legs wobbled. She knew she should be pushing him away but she couldn't.

He lifted his head, his breathing ragged. "I want you."

Need clamored though her. Her nails bit into his shirt. "I can't."

"Your body says differently," he said hoarsely.

"I don't let my body rule me." Drawing on all her strength, she managed to step back. "And if that's all you came for, you can leave."

His dark eyes went flat, then he pulled her back into his arms. "Trust is going to be hard for us and it's my fault."

After a second, she put her arms around his waist. "If you're expecting an argument, you've come to the wrong place."

He kissed her hair. "I disagree. I'm exactly where I want to be."

Angelique melted a little more against him. "You must be a dynamite lawyer."

"Why do you say that?" he asked, his hand making slow, lazy strokes up and down the curve of her back.

"That persuasive tongue of yours."

She felt him smile. "So where are we going for our first date?"

"I'm supposed to be writing my dissertation," she told him, enjoying the erratic beat of his heart against her cheek.

"I'm supposed to be going over contracts for a multimillion dollar deal."

Her fingers stroked his chest, toyed with the buttons of his shirt, then regrettably moved on. "Damien, I don't know if we're good for each other."

His thumb and forefinger lifted her chin. His dark gaze bore into her. "The same thought entered my mind, but here I am."

"Here we are."

His head drifted down and he kissed her, his mouth persuading her, then he stepped back. "Since you can't decide, how about dinner tomorrow evening? I'll find a place that's quiet and you won't have to worry about dressing up."

"Damien, I'm not going to your place."

"Couldn't get that one by you, huh?"

She smiled because he was smiling. "Pick another place—one more public—with the same features and I'll be ready at eight."

"I'd better leave before you change your mind." He kissed her on the cheek. "Get back to writing."

She walked him to the door. "Good night."

"Good night and just so you know, I wanted the manicure to be something nice for you, nothing more."

The sincerity in his eyes and voice pulled at her. "I guess I over-reacted."

"See you tomorrow night."

She closed the door and wondered—what had she done?

Angelique desperately needed to talk.

Just after Damien left, while her heart was still beating wildly, her body still tingling deliciously from his touch, Angelique called Kristen. The man had scrambled her circuits and made a mockery of her plan to dislike him.

It was quickly agreed that they'd meet for breakfast at Angelique's place. She'd cook. Her housekeeping might be the pits, but she could cook her behind off.

Shortly after seven Wednesday morning, Angelique and Kristen sat down to a huge breakfast of grilled ham steaks, scrambled eggs, hash browns, grits swimming in real butter, and biscuits light enough to float off the plate.

"Where do you think Damien plans to take you tonight?" Kristen asked, slicing into the ham.

"I haven't the foggiest." Angelique grimaced, her spoon poised at sprinkling brown sugar over her grits. "I spent an hour last night after he left trying to find just the right outfit. I'm still undecided."

"Black is always in order," Kristen told her. "Or wear that white satin wrap blouse over cropped black pants or a sexy black skirt, lots of gold or silver jewelry, heeled sandals. The barer the better, but that's not what's bothering you."

Angelique propped her elbows on the small kitchen table. "I like him. I really like him. I know this could end badly, but it's like I'm rolling down a hill toward a precipice and I can't stop myself."

"I'm rolling right beside you." Getting up, Kristen topped off their coffee cups, then retook her seat. She was as comfortable in Angelique's kitchen as she was in her own. "But I have to admit, even if I could stop, I wouldn't. Rafe needs me."

"At least you have an altruistic reason. All I want to do is jump Damien's bones," Angelique said, disgust in her voice.

"If that's all, why didn't you?" Kristen asked. "You had the perfect opportunity last night."

Angelique opened her mouth, then closed it. "Beats me."

"I'm the last one to try and analyze what you're feeling, but I'd say you want something a little more meaningful with Damien, something that's built on mutual respect and trust," Kristen told her. "You got off on the wrong foot and you're smart enough to realize that jumping into bed with him at this point will just make things more difficult, not easier."

Angelique narrowed her eyes. "You've been reading my textbooks?"

Kristen laughed, then sobered. "Caring about another person makes you more sensitive to what others are going through. I understand now why my family was so understanding when I was a hateful shrew after Eric and I broke up."

"Where's the creep now?" Angelique asked, sipping her coffee.

"I don't know, and I stopped caring long ago," Kristen admitted, glad it was the truth.

"My professor got one of the students pregnant the year after I graduated. He lost his tenure, there was a big scandal. He left town."

"We're better off without them," Kristen said.

"We have a chance to get it right, but it won't be without risks."

"For the first time in a long time, I'm not afraid." Kristen's face softened. "Sometimes Rafe looks at me a certain way and I forget to breathe and, although he'd never admit it, I can tell he feels the same way." She sighed and set her cup down. "But then he backs away faster than a crayfish. Knowing why he's afraid of opening up to me doesn't make the hurt any less, but deep down in my heart, I feel he'd slice off his arm before harming me."

"You haven't discussed Rafe with me, and I respect that. From being around him a short time I'd have to say he's uncomfortable around crowds and goes to great lengths to avoid them." Angelique stared at

Kristen, not as a friend but as a psychologist. "He's not going to open the door and let you into his life. You'll have to keep knocking it down, keep proving to him that you're there for the long haul, keep reminding him that you're there for him as much as he is for you."

Kristen nodded. "I will. In fact, I'm thinking about going out there tonight and surprising him."

Angelique grimaced. "We certainly didn't pick easy men."

"Are you sorry?" Kristen asked, positive she already knew the answer.

Angelique didn't even have to think. "No."

"Neither am I." Kristen picked up her coffee cup. "To victory."

"Victory." Their cups clinked.

Kristen was busy from the moment she flipped the "closed" sign to "open" until well after one. Jacques had ordered sandwiches from a nearby restaurant, then gone to pick them up. She didn't mind working: it kept her mind from dwelling on Rafe and his possible reaction to her showing up uninvited again.

The front door opened: she looked up, preparing to rise, when she recognized the three teenagers Jacques was mentoring. Her smile broadened. "Hi, guys. Jacques went to get our lunch. He'll be back shortly."

"Actually, we came to see you," Lee said, unwrapping newspaper from the object he was carrying. He placed it on her desk.

Kristen stared at a crude wooden chest.

"What do you think?" Lee asked, his voice anxious.

Kristen's gaze went from the unvarnished wood kept together with oversized nails to Lee. She bit her lip. She didn't want to hurt his feelings.

"She thinks it sucks," Pierre said. "Don't you?"

"Not exactly," she evaded, trying, but failing, to come up with a comment that was honest without damaging Lee's pride. "Did you build this?"

"We all did." He picked up the lopsided box and examined it closer. "The man at the lumberyard let us have some scraps for free. We had to buy the nails." He squinted, then set the box back down, this time beside Kristen's writing box. "I was thinking paint would help, but not anymore."

"Rafe's been making furniture for years. Plus, he had the tools and machines. A few are bigger and taller than I am," Kristen told them.

"I bet if we had those tools we could have done a better job," Pierre said. "You think he'd show us?"

"I'm not sure," Kristen said slowly, watching the disappointment spread across their faces. "He's a private person, but he did say he'd loan you some of the books he has." Their expressions closed immediately. "What's the matter?"

"Nothing," Lee said. "Gotta run. Tell Mr. Broussard we came by."

"You forgot your box," she said when they turned to leave.

"Yeah." Lee came back, picked it up, then dumped it into the trash can.

Kristen was stunned. "Why'd you do that?"

"Because that's where it belongs. In the trash." The door closed and they were gone.

Kristen got the distinct impression that Lee felt the same way about himself.

His expression pensive, Jacques held the poorly made box in his hand. "This is the first time any of them have tried to do anything besides try to act macho."

Sitting at the small, all-purpose table in the storage room in the back, Kristen folded her arms over her chest and leaned back in her chair. "I told them Rafe offered to loan them his books, but it was as if I'd insulted them."

Shaking his head, Jacques set the box down and reached in the plastic bag to hand Kristen her grilled-tuna sandwich. "Lee's dyslexic. Pierre and Michael read, but on a second-grade level. All three were passed from grade to grade. They're in the same neighborhood and hang out together because they know each other's secrets."

"That's horrible," Kristen said, incensed on their behalf.

"They're getting the help they need now, but I'm afraid it may be too little too late. I'd push them to go to college if I thought they could make it. They haven't learned the discipline nor do they have the academic skills. In the eleventh grade, the odds are stacked against them that they'll catch up." Jacques put his lunch in the refrigerator. "Without a trade they'll never be able to rise out of the poverty they were born in."

"Like carpentry?" Kristen asked, not bothering to unwrap her grilled-tuna sandwich.

"If you'll excuse a pun, they're sharp kids with inquisitive minds," Jacques told her. "All come from large families. Lee and Pierre live with their mothers. Michael with his mother and father, but none of their parents seem able to give them the support and direction they need. I can't criticize them. Putting food on the table and keeping a roof over their heads probably takes all their energy. I saw Rafe and thought he might be able to help. I still do."

Kristen's hand traced the side of the unvarnished box. She couldn't get Lee's last remark out of her mind. He reminded her of Rafe, putting on a brave appearance and hurting inside. "I'll visit Rafe tonight and talk to him."

"Tell him I'll pay for any supplies they'll need, and of course for his time."

"I don't think any of that will be a consideration in his decision," Kristen said.

"What will?" Jacques asked.

"This." Kristen picked up the box.

Determined to make the art council meeting at Claudette's house on time, Jacques shooed Kristen out the door fifteen minutes before closing time. He was the first member of the fund-raising committee for the annual Christmas benefit and auction to arrive. He'd dreaded and anticipated this moment all day.

He was shown immediately to the drawing room with its vaulted ceiling, Persian rugs, and antique furniture. Claudette was alone.

"Hello, Jacques," Dressed in a slim-fitting, cream-colored dress, she offered her cheek and her hands.

"Hello, Claudette." Her skin was fragrant and warm, her hands cold. He frowned when he saw the lines of strain around her mouth. "Where's Maurice?"

Her delicate brow lifted at the harshness of his tone. "In the study. He's working." The astonishment must have shown on his face. "I had to practically drag him out of the office this afternoon."

"Then why does that make you so sad?" he asked before he could stop himself. Her hand jerked slightly in his. She tried to pull them free, but Jacques's hold tightened. "We're friends. I care about you." *Too much.*

"Then you'll let the matter drop," she said, her voice not quiet steady.

"No. Not this time. You've gone through so much losing Claude— you deserve happiness."

"I am happy." She pulled her hands free and stepped away to take a seat in the deep burgundy leather wing chair that had been her father's favorite. Her hands cupped the rolled arms. "I wasn't sure you would be able to make it tonight."

Jacques stared at Claudette. She looked fragile and vulnerable. She'd looked the same way after losing her father. Now wasn't the time to push. He took a seat and accepted the change of subject. "I promised to help with the benefit and I will. I'll always be there if you need me. Any time. Any place."

Her eyes widened as if she'd caught the undercurrents of his true feelings for her.

Jacques kept his gaze on her, refusing to look away or back down. He'd honor her marriage vows, but he wanted her to know she only had to ask if she wanted his help.

Whatever her response might have been, it was interrupted by the appearance of a couple on the art council committee. Claudette got up to greet them and Jacques did the same. Almost immediately, another member was shown in, and Jacques knew that he wouldn't have any more quiet moments with Claudette.

A couple of times that night, when he turned to her, she'd look away. Jacques didn't know if it boded well or ill.

fifteen

❧

"The students Jacques is mentoring made this. What do you think?" Kristen asked.

A frown worked itself across Rafe's brow as he stared down at the rectangular box on his worktable. The unvarnished, misshapen wood was splintered at the sides from nails too large, the hinged top overlapping. He didn't know exactly what to say.

Kristen sighed. "Your reaction is exactly the same as mine. I didn't want to hurt their feelings. Then Lee sat it beside yours, and I didn't have to say a word."

Uneasiness moved through Rafe. He knew what it was like to have your work criticized. His father had taken delight in belittling him over the simplest little thing. He could never please him no matter how hard he tried. He'd finally stopped trying.

Rafe shook off the memory. "He shouldn't have done that. I took shop my last two years of high school and worked with a furniture-maker for five years before I struck out on my own. It's next to impossible to make a good piece without the right tools."

"Jacques said this is the first time they have shown any interest in anything besides being macho, but Lee got angry and threw it in the trash. I fished it out."

"I'll get you the books." He started toward the stairs, but her hand on his arm stopped him. He tried not to jump at the spiral of heat her touch caused.

Her face was unbearably sad. "It won't do any good," she said, then explained about their reading difficulties. "That's why Jacques and I feel that they need to learn a trade."

He stared down into her soft eyes. For the first time in years, he wasn't able to rule his thoughts. Kristen kept intruding. He hadn't been able to deny the pleasure seeing her had brought a short while ago. She lit up his solitary world.

"You don't know what you're asking."

"I do," she said, her gaze locked with his. "I'm asking you to help three teenagers who have nowhere else to turn."

Shaking his head, he moved to the lengths of wood he'd cut for the shelves in the highboy. "I don't like working around anyone."

"I thought you had an assistant."

He wished she wouldn't stand so close. Even with all the sawdust, he could still smell the exotic fragrance of her perfume. "Jim Dobbins just does a bit of the sanding and varnishing. I work alone."

"Rafe, they need to see what hard work and determination can accomplish." She looked around his shop. "You did this despite what must have been tremendous odds. You didn't give up or blame others, you just did it."

His fingers bit into the wood. Oh, he'd blamed and he'd hated. He'd succeeded because he was determined that he'd honor his grandmother's memory and the faith she'd always had in him, and to show his father that he'd been wrong about him being worthless. "They may not want it as badly as I did."

"One hour of your time is all I'm asking," Kristen said. "If you don't feel they're sincere, I won't ask again."

He placed the wood on top of another piece, marked his cut, then turned to her. "Why are you so adamant about this?"

"Because I know what it is to want something and not know how to go about getting it, to be afraid of failing." Her beautiful face was sad, wistful. "Like you, I was valedictorian of my high school class. And unlike you, if I died tonight I'd leave nothing tangible behind. Nothing would mark my passing through this life."

A chill swept through him. He grabbed her arms before he counted the cost. "Don't you say things like that." He shook her once as if to punctuate his order. "Ever."

Her hand tenderly cupped his cheek. "I didn't say no one would care."

He swallowed the hard knot in his throat, struggled not to turn his head and kiss her palm, not to drag her into his arms. "This is really important to you, isn't it?"

"Yes."

He dropped her arms and stepped back while he was still able. "All right."

She launched herself into his arms. "Rafe! Thank you!"

Need slammed into him like a jackhammer. With her talk of death he was too weak to deny the urgency clamoring through him. His arms closed around her, drawing her to him. He'd been allowed to touch heaven twice.

She leaned her head back, grinning up at him. "You won't be sorry."

The only thing he was sorry for was that one day she'd move on with her life . . . without him. "There'll be rules and regulations. First, those baggy clothes have to go. They have to wear safety equipment and the first time one of them starts horse-playing in here, they're out."

"Yes, sir." She grabbed her purse. "If you'll give me a list, I'll pick up the things they'll need tonight. Jacques is footing the bill."

He glowered down at her. "You aren't going wandering around Home Depot this time of night."

She checked her watch, then rolled her eyes. "Rafe, it's barely eight."

"And men are coming in there off jobs getting supplies for the next day. The parking lot is always busy, and once you get inside, you won't know where to find anything."

She sighed dramatically. "Well, Rafe, I guess there's only one answer."

"What?" he asked, sure she'd listen to reason.

"You'll just have to go with me."

He blinked, barely able to keep his mouth shut. *He should have known better. This was the new Kristen.* "Come on," he said with a sigh. "The truck is in the back."

Angelique was ready. She'd even cleaned up the living room. Then she answered the doorbell and her heart raced. Dressed casually in a navy blue sports coat and tan slacks, Damien still exuded a raw power and masculinity. "Hello."

"Hello, Angelique." His dark gaze swept caressingly over her hair pulled up on top of her head, past the hint of cleavage in her wrap-style blouse to her form-fitting black capri pants and her black, high-heeled sandals. "You're beautiful."

She'd received hundreds of compliments about her looks, but none had ever made her insides quiver like gelatin or pleased her more. "Thank you." She went to pick up her purse off the sofa. "I'm ready."

"Not quite." With an easy motion, he pulled her into his arms and kissed her, long and leisurely. "Now I might be able to sit through dinner like a gentleman."

Angelique strove for calm as they left her apartment and Damien checked to make sure the door was locked. "Where are we going?"

His hand slipped possessively around her slim waist. "To a place where I can enjoy you."

Her startled gaze flew up to his.

Laughing, he hugged her to him. "That delight comes later. For now it's a quiet dinner at the Palace Cafe."

Angelique felt her heart do a silly little dance as the sound of Damien's rich laughter flowed over her. She was going faster and faster down that hill.

Outside, Damien escorted her to a sleek, gray Maserati Spyder in the visitors' parking area. Her eyes widened. Inside the flashy Italian classic, she glanced over at him as he slid his long, powerful body into the low seat beside her. He looked as beautiful and as powerful as the car. "I pictured your car being staid and conventional."

Shifting the vehicle into gear, he backed out. The motor roared. "I've always had a passion for fast cars. I like opening them up, feeling their responsiveness beneath me." He threw a seductive glance her way. "There's only one other feeling that can possible compare with it."

Angelique's breath caught. Her nipples pouted. Her body tingled in a place it had no place tingling on a first date. Defensively she pressed her knees together and tried not to think of her body beneath Damien's, her legs wrapped around him.

"Aren't you going to ask what?" he said after a moment, stopping at a signal light.

"I'm not touching that," she said, then groaned.

He ignored the green light and the car behind him honked. "Oh, I wouldn't bet on it."

Since Angelique wouldn't, either, she sensibly remained quiet as Damien finally sped off.

Kristen had never experienced shopping with a man except when she'd helped Adam prepare a cozy dinner for Lilly the night he proposed. Although he didn't have his sight, he'd been exacting in what he wanted. Rafe was the same way. There was no leisurely stroll down this aisle or that. He'd gone directly to the items he'd wanted, tossed them in the wheeled shopping basket, and set off to get in the long line at checkout. Then she'd seen the light fixtures and suddenly had another agenda.

"Let's go down this aisle," she said, not waiting for him to follow.

Light fixtures hung from the recessed ceiling, sprouted from the wall display, or sat on the floor. All were lit and shone brightly. She could picture the flowered chandelier over his kitchen table.

"Why are we stopping here?" he asked.

She fingered the forged iron candlestick floor lamp that would be perfect by his chair in the living room. "Isn't this nice?"

He shrugged. "I guess. Come on before the line gets longer. I don't like you being out this late on the road."

Ignoring him, Kristen went to the glass lamp shaped like a pineapple with sculptured brass leaves. "This would look wonderful with a couple of brass candlesticks and perhaps a little crystal bowl of vanilla potpourri."

He finally seemed to be paying attention. "You need a lamp?"

"I might," she evaded. "Let's go look at the wallpaper."

Frowning, he fell into step beside her. "You're thinking about redecorating your place?"

Casually, she placed her hands beside his on the handle of the shopping cart, felt the brush of his shirtsleeve against her bare arm. "Could I count on you to help?"

He stared down at their hands inches apart a long moment before he lifted his head. "You can always count on me, Kristen."

There was such a yearning in his words that Kristen felt her throat tighten. Wanting to step closer but aware that she couldn't, she simply nodded. *One day.*

The Palace Cafe, with its rich cherry walls, high-backed leather chairs, and black wrought iron wall-sconce lighting had a sweeping view of busy Canal Street, yet still maintained a quiet atmosphere. Angelique wasn't surprised when the maitre d' greeted Damien by name or that they were seated immediately at an intimate table draped with a white linen tablecloth. What shocked and delighted her was the snowy white orchid by her plate.

"It's beautiful." The tips of her fingers lightly touched the soft petals. "Thank you."

"I want you to enjoy yourself tonight, enjoy being with me," he told her, accepting the oversized menu.

She accepted her own leather bound menu. "You're off to a good start. I can't wait to see what's next."

What came next was impeccable but friendly service, a superb dinner of steak and Maine lobster, and a wine so smooth it tasted golden. A jazz trio played softly in the corner of the restaurant.

"This was wonderful. Thank you," Angelique said, sipping her coffee, feeling relaxed and mellow.

"You're welcome." He nodded toward her cup. "You're sure you don't want another glass of wine?"

She shook her head. "Not if I want to get up and go to work in the morning."

"How long have you worked at the rehab center?" He braced both arms on the table.

"A little over a year," she answered, enjoying the shadows cast on his face by the small, flickering candle in the middle of the table. "How long have you been with Thibodeaux?"

"Twelve years. I was recruited in law school and have been there ever since."

She set the china cup aside. "Did you ever think of following in your father's footsteps?"

Regret crossed Damien's face. "Perhaps for a short while when I was young, but never seriously. He accepts that, and I'd like to think he's proud of me."

"I think you can safely say he is," she said with a smile.

"He hasn't always been." He reached across the table and took her hand in his. "He wasn't too pleased about the way I acted toward you."

The memory still had the ability to hurt, so she shrugged it away. Instead she tried to get used to the excited little thump in her chest. "You were only trying to protect him. I respect you for that."

His grin was slow and lazy; he kissed her hand. "Thanks for not socking me."

Shivers raced over her body. If he kept looking at her like that, she'd forget where they were. "That's reserved for Maurice," she said, then could have bitten off her tongue when Damien stiffened.

"What is he to you?"

"Nothing." She tried to pull her hand away and found it trapped.

"The night after you left me at The Inferno, he came in with another man. Had he been there before?" he asked tightly.

"What you're asking is had he been there before to see me?"

"Has he?" he bit out the words.

She snatched her hand free. Her eyes were hot, her voice cold as ice. "No, but you don't believe me, do you?" He waited a beat too long. "You can't forget, can you?"

"I thought I could," he answered honestly, feeling his stomach knot.

Calmly, she placed her napkin on the table. "This was a mistake. I'd like to go home now."

"Angelique . . ." he began, but he was talking to her back.

Cursing under his breath, he threw some bills on the table and tried to catch up with her. A large party came in the door just as he was going out. By the time he made it outside she was nowhere in sight.

Kristen refused to think of her actions as sneaky as Rafe placed the last of the three boxes in a back corner of his shop. "Thank you for keeping the lamps for me, Rafe. I don't have any storage space at my place."

He straightened. "No problem. Just keep your receipt in case you change your mind about anything."

"I won't. I know exactly where they're going," she said, then started for the front door. "I'd better go. I'll bring the boys by around seven tomorrow night."

He rubbed the back of his neck. "I don't like the idea of you having to chauffeur them here, then back home."

Kristen already had her answer planned. She was driving the boys and spending as much time with Rafe as possible. "Jacques likes to close the shop and, if a customer is there, it will be even later than seven."

"He should have thought of that before he wanted the boys to come out here," Rafe said, still unhappy with the idea.

She started through the work area. "Jacques isn't worried about me."

"Maybe he should be," Rafe replied.

Kristen smiled up at him as they entered his office. "Thanks for caring, but I'll be fine."

Rafe grunted. Outside he opened the BMW's door. "I still think I should follow you home."

"Nonsense. You have work to do. I don't want to take any more of your valuable time." Getting in, she closed the door, started the motor, then activated the window to roll it down. "Good night, Rafe, and thanks again for everything."

"Call when you get home," he instructed.

"I will." Putting the car in reverse, she backed up, then headed down the driveway to the street. In the rearview mirror she saw Rafe unmoved, watching her.

Damien cruised Canal Street before going to Angelique's apartment. His concern for her grew as he rang the doorbell and there was no answer. "Angelique. Just let me know if you made it home all right."

He pressed his hand against the door. "Angelique."

Grimacing, he went to Kristen's apartment and knocked. There was no answer. Hands shoved in his pockets, he left and went back to his car. How could an evening that started out with such promise end so messed up?

"You screwed up. That's how," he muttered, starting the Maserati and pulling off. He didn't realize where he was going until he parked in front of the black wrought iron gate of his father's house in the Garden District.

His hand swiped over his face. He hadn't run home to his father with a problem . . . since he'd thought they were interested in the same woman. Here he was again . . . because of the same woman.

He got out and went up the walkway to the wide wooden porch. Two huge, ruffled ferns swayed gently in the cool evening breeze. In one corner, he could see the white wicker furniture his mother had pampered and loved to sit in with his father. His father might care for Claudette, but he'd never forget Damien's mother. Damien rang the doorbell.

Jacques opened the door, saw Damien's troubled expression, and knew his son had a serious problem. "What's the matter?"

"Am I that obvious?" Damien asked, closing the door behind him.

"I'm your father," Jacques said, then, "Angelique or Thibodeaux?"

Damien stuffed his hands into his pockets. "I took her out tonight and made a mess of it."

"Like father, like son. Come on into the study. I need a drink myself."

Damien cast a sideways glance at his father's unhappy face. "The committee meeting or Claudette?"

Jacques waited to answer until he had poured them both a drink. "I've never seen her look so tired and strained. Not even after Claude died." He handed Damien his drink, then took a sip of his Scotch and soda. "I won't ask you to break client confidentiality, but I will ask you to be there for her."

"I will, Dad. You can count on it."

"Thanks." Jacques took his seat and crossed his legs. "Now, what about you?"

"I'm not very proud of myself." Damien rolled the glass between his palms. "I thought I was all right with her past, but she mentioned a man's name who is an associate of the firm, a man I don't think very highly of, and I lost it."

Jacques studied his drink, then glanced up. "I don't suppose she told you how she knew him?"

"No."

"Are you afraid she did more than dance for him?"

Damien's head snapped up. His eyes were glacial.

Jacques stood and put his hand on Damien's bunched muscles in his arm. "How many women would you say you've been intimate with?"

Shocked embarrassment widened his eyes. "Dad!"

Jacques was unfazed. "What do you think the odds are that you'll meet one of those women again?"

"It's not the same," Damien said, his mouth in a tight, narrow line.

"Damien," Jacques said patiently, "memory is a strange thing. We tend to forget the good and remember the bad. I may be sixty-one, but I remember my youth and I'd be a liar if I told you there weren't a couple of lustful flings. Since we had our first talk about sex when you were fourteen, I daresay you've had more than a couple."

"Geez, Dad!"

Jacques grinned. "Thought so. So don't start casting stones that may boomerang back at you. If Angelique's past bothers you, talk about it before it causes a wedge between you."

"She told me she'd never been with the man, then left me at the restaurant when I tried to talk to her."

"From what I'm hearing, you'd said more than enough." Jacques shook his head. "I'd rap you on the head, but you obviously feel bad enough."

"I blew it, didn't I?" Damien said.

"You're a brilliant lawyer, Damien. I'm sure you'll figure out how to present your case."

He nodded, feeling better already. "I'd appreciate it if you'd call Kristen and see if Angelique made it home all right."

Jacques went to the phone on his desk and began dialing. "After you find out, then what?"

"Throw myself on the mercy of the court, what else?"

sixteen

"Angelique, I'm sorry," Kristen said on seeing the misery in her best friend's face when she answered her door. Kristen had been four blocks away when she'd received Jacques's call on her cell phone. All he would say was that Angelique's date with Damien had ended badly, and his son wanted to make sure she was safe after going by twice and getting no answer at Angelique's door.

Angelique, her long hair tumbled around her face, swiped at the tears cresting in her eyes. "I'll get over him."

"Let me make you some hot chocolate," Kristen said, closing the door behind her and leading Angelique to the sofa.

She balked. "I don't want to sit down."

"Then come into the kitchen with me." Still holding Angelique's arm, she headed for the spacious kitchen.

"Why can't I pick a good man to care about?" Angelique asked, swiping at her face again as she leaned against the blue tiled counter.

Kristen paused while reaching for the special blend of cocoa in the overhead cabinet. "You want to talk about it?"

Angelique folded her arms and shook her head. "It doesn't matter."

Setting the tin can on the counter, Kristen opened the refrigerator. Angelique might not be the best housekeeper, but her pantry was always neat and usually well stocked. "If that were so, you wouldn't be miserable, and he wouldn't be worried about you."

Angelique's head came up. "What?"

Placing the milk beside the cocoa, Kristen went to her. "I was four blocks away when I received a call from Jacques. Damien had him call me because he'd been by twice and no one answered the door. He was worried."

"I had a hard time getting a cab. I only arrived five minutes before you," Angelique explained. "He probably didn't come by at all. Just wanted his father to think he had."

As if to dispute her, the doorbell rang. "Want to bet that's him?" Kristen asked, lifting a dark brow.

Angelique's arms tightened around her waist. "I don't want to see him."

"We both know that's not true," Kristen said gently. "If you can work this out you'll save yourself a lot of misery."

"Or give myself more?" Angelique said, her voice a thin whisper of sound. "He can't deal with my past."

Kristen took her best friend's arms. "I seem to remember a very wise psychologist advising me to knock down the door of someone who was caught up in their past." She leaned her head in the direction of the sound of the front door. "I believe Damien is doing that literally."

"He's the one who can't forget the past," Angelique said.

"Then help him. Show him the woman you are, not the one he thinks you are."

Angelique's expression turned mutinous. "I won't explain myself to anyone! He takes me as I am or not at all."

"Then give him a chance to learn who you are. The Angelique I know wouldn't be afraid to see any man," Kristen challenged.

Angelique snorted. "A three-year-old could see through that one."

Kristen was undisturbed. "True, but am I wrong?"

"No." Angelique made a final swipe at the tears on her face. "Maybe you should try your hand at counseling."

Kristen smiled. "I'll stick to art." She nodded toward the front door again. "I don't think he's going away."

"If he blows it this time—" There was no need for her to finish.

"We'll have a session thinking of nasty things to happen to him, but somehow I don't think he will. I'll let myself out," Kristen said. "To-morrow morning breakfast is at my place." She went to the front door and opened it. An anxious Damien stood in the doorway.

"Is Angelique all right?"

"She's been better." Kristen stepped aside to let him enter.

His mouth tightened with self-derision. "That's my fault, but it won't happen again."

"I hope you mean that."

"I do," he told her.

"Good. Don't make me sorry I talked her into seeing you."

"I won't. Thanks."

Kristen noted the way his gaze kept searching behind her, the lines of worry etched in his face. "She's in the kitchen. I was about to make her some cocoa."

"I can do it," he said.

Kristen's eyebrow lifted. "Is that your way of telling me to go home?"

He stared directly at her. "I'd like to talk to her alone, if you don't mind."

"It's not instant."

"How hard can it be?" he said, edging toward the kitchen.

"I think I'll let you find out." She opened the front door wider. "Damien, if you make a misstep this time, nothing will help you."

"I won't," he told her with complete confidence.

"Good night."

"Good night." As soon as the door closed, Damien headed for the kitchen, not sure what to expect. Seeing the mixture of anger and hurt on Angelique's face, her arms folded defensively, tore at him. "I'm sorry. I didn't mean to insult you."

Misery stared back at him. "I won't explain myself or take accusations from anyone who tries to make me feel less than I am."

Horror crossed his face. "I wouldn't do that."

Her arms fell to her sides. "That's exactly what you did. How do you think I felt, knowing you think I'd sell my body?"

Damien blanched.

"This isn't going to work out. I think you need to leave."

"Angel—"

"No more," she interrupted, then started to brush by him. He caught her arm.

"Please listen to me."

"Turn my arm loose," she said tightly.

Damien could feel the situation slipping away from him again. "Ah, hell. I was out of line. I apologize."

"Not good enough."

"What do you want from me?"

"My arm and for you to get the hell out of my life."

His fingers uncurled.

Her head aching as much as her heart, Angelique went to the door and opened it. "Don't come back."

He followed her out of the kitchen, then stopped ten feet away from the front door. He looked everywhere, then stared directly at her and took a deep breath. "I was jealous."

Angelique's gaze jerked toward him.

Damien shifted from one handmade Italian loafer to the other. "It won't happen again."

He was telling the truth. He was too annoyed at himself not to be. Suspicion crept into her mind as she remembered their last conversation. She closed the door. "You don't like Maurice either, do you?"

His eyebrow shot up. "Kristen said she was about to make you some cocoa. I told her I'd do it for you."

"I know why I don't like him, but what's he done to you?" She wasn't going to let him evade the issue. He might know something that could get Kristen's job back and nail Maurice's sorry hide to a wall.

"I'll go make the cocoa." He started toward the kitchen.

"Come back here," Angelique called, then went after him when he kept going. She found him opening the bottom cabinets. "What are you looking for?"

"A kettle or a pot."

She rolled her eyes, then moved him aside to get two mugs from the overhead cabinet. "Nuking is faster and less mess to clean up."

He took the mugs from her. "What's next?"

"Answers would be nice."

"Maurice is the husband of a woman I admire and respect, a woman who is my boss, and therefore they're both sacrosanct." He put the mugs by the cocoa and milk and began opening drawers.

"Did you know your lips pucker when you say his name as if you have a bad taste in your mouth?" she said. She wondered if the reason was because he'd learned of his father's affection for Claudette or if it was an entirely different matter.

He opened another drawer. "I hadn't noticed."

Angelique wrinkled her nose. He certainly could be close-mouthed. Guessing what he was searching for, she handed him a spoon.

"Thanks." He opened the lid. "How much?"

"You ever cook for anyone?" she asked, almost sure of the answer, and just as sure that she wasn't going to get an answer to her question about Maurice.

"I made my mother tea when she was ill," he answered softly. "She liked to sit outside in her garden on clear days, and Dad and I would sit with her and read her poetry."

Angelique's heart ached for him and his loss. "You miss her."

"I'll always miss her. She was great. Five-feet-two and a hundred pounds of pure energy and love." The smile that slowly blossomed was full of good memories. "But she had a temper. You remind me of her."

"Me?"

"She didn't take crap from anyone." He screwed up his face. "Including me."

Angelique grinned. "That's my kind of woman."

He grinned back. "Once Dad was out of town on a business trip and, feeling grown at sixteen, I didn't call and tell her the guys and I were going for a burger after football practice. It was almost eleven when I got home. Two hours later than usual on a school night."

Angelique leaned against the counter, imagining what her "parents" would have done to any of their "children" who didn't obey their rules. "What happened?"

"She met me at the door with my tennis racket and a chair to stand on while she chewed me out about responsibility and worrying her. Since I was close to six feet, she said she needed to even the odds. Every time I tried to explain she plunked me on the head with the netting of the racket. It finally settled in my thick skull that she had been worried sick. When Dad got home the next day, he tore into me again." Damien rubbed his head. "I should be brain-damaged, as many times as I've been hit over the head."

"They did it because they loved you," Angelique said, longing in her voice. "You don't know how blessed and fortunate you are."

"Yes, I do." Damien set the cups aside. He'd give anything to have been there for her. "I'm sorry, Angelique."

She had learned over the years to shrug off her parents' abandonment. Tonight she couldn't. "I don't remember very much because I was so young. The social worker told me I didn't talk for the first couple of months because I thought the reason my father left me was because I made too much noise." She shuddered. "I remembered playing and my mother telling me to be quiet so I wouldn't wake my father. I thought if I kept quiet they'd come for me. They never did."

"Oh, baby," he said, drawing her into his arms.

She squirmed and his hold tightened until she relaxed. His hand stroked her unbound hair, the curve of her back, trying to give comfort and reassurance.

"I don't want your pity. I don't want anyone's pity."

"You're not getting any." He lifted her chin. "Do you realize what you've accomplished despite the curve life threw at you? You've succeeded when others with so many opportunities failed. You refused to let life get you down. You survived."

She stared straight into his eyes. "I only danced. Nothing more."

His steady gaze never wavered. "I wish I could say it didn't matter. I can't because it does matter and it makes me feel petty and selfish, but I'm a possessive bastard. I like being first and I don't share well."

Angelique settled more comfortably against him. "And I've had to share all my life. There's nothing much that I've been able to claim first."

"We'll have to work on changing that." Damien brushed her hair from her face. "Has a man ever made you cocoa?"

The corner of her mouth curved upward. "No, and certainly not one in a tailored sports jacket and silk tie."

"Good, then have a seat." Pulling out the chair, he gently urged her to sit down, then went to the counter. "How many spoons?"

Angelique laced her fingers together and propped her chin on top. "Two and just a little milk at first until you get it mixed, then add the rest."

"Got it." Damien did as instructed, then put it in the microwave and glanced over his broad shoulder.

"Twenty-five seconds."

He punched the time in and watched until the timer went off. Retrieving the stoneware, he went to the small table and placed the blue mug in front of her, then waited expectantly until she sipped.

She smiled at him. "I couldn't have made it better myself," she said, meaning it.

He pulled a chair beside her and sipped his own drink. "This is good stuff."

Angelique eyed him over the rim of her cup. He looked absolutely perfect, so what was he doing in her subleased apartment drinking cocoa instead of thirty-five-year-old Scotch? "But not what you're used to?"

"No, but I'm a man always open to new experiences," he told her, watching her as he drank.

Her heart thumped and she looked away. "I'm still not sure we shouldn't call it quits tonight."

"I am." His hand closed over hers on the table. "I have a handle on it now."

"My past or on being jealous?" she asked, still unable to believe it. "You could have your pick of women. You're rich, successful, and relatively good-looking."

He rubbed his chin. "Only relatively good-looking?"

She wrinkled her nose and took the top off the snowman cookie jar her foster mother had made in ceramics class for each of her six girls ten years ago. Unzipping a plastic bag inside, she dug out a piece of fudge and handed him one. "Do you ever answer a question the way the rest of us do?"

He studied the nut-stuffed candy before looking at her. His face grew serious. "When I first saw you, I couldn't believe you were quite real. You were so beautiful. There was something about you that pulled at me. Still does. You're courageous, intelligent, loving. Those qualities far outweigh anything I've done. So Angelique Fleming, what are you doing sitting here with me?"

She couldn't speak. She didn't want to admit how much his words meant to her. "I-I don't know."

He took her unsteady hand and kissed the inside of her wrist, feeling her pulse leap beneath his lips. "Then why don't we find out together?"

She gazed at him and felt herself weakening. Since when had she been afraid to take a chance and tackle the unknown? "Just in case, I think I'll shop for a tennis racket or see if your father has one I can borrow."

He chuckled. "Dad would be only too happy." He gestured toward her cup. "Drink up. I don't want my first effort to go to waste," he said, then bit into the fudge. "This is good. You make this?"

"Mama Howard, my foster mother," she said. "I was stuck for a while on my dissertation last week and called her. I asked for fudge to get me going."

"You're doing all right on it, aren't you? Your advisor is helping, isn't he?"

The concern in Damien's face warmed her heart. "I meet him on Monday and I'm doing fine."

He reached for another piece of fudge. "When do you defend your dissertation?"

"Summer's end."

Damien paused with his hand in the jar. "This summer? Dissertations usually take a year to write."

"I can do it," she said, ready to defend her actions the same way she had to her advisor in the psychology department. "I've known what I wanted to write about since I wrote the thesis for my master's two years ago, which I wrote in two weeks and received an A. I've finished all my course work. I work better under pressure."

Damien closed the lid without taking any candy. "Why the rush?"

"I have an agenda. I'm twenty-seven. By the time I'm thirty I want to have established a thriving practice. I don't have any time to waste."

"If anyone can do it, you can," he said.

She hadn't realized she had been holding her breath waiting for his approval until he gave it. "Thanks."

"Do you think you'll have time for me *and* writing your dissertation?"

Pleased and surprised he'd been sensitive enough to ask, she said, "I think I can fit you into my schedule. I don't want to miss the opportunity to use that tennis racket."

He laughed. "You certainly know how to keep a guy on his toes."

She smiled. "Since I haven't dated much since my undergrad days, it's nice to know I haven't lost my touch."

His laughter died and he simply stared at her, his expression hardened. "Who was he and what did he do?"

Angelique considered not telling him the truth, then recalled her promise to be honest. When she'd finished telling him about the affair with her history professor, she said lightly, "I don't suppose you have a story about some old girlfriend who did you dirty?"

"Sissy Myerson dumped me the day before the prom for another guy. Melody Scarsdale married on me. There were too many to count who wanted my bank account and not me." His hand stroked her cheek. "I'd say we're better off without them."

"Much."

His hand curved around her neck and drew her toward him. Their breaths mingled. Her eyes closed just before his lips touched hers. Each tasted the rich, dark chocolate and the taste that was uniquely theirs, intoxicating and boldly enticing.

Each took their time savoring the other as their tongues mated and learned the alluring taste of the other. The heat built slowly until both were straining to get closer. His hands closed around her waist, drawing her to him. With a little moan, she went. Finally, he lifted his head, his breathing off-kilter.

"If I chew nails and stay away from you for a couple of days, can we spend Saturday afternoon together? We can go swimming in the pool at Dad's house, have a late lunch, then wander around the French Quarter like tourists."

"I'd like that."

"Good. I'll pick you up around one. And so you won't forget me." His mouth closed over hers again, warm and insistent. Reluctantly, he pulled away and stood. "I better say good night while I can."

Once Angelique was sure her legs would support her, she followed him to the door. "Good night, Damien."

"Good night." His hand curved around her neck, threading his fingers through her hair. "You won't be sorry." The kiss was quick and potent. Releasing her, he was gone.

seventeen

Kristen arrived at work with a smile Thursday morning. Angelique had been ecstatic when she'd come over for breakfast that morning. It looked as if she and Damien were going to be able to work out their problems. Kristen couldn't be happier for her friend.

The bell jingled as she opened the front door. Jacques glanced up from dusting a mounted panel painting by Benson, a twentieth-century artist. "Good morning."

Straightening, he returned her smile and greeting. "Thanks for your call last night. Damien called a little after I'd hung up from talking to you."

Kristen put her purse away and crossed to him. "I thought he might, but I didn't know how long it would take him to get out of the doghouse with Angelique. In the meantime, you'd worry."

"You're right. No matter how old, they're still your children."

She nodded. "So my mother and stepfather tell me all the time. You want me to finish that?"

"I can manage. You have enough to do." He moved to a still life by Pippin, a gifted, self-taught artist who'd worked independent of the academy of art.

"I don't mind." She glanced around the gallery. "I love working here. Besides, I'd like to take off early tonight."

"No problem. I can handle it."

"Aren't you going to ask me the reason?"

Jacques carefully ran the soft cloth around the original frame of the nineteen-by-nineteen-inch, oil-on-canvas painting, a still life of a bouquet of flowers. "My best guess would be that you're seeing Rafe."

"Right, and guess who I'm taking with me?"

"I don't—" Jacques stopped finally and looked up, his eyes widening. "He's going to work with the boys?"

Kristen smiled broadly. "Last night we picked up their safety equipment. If you can get permission from their parents, Rafe is expecting them tonight around seven."

"That's wonderful!" Jacques said and went to the phone. "I don't think I'll have any problems getting their parents' consent. I'll give you a check for their equipment."

"Tell them that Rafe said they can't wear loose-fitting clothes in the work area because it's too dangerous, and no playing. The first infraction and they're out. No second chance," she said.

"I agree. Sometimes you get only one chance in life and it's up to you to take advantage of it," he said with meaning as he picked up the phone. "I'll make sure they understand that. But I can take them to Rafe's warehouse tonight."

"I'd like to, if you don't mind," she said, lacing her fingers together.

Jacques stopped dialing and replaced the receiver. "They're my responsibility. They can meet you here, but I don't like the idea of you having to drop all three of them home."

"Please. It's important to me."

He studied her closely. "Don't tell me Rafe is as dense as Damien?"

She sighed. "Damien has at least shown an interest in Angelique. Rafe is still fighting."

"You aren't going to let that stop you, are you?"

"No," she answered without the least hesitation.

"Good. You call me when you leave Rafe's place and I'll meet you at your apartment and take the boys home. That way I won't worry, and he won't worry or think I'm uncaring for letting you be on the streets alone at night."

"He was a bit concerned," she admitted.

"He had a right to be." Jacques picked up the phone. "Despite New Orleans' good-time image, crime happens here. I'm going to do my best to see that the boys don't go that way."

"You will, Jacques."

"I'm going to try. It's about time I won one."

Frowning, Kristen wondered what he meant, then he was talking on the phone to Pierre's mother. The bell rang and she went to answer the door, happy that she was going to see Rafe tonight.

Rafe was nervous. He hadn't been able to concentrate on the ten-drawer walnut chest he was making. Why had he let Kristen talk him into this? He knew nothing about teaching, especially teenage boys. He didn't have the patience. He'd lose his temper and then Kristen would see the type of man he was.

His hand gripped the wood. Then *why*? The answer wasn't comforting. He wanted her approval, wanted her near although he lived in fear that she might see the real person instead of the one she thought he was. He never wanted to see again the shock and fear he'd seen on her face that Sunday afternoon when she'd asked about his father.

Just as he never wanted to see his father, a man who hated his son and never passed up an opportunity to belittle or strike him. Rafe had wasted too much time trying to figure out why, from his earliest memory, he was treated with such abhorrence and his younger sister, Shayla, was always loved and pampered.

In the eleventh grade he'd cut classes because he was too ashamed of his ragged clothes and worn-out tennis shoes. Lilly found him hiding out back and told his grandmother.

He hadn't wanted her to know her son could be so mean. She'd taken Rafe to the store and bought him a new pair of tennis shoes and clothes with part of her social security check. He hated that just as much, hated taking money she'd needed.

He hadn't seen or heard from his father or sister since he'd testified. Lilly had talked him into writing Shayla; his letter had come back unopened. His father hadn't been able to stay in their rural town of Little Elm after he was exposed. An abusive husband and father certainly hadn't been able to remain on the deacon's board. Rafe didn't know where he'd gone and couldn't care less as long as he never had to see him again.

The sting of the wood biting into his hand jerked him back to the present. He stared down at his trembling hand and tried to control the rage swirling through him. He was an outsider, always was and always would be.

He was his father's son. No matter what he did, he couldn't change his genetic make-up or his disposition to cruelty; fighting it would only lead to false hopes and unfulfilled dreams. Statistically, he was a walking time bomb. There wasn't a question if he would blow, only when. His solitary life was as much to protect others as it was for him to find what peace he could.

Now he'd let Kristen change that.

He heard a car motor and placed the wood aside, then flexed his hands and stood. He could do this. He didn't have a choice. He was trapped by the undeniable need to be with and please Kristen . . . and by the bad blood of his father.

Kristen hadn't expected Rafe to meet them with open arms, but she hadn't expected him to look like he was ready to toss them all out on their ear, either. The boys sensed it because their excited chatter abruptly stopped.

"Hello, Rafe. I hope this is a good time," Kristen said. She opened her purse and deliberately handed him the umbrella to hold while she dug around inside, giving him and the boys time to relax. "Here is the check for their equipment. Jacques said if they need anything else, just give me a list and he'll get it."

"I don't want it." He handed her back the umbrella and looked behind her to the three silent, watchful boys.

Kristen tried again. "They're dressed as you said. What would you like to do first? Go over safety or equipment? I bet I remember some of it." She stepped around him and pointed. "That's a lathe. It's used to turn legs like those on Jacques's desk."

He jerked his gaze back to her. "You remembered."

She laughed at his incredulous expression. "Of course I remember. Once something is in my head, it's there forever."

His expression grew even more troubled.

Kristen thought fast. "Have you seen the alligator again?"

"Alligator?" Pierre repeated, excitement in his voice. "There's gators around here?"

"*Was*," Rafe answered. "I saw him once about three weeks ago."

"Did you look today?" Lee asked.

"No, but I guess we could start with the tour out back and you can see for yourself," Rafe said slowly.

All three charged forward.

Rafe held up a hand and they stopped. "If he is there, we come back inside immediately and Kristen stays by the door."

"Rafe—"

He simply looked at her.

"I'll stay by the door."

Rafe glanced at the boys and correctly called each one by their name. "When we get back and we go over the equipment and the safety rules, then I thought we'd look at a couple of projects and agree on one. Maybe something for your mother?"

"I promised my boo a box," Pierre said.

"Since my old lady dumped me, I'm easy." Lee shrugged.

Michael did the same. "I don't have time for chicks, so the same goes."

Kristen frowned. "Guys, the box Rafe made for me took a great deal of skill and time. Perhaps you should try a plaque or something simple."

"I can learn," Lee said, proud and belligerent.

"I'm not saying you couldn't do it, but it would take all summer and into the fall," Rafe told them. "You'll only have so much time to work and there may be days when I might not be able to meet with you."

"How many hours did it take?" Lee asked, apparently still not convinced.

Rafe's gaze flickered to Kristen, then away. "About thirty, I guess."

"Thirty," Kristen squeaked. "You gave it to me four days after I went to work at St. Clair's."

"I don't sleep much, and I wanted you to have it," he explained.

"Oh, Rafe," she said, her eyes soft. "I'll treasure it always."

Feeling himself being pulled into the depths of her eyes, Rafe looked away and caught the boys' interested looks. He strode briskly to his workbench. "Come with me, and don't touch anything until I tell you. I have an idea for a design that I think we could finish in three to five weeks. That's another thing; always give yourself time in case problems come up."

At the end of the long, wooden bench, he placed a large sheet of drafting paper on top. Taking a pencil from a nearby white mug, he quickly sketched the outline of a small box that appeared to be half the depth of a shoebox and twice as wide. He then shaded the inch-wide strips to indicate different types of woods, talking as he worked.

"Until you're sure of where you're going and maybe even before then, sketch out what you want. Seeing it in your mind is good, being able to put it down on paper better, but having the ability to bring it to fruition is what it's all about." He made a few more strokes, then tapped the pencil on the drawing.

The three young men and Kristen crowded around to see what he had created. In their jostling, they pushed Kristen closer to him. This time, even if he'd wanted to, he couldn't move away from her. The young men hemmed him in. He felt an inescapable yearning to lean closer to her.

Instead he shut off his mind and went over how the box was to be made. "You'll have to join or glue scraps or rips to a consistent thickness, then put them in a clamp to set. We'll begin construction with the glued-up panel and from that you'll cut the top and bottom."

Rafe went to a corner in the back of the room where there were scraps of woods, from oak to maple to walnut. He hunkered down and picked up pieces of burled oak two feet long and five inches wide. "I saw a cross section of wood that was made into a one-of-a-kind box. If we can find enough for each of you, you'll have top quality wood and we can design a box for each of you."

The three hunkered down.

"This piece of wood came from a damaged chest that was over a hundred years old. I'd thought about using it for inserts that could up the price on a piece a hundred dollars or more." He picked up another length of wood. "Cherry. Not as old, about fifty years, but still valuable. It would make a beautiful shelf in a powder room."

As he had hoped, the boys' interests were piqued and they began picking up pieces of wood and wanting to know the type of each and what it might be used for. Rafe listened patiently and answered their questions. "You want to go outside to look for the alligator or learn the equipment so we can get started?"

"The equipment," they said almost in unison.

Rafe nodded his approval and pushed to his feet. "Some people never learn that sometimes you have to put aside what's fun for what's important. Let's go over your safety equipment, then the machinery." He looked at Kristen. "Since you're going to be here, you listen, too, and I want you to wear earplugs and goggles when we're working."

"I thought I might sit upstairs and read while you're building things," she said innocently.

Rafe wasn't fooled. "No."

"Rafe—"

"No."

She sighed. "I'll try."

The boys looked in puzzlement from one to the other. "Rafe doesn't want me doing any more decorating in his apartment," she explained.

"The curtains were enough," he said, trying not to think how much he enjoyed not just the curtains, but that she had thought enough of him to take the time and make the effort to find and hang them, even if the encounter had almost given him a heart attack. "Put your hair up. I don't want it getting caught in the machinery or getting in the way."

Kristen shoved the strap of her bag on her shoulder, then took the heavy strands in her slim hands and began deftly plaiting them. "I'll remember next time."

Rafe watched in fascination as she quickly did her hair, almost hating to see the lustrous black strands bound.

Finished, she held the end. "Do you have a rubber band?"

Rafe took one from a set of rolled blueprints and handed it to her.

At that moment her bag began to slide from her shoulder. She grabbed it with one hand and with the other kept a grip on her hair. "Can you please do it for me?"

He didn't want to touch her hair, feel the heavy weight in his hand, but it didn't appear as if he had a choice. It was as silky and as soft as he'd feared. His rough hands lingered over the task and he wished he could let his fingers glide through the strands, take it back down, feel it on his bare skin, breathe in the scent.

He could do none of those things. Ever.

Cursing himself for even thinking such thoughts, he quickly looped the band around the end of her hair and let it drop over her shoulder. The end hung just below her breasts. He swallowed. Hard.

"Thank you." She went to the rips and began searching through the wood.

He stared at her. "What are you doing?"

She glanced over her shoulder at him. "I thought I'd make one, too, since I won't be doing any decorating."

Rafe frowned down at her, but she had already gone back to sifting through the wood. He wasn't sure how he'd handle working with her but, as she began matching beech to walnut to Brazilian rosewood, he didn't think he'd have much choice.

She came gracefully to her feet. "I've made my choice."

"Can we start tonight?" Lee asked.

"Yeah, that would be way cool," Pierre said.

Rafe had to admire their enthusiasm. "I try to buy the hardware first, unless I have a good idea of how the mechanism is going to work."

"I thought we would get started tonight," Lee grumbled.

Rafe looked at the disappointed young man, then at the other two boys. "No one is touching a piece of equipment, not even a hammer, until I'm sure you know what you're doing. In high school it was three weeks before my shop instructor let us start on a project." He hurried on as they grew more sullen. "You'll move faster because, unlike Mr. Thompson, I have three—"

"Four," Kristen interrupted.

"Four students who want to learn," he amended, not glancing at Kristen. "Instead of twenty-three hardheads who are there for what they thought was an easy credit toward graduation."

"I take it they were in for a rude awakening?" Kristen asked.

"Mr. Thompson didn't believe in easy, but he was a darn good teacher. I hope I remember what he taught me." He glanced at the boys. "I'll pick up the hardware tomorrow and have it for you when you come back next week."

"What am I gonna tell my boo, man?" Pierre asked. "She'll think I was just fronting about making her a box. I took her to see one and everythin'. This other dude is in her face, trying to hit on her."

"What if you showed her the design?" Rafe asked. "I could make each of you a copy and put your name on it."

Pierre's dark head bobbed. "Yeah. That might work," he said, considering. "Could I take a piece of the wood?"

"I don't see why not, and when you come back, I'll have the hardware." Maybe by then he'd also have his own emotions under control so he could work closely with Kristen.

"Rafe, you don't have to do that," Kristen said, still holding her wood. "If you'll tell me what we need, we can stop by the hardware store on the way back."

"That would be tight." Lee bobbed his head.

"I want one with a heart on it." Pierre shaped the design with his hands.

"A car or a dagger." Michael grinned, hooking his thumbs upward.

Rafe turned to Kristen, his face set. "You know how I feel about you going there this time of night."

"They'll be with me so I'll be perfectly safe."

There was a chorus of agreement from the boys. "Can the three of you fit in the back seat of her car?" Rafe asked.

Unsure of what was going on, they glanced among themselves, then nodded.

"Good. We'll go over the safety equipment, rules, and the machinery, then we'll all go to the store." As if the matter were settled, Rafe walked toward the workbench, unaware of Kristen's satisfied little smile.

eighteen

Comfortable in chaos, Angelique, in shocking-purple knit booties, sat with her back propped against the sofa in the living room and no less than a dozen textbooks scattered around her. She'd come home directly from work, fixed herself a bowl of leftover gumbo, then hit the books. She'd skated on thin ice before where deadlines were concerned, but thank goodness, had never crashed through. She was determined that come July 26, she was marching down the aisle.

She hadn't been blowing hot air when she told Damien she'd written her thesis in two weeks. Her oldest "sister" managed a hotel in Shreveport, and Angelique had gone there to hibernate and write. A dissertation might be more difficult for others to write, but not for her. The topic was too close to her heart for her to fail.

Perhaps her disastrous affair with her professor in college had been the basis in the beginning for her wanting to expose man's duplicity, but since then it was more to reveal the inequality in the way women were treated, the double standards from employment to health care. She couldn't wait to expose men like Judge Randolph.

Men might be considered the dominant one of their species, but women were more cunning and resourceful. They had to be if they were to survive, but that survival was sometimes not without a very high price tag.

A man could be intimate with a hundred, a thousand, women and receive a pat on the back from his chums, be revered and called macho or a stud. If a woman did the same, at best she'd be called promiscuous, at worst a slut.

The reason for a woman's behavior never entered into it. No one stopped to think that she might have hungry children to feed or self-hatred of herself and men because of being sexually abused as a child, or that perhaps she hadn't been taught to honor her body, or that she was brainwashed by a no-good man, or if she just happened to enjoy sex the same way men did. Only her actions were seen, and each time she was condemned while the man was praised.

Angelique's dissertation wouldn't change the way people thought, but she hoped it would give people a thing or two to think about. She already had a couple of radio interviews lined up. She also planned to submit it to several magazines. No, she wasn't about to fail.

Just as she was dragging a four-inch-thick textbook into her lap, the doorbell rang. Figuring it would be easier to answer and get rid of the caller than to let it keep ringing, she put the book aside and rose to her feet. Going to the door, she pulled her worn, oversized sweatshirt down over her cut-off-clad hips.

Pulling open the door, her heart jolted. "Damien."

He looked absolutely mouth-watering. The man knew how to wear a suit, and she'd just love to rip it off him.

"Good evening, Angelique," he said, his gaze roaming over her face and down the long length of her bare, shapely legs with unmistakable approval. "I was in the neighborhood and had a sudden craving for something sweet."

She smiled in understanding. "Mama Howard's fudge is addictive." Opening the door wider, she stepped back, then closed it after him. "Come on in. I'll get you some to take home."

"I wish that were possible."

Her breath caught at the hot desire in his eyes. "D-Damien."

He pulled her into his arms. His mouth took hers in a hot, erotic kiss that curled her toes and had her straining to get closer. His hand swept under the sweatshirt to her bare skin. He sighed and she groaned when his hand closed over her unbound breast. It swelled. Her nipple peaked.

Reluctantly, he pulled the sweatshirt down, then drew her to him. They both trembled. "Your mother's fudge has nothing on your mouth."

"Nor on yours," she said breathlessly.

He stepped away. "Perhaps I should pick you up Saturday for break-fast."

She smiled up at him playfully. "You don't think you'll get tired of feeding me?"

"Not if we had each other."

"D-Damien," her voice and body shook.

"One it is, then." He brushed a strand of auburn hair behind her ear. "How is the dissertation going tonight?

She started to tell him about the slant of her dissertation, then changed her mind. Damien was one of those men who, while he admired cour-age in anyone, believed a woman should always act like a lady. Often that wasn't possible. "Great. So get out of here and stop distracting me."

"I like distracting you, but I'll go. Good night, *chère*."

The endearment caused her smile to wobble. "Good night, Damien." Angelique closed the door behind him and leaned her back against it.

She picked up speed going down that hill every time she saw Damien. She could only hope and pray there wasn't a cliff waiting for her.

Shopping with three teenage boys was an experience Kristen wasn't sure she'd want to repeat anytime in the near future. She should have known when they came out of the car with their shirttails hanging out and pants bagging. Rafe had taken care of that by telling them they either fixed their clothes or they were going back to the shop. With what she thought was only grumbling to save face, they'd tucked, pulled up, and belted.

Foolishly, she'd thought that was the end of it until she'd seen their skip-slid walk, and the way they turned in a complete circle when a young girl passed. Since the boys were good-looking kids, the girls giggled or gave come-hither looks Kristen wasn't sure she could dupli-cate. That time a hard glare from Rafe had done the trick.

Once they stood in front of the twelve-foot-long shelf of hardware, all playfulness left. Rafe explained again about the construction of the box, the hinges and lock needed. Big and flashy was their first pick, until Rafe pointed out that the screws needed would split the wood and distract from the simple beauty. He made suggestions; they considered, then they made suggestions of their own. No one wanted his outside lock to look like the others.

Kristen marveled at Rafe's patience. He didn't appear to mind all the questions or asking for advice when they usually ignored it. Finally, they all decided on their faceplate and key. All of them were grinning.

"This is going to be phat."

Rafe assumed that was good, and looked at Kristen, who had waited patiently for them to finish. "You decide?"

She held up her choice, an old-fashioned, elongated brass key and faceplate.

"Good choice. It's getting late." He took her by the arm. "Come on, let's go to the check-out."

At the cash register, he reached for Kristen's hardware. She held it away from him. "I'm paying."

Positive there wasn't any use in arguing, he turned to the boys and found they were just as stubborn. "We got it, man."

Rafe understood pride. It was what caused him his greatest agony and what kept him going when he wasn't sure he could make it. Yet, unsure if they had looked at price during their selection, he said, "If you're a little short I'll make up the difference and you can pay me next week."

Once again, they glanced at each other before agreeing. "Aight."

He handed them his discount card. "My grandmother taught me never to pay the full price unless you had to."

"Sounds like my mother," Lee said, taking the plastic card.

They searched every pocket and counted pennies, but they had enough. Clutching their plastic bags triumphantly, they proudly strolled from the store.

"I knew you'd understand them," Kristen said as they walked behind the boys in the parking lot. "I'm glad you came."

Yes, he understood pride; he also understood that Kristen made it too easy to forget his past.

Saturday morning Claudette woke up in bed alone. She sensed it even before she opened her eyes and rolled over to find the space beside her empty. Perhaps Maurice had awakened hungry and gone downstairs for breakfast.

Clinging to the thought like a frightened child to its mother's skirt, she drew on a robe and went in search of him. She gave no thought to the fact that she had never dared leave her room until she was dressed. Her parents had never wanted her to look less than her best.

Her hand on the railing, she hurried down the stairs and into the small dining room where she and Maurice took their meals. Empty. She whirled and went down the hall toward the study. She opened the door. Her gaze searched the high-ceilinged room. He wasn't there. Her heart sank.

Slowly she walked to her father's—no, *Maurice's*—desk. Her hands trembled as she shoved papers aside. She didn't have to round the desk to know that they were the same papers he'd been working on for the past two nights at home.

"Mrs. Laurent."

She whirled, inexplicably feeling guilty.

"I'm sorry. I didn't mean to startle you," the maid said. "Before he left, Mr. Laurent said we were to let you sleep."

She hated to ask, but she had no choice. "How long ago did my husband leave?"

"About an hour ago. He also said to tell you, in case you didn't see it, that he'd left you a note on the secretary in your room."

"I hadn't. Thank you." Clutching her silk robe, Claudette went back up the stairs and straight to the century-old secretary that had belonged to her grandmother. Propped in the middle was one of her note cards, resting against the single wedding picture Maurice had allowed to have taken the day they were married.

She snatched up the note, read it, read it again, then sank into the gilt chair. The heavy vellum crumpled in her hand.

I have a business lead. See you tonight. Love, Maurice

She'd cleared her calendar for them to spend the day together, asked Bridget to prepare a special dinner, had tickets to the theater tonight, had bought a new gown. Paper crinkled as she clutched the note in her hand.

All for nothing. Then she thought of the overwrought picture she must have made in her robe, running through the house, frantically searching for her missing husband.

Foolish. Foolish woman, and the house staff would know exactly how foolish when Maurice didn't show up. She had to get out of here, but where could she go?

It was going to be one of those clear, beautiful days. Kristen could tell that when she woke Saturday morning and looked out her bedroom window. Smiling, she showered and quickly dressed in tan slacks and a short-sleeved white blouse. June in New Orleans was sultry. Seeing that she had forty-five minutes before Rafe was to arrive at nine, she laughed at her own eagerness and went to wait in the living room.

Waiting, she decided to do what should have been done long ago. Before her courage failed, she dialed her mother's number. Both she and Jonathan were early risers.

A breathless voice answered on the fifth ring. "Hello."

Kristen's timing was off again. "I'll call you back."

Laughter filtered through the line. "Good morning, sweetheart, and don't you dare. You're up early," her mother said.

Kristen settled back into the corner of the sofa. "Rafe and I are going antique-hunting."

Bed covers rustled. "It's about time you two got to know each other better."

Kristen debated if she should admit that for her it was more than that, then decided to keep her own counsel. "Yes, it is."

"Anything in particular you're looking for?" her mother asked.

"A sleigh bed for Adam Jr.," she answered. "Lilly asked me to keep an eye out for one."

"He's such a wonderful little boy. I'm trying to talk Lilly and Adam into letting him spend a week with us this summer." She laughed. "They both keep making excuses. Lilly told me she's sure she's going to cry when he goes to kindergarten next year."

"Adam didn't spend that long with Grandfather and Grandmother Wakefield until he was six and you and Dad went to a conference in Belgium," Kristen reminded her.

Her mother laughed. "I was hoping you wouldn't remember your father telling that story. Adam reminded me of the same story when we talked last night."

With one eye on the clock, Kristen asked, "Everything all right?"

"Fabulous. It's wonderful knowing your children are doing so well in life. Adam's practice is thriving and so is Lilly's business. You're making headway with your nineteenth-century paintings. By the way, have you had time to contact Paulette Banks about her painting?"

Here it was. "Not yet. I've been rather busy." Her hand flexed on the phone. "I changed jobs."

There was a brief pause. "Oh."

"Yes," Kristen said, trying not to fidget or think she'd disappointed her mother. "I work at St. Clair's, a well-known art gallery featuring a wide range of African-American art as well as traditional artists on Royal Street in the French Quarters."

"Do you like it?"

"I love it," Kristen answered, becoming more assured. "I'd met the owner before, and when I went in to interview for the job the shop was so busy I put down my purse and started assisting a couple." She related the details of her first sale. "At St. Clair's, I get to talk with the customers and discuss art. At the museum I was usually stuck doing administrative duties. Jacques, my boss, is wonderful to work for. I go to work smiling every day."

"I can tell, and that's what's important. The best part is that you won't have that Dr. Smithe to contend with."

Her mother had come to New Orleans with Jonathan on several occasions and visited the museum while she was at work. Dr. Smithe had been barely civil. "That's one of the great benefits."

"You're a smart woman. I'm glad you found a job you love," her mother said. "Now, when are you coming for a visit?"

The last of the lingering tension eased out of Kristen's shoulders. Her mother trusted her to make the right decision. She always had. Why had it taken her so long to realize that? "Not for another month or so, probably."

"Then we'll have to visit you if you can't manage it soon."

"I'd like that." The doorbell rang. She glanced at the clock. Rafe was almost thirty minutes early. "Rafe's at the door. I'll talk to you next week. Tell Jonathan hi for me."

"You know perfectly well he's sitting here beside me."

"Hi, pumpkin," Jonathan said. "I'm glad you found a job you love."

"Me, too. Love you both, 'bye."

" 'Bye."

Hanging up, she went to answer the door. An uncertain Rafe stood there.

"I'm early," he said by way of greeting.

"You're exactly on time." Taking him by the arm, she pulled him inside and closed the door. "I just got off the phone with Mother, and I told her about leaving the museum. She and Jonathan were happy for me."

"You tell them why?"

Making a face, Kristen picked up her large, black bag from the sofa and slung it over her shoulder. "No, because I didn't want them on the next plane here. Besides, I'm pleased with the way things turned out."

He stared down at her in complete bafflement. "You can't be serious."

"I am." Hooking her arm through his, she took heart that he didn't stiffen. "Claudette will wise up sooner or later and Maurice will get his. In the meantime, I'm working at a job I love, have a fabulous boss, and best of all, I made a wonderful new friend."

"Who?" he asked as they left her apartment.

She smiled up at him. "You."

Rafe didn't want his chest to swell with pride or a smile to grow on his face, but he was powerless to keep either from happening. No matter how he fought letting Kristen matter to him, he hadn't been successful. So the only thing left to do was just keep things in perspective. She was a friend, nothing more.

"I found out the Catfish Shack serves breakfast. You want to eat there?" he asked as they stopped in front of the elevator.

"That's a marvelous idea," she said, stepping into the chrome-and-glass elevator.

• • •

The buxom waitress at the Catfish Shack recognized Rafe and Kristen immediately. Grinning broadly, she showed them to a small table, proclaiming that they were going to turn into regulars as they sat down. She could always tell. Rafe's dark eyes widened at the announcement—then he became intensely interested in the small selection on the slate menu.

The friendly woman winked at Kristen and she winked back. She fully believed she was making progress knocking down Rafe's doors and she planned to continue. "I'm starved. I'll have ham, scrambled eggs, hash browns, French toast, juice, and coffee. How about you?"

His head popped from behind the slate to stare at her in astonishment.

"What?" she asked.

"Nothing." He shifted in his cane-backed chair, then handed the menu to the waiting waitress. "I'll have the same, except I'll have apple juice."

"Gotcha." Collecting the menus, she left.

Bracing her arms on the small table, Kristen linked her fingers together and stared at Rafe. Her lips twitched. "Now that she's gone, you can tell me that you think I'm a pig when it comes to good food."

"It's just that you remind me of a polished teak statue of a woman I saw in an art gallery. You're both so elegant and graceful." He shrugged. "It's hard to imagine you having a big appetite."

His words went straight to her heart. Kristen strove to keep her expression unchanged and her arms from reaching across the small table to hug him. "I didn't until lately. I'm enjoying life more and my appetite reflects that."

"You deserve to be happy." He placed his forearms on the table. "You were always so quiet at your family gatherings."

"Here's your coffee and juice," the waitress said.

"What did I tell you about that?" Kristen asked as soon as the woman moved away, then noted his obvious confusion. "You are a part of this family."

He glanced away. "Not really."

Kristen didn't resist this time: she reached out and placed her hand on top of his. He jumped at the contact. His head came up. Beneath her hand, his quivered, but he didn't pull away.

"Rafe, that's not true. You matter to us and you've proven that we matter to you. If you think otherwise, you do all of us and yourself a disservice." Reluctantly, she pulled her hand away, sat back in her chair, and tried to bring some lightness back into the conversation. "You don't want me to tell Lilly on you, do you?"

He almost smiled. "No, she'd get on me. She's always been in my corner."

"That's the type of person she is." Kristen picked up her coffee cup, a heavy white stoneware mug. "I'm happy she and Adam found each other."

He seemed to take a moment to digest what she had said as he added two sugars and cream to his coffee. "When I came for the wedding and saw how wealthy Adam and you all were, I was worried that he was just grateful for her help while he was blind. Then I saw them together and knew he really cared about her." His large hands curved around the mug. "I saw how the rest of you accepted, even loved Lilly and I knew I didn't have to worry about her anymore. She'd found the place where she belonged and was wanted just for herself."

The longing was back in his voice. Kristen recognized it because she'd heard the same longing in her own voice at one time. "You will, too. I think I already have."

He couldn't mask the surprise on his face or the hope that was quickly banked.

"Here you are." The woman placed two oval-shaped platters wider than Kristen's hand on the table. Both were heaped with food.

Kristen glanced at Rafe. "Just call me Ms. Piggy."

He grinned at her. "I may not know much about women, but I do know that could get me into trouble."

Kristen returned the smile, treasuring it, then bowed her head for him to say grace. He was getting there.

Their first stop at an estate sale yielded little. The reportedly antique furniture was little more than pressed wood. At the second stop thirty minutes later, the furniture wasn't much better. Kristen hadn't expected to find anything their first time out and told Rafe as much as they crossed the lawn, heading to his truck parked on the side of the two-lane blacktop.

"This might take a while. I hope you don't mind."

Taking her arm, he steered her around two small children running to catch up with their parents. "I have time. I'm ahead of schedule on my next three projects."

"I can certainly see why your work is in such demand after today." She climbed into the truck. "Mrs. Oliphant stopped by the gallery the other day and said she'd been by your shop and ordered a tea box and a chest."

He propped his hand on the open door frame. "I gave her a card and she said she already had one. Then she said she thought I should discard my old ones because my new ones on the heavy paper with old English printing were so much better."

"I, er, ah, intended to tell you about that." She really had.

"I guess you forgot." Closing her door, he went around and got inside.

"Are you upset with me?" she asked, a little worried. Things had been going so well between them.

Fastening his seat belt, he started the motor, then glanced at her. "Friends help friends. Isn't that what you told me?"

"Yes, but I wasn't sure you were listening." She grinned at him. It was going to be all right.

"I was." Checking the rearview mirror, he pulled off. "Where to next?"

She checked the map she'd printed off the Internet. "Another estate sale about five miles from here."

"What time do you have to be back?"

"Not until three," she said, looking out the window at the denseness of the woods and the intense greenness. "Jacques gave me extra time since I'm working with the boys."

"Sounds reasonable. I guess I'll have to feed you again before I take you back," he teased.

"I wouldn't be a bit surprised." Of course that meant they'd spend more time together. The day was turning out to be as beautiful as she'd hoped.

nineteen

Damien had everything ready. The wine was chilling, a scrumptious lunch would be waiting after their swim, and the speaker system allowed soft music to drift out to the pool. He'd shown Angelique to the guest bedroom upstairs so she could change, then he'd come back downstairs.

The weather was cooperating. It was one of those clear days when the sky was so blue it almost hurt your eyes. The soft scent of the flowers in the well-tended gardens his mother loved so much drifted out to him. The vibrant hues of purple and red were startling against the lushness of the green leaves.

"I'm ready."

Damien jerked around and his heart actually stopped, then galloped like a racehorse coming down the final stretch at Louisiana Downs. His throat dried and he was glad he'd kept on his robe. His reaction to her was instant and fierce.

She wore a deep tangerine two-piece suit that made her golden-brown skin lustrous. A knotted sarong in a bold tropical print was tied at her waist. The top was modest by most standards, but for a man who'd wanted a woman as much as he wanted Angelique, it was pure torture.

The smile on her face died. "Please don't look at me like that."

"Can you change how you look?" he asked, coming to her.

"Of course not."

His arms slid around her small waist, he nibbled on her ear. "Then I guess I can't change how I look at you."

Feeling herself slipping under his spell, Angelique pushed away. "You promised we'd go swimming."

He untied his robe and tossed it on a chaise longue. "So I did."

Now it was Angelique's turn to stare. He was magnificent, with rope-hard muscles and a wide chest tapering to a trim waist and long, powerful legs. She caught herself and snapped her mouth closed. He was grinning at her. She blushed, but returned his grin.

"Come on, I'll race you to the other end and back." Giving her just enough time to untie her wrap, he took her hand and ran with her toward the clear, blue waters of the pool.

A few steps before they reached the tiled edge, he released her hand. He dove into the water mere seconds before her. Damien blinked in astonishment to see Angelique beside him when he broke free of the water. She quickly pulled ahead of him. He went after her.

He didn't catch her until they reached the other end of the rectangular pool. He pushed away and pulled ahead on the way back. Twenty feet from the end of the pool and victory, he glanced behind and didn't see her. His blood chilled. He paused, treading water: he was about to dive beneath the surface when he heard a giggle and turned to see Angelique near the end. He raced after her, knowing he wouldn't win.

She waited for him at the end, one hand on the lapis blue tile surrounding the pool, the other rippling through the water as she floated. "You lose."

"You cheated." He placed his hand beside hers.

"I did not."

"I was worried about you," he said, trying to get his heart to stop drumming in his chest. "I thought you were in trouble and had gone under."

Her satisfied smile faded into one of regret. "Oh, Damien, I didn't think about that. There was a YMCA down the street from our house in Baton Rouge and usually one or the other of us worked there so we always had access to the pool whenever we wanted."

"So you can swim like an eel and you cheat," he stated bluntly.

She wished she could tell from his bland expression if he were angry. "Some of my brothers and the other guys were stronger swimmers so we girls had to even the odds some way."

"Winning is the bottom line then?" he asked, continuing to watch her closely.

Angelique grew more nervous by the second. No one had to tell her that Damien was the straight-and-narrow type. "It was a joke."

"Damaging a man's pride is no joke," he said. "I'm trying my best to impress you and you beat me. How is that supposed to win me points?"

Seeing the teasing glint in his dark eyes and hearing the laughter just beneath the surface of his words, Angelique relaxed and swam away, doing backstrokes. "You'll think of something."

"Count on it." Damien sank below the surface and emerged directly behind her. He stretched out his body so that her back was against his chest, her legs resting lightly on his. The water gave their bodies an erotic buoyance as they brushed teasingly against each other as Damien propelled them across the pool.

He turned her into his arms. "Wrap your legs around me."

She did as he asked without hesitation. She felt the rigid hardness of his manhood pressed against the junction of her thighs, felt her own body quicken in response. Then his mouth, hot and avid, was on hers. The kiss boldly stated his desire and mirrored her own. She clung to him.

Damien lifted his head, his eyes fierce with passion. There was no need to say a word. Each knew the outcome when his mouth slammed down on hers. She moaned deep in her throat.

Reaching the edge, he untied her swim top in the back and shoved the material over her shoulders. Damien sucked in a ragged breath. Her breasts were glorious. Lush and golden, they'd tempt a saint and he had never been known to be one. Wanting to take a pouting nipple in his mouth, but not sure if he'd want to stop even in the next century, he turned and vaulted out of the pool. If he didn't get inside her soon he'd explode.

In a matter of seconds he had pulled Angelique out as well and into his arms. He hurried toward the terrace. She wrapped her arms around his neck and kissed the curve of his jaw beneath his ear. He groaned and increased his pace as she nibbled on him, driving him crazy.

He was practically running when he passed the living room. Vaguely he heard the phone ring. Two desperate steps away from the stairs, a hundred steps—shorter, if he ran—from his old bedroom, he heard his father's frantic voice.

"Damien. Damien, are you there? This is my third call. I need you."

He almost stumbled as he jerked around in mid-stride. His always calm, unflappable father sounded frantic. Fear punched Damien in the gut. Quickly placing Angelique on her feet, he grabbed the extension on the hall table by the stairs.

"Dad, I'm here. What's the matter? Dad, what is it?"

"Thank goodness. The woman I hired got sick and had to go home. The gallery is swamped. I hate to ask, but could you come down? Kristen isn't due back until three."

Damien took several deep breaths, then several more, trying to control the desire that still raced through him. He looked at Angelique, who was retying her top, and accepted his fate. "I'll be down as soon as I can shower and change."

"Thank you—please apologize to Angelique for me."

"I will." He hung up. "Dad needs me to work at the gallery," he told Angelique. "The woman he hired got sick. I have to go. I'm sorry."

"You have nothing to be sorry for. If Jacques needs you, then you have to go. You go on. I'll change and call a cab."

Her wet bikini clung to all the places he'd like to. He could still recall the exotic taste of her, her incredible heat and responsiveness. His body hardened. She wasn't getting away from him. "You're going with me."

Her eyes widened. "I don't know anything about art."

"Dad and I will handle the serious customers while you keep the others charmed." Catching her hand, he went up the stairs to take a very cold show . . . unfortunately, alone.

Claudette spent the morning and early afternoon shopping for clothes she didn't want, considering furniture she didn't need, and it was still only a little after two. Strolling down Royal Street, stopping occasionally to peer into one of the shops, she wondered how she would fill the rest of the hours.

Thank goodness the day was clear and the streets crowded with tourists. Locals didn't venture out to the French Quarter on a Saturday unless they had to because of the congestion. Therefore, she was reasonably sure she wouldn't see anyone she knew. But just in case, she wore her shades and a light blue scarf, the same color as her pants suit, draped over her hair and looped around her throat. She wasn't as concerned with fashion as she was with obscuring her identity.

She'd give it another hour or so and then she'd go to a movie or something. It would be better than aimlessly wandering the streets.

Crossing the street with a group of laughing pedestrians, she didn't pay much attention to where she was going until she saw Jacques Broussard's sign for his art gallery two doors down. She stopped, almost causing the couple behind her to bump into her. Mumbling her apology, she stepped closer to the glass front of Sutton Antiques and pretended to be interested in the collection of Lladro porcelain displayed in the window.

She didn't want Jacques to see her. Something about the intense way he looked at her, the tender way he held her hand the other night at her home made her wonder if he suspected, as others of her friends did, that her marriage was in trouble. Her lips pressed into a tight seam. He probably did.

He'd had a beautiful marriage. He and Jeanne had the kind of marriage that Claudette had wanted, the kind she thought she had.

Claudette snuck a peek in the direction of St. Clair's just as the door to the gallery opened. Out came a woman and behind her was a man carrying a painting. All Claudette could see were his hands and his body from the waist down. He turned and looked directly at her.

Hoping he wouldn't recognize her, Claudette didn't move. She thought she had succeeded until he placed the painting in the back seat of the car parked in front of the shop, then walked directly to her.

"Hello, Claudette."

"Hello, Damien. I didn't know you moonlighted," she said, trying to keep her voice amused rather than guilty.

He smiled, but he watched her closely. There was a pinched look around her mouth that he saw more and more these days. "Dad needed me. The woman he hired became ill and had to leave."

"Kristen isn't here either?" Claudette asked.

At the sharp tone in her voice, he looked at her strangely. "She's off until three. I meant the woman he hired to fill in for her."

"Oh," she said, not sure how to cover up her reaction. "I'd better be going."

"If you can spare a little time, Dad could use your help. I'm kind of rusty."

She tugged nervously at the silk scarf at her throat. "I don't know."

He took the decision out of her hands. "Come on. You can't do any worse than I'm doing."

Inside the shop, people were everywhere, meandering through the gallery, clustered in front of various art pieces. "Take your pick. Just keep them entertained until Dad can get to them. If you'll excuse me, I'll go find him and tell him you're here."

Leaving Claudette, he found his father and a rotund gentleman in front of a still life by Roesen. "Could you please excuse us for a moment?" Damien asked, then drew his father aside when the man nodded. "Claudette is here. I'm trying to get her to stay and help—then perhaps you two can talk later."

Jacques immediately looked around and tried to peer through the milling crowd. "Where?"

"I left her up front."

"Where's Angelique?" Jacques took a step toward the front. He saw Claudette glancing around nervously. Angelique was several feet away. "If she sees Angelique, she'll leave."

Damien's eyes went hard. "Why? What aren't you telling me?"

"I don't have time to explain. Just see that they don't meet."

Damien started toward them, but even as he did, Angelique moved toward Claudette. It was too late.

Angelique had seen Damien come in with Claudette. The reluctance on her face had been obvious. The determination on his face was just as clear. Since her husband wasn't with her, Angelique could only assume that perhaps Damien knew how his father felt about her and he was trying to do a little matchmaking.

Angelique liked Jacques, and she was relatively sure that if Claudette saw her she would remember her. A second later she'd head right back out the door. Not wanting that to happen, Angelique had moved into a circle of people discussing a painting, her attention ricocheting between Damien and Claudette.

Claudette kept fidgeting with the scarf at her throat and biting her lower lip, gestures Angelique would not have expected from the poised woman she'd seen the night of Jacques's party. The reason could be business-related, but according to Damien, her firm was doing fantastically well. That left a lot of other reasons but since she was married to a user like Maurice and Kristen thought Claudette was too sharp to stay blind to his duplicity for long, maybe she had finally begun to see her husband for the loser he was.

Just then, Claudette turned toward the door and Angelique saw Jacques's chance slipping away. She left the crowd without thinking and hurried to catch up with Claudette. "I hope you aren't leaving, Ms. Thibodeaux."

Claudette froze and then turned. Angelique knew the exact second the other woman recognized her. Her lips tightened, her body stiffened. But if Kristen was also right about the other woman being a class act, her breeding would show and, no matter how distasteful, she wouldn't walk off or create a scene.

Keeping her friendly smile in place, Angelique extended her hand. "I'm Angelique Fleming."

The hand that lifted to Angelique's was as cool as the smile.

Angelique was undaunted. She'd played to a hostile audience before. "I have to tell you I was delighted to see you come inside with Damien. Jacques desperately needs someone's help. I've spent most of my time in academic circles, and know nothing about art."

Claudette glanced around, as if looking for someone to rescue her.

"Kristen tells me you're the best. She admires you greatly."

Claudette's attention snapped back to her. In her black eyes, Angelique saw confusion and suspicion.

"Kristen has moved on since leaving the museum and loves her job here. Jacques thinks the world of her. I'm told sales have doubled since she's been here." She glanced around the bustling gallery. "Although she may have to go some to beat his sales today. He's such a wonderful man, don't you think?"

For the first time, Claudette looked at Angelique more closely. "Are you a friend of his?"

Angelique thought it was a good thing it was summer or Claudette's tone would have frozen her on the spot. "I wish I could say yes, but I'm more of an acquaintance through Kristen. We live next door to each other. Today she went antique hunting to find a sleigh bed for her nephew. She's very close to her family."

Claudette's brow arched as if she couldn't tell if Angelique was making a statement or a threat.

"I see you two have met," Damien said, walking up to them and sliding a possessive hand around Angelique's waist.

Claudette noted the gesture. Her cool gaze went to Damien. "I forgot I have an appointment."

"Please don't go," Angelique said before Damien could speak. "You're the perfect solution. Especially since I have some bad news for Jacques."

"What bad news?" Damien demanded, dropping his arm to angle his body toward Angelique and stare down at her.

Claudette didn't say anything, but her alertness sharpened.

Angelique sighed dramatically and hoped Kristen didn't decide to return early. "Kristen called a short while ago. It doesn't look like she'll be able to get back today, after all. I hadn't the heart to tell Jacques yet. Especially since I have an unexpected appointment with my advisor for my dissertation in thirty minutes and I have to leave."

"Damien will be here," Claudette pointed out.

"I'm practically worthless," Damien said, disgust in his voice. "I'm familiar with some of the artists, but not all. I realize you have a busy schedule, Claudette, but Dad really needs you. At least you've been in sales—I never have."

Trying to think of a gracious out, Claudette glanced around the gallery, then fidgeted with her scarf again. "Perhaps we could call someone else."

"In the meantime, what do we do about the customers here now?" Damien asked.

As if to punctuate his statement, a middle-aged woman in a black Chanel suit approached him. "Excuse me, but I noticed you helping a woman earlier," she said. "My mother is getting tired of waiting and frankly, so am I. There was a painting that I was interested in for her birthday."

"Certainly. I apologize for the wait," Damien said. "The salesperson became ill and I've just learned the person scheduled to come in has been delayed, but I'll be happy to assist you in any way I can."

She frowned. "Who are you?"

He bowed his head. "Damien Broussard, the owner's son."

The woman's frown didn't clear. "Mama wants to know about Ellis Ruley's painting. She said it looks like it was painted on discarded containers. Is she right?"

Damien looked at Claudette. The woman looked at her as well.

Claudette moistened her lips. Swallowed. Damien continued to look at her expectantly.

"I don't know about that particular painting," Claudette slowly answered, her breeding kicking in. "I'd have to look at it, but he did use cast-off materials in his work. He's noted for his peaceful and pastoral scenes. People who enjoy nature are drawn to his work."

The woman's eyes lit up. "Mama loves her garden. She'd spend all her time in it if she could."

With an elegant movement of her hand, Claudette swept the scarf from her head. "Then she is looking at the right artist, although another unschooled artist of his period was Minnie Evans. Her work abounds with images of flowers, although I'm not sure Jacques has any of her work." As the woman's frown returned, Claudette added, "I'm a friend helping."

"And doing a beautiful job. Thank you," Damien said, then explained further to the prospective client. "This is Mrs. Thibodeaux Laurent. She's on every major art board in the city and three or four around the state."

The woman's eyes rounded. "Me and Mama certainly picked the right gallery to buy her painting."

"*Merci,*" Claudette said with a graceful nod. "If you'll lead me to your mother, I'll be happy to assist."

The two women walked away, chatting. As soon as they did, Angelique started toward Kristen's desk to get her purse, but Damien stopped her. "Not so fast. What's this about an appointment?"

"Shouldn't you be working?"

"Answer my question so I can," he told her, still unsure exactly what was going on, but certain he wasn't going to like it. "I went along with your story because Dad needs Claudette's help. You were to meet with your advisor Monday."

She glared at him. "Stubbornness is not an endearing trait."

"Angelique, people are waiting." His response was immediate and expected.

"Let's just say that if I stayed Claudette wouldn't and, as we both just found out, she's more helpful than I am so I'm the one who should leave," she said. "And before you start asking more questions, that's all I'm going to say on the subject."

He'd press her for the truth if he thought it would do any good, but somehow he knew it wouldn't. He didn't think he'd get any answers from his father, either. "We're going to have a talk when I see you again."

Her eyebrows lifted regally. "Are we?"

His hands fell away from her arms. "Count on it."

"Then I guess I'd better go home and work on my dissertation." She went around the desk and took her purse from the seat of the chair.

"If it's all right, I'll have Sarah bring over what was to be our lunch to your place." He planned for them to take up where they had left off. The pulse in her throat fluttered and he wished he could kiss her there.

Her nostrils flared delicately. She licked her lips, swallowed. "That's too much trouble. I'll fix something."

"All right." With what he thought was admirable control, he walked her to the door without gritting his teeth. "Kristen didn't call, did she?"

She didn't even hesitate. "No."

"Thanks." He kissed her on the cheek. "I'll see you later."

Rafe had just pulled into the parking lot of a restaurant outside New Orleans' city limits when Kristen's cell phone rang. It didn't take her long to get the gist of the call. In Angelique's opinion, a wealthy, influential woman like Claudette didn't wander around on a Saturday afternoon looking nervous and lost if all were well.

"Do you think she's having problems with Maurice?" Kristen wanted to know, very much aware that Rafe had tensed beside her.

"That's my take on it," Angelique replied. "She'd probably deny it with her last breath, though."

"I still don't understand why you wanted her to work in my place."

"Can Rafe hear me?"

Kristen threw a quick glance at Rafe. He watched her intently, but she doubted if he could hear what Angelique said. "No."

"I was trying to help Jacques. He's in love with Claudette."

"What?" Kristen exclaimed. "You've got to be kidding."

"What is it?" Rafe asked, turning fully toward her and touching her arm.

"It's fine. I must have a bad connection," she told him, then to Angelique, "Please repeat what you just said."

Angelique laughed. "You heard right and if you let on to him that you know, I'll never cook for you again. Have fun the rest of your day off. Since Damien is coming over later, I certainly plan to." She hung up.

"Kristen, what's the matter? Is everyone all right?" Rafe asked, his hand still on her arm.

"Yes." Deactivating the phone, she put it into her purse, then turned toward him, her own plans growing. "It seems I have the rest of the day off. If you don't mind, I'd like to spend it with you. I could go with you on your deliveries and keep you company. Afterwards, we could see a movie if you aren't too tired."

Uneasiness crossed his face. His took his hand from her arm.

"Or maybe not." She got out of the truck and closed the door, her appetite suddenly gone.

He caught up with her as she crossed the parking lot. "The deliveries will take the rest of the day and well into the night. You'd be bored."

"I enjoy being with you and I'd get to see the reaction of your customers when they see your work," she told him, stepping onto the sidewalk, which curved to the back of the steak restaurant. "That has to be a proud moment for both of you."

"It is," he said in amazement. "How did you know that?"

She stopped and turned to face him. "You put your heart and soul into every piece you make. I saw the way you waited for my reaction when you gave me the writing box. Your work is as much a part of you as your arms and legs."

He shoved his hands into his pockets and looked away.

She wanted to touch him, hold him, but he had to make the next move. She started to turn away.

"What kind of movie?"

Kristen's voice was breathless when she answered. "We'll get a newspaper and decide."

"I haven't been to a movie in years." His hand closed gently around her upper forearm and they continued toward the front door. "I might go to sleep on you."

He was trying.

She smiled softly. "Just so you don't snore."

twenty

❧

"I don't know how you got Claudette to stay, but I'm thankful to both of you," Jacques said two hours after Claudette's arrival, when things were beginning to settle down. There were only about ten people in the gallery. Most were browsing.

Claudette was in a deep discussion with two elderly women on the work of a native of Orleans, Archibald J. Motley Jr., whose controversial 1927 painting of *Stomp* depicted the joy of African-Americans dancing at a cabaret. Many African-Americans at the time thought the painting was too stereotypical, that it would lessen their chances of entering mainstream white society. "You were both invaluable."

"Don't thank me," Damien said, leaning casually against the desk. "It was Angelique who kept her from leaving—then the woman asking for help on a painting by Ruley cinched it."

Jacques looked up from finishing writing an order. "Why didn't you answer? You have a couple of his pieces. As I remember, you liked the fact that he was a non-conformist."

Damien straightened and flicked nonexistent lint from his wheat-colored sports jacket. "I thought Claudette could do a better job. Since the woman bought the painting, I guess I was right."

"Times like this, you make me extra proud," Jacques said, coming to his feet. "Now get out of here, and thank Angelique for me."

"You don't have to tell me twice. I asked Sarah to put the wine and food in the refrigerator. Angelique is cooking for us, so help yourself." Damien started for the door, then turned back, a pained expression on his face. "Dad, are you sure you're going to be all right?"

"Don't worry. I won't interrupt you at a crucial moment again."

"Dad!" Damien flushed and quickly glanced around.

"Go!"

This time Damien didn't stop.

Jacques adjusted his conservative blue silk tie, brushed his hand over his navy, one-button suit jacket, and started toward Claudette, his concern for her increasing with each step. Free time was a commodity that was probably unheard of for Claudette. Besides running a thriving business, she was on enough boards and committees for three women, yet she had spent the past two hours helping in his gallery. Although he was extremely grateful, he couldn't help being anxious about the implication.

One thing he knew for certain—Claudette needed a friend and he planned on showing her that he'd be there for her no matter what. "Good afternoon, ladies. Mind if I join you?"

One of the older women pinned him with a shrewd look. "Only if you agree with us that Motley's paintings showed black culture as it was." She jabbed a white-gloved finger in Claudette's direction. "Like this intelligent young woman said, sometimes it's uncomfortable to be confronted with the truth, but the truth is the truth and denial won't change it."

Jacques's attention immediately switched to Claudette. He wondered if she could use the same clear-headed judgment when it came to Maurice. He couldn't discern anything from her slightly amused expression. Only time would tell.

The only reason Damien didn't speed was because he didn't want to end up in a hospital bed instead of Angelique's. He'd wanted a woman before, but never this badly.

He careened into a visitor's parking space, hopped out of his car, and sprinted toward the glass doors of her apartment building. The doorman held the door open for him. Damien made a mental note to tip him on the way out. He wasn't stopping to do it now.

He punched the elevator button and breathed a sigh of relief when it opened immediately. Inside the chrome-and-glass enclosure, he paced. As soon as the doors opened on the second floor, he was out like a shot.

His long-legged strides quickly carried him down the hall to Angelique's door. He rang the doorbell. When she didn't answer immediately, he knocked. Seconds ticked by and no answer.

Damien stared at the door in disbelief. She couldn't do this to him. Closing his eyes, he braced his hands against the door. Why wasn't she home, waiting for him? She knew he was coming. The thought had no sooner formed in his mind, then another took its place.

A chill whipped though him. What if she wasn't all right? He was reaching inside his pocket for his cell phone when the door opened.

"Damien. Sorry, I was on the phone with—"

That was as far as she got. He hauled her into his arms, crushing her to him. His mouth took hers in a kiss filled with desire and long-suppressed hunger.

After a long time, he lifted his head, his breathing ragged, his hands braced on her slim hips. "You are going to turn me into an old man, worrying about you."

She tightened her arms around his neck and brushed her lips across his chin. She smiled seductively up at him. "Not too old, I hope."

His eyes blazed. With her still in his arms, he took the couple of steps to bring them inside her apartment, and then slammed the door behind him. "I haven't been able to get you out of my mind."

"Same here. I wrote exactly two pages."

His mouth took hers again in a soul-searing kiss. Then he feasted on her enticing lips, the sweet curve of her cheek, and the delicate rim of her ear. Each kiss fueled the hunger that grew steadily within him.

His head lifted. His breathing was ragged. "I think we have a problem."

Her mouth was doing its own feasting. "Not from where I'm standing." Her tongue grazed across his lower lip, causing him to shudder.

"I don't think I'm going to be able to wait much longer."

She lifted her head. "In a bit of a hurry, are you?"

"Yes." He was barely able to speak. She took his breath away and made him rock hard. Her sensuality and beauty called to him as no woman's ever had.

"Then it's a good thing I am, too." She jerked his shirt out of his pants.

"Thank goodness," he groaned before he took her mouth again. His hands tried to blindly unbutton and unzip without taking his mouth from hers, and at the same time guide them to the bedroom—or at least what he hoped was the right direction.

They bumped into the sofa, a chair. Angelique giggled until Damien nipped her on the neck. She moaned and worked faster to get his shirt off. The best she could do with his tie was slide the knot down. She wasn't letting go of him until it was absolutely necessary. Kissing him was like taking a bite of chocolate. One taste was never enough; you had to taste it again and again.

Somehow they worked their way down the hall. Damien wanted to weep when the first room turned out to be her office. It looked as if a hurricane had swept through it. He came up for breath. "Please tell me it's not much farther."

Off came his tie. "I'll make it worth the wait."

Damien snatched her up in his arms and practically ran to the last room down the hallway, where he came to an abrupt halt. The room had been set for love and seduction. The ecru comforter on the king-sized bed was turned back invitingly; the mini-blinds beneath the tailored blue casement were closed so that only splinters of light reached inside. Candles glowed around the room. The intoxicating scent of hyacinth filled his nostrils.

"Do we still have a problem?" She unbuckled his belt.

"Not at all." He continued to the bed and sat down, pulling her down beside him. He took her face in his hands and tenderly kissed her lips. "In case I get carried away later."

She opened her mouth to speak, but his mouth on hers silenced her in a kiss that made her body hum. Her tongue sought his greedily, tangling with his, dancing with his, dueling with his.

He eased her back on the bed and she went, her eyes closing as his hands splayed on her bare abdomen as he lowered her panties. Anticipation and heat swept through her. She arched against him, moaning his name as he found her damp and hot. She wanted to tell him to slow down and let her savor each new emotion he wrung from her.

Then she was beneath him. Their eyes met as he prepared himself. Her breath caught at the naked desire in his eyes. Moments later she felt herself being filled by his hard length, aroused by the incredible heat of him. Pleasure swept though her as he stroked her, rocked inside her again and again. The pace he set was relentless and thrilling. Her long legs locked around his waist, drawing him closer, deeper still.

The edges of reality blurred. Angelique clung to Damien as desperately and as passionately as he clung to her. They shattered together.

Claudette told herself that she would leave St. Clair's as soon as Jacques returned from carrying a purchase to a customer's car. It was almost five. She should have left hours ago. Yet, she'd stayed.

Staying busy had helped keep her mind off her problems, plus she'd had the twin joys of helping Jacques and talking about art. But now that she was alone in the gallery, her worries crept back. Try as she might, like wisps of fog, there was nothing she could do to push them away again.

In the past, art and music had always soothed and calmed her. Since she was a child they had been her companions, her solace. Her parents had loved her, but they hadn't been demonstrative. Casual touches and praise weren't in them, but they never missed an event she participated in. Each school year they obtained a schedule and planned their business and social obligations around it. They'd expected her to be self-reliant and self-possessed. Decorum was always maintained, no matter what.

She had been so afraid of disappointing them that she never dared risk voicing any of her insecurities about living up to their expectations. Perhaps that was why James appealed to her. She didn't have to pretend with a rebel like him. She could relax and not always be on guard against saying the wrong word, doing the wrong thing.

Claudette wrapped her arms around herself and admitted there was another reason for her attraction to James. He made her body tingle with desire. She'd grown up starving for affection and he was a master at knowing just the right place to touch with just the right amount of pressure. The second time she'd snuck out of the house to meet him, she would have gladly given her virginity to him in the back seat of his car. It was James who had stopped.

"We can't. For once in my life I'm going to do the right thing." He'd held her tightly and they had planned for their future. She had been scared but happy as she slipped out of the house a week later, knowing she'd return as Mrs. James Cassell. But there was no future for them—only lies and deceit.

Two days later James had dumped her at her parents' house, saying he wasn't cut out for marriage after all. Despite her tears and begging, he had driven away without a backward glance. She'd never seen him alive again.

Her eyes shut tightly for a moment. She had raced headlong into doing the very thing she had fought against. She had disgraced herself and the Thibodeaux name. Afterwards she had pulled into herself even more, determined to mold herself into the daughter her parents could be proud of. Music and art had influenced her even more. They'd become her passion and her unshakable solace. Until now.

Neither the haunting violin strings of *Madama Butterfly* nor the graceful serenity of a mahogany statue, *Woman Resting*, by one of her favorite artists, Elizabeth Cattlett, helped ease the disquiet that had nipped at her heels since she had awakened alone in bed this morning. She had always identified with Cattlett's strong sense of purpose, her unshakable belief in herself. Until now.

After only four short months, she had to admit her marriage was in trouble. Denial was no longer possible, and with that came more questions. Had the problems developed because of something missing in her, or had she let another man's charm fool her? Turning away, Claudette moved toward the front of the empty gallery. Feeling adrift, her restlessness increased and so did her loneliness.

There was no one to share her troubles with. No one she could show her weakness, her doubts to. To the outside world she was invincible and in total control. And no matter what, she had to make sure that image remained. Her father had entrusted more than a business to her: he had entrusted the Thibodeaux name.

Failure was unthinkable. She just had to figure out her next move.

If she went home, she'd have to deal with the sympathy of her staff and her own unwanted thoughts. She'd swallowed her pride and called her home when Jacques had left to help the customer. Maurice wasn't there, nor had he called. Pretending she expected as much, she'd given them the gallery's phone number. She'd heard the pity in the housekeeper's voice when she said she'd give it to him as soon as he came in.

But how long would that be? *Where was he and what was he doing?*

Uncomfortable with the answers she kept getting, she was thankful when Jacques reentered the gallery. With an effort she plastered a bright smile on her face. "You get everything taken care of?"

"Yes," he said, flipping the "open" sign to "closed."

"Jacques, you don't have to close early," she said. "I'll stay and help." *No one is waited for me at home.*

He smiled warmly at her, crossed, and took her hands in his. "We've worked hard and I'm tired. You must be, too."

"A little," she admitted, but she was more concerned about going home to an empty house and the doubts troubling her.

"I thought so, although you look as lovely as ever," he said with his usual gallantry.

Unexpectedly, Claudette felt her cheeks grow warm. She pulled her hands free. "Thank you."

"Now, where would you like to go for dinner?" he asked, determined that she end the afternoon pleasantly. "And I won't take no for an answer. After taking your entire Saturday afternoon, the least I can do is feed you. If I remember, the last time the art council met at The Palm for a planning session, you ordered redfish with crabmeat jaime."

She couldn't keep the surprise or the pleasure from her face. "The Palm doesn't open until seven."

Jacques nodded and started toward the back of the gallery. "I don't think either of us can wait that long. We can eat at my house, compliments of Damien."

She frowned. "I don't understand."

"Let me set the alarm and I'll explain on the way to my place." He disappeared into the back room.

Claudette bit her lip, then decided dinner with an old friend was better than dealing with her absent husband and her own insecurities. Much better.

• • •

When Jacques and Claudette arrived at his home in the Garden District, he'd shown her to the powder room, then went to the patio to see that everything was ready for their meal. He'd called Sarah, his full-time housekeeper, from the gallery when he was in the back setting the alarm. She'd been with him since Damien was born. He hadn't a doubt she'd follow his instructions implicitly.

His steps had a certain spring to them that had been missing lately as he crossed the flagstone terrace and went down the three stone steps. Thirty feet ahead of him was the cool, beckoning water of the rectangular swimming pool. To his immediate right, beneath a canopy of evergreens with a backdrop of flowering shrubbery and plants in hues of red and burgundy, was a serving cart. Next to it was a table covered with Irish linen. On top was a small bouquet of flowers, bone china place settings, delicate crystal stems, and the sterling his wife brought out for special occasions.

Jacques recognized the label of the wine in the standing ice bucket. Damien had certainly wanted to make the afternoon special. Jacques wondered if his son usually went to this much trouble, or was Angelique that special to him.

"He must really like her."

Jacques turned to see Claudette at the top of the terrace steps. In her face he saw something he'd seen too much of lately. Uncertainty. "I think he does."

Slowly, she came down the steps. "How do you feel about that?"

"I like her." Jacques took Claudette's trim arm and led her to the table.

She looked over her shoulder at Jacques as she sat in the white wrought iron cushioned chair. "How long has he known her?"

"A couple of weeks," Jacques answered, serving them shrimp salad with tropical fruit. After he filled their gold-trimmed flutes with champagne, he took his seat. "They met at the gallery when she came by to see Kristen. They're neighbors and best friends."

Claudette paused as she reached for her apricot-colored cloth napkin, then picked it up. "I see."

Jacques decided a quick change of subject was in order. He said grace, then picked up his fork and speared an opalescent pink shrimp dressed with spicy, sweet-and-tart vinaigrette. "Damien tells me the company is thriving under your leadership. Claude would be proud."

Her dark eyes lost some of the unhappiness. Her stiff shoulders relaxed. "Thank you. Coming from you, that means a lot."

"No one ever doubted your capability, and you've proven they were right," he said truthfully. She needed bolstering more than he needed to raise the possibility in her mind that her husband was a liar and philanderer. "What's next for the company?"

"We're after Hughes, an accounting firm with ten thousand employees across the country," she told him, finally beginning to eat.

"Interesting. Tell me more." Jacques listened as she did just that. He was determined to keep their conservation on safe topics.

As their dinner progressed, he took satisfaction from noticing that she relaxed more and more as the sun slipped below the horizon. If he couldn't offer his love openly, at least he could help her find peace for a short space of time.

When they'd finished their meal, Sarah cleared the table, replaced the bouquet with a hurricane lamp, then served chilled Cointreau. The yard lights and those meandering on a path bordered with begonias and caladiums winked on. "Would you like to go inside or stay out here?"

Claudette sipped her wine contentedly. "Here, if you don't mind." She glanced around the well-tended yard. "You've kept the grounds as beautiful as when Jeanne was alive."

"I try." He nodded toward a five-foot lemon tree with its branches loaded with glistening yellow fruit. "She brought that home in a three-inch pot. Nothing she loved more than her garden."

"Except you and Damien," Claudette said quietly.

Jacques brought his attention back to Claudette. "We loved her, too. She was a wonderful woman."

Claudette absently twirled the stem between her thumb and forefinger. "I used to envy her ability to have a family and a career working with you in the gallery, but everyone always knew her family came first."

"With Claude, the family business came first," Jacques reminded her unnecessarily. "You were raised with totally different family concepts."

"I suppose, but I often find myself wishing family and business could have had a better balance." Claudette stared into the distance. "It has to be wonderful knowing there is someone who will drop everything and rush to your aid, as Damien did today."

Jacques took a chance and placed his hand over Claudette's, then waited until her startled eyes turned to his. "If you ever need me, you only have to ask. I'll be there."

"Take your hand off my wife."

twenty-one

Jacques and Claudette jerked toward the sound of the strident voice and saw Maurice stride angrily down the stone steps toward them. Jacques's housekeeper remained on the terrace. Obviously, she had been escorting him to Claudette and Jacques.

Undaunted, Jacques came to his feet. If Claudette hadn't moved her hand he wouldn't have. They had nothing to be ashamed of. "Maurice," he greeted curtly.

Maurice's hard gaze drilled into Jacques: then he focused the full force of his displeasure on Claudette. "So this is what happens when I'm out of town on business?"

"Claudette and I had just finished dinner and were relaxing," Jacques said, not about to back down or see Claudette maligned, especially by her philanderer of a husband. "Anyone who knows Claudette would never think otherwise. You owe her an apology."

"Apology!" Maurice spluttered, glaring at Jacques. "I know what I saw."

Claudette finally spoke. "You saw a friend offering another friend comfort." Her head lifted regally. "Jacques and I have been friends for years and to question his integrity is unthinkable, as is questioning mine. How dare you come into his home with such an accusation!"

Maurice blinked, obviously taken aback by his wife's defense of Jacques as much as by her annoyance with him. She had always sought to placate him, no matter the situation. His mouth tightened into a thin line of annoyance at being reprimanded in front of a man he intensely disliked.

"Did you come in the car?" Claudette asked, picking up her purse from the table.

"Yes," he said curtly.

She turned to Jacques, her face softening. "Thank you for a wonderful evening." Leaning over, she brushed her cheek against his. "I'll remember. Good night." Not looking at Maurice, she started toward the terrace, stopping only long enough to thank the housekeeper.

Jacques smiled and picked up his wine. Now that was the Claudette he knew, admired, and, yes, loved. "If you don't want to take a taxi home, you'd better run after Claudette." His smile broadening, he took a casual sip of the Cointreau. "I don't think she's going to wait for you."

Maurice said a foul word, then turned and ran. Jacques's laughter was like a prod to his back.

As Maurice came out of the house, it didn't help that Simon, their driver, hopped out of the Rolls to open the door for Claudette, then got back inside and pulled off. The bastard had seen him. Hell, even if he hadn't, Claudette could have said *something*.

Maurice had to lower himself to run after the car and bang on the back fender for Simon to stop. As it was, the car traveled several feet before pulling up to the curb. He wanted to take his time, but didn't dare. With each step his anger at Claudette and the situation that left him dependent on another woman for his livelihood grew.

He jerked the door open and got in. Simon certainly wasn't going to open it. He had been surly and disrespectful when Maurice told him to get the car and drive him to Jacques's house. Maurice had intended to discuss the man's impertinence with Claudette. Now he had bigger fish to fry. He slammed the door shut.

Claudette, her legs crossed demurely at the ankle, was reading *Money* magazine. In deference to the night, she had flipped on the special reading light. She'd told him that her father had taught her never to waste time simply riding in the car. He tried to remember if she had continued the practice while they were dating or married, and couldn't.

Unease slithered though him. After all the drama he'd gone through today, trying to pacify Ann and get her off his back, he didn't need any more woman problems. He certainly didn't want to end up where she was. He shivered and forced his mind to concentrate on Claudette, his way out.

That prick Jacques had the hots for her. Maurice had noticed the way he looked at her. Maurice had privately hooted about it. Jacques probably couldn't get it up with the help of a forklift and a shipload of Viagra.

Maurice had also picked up on what Jacques thought of him. The bastard hated Maurice's guts. Like he'd give a good goddamn. His only concern was Claudette.

He was her husband and he was going to make sure nothing and no one came between them. Ann's ranting had made that imperative. The moment he'd arrived home tonight and found that Claudette had been gone most of the day, and learned where she was, he'd ordered the car brought around. He'd planned to show Jacques how much control he had over his wife. It had blown up in his face. For the first time, Claudette hadn't rushed to reassure him.

He took a few calming breaths, then several more. Although it galled him to apologize, he couldn't see his way around it. Nothing could interfere with him becoming a full partner.

"Claudette, I'm sorry. It's just that when I arrived home tonight and didn't find you, I was extremely disappointed." His voice dropped to a soft croon as she turned another page in the magazine. "I wanted to be with you. Then, to find another man's hand on you . . . You can't blame me for being jealous of my beautiful wife."

She finally turned toward him. Even in the dim light, he could see the bland expression on her face. Something like fear went though him. "Strange. You knew I had cleared my calendar to be with you and yet all I found was a note when I awoke. That doesn't sound as if you wanted to be with me."

He'd had to go to Atlanta and deal with Ann. He wasn't going to end up like her. "I had a chance to clench a deal. I thought you'd understand and be proud."

"Did you?" she asked.

"No. Not yet." He didn't even flinch at the bold lie.

"Whom did you meet?" she asked.

"A company on the East Coast." Another lie rolled easily off his tongue. "They don't want their name mentioned just yet."

Her perfectly arched brow lifted. "Surely that restriction doesn't apply to the owner and CEO of the firm?"

"I'm afraid it does, darling." He tried to put just the right amount of teasing banter in his voice. "But it's a large, well-established firm, and should generate millions for Thibodeaux."

"I assume you put your expenses on your business account?" she asked, once again returning her attention to the magazine.

Maurice frowned, trying to figure out if the question was an idle one. "No. Since it's just speculation, I put it on my personal account."

Claudette glanced back up at him. Her black eyes narrowed.

Maurice remembered a moment too late that he didn't have an account outside of hers. He'd transferred the high balance of his two credit cards to her. She hadn't appeared to mind. She was the primary cardholder of the platinum American Express card in his wallet. One call from her and he couldn't charge a dime.

"Next time, please use the business account," she said. "It will make it easier when it's time to do the taxes."

He sighed inwardly in relief. "No problem." Smiling, he reached for her hand.

At that moment the car came to a stop. She leaned forward to put the magazine back, then picked up her purse and turned expectantly toward the door, leaving Maurice's hand in midair. His empty hand fisted.

Her door opened and she got out, thanking Simon as she did so. The door shut with a soft thud.

His mouth tight, Maurice opened his own door. Simon wasn't going to. The bastard would probably take the car to the garage and leave him sitting there all night.

He was barely on the curved driveway before the Rolls took off toward the garage in the back. Maurice turned to see Claudette enter the house without a backward glance.

So she was mad. She wouldn't be that way for long. He knew exactly how to put a smile on her face.

Sure of his sexual prowess, Maurice leisurely strolled up the walkway toward the mansion and the riches he deserved.

Angelique felt deliciously boneless. The sun had long since gone down. The only light in the room came from the grouping of three pillar candles on the triple dresser in front of the bed. The others had spluttered out. She felt contentment all the way from the top of her head to the soles of her feet. She was sprawled atop the reason: Damien's hard body. Her leg was sandwiched between his muscular thighs, her head on his wide chest.

"You haven't gone to sleep on me, have you?" he asked, his hand gently stroking her hair.

"Ummm," she murmured, too languid to speak.

"You hungry?"

She had just enough energy to angle her head up toward his handsome face and inventive mouth. "Starving. Since you owe me lunch and it's way past dinner, you should be the one to get up and go get the food."

"If I thought my legs would support me, I would." Smiling, he grasped her just below her breasts and pulled her up to eye level. The friction of their bodies caused both of them to moan.

"That's what got us into trouble last time," she reminded him, running her tongue over the seam of his mouth.

"I'm all for that kind of trouble." His hands closed over her hips, pressing her gently against his burgeoning arousal.

"If one of us doesn't show some restraint, all they'll find is skeletons." Angelique whimpered as Damien rocked against her. Her nipples hardened. Unable to resist, she moved the aching peaks against his hair-roughened chest in sweet agony.

"But we'll be grinning from ear to ear."

"You think?"

"Let's find out." He sheathed himself, then brought them together. As before, everything but the two of them locked in passion and need ceased to exist.

· · ·

"We survived." An hour later Damien reached for another chicken strudel wrap.

"Barely," Angelique commented from beside him on the bed. A tray of finger foods was balanced between them. She'd been on target when she had decided to prepare food that didn't need to be heated. Damien had been a thorough and demanding lover, and she'd relished every exquisite second of it.

He made her feel deliciously wicked, as if she could take on the world. Having him in her bed was proof of that. Damien was in a class by himself. Finding a balance between two strong-willed people was going to be a challenge, but it certainly wouldn't be boring having him around.

She chose a cube of Brie and popped it into her mouth. She didn't remember ever being so hungry or enjoying food so much.

He polished off the sandwich and picked up his wineglass. "You about through?"

The husky undertone in his deep voice caused Angelique to glance up. Her breath stalled as she gazed into his dark eyes. Her insides quivered at the sensual promise she saw. "Stay away from me until I've finished eating."

"I'm finding that hard to do." He frowned at her as if he were surprised by the revelation and was none too happy about it. The grooves in his brow deepening, he set the wineglass down.

Her ravenous appetite vanished. Disappointment bloomed. She tried not to let his reaction hurt, but couldn't quite manage. He didn't want an emotional involvement, just sex. So she'd made a mistake. It wouldn't be her first.

Although she didn't want it, she took an inordinate amount of time choosing a green grape from the fat cluster on the tray. "You'll have to. I have to finish my dissertation, remember?"

"So where does that leave us?"

Wishing "us" meant more to him than just his sexual partner, she plucked a plump grape, pleased her hands were steady. "We'll see each other when time permits, of course."

"Which would be?"

Her brow lifted at his brusque tone. "Don't get snippy with me, Damien."

"I just asked for clarification," he said, all languidness gone from his body.

"Clarification!" she snapped, setting the tray aside. "You mean you want the specific time and the hour you can come by and we can have a round or two in bed?" She turned to get up, but instead found herself flat on the bed, Damien's body on top of her, his angry face inches from her.

"What the hell got into you?"

Her eyes shot sparks. "Get off me and get out!"

His eyes narrowed, and then he rolled over and came off the bed. She tried not to look, but couldn't help herself. Her eyes were drawn to his hard body, the delineation of muscles, the tapering of his narrow waist.

He snatched his pants off the floor, then glanced toward her. She was unable to hide her desire for him or the pain his leaving would bring. "Hell!" He tossed the pants aside and climbed back on the bed and gathered her in his arms, easily overcoming her halfhearted attempts to push him away.

"You mind giving me a hint as to what I did or said wrong so I won't make that mistake again?" he asked, then tenderly kissed her forehead.

She shook her head. So she was weak where he was concerned. "I'm just tired."

He stared down at her, trying to see the truth beyond her words. She tucked her head. He wouldn't be worth spit as a lawyer if he didn't see through her evasive tactic. "I don't know where this is going, but if it was just for sex, then neither of us would have to look far to find another partner."

His words stabbed her in the heart. Again. She pushed out of his arms and sat up. "What's stopping you?"

"You are." His hand gently touched her face. "You are," he repeated softly, his dark eyes staring intently into hers. "You drive me crazy thinking about you, you drive me crazy worrying about you, you drive me crazy when I'm inside you, hearing you call my name. *You're* what's stopping me."

A curious warmth curled though her, a need that grew with each passing second. *Precipice straight ahead.*

"Do you think you could squeeze out time for a luncheon or dinner date on Wednesday. Then maybe I could last until Saturday or maybe Sunday brunch." He brushed her tumble of hair away from her face. "I have a lot of paperwork these days. Maybe we could do study dates. How about it?"

Angelique stared up at him. No one had to tell her that Damien could have his pick of women. If all he wanted was a fast tumble, many would be only too happy to oblige. If he wasn't entirely comfortable with the intense sexual attraction between them, he *was* there with her. "If I get enough work done, maybe we could go out to dinner Wednesday."

"It's a deal." He began kissing her ear, her neck, working his way down as he pulled the robe away from her body.

"D-Damien."

"I'm right here." He nuzzled her breast.

She would have giggled at the absurdity of his answer, but he laved, then blew on, her nipple. She almost came off the bed. "W-what are you doing?"

"Fortifying myself for my four-day fast. Any objections?" His mouth closed over her nipple.

She sucked in a sharp breath and clasped his head, holding him closer to her breast. "None at all."

Maurice couldn't understand it. Nothing he said or did worked on Claudette. She remained aloof and so sickeningly polite he wished he could pitch her out their second-floor balcony window.

Gritting his teeth, he got into their bed. Claudette remained at her dressing table, brushing her hair. He snorted. As if that would make a difference at her age. Just wait until he got her into bed. He'd ride her until he had her moaning, like he had on their wedding night. Probably the first orgasm she'd ever had. He'd have her wrapped back around his finger. He had to. The consequences were too horrible to think of.

Finally, Claudette laid the sterling brush aside and turned off the crystal lamps on either side of the vanity. Maurice sent her a welcoming smile, but she was buttoning the sleeve of her silk pajamas and didn't see it.

She won't have those on for long.

By the king-sized, antique bed, she dropped to her knees and bowed her head. His mouth tightened even more. He'd never been a religious person. A man made his own luck, not some all-seeing, all-powerful god. Maurice could only depend on Maurice.

Rising gracefully, she turned off the brass lamp on her side of the bed and slid beneath the down covers. "Good night, Maurice." She turned her back to him.

Undaunted, he began sliding toward her. Claudette wasn't the aggressive type. He'd surreptitiously removed his pajama bottoms after climbing into bed. He was hard and ready. His Jimmy never let him down when it was time to perform.

He touched her on the curve of her shoulder, the back of her neck, the hollow of her throat, finally stopping to close his hand over her breast. She might be old, but her breasts remained firm. "I love you, Claudette."

"I have a headache."

His hand, his entire body went still. She couldn't have surprised him more if she had gone down on him. "W-what?"

Her weary sigh drifted between them in the darkness. "Too much wine." She yawned. "Good night. I'm glad your trip was successful."

He quickly withdrew his hand, wondering if she had felt the slight jerk when she mentioned his trip. "Yes. So am I." He scooted back to his side of the bed, belatedly remembering to say, "I hope you feel better."

"I'm sure I will. Thank you."

There it was again, the polite, cool voice. He wanted to shake her reserve. He didn't have to think long to figure out how. "Jacques wants you for more than just a friend, you know," he told her, then waited for her denial and defense.

None came.

"Didn't you hear me?" he snapped out.

"What?" she said and yawned again. "I must have drifted off. Did you say something?"

She couldn't have fallen asleep that quickly. Could she? "Nothing. Good night." Maybe it was for the best that she hadn't heard. He didn't want to give her any ideas. She was his ticket out of a butt-load of trouble, and no one was getting in his way.

twenty-two

Kristen had known she'd be right. People had glowed with as much pride as Rafe did on seeing the furniture he'd made for them. It was obvious from his pleased expression that he appreciated their praise, but even so, he never wanted to linger and chat. Each time it happened, Kristen's heart ached a little more for him. She'd never met a man who needed love so much and was so afraid of reaching out for it.

Their third and last stop was in Lafayette, two hours west of New Orleans, to deliver a cedar chest to a young couple. By the time Rafe had finished removing the heavy packing quilt from the cedar chest in the nursery, seven-months-pregnant Gloria Sanders and her husband, John, were on their knees on the other side of Rafe. The happy woman kept running her hand over the gleaming wood.

"It's beautiful. Just the way I envisioned it," she choked. "You got every detail just the way I remember. Even the hand-carved tulips my grandmother loved on the front panel."

John hugged his wife to his lanky frame and kissed her dark hair. "If you cry, you'll warp the wood."

Gloria brushed tears away from her dark eyes and glanced up at Kristen. "You must think I'm silly for crying, but the chest my mother gave me before she died was destroyed in a fire last year. I grieved over that chest. It was like losing my mother all over again."

She glanced back at the chest, her eyes misting again. She put one hand on top and the other on her rounded stomach. "I wanted this before I had my first child. It's a girl. My daughter, then her daughter, will fill this with their hopes and dreams, just as I did. The tradition my grandmother started will continue. The loving legacy will continue."

Rafe's hand clenched on the padded blanket. The couple was looking at each other and didn't notice. Kristen did, and her heart went out to him.

John helped his wife to her feet. "Thank you, Rafe. I heard you were the best."

"I want to build the best and I want it to last," Rafe said quietly. He stood and folded the blanket. "I don't guess there's any reason to ask, if you decide to sell it, to contact me first."

Gloria glanced at the chest again, then around the room with the animal-print wallpaper, before facing Rafe. "No. Not in the least."

"We'll be going, then." Rafe tucked the blanket under his arm and reached for Kristen.

"Won't you stay?" Gloria asked, following them to the front of the house. "Some of our friends and relatives are coming over a little later to see it. I'd like them to meet you."

Rafe's eyes went wide. "Eh, thanks, but we have to be going. It's a long drive back."

John pulled a check from the pocket of his shirt and handed it to Rafe. "I understand. Thank you for delivering it so late."

"I knew she wanted it and I wanted her to have it." Rafe exchanged the check for a receipt he'd already prepared. "Good night."

"Wait!" Kristen cried as they started off the porch. She dug in her purse and gave the man a few of Rafe's new business cards. "For your friends and family."

Rafe's mouth twisted wryly. "My PR person," he explained and continued with Kristen down the steps to his truck. Opening the door for her, he helped her inside, then stored the packing blanket and climbed into the driver's seat. "You hungry or thirsty?"

"No. I'm fine." She twisted in the seat toward him, enjoying his strong, handsome profile. "Surprise."

His mouth quirked. He started the motor and backed out onto the street. "Try to get some sleep. I'll wake you when we get to your place."

Kristen started to tell him it was barely ten and that she wasn't sleepy; then she thought of the enticing possibilities. Placing her large bag on the other side of her, next to the door, she scooted closer to Rafe and placed her head on his broad shoulder.

He jumped and stared down at her.

She had expected as much, and patted back a yawn. "Hope you don't mind. I have a fear of going to sleep on the door and falling out."

His gaze snapped from her to the door. He punched the automatic door lock. "N-no."

"Thanks." She rubbed her chin on his shoulder, adjusting her body to his, and closed her eyes, her hands primly in her lap.

The heat from his body seeped into her: she felt the hard outline of his thigh next to hers, smelled his spicy cologne. Awareness hit her and so did the need to touch him, feel his mouth on hers. She clasped her hands together.

Perhaps this wasn't a good idea after all. She was about to move away when she remembered Rafe's tortured face when the young woman mentioned *legacy* and *tradition*. He fought one and didn't think he would ever have the other. If she had any say in the matter, Rafe would know that he had his own legacy and tradition. Maybe, just maybe, she'd be there to share it with him.

Her warm breath bathed his neck, her soft breast pressed against his arm, her hand rested on his thigh. She was torturing him, and he welcomed each sweet, agonizing second. Wanting to steal each precious moment with her, he drove fifteen miles below the posted speed limit.

Kristen could never be his, could never be more than a friend. He knew that in his mind, tried to accept it, but some part of him refused to acknowledge it.

That rebellious part of him longed to take her home with him, to take her in his arms and to his bed. He'd awaken her with tender kisses; she'd smile up at him and welcome him into her arms, into her heart and body.

Rafe's hand flexed on the steering wheel as he exited off the ramp in New Orleans. It was an impossible fantasy, one that could never come true. His course had been set long before he was born. He had bad blood. No matter how he wished it were different, he couldn't change what was.

He'd never see Kristen's eyes light up with love for him, never share a life with her, never see her body grow round with their child. He couldn't change fate.

Gripping the steering wheel, he pulled into a parking space in her apartment and shut his eyes, but was unable to shut off the thought of her eventually loving another man, having his child.

She twisted in the seat more fully toward him. Her slim hand slid perilously close to a part of him that he wanted to bury deep inside her silken heat. He caught her hand before she touched something that would embarrass her and send him over the edge. "Kristen, we're here."

"Ummm," she said, turning her body more into his, her arms going around his neck, her mouth moving closer to the open collar of his shirt. "Rafe."

Hearing her murmur his name sent a shaft of need and longing through him. His eyes shut. Slowly his arms crept up and around her, even as he told himself to stop.

She quieted immediately. Not so his heart. It thundered wildly.

She was so soft, so loving and giving. Why was it his fate to be the son of a cowardly bastard? This time he couldn't help the rage that swept through him or the sudden tightening of his arms because of what had been taken from him, because of what would never be his.

"Rafe?"

He heard the sleep-drugged voice, but also the uncertainty. Immediately he loosened his hold and set her away. "We're here."

"Is everything all right?"

He refused to meet her eyes. "Sure." He got out of the truck and opened her door. "Come on, let's get you upstairs and to bed."

"You're the one who needs to be in bed. I slept." She punched in the code to the lobby door. The doorman went off at midnight and came back on at six.

"I'm used to late nights," Rafe said, his voice gritty. He followed her into the elevator.

"Thank you for taking me with you," she said, smiling up at him.

He nodded, staring straight ahead, glad she lived on the second floor. When the chrome-encased doors slid open, he took her arm and stepped off. Silently he walked beside her to her apartment and then waited while she opened her door.

"Rafe, are you sure everything is all right?" she asked.

The uncertainty in her voice tore at him. He glanced at her, then quickly away. "Sure."

"Do you want to come over tomorrow and watch a movie or something?"

"I'll be busy." He stuck his hands in his pockets and looked anywhere but at her. *Just go inside. Please.*

"I'll bring you lunch, then."

"No!" he said, then cursed under his breath when he saw the hurt on her face. She was tearing him apart, but better that than him ever hurting her. "I meant, I want you to rest. I dragged you all over the place today."

"I enjoyed being with you," she said, a half-smile on her tempting mouth. She looked up at him as if she'd never get enough.

Rafe's fists clenched. "I'd better be going."

Her smile faded. She swallowed. "Good night. I'll see you Monday night."

"Good night."

Kristen finally went inside and closed the door softly behind her.

Rafe spun on his heels and strode down the hall, his thoughts on a man he couldn't forget, couldn't stop hating.

Old man, if I ever see you again, I'm keeping my promise. Only one of us will walk away. And for all the hell you've put me through, it won't be you.

Maurice woke up in bed alone. Instantly uneasy, his head turned on the pillow, knowing as he did that he wouldn't see Claudette. He sat up beneath the mound of luxurious bedding that cost as much as a month of his old salary.

She'd awakened before him lots of times, but always, always, she'd kissed him good-bye before she left to go downstairs or to the office. He knew because, despite her tiptoeing around, he was a light sleeper and woke up. This morning he hadn't.

He got out of bed and checked her bathroom. The elegant bathroom in gold and creamy marble was empty. No steam coated the mirrors.

Freshly used bath towels hung neatly on the rack behind the six-foot garden tub.

His first thought was to go downstairs and find her. Common sense made him go instead to the armoire she'd put in her room for his clothes. He couldn't let her know that her actions last night concerned him.

He chose a new three-thousand-dollar, three-piece charcoal suit with a cream vest. The cufflinks in his French cuffs were 24K. He'd always had an eye for style. He just needed the means.

Thirty-five minutes later, freshly showered and dressed, he descended the stairs, expecting to find Claudette in the dining room or in the study. She was not in either place. He stood in the study with its dark-stained paneled wall and heavy furniture and stared at a picture of Claude Thibodeaux over the hand-carved mahogany mantel of the fireplace done by one of their ancestors. There was no give in the strong, austere features of Thibodeaux. Maurice hated and envied him.

"I'll have it all." Maurice strode to the bellpull by the damask draperies and jerked. Five minutes later, he pulled again. He was about to go find the maid when the door finally opened.

"Yes, sir?"

His irritation inched up a degree. It was Bridget, the cook. She disliked him, though she hid it from Claudette. "Where is Mia?"

"She's busy. Can I help?"

It was just as obvious that the place she wished she could help him to was hell. Had Mia told her about their little encounter in here last week? No, she was too afraid of being fired. "Where is Mrs. Laurent?"

"Out," came the succinct, and if he wasn't mistaken, pleased reply.

"Where?"

She folded her arms across her nonexistent breasts. "The cemetery and then church."

Claudette visited the mausoleum weekly. He thought it was morbid to be buried on top of another person and wasteful to spend hundreds of thousand of dollars on a crypt. He wouldn't have to worry about that for a long, long time. He had a long, wealthy life ahead of him. "I want eggs Benedict and fresh fruit for breakfast. Bring me the paper."

The smile on her homely face was slow and aggravating when it finally arrived. "Ms. Thibodeaux gave the staff the day off. I was just leaving."

Shock snapped his head back. "She's never done that before. You're lying!"

Bridget put her hands on her narrow hips and gave him the once-over. "Now, if that isn't calling the kettle black!"

"What!" he exclaimed, angered by her impertinence.

"My ride is waiting for me." She turned on her spotless orthopedic shoes and closed the door behind her.

Maurice couldn't believe it. He stalked across the room and jerked the door back open. "Come back here!"

She stopped in the wide hallway to face him. "Believe me, you do not want me to come back there."

"You're fired! You hear me? Don't come back!" he yelled, but he was talking to himself. She had already turned a corner and disappeared. Just wait until Claudette arrived. He'd have them all fired. All except Mia. He had plans for her.

Instead of sleeping, Kristen had tossed and turned most of the night. She couldn't get the nagging suspicion out of her mind that something important had happened between her and Rafe when he brought her home. But try as she might, she couldn't remember what it was.

Sitting in the living room Sunday morning, she stared out the window at the bright day, a startling contrast to how she felt. Her gaze drifted to the phone on the end table beside her. During the course of the morning she had picked it up at least five times to call Rafe, and each time she had put the receiver back down.

He didn't want to see her.

The thought wounded her deeply. But more than that was the unforgettable memory of the agony in Rafe's face last night. If she could only remember. Her fingers massaged her temples as if that would help. Perhaps when Angelique came over she could help trigger Kristen's memory.

On Sunday mornings they usually had coffee together, then went to church, and afterwards, brunch. But it was 8:45 and she was already fifteen minutes late. Kristen wasn't about to call and see if she was coming. Damien might have slept over.

Eyes closed, Kristen leaned her head against the cushioned back of the chair. At least one of them was happy.

The sound of the doorbell snapped her eyes open. Standing, she quickly crossed to the door. She didn't relax until she saw the smile on Angelique's face. It quickly faded.

"What happened?" Angelique asked, shutting the door behind her.

Kristen felt tears prick her eyes. "I wish I knew. Everything was going great until I woke up with him refusing to look at me." Her hand speared through her hair as she sat down on the sofa. "Before then, I was having this wonderful dream of being in his arms."

"Woke up where?" Frowning, Angelique sat down beside Kristen. "Back up and tell me everything from the start."

Kristen did as she requested. "I don't know what to do now. I don't want to make him unhappy."

Angelique crossed her long, shapely legs. Her short, white skirt slid up. "Maybe it wasn't a dream."

"What?"

"What if you *were* in Rafe's arms? What if you're the temptation he can't resist?" Angelique asked, tapping her lower lip with her fingertip.

Kristen's heart leaped with hope and excitement. "You think?"

Slowly, Angelique nodded. "The times I've seen him with you, he's pretty protective. If there is something in his background that makes it difficult for him to reach out to another person, it also makes him feel as if he's unworthy of happiness."

Rage went through Kristen. His father. "The bastard!"

"You aren't talking about Rafe, are you?" Angelique guessed correctly.

"No, and I can't discuss it. Thank you." Kristen stood. "We better hurry if we're going to make it to church."

Angelique slowly came to her feet and stuck her small, red leather clutch beneath her arm. "I debated if I should go today."

Kristen grabbed her own turquoise bag that exactly matched her suit and shoes. "Why? You need the time on your dissertation?"

"Damien didn't leave until almost two this morning."

Kristen whooped and linked her arm though her best friend's. "I have a feeling if that kept people away from church, attendance would drop sharply."

"I like him. I really like him. This isn't a whim or just sex." Angelique bit her lower lip.

"I know," Kristen said, seeing the fear in Angelique's face, hearing it in her voice. "Hopefully, someday we'll look back on this and laugh."

"If not, we'll hunt Damien and Rafe down and make them pay for breaking our hearts," Angelique said, her gaze narrowed.

"Exactly."

Laughing, they went out the door.

twenty-three

When the sun sent its rays into Rafe's shop early Sunday morning, he was there working. He hadn't even attempted to go to bed. He'd known it would be pointless. With every breath, he inhaled Kristen's exotic fragrance; when he brushed shavings away, he recalled the softness of her skin; the curve of the cabriole leg reminded him of her graceful body. She invaded his mind, and there didn't seem to be any way to keep her out.

The phone rang and he was unable to stop the leap of his heart, the hope that sprang within him. *Kristen.*

His body paused as if frozen as he counted the rings. Two. Three. Four. He heard the click of the answering machine picking up the call.

"Rafe, this is Shayla."

He turned wildly toward the phone at the first sound of his sister's voice. He hadn't heard it for seven years, hadn't heard her say his name for eight.

The last time he'd seen her was at his father's trial during his divorce from Lilly. He'd testified against the bastard and Shayla had turned against him. She only knew their father's love and gentleness. Not the back of his hand, the sting of his belt, the hurt of his words.

"Daddy's sick. Real sick. Cancer." Her voice broke, then continued. "He wants to see you. You have to come. Please, Rafe. He didn't mean it."

Didn't mean it! He laughed until tears streamed down his cheeks. That man had marked his skin and his soul, and he hadn't meant it.

"He's at M.D. Anderson in Houston." She gave the phone number of the world-renowned cancer center and his room number. "You have to come. He's forgiven you."

"Forgiven me?" Rafe cried incredulously. "For showing the town what a cruel coward he was and not the pious deacon he pretended?"

"Now it's your turn," she continued. "Grandmo—"

"Shut up!" He sent the cabriole leg flying against the wall. His tenuous control had snapped at the casual mention of his grandmother who had prayed and grieved for the son she'd loved to no avail.

At a time when divorce had been unheard of, she'd moved from Chicago back to her hometown of Little Elm with her two small children to get them away from her abusive husband. Her faith had sustained her when her husband died in an automobile accident six months later, and when her oldest child died of rheumatic fever within a year of his father. The son that had survived turned out to be just like his father. She'd always regretted that she hadn't seen through her husband, regretted that she hadn't been able to save her youngest son.

She had been so full of love. She loved her selfish granddaughter although Shayla had been too busy with her husband in Houston to visit her grandmother during the last year of her life. Their grandmother had never said one bad thing about Shayla.

"Grandmother would want you to come. You know she would."

Realizing the answering machine would record as long as she talked, he headed toward the back door. His sister's pleading voice grew fainter and fainter until he stood in the bright morning sun, breathing in the fresh air, not the stench of hate and cruelty that had been his father's legacy to his oldest child and only son.

"If I see him it will be to send him to hell quicker."

His hands clenched and unclenched. He turned one way, then the next, not knowing where he wanted to go or what he wanted to do. All he knew was that his sister's phone call had plunged him into misery and memories.

"You bastard! You fucking bastard! I hate you! You hear? I hate you and hope you die screaming!"

Rafe took off running, unaware that tears were coursing down his cheeks. He fought the thick underbrush as much as he fought the memories that washed over him. He stumbled, righted himself, then batted away branches and bushes that tried to impede his headlong flight until his lungs and legs protested and he could go no farther. He dropped to his knees in the deep shadows of the woods. His shoulders shook from the sobs that racked his body.

The phone call had dropped him into hell and he wasn't sure he could climb out again.

Her phone was ringing when Kristen let herself back into her apartment. Waving good-bye to Angelique, she closed the door and rushed across the room. "Hello," she answered, still in good spirits after church and a crazy, fun time with Angelique at a champagne brunch at Brennan's. They'd eaten in the courtyard and pigged out on Bananas Foster, enjoying themselves thoroughly.

"Kristen, thank God!"

Her smile froze at the frantic sound of Lilly's voice. "What is it?"

"It's Rafe—"

"No!" she protested, her knees turning to water as she sank to the floor. "No!"

"Kristen, he's not hurt," Lilly rushed on. "At least not in the physical sense. Kristen, did you hear me?"

The fear slowly receded. She pulled her legs under her. "I'm sorry."

"I love you for caring," Lilly said, a catch in her voice. "He'll need all of us who love him, if he's to get through this."

"What happened?"

"His sister called him this morning instead of waiting as I asked her until I could fly down and be with Rafe in person to tell him. His father is in the hospital, dying with cancer. They only give him a couple of months at the most. He wants to see Rafe."

"After what he did to Rafe?" Kristen yelled, coming to her feet.

"Abusers can be healed, Kristen."

"You think that makes up for what he did to Rafe, the hell he put him through, continues to put him through?" she raged, stalking across the room with the cordless phone clenched in her hand. "Rafe is by himself because of what his father did to him."

"And the only way Rafe will be free is to forgive him and move on. I know."

Kristen closed her eyes. Lilly had been abused as well. "I'm not sure I'd have it in me to do what you've been able to do."

"It wasn't easy, and I might not have if not for Mother Crawford. She taught me what love and faith were all about. Then I met Adam and I wanted him more than I wanted to hang on to my hatred."

Kristen immediately wondered if Rafe's feelings for her could help him to heal. "Have you talked with him?"

"No, and I'm worried," Lilly admitted. "I've tried to call since Shayla called an hour ago. His answering machine keeps picking up. He doesn't answer his beeper. He never does that. I'd fly down, but Adam Jr. has an ear infection. His fever just broke this morning. I can't leave him and I can't take him on the plane."

Kristen easily heard the distress in her sister-in-law's voice. She loved both of them, her stepson and her son. "I'll go out to his place."

"Thank you. I was hoping you could." There was a long pause. "Kristen, there is something you should know first. He may be upset. If he is, I'm not sure how he'll react. Adam would fly down, but he has two critical surgeries tomorrow that he can't reschedule."

"I'll be fine," she said, her concern for Rafe overshadowing everything else. "I'll call you as soon as I can. Kiss Adam Jr. for me."

"I will. Adam wants to talk to you."

Kristen didn't have to guess what he wanted. He was the proverbial big brother. The cordless in one hand, she went to her bedroom, her other hand freeing the buttons on her suit jacket.

"Kristen, I know you two are becoming friends, but he has a lot to contend with right now."

"I'm aware of that." Switching the phone to the other ear, she pulled off her linen jacket; her skirt followed.

"He's a good man, but he's hurting. I don't want him to hurt you," Adam said flatly.

"You were hurting, too, when you lost your sight." She reached in her closet for a pair of trousers and a sleeveless cotton blouse. "You never took your anger out on Lilly or any of us physically, and neither will Rafe."

"You don't know that," Adam told her, his voice taking on a bit of an edge.

Kristen stuck the phone in the crook of her neck, took off her stockings, then reached for her slacks. "I do. I'm not afraid of Rafe. I'm not the little girl who's afraid of facing the world anymore. Rafe's my friend. He was there for me, and I plan to be there for him."

"What are you talking about? What happened?" A sudden sharpness entered his voice.

"I'll explain later." She shoved her arm into her blouse. "Just know I'm happy and finally finding my way. You and Mother can't be with me all the time. It's way past time I did things on my own. I may make mistakes, but this isn't one of them."

"Sounds as if you grew up on us when we weren't looking," Adam said slowly, the concern in his voice lessening. "Call."

"I will. Thanks for the note of confidence, and tell Lilly not to worry. 'Bye." Disconnecting the phone, she pitched it on the bed and was out the door.

Rafe had no idea how long he stayed in the woods. He staggered to his feet, tried to get his bearings, then started back. It was an effort to put one foot in front of the other. He felt old and useless, and so tired.

He broke from the clearing and saw the last person he wanted to see. She started running toward him, her beautiful face pinched with worry. He backed away.

Wide-eyed, she stopped in front of him. Her hand lifted toward his face. He flinched.

"Let's go inside," she said, her voice shaky.

"Go home."

"I'm staying."

He didn't doubt her. Weaving on his feet, he started back into the woods. He hadn't gone ten feet before he sensed her behind him. He whirled, rage pouring through him. "I told you to leave!"

Her delicate chin jutted. "I can be just as stubborn as you."

Once he might have doubted her, but in the past weeks Kristen had shown him a strength and courage he hadn't known she possessed. She was dressed in a white sleeveless blouse and coral-colored, silky-looking pants that would offer no protection against the thick underbrush. The strapless coral sandals on her narrow feet weren't much better. Even now he felt the stings on his own face and hands, and he was a lot tougher and wore more protective clothes.

Told you you'd hurt anything you touched. Believe me now?

Rafe turned away, bile and rage bubbling up in his throat. "Kristen, just go."

"Friends help friends."

He wished he didn't want her friendship, didn't crave her smile and her carefree laughter. Afraid if she didn't leave soon, he'd weaken and grab her and never let her go, he faced her. "I don't need anyone."

She didn't even blink at his biting tone, the rage emanating from him. She simply took her cell phone from the little bag dangling from her shoulder and punched in a number, all the time her gaze locked with his. "Lilly, he's all right except for a few scratches on his face and hands from a walk in the woods. We're going inside to get them cleaned up and I'll call later." She deactivated the phone and put it away. "Let's go, Rafe."

"I don't need you." His voice sounded hoarse and scratchy.

"That's debatable." She reached for him.

Again he flinched.

Her arm remained extended toward him. "I'm not leaving until your injuries are taken care of."

Why did she have to be so stubborn? Why couldn't she understand that he felt unclean, embarrassed, and oh, so damn lost and alone? Why couldn't she understand she was everything he wanted and everything he couldn't have and it was ripping him apart?

"Would you rather have Lilly worrying about you while Adam Jr. has an ear infection and is running a temperature?"

"Adam Jr. is sick?" Worry replaced the desperation in his eyes.

Compassion shone in her face. "Do you think if you needed Lilly, anything less than Adam or Adam Jr. would keep her from being here?"

He felt as if he'd been sucker-punched in the gut, his darkest shame revealed. "What did she tell you?" he asked, stalking to her. "What did she say?"

Kristen gazed up at him without flinching from the savagery in his face. "She's been trying to reach you for most of the morning. She was worried, and I offered to come and check on you."

His relief was so great, he almost dropped to his knees. She didn't know the disgrace he lived with daily.

"Now, can we go inside and get you cleaned up?" she asked casually, shoving the strap of the handbag up over her shoulder.

"I can do it," he said.

"But I can do it better. Besides, you heard me promise Lilly." Her hand closed slowly around his arm. She felt the flex of tense muscle and tried to slow her racing heart. It had taken every ounce of her control not to cower when he had asked why Lilly had called.

"Have you seen your alligator lately?" She glanced around, then started toward his shop.

"No," the answer was clipped. It didn't invite conversation.

"Good." With her free hand she opened the back door and followed him inside. "I bet you haven't called the zoo about gator repellent, either." She continued as if not expecting an answer. "Adam Jr. will probably love hearing about it."

Rafe grunted.

"Probably ask if you and he could trap it." She thought he'd balk at the spiral staircase. He didn't. "I can picture it now. He'd use that computer he loves to be on to learn all about alligators, then he'd talk you into scouting the area and camping out all night to catch it."

Rafe opened the door to his upstairs apartment. "He's smart."

"Just like his big brother." The muscles of his arm flexed beneath her fingertips.

With ridiculous ease, he twisted free. The harshness was back in his face. Kristen could have cried. Adam Jr.'s father loved him; Rafe's father had abused him. "Come on into the bathroom."

"I can manage," Rafe said, his voice cold, inflexible.

"Let me help," she said, unable to keep the quake out of her voice.

A muscle leaped in his bronzed jaw. "If you're afraid of me, why are you here pushing it?"

Her eyes widened. She punched him square in the chest with her small fist, surprising them both. "I'm not afraid of you! I don't know why you keep bringing up such an idiotic idea."

"You're shaking in your high-priced shoes, that's why!" he boomed back, angry with her and the impossible situation.

She hit him again. "Concern. Not fear. Look at you!" She gestured wildly. "Your beautiful face is all scratched up." She picked up his hands. Hers trembled. "So are your hands, and they have to hurt."

Not as much as the ache in my heart for you, he wanted to say. Tears formed in her eyes and he panicked. "Don't cry."

Kristen freed his hands and brushed angrily across her face. "I wouldn't cry over a hard-headed man like you."

He couldn't help it; he brushed her hair away from her face. She was so beautiful. "Good."

"Well, go ahead and get cleaned up." Swiping impatiently across her face, she turned toward the tiny kitchen. "I could use some iced tea. You got any?"

"In the cabinet to the right of the sink."

She opened the bottom cabinet for a pan and filled it with water. On tiptoes, she retrieved the box of tea from the upper shelf, then turned toward him. He remained unmoving. "Those scratches won't get cleaned by themselves."

He started toward the bathroom, telling himself that he had made the right decision to do this himself, that he didn't want Kristen touching him—and knowing he lied.

When Rafe came out of the bathroom after showering and changing clothes, she was gone. His gaze quickly surveyed the room. It was as empty as it had always been.

He headed where he always did when he was troubled, his shop. His feet pounded on the stairs as he quickly went to the bottom floor. Had he really expected her to hang around a man who couldn't even offer her gentleness?

He was several steps away from the stairs when he heard the mutters.

He spun, his pulse pounding, and saw Kristen surrounded by three open boxes and an assortment of lamp parts.

With a screwdriver in one hand and a piece of paper in the other she glared up at him. "It's about time you showed up."

He didn't even know he was smiling as he went toward her and hunkered down in front of the carnage. "You're supposed to assemble one at a time."

She blew her long, black silky hair out of her eye. "I'm aware of that, but when one wouldn't act right, I got another one, and before I knew it I had this . . . this . . ."

"Mess."

Her eyes narrowed. "Let's see how *you* do." She handed him the screwdriver and three sets of instructions, then picked up her glass of iced tea.

The only spot free of parts in the circle around her was next to her. He didn't hesitate. "Move over."

He stepped over the entrails of three lamps and came down next to her, crossing his legs under him. "Which one first?"

"Doesn't matter." Leaning closer, she peered at the instructions for the crystal-and-brass pineapple lamp.

Rafe smelled the floral fragrance in her hair, felt the brush of her bare arm against him. Desire was there, but so was another curious emotion he'd never experienced before. "That tea looks good."

"Yours is on the kitchen table. You want some of mine?" she asked.

He took it without hesitation and took a long, satisfying swallow, then handed it back to her. It tasted sweet, just as he'd imagined her lips would taste. "Thanks. Now let's see what we can do to untangle your lamps."

In less than thirty minutes, Rafe had the three lamps together. Kristen stared at them in disbelief. She'd deliberately mixed up the parts so they could spend more time together. "I can't believe it."

Rafe shrugged. "They were easy."

Kristen stared at him.

"I'm used to following blueprints," he said quickly. "You want to put them in your car?"

She bent to pick up the boxes they'd come in. "I just wanted to see what they looked like assembled. Can they stay here?"

"Sure." He took the box from her and picked up the other two. "I'll put these out back."

"Thanks." She wanted to stay, but she was already an hour late for work. As it was, she had to go by her place and change into less casual attire. She hadn't been able to leave until she was sure Rafe would be all right. "I'll see you later then."

"Yeah."

She stared at him, wishing she had the nerve to close the distance between them, to kiss each scratch that marked his face. "Good-bye, Rafe."

"Drive carefully." He wrapped his arms around the cardboard when he wanted to wrap them around her.

"I will." She started toward the door, feeling satisfied that he no longer wore that haunted look on his face.

Rafe watched her go, observing the unconscious grace, elegance, and beauty of her slim body. And so much heart, with an endless capacity to love. It occurred to him that there was more than one kind of hell: the hell his father put him through when he was growing up, and the hell of caring for a woman who could never be his. Both could destroy him. He just had to make sure neither did.

Laying the cardboard on the workbench, he went to the answering machine in the corner of the shop, took out the tape, and tossed it in the trash. Some hells he knew how to deal with.

twenty-four

Kristen made it to work two hours late. Opening the gallery door, she didn't know if she'd find the usual calm Jacques or an out-of-sorts boss. He answered that question when he excused himself from the man he'd been speaking with and came to her.

"Is everything all right?" he asked, his concern obvious.

She might have known. "Fine. I'm sorry to have left you shorthanded for two days in a row."

The frown on his rounded face smoothed into a pleased smile. "Yesterday turned out quite nicely and, as for today, it's been slow. If you want to leave, you can."

She stared at her boss. There was definitely something new about him that hadn't been there the last time she'd seen him. It didn't take long to recall what Angelique had said about him and Claudette. "I'm fine. Thanks for asking."

"Good, I'd better get back to Kenneth. He's looking at the Arthello Beck. If it sells, we can close the shop for the rest of the day."

Kristen smiled as he walked away. They were a party of three, trying to find their way in love. Going behind her desk, she put her purse in the drawer. Her gaze was drawn to the writing box Rafe had made for her. Her hand stroked the smooth wood, much as Rafe's must have while he was making it. He created such beauty and was unable to see it in himself.

Someday he would. She wouldn't think otherwise.

Seeing Jacques and the customer move out of sight in the back of the gallery, she decided it was as good a time as any to call Adam. He'd been champing at the bit to talk with her both times she'd called Lilly to get a report on Adam Jr. The only reason why she'd put Adam off was to tell him it was too involved to go into over the cell and she'd call him as soon as she could.

Oddly, as she dialed she found herself more concerned about Adam wanting to interfere in her life than she was by what he'd think of her. Somewhere in the past weeks she'd developed a backbone and thrust aside all the insecurities she had harbored for as long as she could remember. Her family loved her and she was blessed to have them.

"Kristen, what's this about Rafe being there for you?" Adam asked the moment he came on the line.

Keeping her eye on the back of the gallery, she told him everything about the night Maurice tried to seduce her. Adam was livid. Hearing that Rafe had knocked Maurice out cold helped to ease some of his anger.

"Rafe came to help without a moment's hesitation. He was the one who found the ad for St. Clair's. I can no more walk away from him than I could you," she finished quietly.

"You've really grown up on me," he said softly.

Her lips curved into a pleased smile. Her fingers stroked the wood. "It's about time. But, please, do me a favor and don't mention this to Mother."

A chuckle came through the line. "She'd have Maurice for dinner."

"That she would, and as satisfying as it might be to watch, Claudette doesn't deserve the humiliation just because she fell in love with the wrong man," Kristen said, recalling her own infatuation with a man who wanted to use her, not love her.

"You never told me what happened that night you came back early from New York. I figured you saw Eric and it didn't turn out well. You might as well know, although I hurt for you, I wasn't sorry to see you break up with him," Adam said. "Jonathan didn't think much of him."

That said it in a nutshell. Her stepfather and Adam were in perfect sync. They respected and loved each other deeply. Adam had given his blessing to their mother's and Jonathan's relationship from the first. "Jonathan likes Rafe."

"I do, too. Even more after what you just told me. I now realize you would have gone anyway, but thank you for going out there. Lilly won't worry as much now."

Through the plate glass, Kristen watched a couple stop and share a passionate kiss. Love seemed so easy for some and so difficult for others. "You love her."

"She's my soul mate."

Was Rafe hers? Laughing, the couple moved on. Kristen felt a prick of loneliness and caught back a sigh. "Good-bye, Adam. Kiss Adam Jr. for me."

"I will, and you might as well know, the minute Maurice is exposed, I'll be standing in his face." The line went dead.

Kristen replaced the receiver. Jonathan would probably be waiting his turn when Adam finished. Having a protective, loving family had its advantages.

Damien was restless, a noticeable and annoying first for him.

He couldn't concentrate on the contacts in front of him. He'd shuffled the papers, reread them, and still hadn't gotten further than the second page of the thirty-page document in the last half hour. Considering he had to present an evaluation of the contract to Claudette and the executives of Thibodeaux at nine the next morning, he had a problem.

Instead of the words, he saw the alluring face of a woman who intrigued and annoyed him, heard the beckoning sound of her sultry laughter, felt the passionate heat of her body burning into his, felt his body respond. Damien threw the contract down on his neat desk in disgust at himself. No woman, no matter how beautiful, how great in bed, had ever interfered with business. He appreciated women, respected then, but that was the extent of it . . . until now.

Rearing back in his executive chair, he whirled toward the immense plate glass window in his home office that offered a commanding view of the Mississippi River. In the distance he could see the chimney stacks of the steamboat *Natchez* docked and waiting for the first launch of the day. Speedboats and jet-skiers plowed through the pliant waters, relishing what was shaping up to be a great summer day.

As for himself, he didn't mind being inside. He'd learned long ago to forgo pleasures.

Or thought he had.

He glanced back at the contract, but made no move to pick it up. Instead of working, he wanted to see Angelique and not just to take her to bed, although he got hard just thinking about her. He'd told her he'd leave her alone until Wednesday. It was only Sunday and he was weakening already.

He could sit here and worry about his lack of restraint or go see her. The thought had barely registered before he was up and heading for his car keys in his bedroom. The masculine room done in chocolate and ecru was as spacious as the other open areas of the apartment.

Keys in hand, he stuck the contract in his briefcase. He could always do the "I was in the neighborhood" excuse. Only slightly less annoyed with himself for thinking of telling a lie, he left.

Less than fifteen minutes later, Damien rang Angelique's doorbell. He didn't expect it to open almost immediately or to see the annoyance on her face go from surprise to pleasure in a heartbeat. He attributed the erratic thud of his heart to shock that she had answered so quickly.

"Hello," he said, trying for a casual approach. "I was in the neighbor—" He sighed. "That's not true."

Apprehension washed across her face. She caught him by the arm and tugged him inside. "What's the matter? Is it your father?"

Her distress touched him deeply and gave him another out, if he wanted to take it. "Dad's fine. It's his son."

Her puzzlement increased. "Jacques has another son?"

He was making a muddle of this, but how did a man admit to a woman that he hadn't been able to stay away from her for more than eleven pitiful hours? "I'm talking about me."

She looked at him closely. "Damien, I'm going to think you're a prime candidate for me professionally if you don't start making sense."

Since his behavior wasn't making sense to him, he could hardly explain it to her. Searching for a way out, he glanced behind her into the living room. Books, magazines, and papers were scattered around the couch. A laptop sat in the center. "Looks like you've been working on your dissertation."

Her hand started to plow through her hair, discovered the scrunchie, then impatiently tore it free. The thick, luxurious hair tumbled down her back and around her face. "Yes."

For a man who had never been jealous or tried to compare himself with others, he felt a spurt of annoyance that she could work while he couldn't. He moved toward the books and picked up a textbook that was as thick as any he had studied in law school, but certainly not of the same subject matter. *Sex Through the Ages.*

"I'm doing a comparative analysis."

He might have gotten caught on the interesting subject if he hadn't heard the irritation in her voice. "Problems?"

She folded her arms. "Nothing I can't handle."

"What is it? Maybe I can help."

She took the book out of his hands. "I don't think that's possible."

"I may be in law, but I'm used to reading technical papers and doing analysis," he told her, beginning to feel better. "I bet I can help."

Her eyebrow arched over the most beautiful hazel eyes he'd ever seen. "Pretty sure about that, are you?"

"I am," he said with absolute confidence.

She placed the book on the cluttered table before she looked back up at him. "I've worked my butt off to get my doctorate. I have my plans laid out, and now that it's within reach, there's an unexpected problem."

The way she was glaring up at him, he strongly suspected what her problem was. He was definitely feeling better. "I've worked very hard to get to my position as chief counselor at Thibodeaux. I have a contract in my briefcase that I have to give a report on in the morning at nine and it took me thirty minutes to read two pages, and I have absolutely no idea what is on them."

They stared at each other. Angelique spoke first. "Try an hour and zero pages."

Damien picked up her hand and brushed his lips across her knuckles. "Looks like we're going to have that study date after all."

Angelique shivered. Desire shimmered in her eyes. "There'll be no touching until we're finished."

Until caught his attention. He released her. "How many pages do you have to do today?"

Her hand raked through her hair. Damien thought he'd like to do that for her. "Ten, but I'd settle for six. The dissertation can vary from fifty to a hundred pages. I'm at twenty, but I want seventy-five, then tighten to fifty."

"Sounds reasonable." Damien nodded toward a small mahogany accent table with gracefully curved legs by the sliding glass doors leading to the balcony. "Mind if I sit over there?"

"I'll clear it for you." She started toward the table.

"I can do it." He set his briefcase on the corner of the sofa. "I'll get a chair from the kitchen."

She bit her lower lip as he went into the kitchen. "Do you really think this will work?"

"We'll soon find out." Returning with the high-backed chair, he cleared the small, oval table of a healthy rabbit-foot fern, two hardback novels, and a shiny assortment of brass candlesticks.

"There's plenty to snack on. Fruit, nuts, and cookies. Crab salad in the refrigerator, if you want something more substantial," she told him.

"I'll be fine," he told her, then removed the contract from his briefcase and took a seat. As if drawn, he glanced over at Angelique on the floor, her back braced against the front of the sofa, her laptop resting against her up-drawn knees. Dressed in another oversized, faded black sweatshirt and blue jean cut-offs, she flipped though the notes in her hand.

Any other woman he knew would be frantic at the thought of him seeing her at less than her best. Not Angelique. She knew her worth and was proud and comfortable with who she was. You either took her as she was or not at all.

He'd take her anywhere and any way he could get her.

Damien turned sideways by the table and stretched his long legs out in front of him, then crossed them at the ankles. He didn't have enough space to put all his papers out; the straight-backed chair didn't conform to his body like his custom-made leather chair at his apartment, but that didn't seem to matter as he settled back, pen in hand, and began to evaluate the contract.

• • •

Damien had expected to finish first and he had. He'd looked over and Angelique had been busy typing into the word processor, her gaze glued to the notes on the floor beside her. Afraid he'd break her concentration if he went to the kitchen, he settled back in his chair, crossed his hands over his flat stomach, and thought of all the ways he was going to make love to her when she finished.

"Stop that! Go get a glass of iced tea and cool off before you break my concentration," she told him, never pausing in her typing.

Chuckling, he stood and made his way to the kitchen. The bright blue room was as neat as her work area was messy. Feeling not the least bit uncomfortable, he prepared a plate of crab salad, fresh fruit, crackers, and iced tea. He was just about to sit down when Angelique entered, rubbing the back of her neck.

"You need to be at a desk."

"Couldn't spread all my notes around, so I borrowed Kristen's laptop." She picked up one of his crackers and took a generous helping of crab salad.

Damien moved behind her and began massaging her neck and shoulders. Her skin was like warm silk. "You're as tight as a taut rubber band."

"A hot shower usually takes the kinks out," she said, eyes closed, her head lolled back against his chest.

His hands paused. "How many pages do you have to go?"

His deep, mesmerizing tone sent desire spinning though her. "I'm finished."

"In that case, I think I have another remedy to relax you even more." He looked at her in a way that made her hot and needy.

His eyes on her, he pulled off his polo shirt, unbuckled his belt, removed a foil packet from his pocket, then pulled off his slacks. His blatant arousal was clearly evident in his black silk briefs.

Angelique's eyes widened. With unconcealed longing, she stared at his powerfully built body. Hunger spiraled though her.

"I've fantasized about this for the past thirty minutes." He slowly came to her, his eyes gleaming. He pulled the sweatshirt from her. He sucked in his breath at the sight of her naked breasts, but he only grazed the tip of one finger across each nipple.

Her knees shook. "Damien."

He unsnapped her jeans, then bent and pulled them off. Still in front of her, he started from her knees and kissed his way up to the place that ached, then progressed past her navel to tease and suckle her breasts. He took his time building a fire inside her that could be quenched in only one way.

"I-I can't stand it much longer."

"You won't have to." He ripped open the foil package.

Angelique watched his every movement, then gasped as she found herself being lifted, then straddling Damien, who sat in the straight-backed chair. His tongue slid into her mouth as his hard length slid into her. His hands cupped her hips, bringing her closer, allowing him to go deeper into her satin heat.

When completion came, she screamed. Damien was right again. His way was better.

Kristen had been gone an hour. During that time Rafe had done more thinking than he wanted. He had also put off the call to Lilly as long as he could. Sitting behind his desk in his office, he stared at the phone.

Lilly had put herself in harm's way trying to protect him too many times not to love and respect her. She'd tried so hard to make the marriage to his father work, to make him love her. Instead, he'd used her goodness to trap her, then abuse her until she had broken free.

Rafe admired her as much for her courage as her faith and determination to turn her life around and find her own happiness. She had, but she had not forgotten him.

He picked up the phone and dialed. He already knew what she'd want him to do—forgive and move on. Just as he knew he wouldn't be able to do it.

Her wide-brimmed lavender straw hat in her hand, Claudette strolled through the beautiful flower gardens on the grounds of her estate. It had been so long since she had taken the time to enjoy them. She had spent a lot of time playing in them as a child, dreaming within them as a young woman, crying in them as an adult. Regardless of the season, there were always flowers or shrubs in bloom.

In the spring the grounds came alive with yellow tulips, azaleas, and flowering dogwoods for a dazzling array of color. This spring she had been too busy with work and being a new bride to notice. Now, in late June, old-fashioned hydrangeas lined the red brick walkway. The numerous beds were bursting with caladiums, begonias, impatiens, and daylilies.

There were five gardens in all, each connected to the other by a walkway, and each richly embellished with fine art pieces collected from around the world, or a sentimental object like the five-foot bronze statue given to her grandmother by her doting husband when she first began to design the gardens.

Her parents had added three water fountains and a more formal garden after their honeymoon trip to the Palace of Versailles. They had wanted to bring the beauty and grandeur of Europe home and had succeeded.

Seeing the wrought iron gazebo, an octagon-shaped structure braced with five two-foot-wide trellises connected by a three-foot circular ring open on two sides, she marveled again that she carried the blood in her veins of the man who had created such timeless beauty.

She'd spent many pleasurable hours sitting at the table with her dolls or her favorite book. Her parents and the staff had always known where to find her if she was missing. Life had seemed so complicated then. She had no idea what *complicated* was. But she had always been keenly aware of her responsibility to her name.

Her fingers closed around the cool metal. Her ancestors hadn't faltered despite overwhelming odds. She couldn't, either. She knew what had to be done.

Honor above all else.

Claudette had barely closed the front door when she saw Maurice coming toward her. His face was tight with anger. "Maurice, what is it?"

"Where have you been?" he snapped. "The servants are all gone and I come downstairs to find you had left without telling me."

"I'm sorry." Her arms went around his neck. Just before they did, she caught the flicker of surprise in his eyes. "You left so early yesterday that I let you rest this morning. Please forgive me."

"O-Of course." His arms lifted to slowly close around her waist.

She leaned back, sliding her hand over the fine wool of his suit coat, and stared up at him. "I should have come inside instead of going to the gardens. Have you eaten?"

The pout returned to his face. "Bridget wouldn't cook. You should fire her."

Laughing, she kissed his cheek. "I can't fire her because she didn't want to cook on her day off. Besides, in father's will, he gave her a job for her lifetime, as he did all of the servants."

"They're all insolent and rude to me," he persisted.

Shock crossed her face. "Then I'll speak to them. You're my husband."

Satisfaction crossed his. "Thank you."

"In the meantime, I'll fix you a late lunch. You can open a bottle of chardonnay and keep me company while I run an idea by you."

"What idea?" he asked, lines running across his forehead.

Stepping back, she looped her arm through his and started to the kitchen. "How does opening a branch in Seattle, New York, or Chicago sound?"

He stopped dead in his tracks. "You serious?"

"Very. I think it's time to expand." She looked thoughtful. "I don't want to present the idea to the board until I have all the details, including the site, nailed down. The only thing is that I don't have time to scout all the areas and work up the prospectus with all these new contracts coming up."

"I could do it!" he quickly said, his excitement clear.

She hesitated. "Maurice, you have so much to do already. You're wooing this new client, plus the work you already have on your desk. Scouting those cities would take three weeks at a minimum. Becoming a partner doesn't mean you have to work yourself to death."

His eyes gleamed. He licked his lips. "Anything for you, my sweet. I'd hate being away from you, but it would be for us."

Claudette's face softened. "I don't know what I would have done without you these past months. Father would be so happy with the way things are going."

Maurice kissed her cheek. "I feel sure he would, too."

"There'll be no stopping us. Do you think you could leave tonight?" she asked, excitement in her voice.

He patted her hand affectionately. "Whatever you say, darling. I'm yours to command."

Claudette smiled back. The overpowering fear that had plagued her lately receded. She wasn't Claude Thibodeaux's daughter for nothing. He had taught her to swim with the sharks and to soar with the eagles. It was past time she remembered and acted accordingly.

twenty-five

❧

Monday morning at nine sharp, Claudette called the meeting of Thibodeaux's top-level executives to order. The first item on the agenda was to tell them that Maurice was on a fact-finding trip for the next week or longer and that all his files were to be given to another agent. When he returned, she'd have some exciting news to share with them.

A few of the executives couldn't hide their surprise and satisfaction upon hearing that he was gone. Was Claudette telling the entire truth or was there trouble in the marriage? Was Maurice on his way out the door? Not by a flicker of emotion did Claudette give them a clue. She was as poised as ever in a turquoise tweed suit. Her eyes were clear and direct, her smile natural and open.

Damien kept his expression carefully blank. He'd spoken with his father this morning—Jacques had told him of Maurice's accusation. Unlike Maurice, his father had a strict moral code. He might care for Claudette deeply, but he'd never act upon it. He just wanted to see that she was happy.

Damien didn't know if he could be that honorable, to sit back and watch another man abuse what he'd cherish. Thankfully, he wouldn't have to put it to the test. He wasn't the sharing type.

"Damien, I hope that frown doesn't bode ill for the Anderson contract," Claudette said from the head of the oval table.

"No," Damien quickly said, dragging his mind back. "Another matter entirely." He rushed on as Claudette stared at him. "Each of you has a copy of the contract in front of you. We'll run through the high points, but I believe we should accept. Please open the Anderson file and turn to page two."

An hour and a half later they wrapped up, voting unanimously to accept the contract as Damien recommended.

"Damien, can I see you for a moment, please?" Claudette asked as people began to file out of the room.

"Certainly." He stuck the papers back in his leather file and took the seat to her right. There was no sense speculating about what she wanted. Claudette didn't waste time beating around the bush.

"You appear preoccupied lately," she said when the door closed behind the last person. "Is it a personal matter or business?"

He rubbed the back of his neck, hoping she didn't see his cheeks flush. They certainly felt hot. "Personal."

"Oh." She glanced away, then back. "I hope you understand that I'm not being nosy when I ask if things are going badly?"

He thought of himself buried deep in Angelique last night and he flushed again. He bowed his head and faked a cough into his loose fist. "No."

When he glanced up, he discovered his cheeks weren't the only ones that were flushed. He was delighted by the discovery. His dad was as old-fashioned as they came. He and Claudette would make a great couple once she came to her senses and dumped Maurice. "By the way, thanks again for Saturday."

"I enjoyed it. St. Clair's is a wonderful gallery."

My dad is pretty wonderful, too. "If you ever find you have any free time on your hands, I can assure you that Dad would welcome you stopping by again."

Her open expression closed. She reached for the folder on her desk and stood. "This is a busy time for the company, as you're aware. Saturday was a fluke. I don't see how I'll have any free time, and if I do, without Maurice here, I'm sure I won't feel much like going out."

Damien came to his feet. The bastard still had a hold on her. "If you ever change your mind, just drop by."

"I'll keep that in mind. Good work as usual, Damien."

Damien watched her walk from the room, head erect, shoulders straight, and shook his head. "You sure picked a tough one, Dad. But then, neither one of us ever liked anything easy."

. . .

Claudette saw the white-handled wicker basket filled with flowering pink azaleas, ivy, and caladiums the moment she opened the door to her office. Her secretary had told her she had a delivery, but hadn't mentioned what it was.

It wasn't unusual to receive unexpected gifts from firms that did business with them or who wanted to do business with them, but they tended to stay away from sending flowers to her for fear they would be viewed as sexist.

Shutting the door, she crossed the office. The distinctive logo of her favorite florist gave no clue. Behind her desk, she pulled the white envelope from the holder, picked up a crystal letter opener, and slit the seam. She read the note written in an atrocious scrawl she had seen many times in the past.

A friend forever. Jacques.

Jacques was always thoughtful and solicitous of others. He'd proven time and again it wasn't blood that made you who you were but strength of character. She had no doubt that Maurice's wild accusation that Jacques had a romantic interest in her was groundless. Jeanne, Maurice's wife, had been a beautiful, vivacious woman who had charmed everyone she met.

Claudette had never lighted up a room with her presence or had men vying to bring her a drink at a social gathering. But she could run a multimillion-dollar company and she knew that was what she'd better get back to, not comparing herself to another woman. Some women could probably do it all, but she wasn't one of them.

Laying the card aside, she reached for a folder on her desk. But the basket of flowers caught her attention again. She touched the delicate pink azalea blossoms, unaware of the wistful expression on her face. Then, picking up the folder, she went to work.

By Monday night, Rafe thought he had his emotions under control and was ready to see Kristen again, but the intense ache he felt the instant she came through the door and into his shop made him realize she'd always touch him deeply, make him want the impossible. Her hair was braided, a long-sleeved, cream-colored blouse draped softly over her high breasts. Her brown capri pants accentuated long legs that would wrap around a man's waist. She'd remembered to dress casually and wear long sleeves to save her arms from flying chips of wood.

Now, all he had to do was save her from himself. Not sure if he was skillful enough to hide his growing feelings for her, he switched his attention to the three young men with her.

He saw the eagerness in their smiling faces, the anticipation in their slight swagger. They hadn't hit enough walls to become discouraged. Rafe hoped they never would.

"Hello, Kristen. Guys. You ready to go to work?"

There was an affirmative chorus, as Rafe had expected. "Good. Since I want to ensure that each of you learns as much as you can as quickly as you can, I've asked my assistant to work with us." He turned to the elderly man beside him. "Jim Dobbins," Rafe said, then completed the introduction of the slim, gray-haired black man in gray-striped coveralls, khaki shirt, and badly scuffed work boots.

"Pleased to meet ya'll," Jim greeted, a gap-toothed smile on his wrinkled brown face.

"First thing we need to do is review safety rules." Rafe expected the groans and ignored them. "Afterwards we'll review the plans and begin work by measuring and cutting the rips to one-inch widths, arrange and cut the desired lengths, then glue up and clamp. When you come back Thursday we'll begin construction of the box walls." He walked over to the workbench and lifted a length of wood. "I think ash will complement all of the wood you've chosen. We'll then mold the top and bottom on a shaper. The bottom will be fastened with screws and that's when you'll be able to see your three-wood box begin to take shape."

"Mine's six," Kristen said, laughing.

Did it sound forced or was it just his imagination? His gaze bounced from her to his assistant. "Jim will help you. Let's get started." Rafe went to the workbench and went over the safety rules and equipment. Not once did he glance toward Kristen. He trusted Jim to guide and help her. What he didn't trust was himself.

• • •

Rafe was avoiding her and there was nothing she could do about it. Kristen kept sneaking peeks at him as he helped the boys, but he never came near her. The couple of times she had started toward him, Jim had stopped her. Not wanting to hurt the older man's feelings, she had let him help her. As the evening advanced, it became obvious to her that Jim was there to keep her away from Rafe.

The back of her hand brushed across eyes that stung with unshed tears as she glued her cherry wood to walnut. She worked by herself on a card table while Rafe oversaw the young men with firmness and patience.

She tried to be happy that they were getting along well, that he'd recovered from the call from his sister, that he must see that he didn't have to be alone. She couldn't. She wanted to bask in his praise, share the warmth of his hand guiding hers to make the exact cut on the wood.

"You're doin' real good, miss," Jim said, standing beside her. "Wouldn't surprise me none iffin you didn't finish first."

Plastering a smile on her face, she looked up. "Thank you. I had a good teacher."

"Him that taught me and gave me this here job," the older man said.

Kristen's hand paused in reaching for the strip of mahogany. "Rafe taught you?"

He nodded his graying head and sat in the folding chair across from her. "I was at the supply house askin' anybody that would stop iffin I could work for them. Social 'curity check is not enough with the high cost of my medicine." His hand rubbed across his thin chest. "Nobody paid me much mind. After a couple of weeks I was about to give up. Rafe came up and said he'd seen me a couple of times and if I was tellin' the truth, he'd like to help."

"What did you do?"

"Took him to my old truck and showed him my social 'curity check stub and the list of my medicines. Been workin' for him ever since." He braced his long arms on the table. "He watches it real close to see that I don't go over what I'm supposed to make so they don't cut my social 'curity none. Buys my medicine or takes me to the grocery store if need be. Don't take much for me to live, but shore is nice knowin' I got a job. A man needs to feel like he's doing somethin' worthwhile. Rafe sees that I do. He's a good man."

Moisture gathered in her eyes again. "I know."

He straightened. His eyes were shrewd behind the plain, black-framed eyeglasses. "Figured you did. My mama always said anythin' worth havin' is worth workin' for. You believe that?"

The huge lump in her throat didn't feel so big anymore. "Yes."

He nodded briskly. "You work on that there box a bit slower then. Wouldn't want you to finish too soon."

"No, I wouldn't," she agreed, unnecessarily rearranging her wood. "Do you have family here, Jim?"

"Sure do." He reached in his pocket and pulled out his worn black billfold. Papers slid out, but he stuck them back and proudly showed her a picture of a plump baby boy and a little girl. "My grandchildren. Nothin' like grandchildren."

Kristen listened to Jim proudly talk about his family and thought that, for Rafe, if he didn't let go of the past, he'd never experience the same joy.

The next day at work, Kristen was unable to get her thoughts off Rafe. She'd spoken to Lilly that morning and learned that he refused even to discuss seeing his father. While Kristen intensely disliked his father for what he had done to Rafe, she had to admit that after seeing Rafe struggle with his rage and his refusal to let anyone get close, perhaps Lilly had been right. He needed to forgive and move on. Until he did, there would be no future for them.

"Kristen?"

Kristen jerked at the sound of her name. Jacques was standing beside her desk. From the way he was staring at her, that had not been the first time he'd called her name. "I'm sorry. What did you say?"

"Is everything all right?" he asked. "You were preoccupied when I picked up the boys, and you're the same way today. I hate to ask, but does it have anything to do with Maurice?"

"No." She hesitated for a moment, then, seeing that the few customers there were browsing, decided to take a chance. "I'm attracted to a man and he's fighting it."

"Ah." Maurice folded his arms and leaned against her desk. "Wish I could give you some advice, but I seem to be having a bit of difficulty in that area myself."

Kristen sighed. "Why is this so hard? My parents knew the moment they saw each other."

"I felt the same way about Jeanne. Perhaps life was simpler than it is today," he reasoned. "Or perhaps it's to make us appreciate love more when it finally works out."

"Until it does, how do you keep from giving up?" she asked, voicing her fears.

He shrugged. "I guess that depends on how deeply you love. Life offers no guarantees except that if you don't try, you'll certainly fail," he said. "Now, I'd better check on the browsers."

Her hand grazed the smooth top of the writing box, as it did more and more frequently these days. She had no thought of walking away. She just had to figure out how to slip past Rafe's defenses. She'd seen the way he looked at her. He cared. Getting him to act upon his feelings, however, was going to be the most difficult task she'd ever set for herself.

Wednesday night at the Club Royal, as Angelique danced with Damien, her head on his chest listening to the comfortable beat of his heart, she had to admit to herself that the possibility of going off the cliff was no longer an issue. She'd already careened off. She, who never thought cell phones were necessary, was seriously considering getting one because she'd missed a couple of his calls.

That in itself made her admit the truth. She loved him. The thought was as frightening as it was exhilarating. She didn't want to be hurt again. They were having a blazing affair, but was that all it was or would it develop into something lasting?

Deep in thought, she lifted her head. She only had to look at Kristen trying to get through to Rafe and Jacques loving a married woman to realize that love wasn't always enough to ensure happiness. Was that what had happened to her parents? Was that the reason her father had dumped her in the bus station like unwanted garbage?

"What is it?" Damien asked, staring down at her.

"Just thinking," she said, placing her head on his shoulder.

In typical Damien fashion, he stopped dancing and led her to their secluded table in the back of the posh restaurant. He seated her, then took his own seat. "So what's bothering you?"

The flickering candlelight cast shadows on his strong face. He was a man who went after what he wanted. But what happened when he didn't want it anymore?

Reaching across the small, white-linen-draped table, he placed his hand on hers. "You know I'll just keep asking."

She wrinkled her nose. "That's what I get for dating a lawyer. I'm not some witness on the stand to badger."

"I never thought you were." He twisted his head to one side. "Are we about to have a fight? If we are, I need to get the check first. No cabs this time. *I'm* taking you home."

She didn't want his sensible words to make her feel childish or his gaze to draw hers. "I was just thinking about my biological parents." Her hand clenched into a fist beneath his.

"You'd like to know the circumstances surrounding them abandoning you?" he asked gently.

"No, I was wondering why love lasts for some and not for others." she answered and watched panic leap into his dark eyes. *Too soon,* she thought. She should have kept her mouth shut.

Damien worked to get his nerves settled. It had been his experience, when a woman introduced *love* into the conversation, it was time to make a fast exit. He saw the waiter and signaled him. By the time the man reached their table, Damien had his wallet out and was avoiding looking at Angelique.

His collar felt tight and he tugged. He never tugged.

Well aware that he hadn't looked at Angelique since she dropped her bomb, he rose to get her chair when he spotted an acquaintance coming toward them. He didn't look at it as a reprieve; at least he tried not to. "Hello, Judge Randolph."

"Damien, I thought that was you," the middle-aged man said jovially, his arm around a perfectly coiffured woman about the same age in a smart raspberry suit. "I believe you know my wife, Helen."

"Yes. Good evening, Mrs. Randolph."

Helen extended her soft, manicured hand. "Damien."

Releasing her hand, Damien turned to Angelique and saw that she was tight-lipped and stared straight ahead. He'd really done it this time. Nothing like making a woman angry. He'd just have to muddle through it. "I'd like you to meet Angelique Fleming. Angelique, Judge Henry Randolph and his wife, Helen. The judge helped me get my first job as a law clerk."

Damien watched in stunned amazement as Angelique sent the judge a look of pure contempt. The older man gasped. In an instant, Damien realized why.

Angelique picked up her purse and came to her feet. "Mrs. Randolph." She tipped her head curtly to the older woman, then stiffly faced him. "Good-bye, Mr. Broussard." Radiating anger, she stalked away.

"A relative or friend of hers must have come before me in court," the judge said nervously, his Adam's apple bobbing up and down. "Happens all the time."

From the knowing look on his wife's face, she wasn't buying it. Damien knew *he* wasn't. "Excuse me. I think my date just left without me."

He hurried out of the restaurant and saw Angelique walking as quickly as possible down the crowded street. He caught up with her a block away. "You're going to give me a complex if you keep walking out on me, and what's with the *Mr. Broussard*?"

"You're not stupid, Damien. Please don't act like it." They reached Canal Street. She lifted her arm for a cab.

His fingers closed around her arm. He cursed under his breath when he felt her tremble. "I'm taking you home."

"If you have questions abut the judge, you can ask them now."

"Your hating his guts about covers it, I think. Let's go." Not releasing her arm, he headed back for his car.

• • •

Angelique didn't say one word during the drive to her apartment. Damien hadn't expected her to. He just hoped when she did she wouldn't lump him with the judge, but he wasn't counting on it. She needed an outlet for her anger and, unfortunately, he was the nearest target.

She stalked across the room as soon as she opened the door to her place, then tossed her bag on the sofa and faced him, her arms folded defensively across her chest. She wasn't going to speak first.

"You denigrated my character tonight."

She swallowed convulsively. "I'm well aware of that."

"I don't think you are." He crossed to her until they were mere inches apart. "How do you think it made me feel to find out that you believe I wouldn't want my friends or associates to know we were dating?"

Her mouth gapped. Her arms fell to her sides. Obviously that wasn't what she had expected.

"I admit to being uncomfortable with your past as a dancer, but that's where it should remain . . . in the past. As my father pointed out, mine isn't the best." He started toward the door. "Get some rest, I'll call you tomorrow."

"You aren't going to ask about Judge Randolph?"

"I don't have the right." He reached for the knob.

"Wait." She went to him. "I've seen him in The Inferno while I was interviewing the girls working there. He's the worst kind of hypocrite. Enjoys lap dances at three hundred dollars a pop, but if one of the girls appears before him in court and even hints she might know him, he throws the book at them." Her hands fisted. "He won't like the possibility of it getting out in his circle on how he gets his kicks."

"And you thought I'd care about his opinion of me?" his voice was dangerously soft.

She tried again. "You said it yourself. He helped you get your first job. You now work for a very old, very established, highly prestigious firm. He still has a great deal of power. Your reputation can't be blemished."

His eyes hardened. "I think you'd better stop or you're going to make me angry."

Why did everything with him have to be so difficult? "Damien, maybe we shouldn't see each other again."

He grabbed her by the arms, his gaze locked with hers. "No one dictates the way I live my life or who I see."

She shook her head, sending her hair streaming over her shoulders. "Randolph is vindictive. If he thinks your association with me might somehow tarnish him, he'd think nothing of ruining you professionally."

"I'm not worried about him and neither should you. Is that clear?"

He'd fight her on this unless she gave him no choice. She was certain Randolph would come after Damien. She couldn't allow that to happen. Her arms went around his neck, her smile tremulous. "Take me to bed."

"Ang—"

She sank against him, her mouth closing on his, taking the decision from him. She gave herself over to him, holding nothing back, committing each touch, each moment to memory, well aware that for his sake it would be their last.

The next morning on the top floor in his corner office, Damien steadily worked through the pile of documents on his desk. He'd always liked morning best and had gotten a head start by arriving at his office at eight instead of nine. It hadn't been difficult. After he'd left Angelique last night, he hadn't been able to get it out of his mind that nothing was really settled between them. He would have discussed it with her, but she'd gone to sleep after they made love. Or had she?

Just before he left her bedroom, he would have sworn he felt her watching him. But when he glanced over his shoulder she lay in bed on her stomach, exactly as she was when he had eased from her. He had wanted to undress and climb back in bed, gather her in his arms, and go back to sleep.

His pen paused. It wasn't lost on him that at the restaurant before Randolph showed up he had been considering a strategic retreat. She had caught him totally off guard by pretending they weren't dating. He hadn't given a damn then or now about what Randolph thought. All he had wanted to do was get to her and show her she mattered to him.

He hoped to hell he had, but there was this nagging doubt in the back of his mind that maybe he hadn't succeeded.

The phone on his desk rang, interrupting his thoughts. He pushed the speaker button. "Yes, Celine."

"Judge Randolph to see you, Mr. Broussard."

Speak of the devil. "Send him in." Disconnecting the call, Damien placed the pen on top of his papers and leaned back in his chair.

Judge Randolph came in with his friendly smile that had helped him remain popular among his peers in the courthouse for over thirty years as a judge. "Good morning, Damien. Thanks for seeing me."

Damien nodded.

If Randolph thought it rude of Damien not to speak or offer him a seat, he didn't appear bothered. He looked around the beautifully appointed office with built-in bookshelves, an entertainment center, wet bar, and small conference table. "This is the first time I've been in your office since I helped you get a job as a law clerk when you were a senior in high school." He turned to Damien. "You've done well for yourself."

"Thank you."

"With Thibodeaux, you're bound to go further. That's why I'm here. I didn't want you to make a misstep."

Damien rocked forward in his chair. "In what way?"

Randolph took a seat in one of the comfortable burgundy leather chairs in front of Damien's desk. "You're like a son to me. I couldn't sleep last night, thinking of how you might have ruined your career by going out with a woman like that."

"I hardly see why my dating a woman working on her doctorate in psychology could ruin my career," Damien said, deciding to give the bastard enough rope to hang himself.

"Is that what she told you?" Randolph said with a derisive laugh. "It seems our meeting was fortuitous. She's nothing but a stripper at The Inferno."

It was becoming harder for Damien to remain seated. The judge's smirking face begged for his fist. "And how would you know that?"

The judge appeared taken aback, then the easy smile came again. "I'm afraid I can't discuss that with you. I'm sure you understand. Just don't see her anymore." He winked. "I'm sure you can find another woman to give you what she was giving you."

Damien came out of his chair as if catapulted and rounded the desk. He had Randolph by the two-hundred-dollar, printed-silk tie before the other man could blink. "Listen and listen good, because I'm only going to say this once. I know all about your visits to The Inferno, the lap dances." Damien watched the judge's eyes go wide. Perspiration beaded on his broad forehead. "Try to discredit Angelique or mention her name except in glowing terms and it will be your career, not mine, that will be in jeopardy. Do I make myself clear?"

"Y-yes," the judge managed to squeak out.

Releasing him, Damien stepped back. "Good-bye, Judge, and remember, if we have to have this conversation again, you'll like it even less."

His hand at his throat, Randolph hurried from the room.

Damien wanted to kick something. Angelique had been right about the pious hypocrite. But what really steamed Damien was that he hadn't been very much better. He'd judged her because of where she worked and not for who she was. Others would do the same.

"Damn!" There was nothing he could do to prevent it except be there for her. Leaving her didn't enter his mind.

twenty-six

❧

"I swear, Rafe must have eyes in the back of his head," Kristen complained, prowling in front of Angelique sitting on her living room sofa. "Tonight I never managed to get closer than ten feet."

In her usual sweatshirt and jeans, Angelique sat sipping bottled water. "You'll just have to blindside him."

Kristen tsked. "Easier said than done. If it's not the boys, it's Jim trying to help me."

"Then that's your answer. Go see him when they're not around."

Kristen stopped pacing. Her eyes lit up. "Angelique, you're a genius."

"Ain't I, though," she said, and took another swig of water.

Kristen finally stopped worrying about her and Rafe long enough to see the misery in her best friend's face. "Oh, no." She went to sit beside her. "I'm sorry, I thought you and Damien were doing so well together."

Angelique began peeling the label off the bottle. "We were until I got carried away and mentioned the "L" word. Damien almost had a stroke."

"That's understandable," Kristen reasoned. She didn't know much about love, but in college she'd heard mentioning *love* was the kiss of death. "Most men react to love the same way if you bring it up."

Angelique stuffed the paper into the neck of the empty bottle. "We might have gotten past that if my past hadn't showed up in the form of the obnoxious judge you saw the night I took you to The Inferno."

"What happened?"

"Reality." Sighing, Angelique sat forward and put the bottle on the cluttered cocktail table. "Damien is the chief counsel with a prestigious, conservative insurance brokerage firm and I'm a former exotic dancer. Seeing the judge made me realize what is bound to happen if this goes any further."

Kristen frowned. She didn't like the way the conversation was going. "You make it sound as if people in positions of authority or people with wealth are narrowed-minded and can't accept a person for *who* they are and not *what* they were."

Her face set, Angelique turned to Kristen. "Can you honestly say that people you know wouldn't look askance at me if they knew how I put myself through my last two years of college—or think that maybe dancing was not *all* I did?"

Kristen tried to think of a way around the damning answer to her question. "They might, but only until they got to know you."

"What about those who won't even try?" Angelique questioned, although each word hurt more than the last. "In the meantime, what about Damien's career? His family and friends?"

"Jacques likes you," Kristen quickly told her.

"That's just one more reason why I can't see Damien again." Needing to do something with her hands, she picked up the bottle again. "I won't hurt him *or* his father."

"Have you told him yet?" Kristen asked

"I tried, but he wouldn't listen." Angelique ripped a strip of paper away with savage force. "He'll have to eventually."

This wasn't the way it was supposed to be, Kristen thought. Love was meant to be forever. "How can you walk away from him when you care about him so much?"

Tears glistened in Angelique's eyes. "It's *because* I care. He shouldn't be put in a position to defend me or be whispered about because of me."

"Don't you think Damien has the right to make that decision?"

"Whose side are you on?" Angelique sniffed. She brushed her sleeve across her damp eyes. "Rational thinking is not what I need to hear right now."

Kristen hugged her. It was all she could think to do. "All right for tonight, but I can't promise I won't bring it up again."

"This is for the best," Angelique said, clutching the bottle in her trembling hand.

Kristen didn't say anything, just continued to offer the comfort of her presence. Love didn't always have a happy ending. Hers might end in tears and heartache as well but, as Jacques said, at least she would have tried.

This is it, Kristen thought as she balanced the two sacks of food atop the pizza box. She took a deep breath, then knocked on Rafe's office door. She'd already peeked through the window and seen him sitting at his desk. He seemed to be just staring at the ledger in front of him. It was time for her to make her next move.

She shifted nervously in the four-inch black sandals with a thin strap across the toe and around her ankle and hoped her clinging, v-necked white knit top was sexy without being obvious. The black miniskirt that stopped six inches above her shaking knees was a new purchase. She resisted the urge to tug it down. Trying to entice a man was new to her . . . and scary. If Rafe didn't open the door soon, she might just run back to her car.

The door jerked open. His hard expression would have made most men run. Kristen thought about it until she looked past the anger to the longing in his dark eyes.

"Hi, Rafe," she greeted cheerfully, entering as if she had every right to do so. "Since we haven't gotten a chance to talk much, I thought you'd like to know that Jacques and the boys' parents are very happy about their progress."

"Where're you going?" he asked. His voice held about as much warmth as an icicle.

"To the kitchen. We can't eat standing up," she said, hoping her trembling legs wouldn't give out on her as she started up the mahogany stairwell to his apartment.

"I'm not hungry."

Her hands gripped the pizza box and she kept going. "You will be once you see what I have." Opening the door, she went to his kitchen. It was as neat and colorless and spartan as the first time she'd seen it.

Placing the food on the table, she went to the cabinet, wondering if he was just a good housekeeper or if he seldom bothered to cook for himself. Looking at the mismatched plates and glasses, she thought it was probably the latter.

Trying to keep her hands from shaking, she took out two plates. "We can eat while we talk."

Placing the plates on the small table, she glanced up. Whatever she had been about to say faded from her mind. He looked so lost and alone. And he'd never admit to it, never admit he needed someone. Needed her.

Taking her heart and her courage in her hand, she went to him, so close she felt the heat from his body, saw her reflection in his tortured eyes. "Maybe if you kissed me we'd both feel better."

His breath hitched. His gaze heated, narrowed. "Go ho—"

"No." Kristen threw her arms around his neck. She had just enough time to see his startled expression before she pressed her lips to his. They were firm and hot.

Rafe lost the battle between one breath and the next. His large, calloused hands clamped around her small waist, jerking her closer to his hard length. Her high breasts firmed and heated against him. His body throbbed.

"Kristen. Kristen," he moaned. He wanted to kiss every sweet inch of her, then start again. He wanted to bury himself in her silken heat until there was no beginning and no end, just each other. He couldn't. He had never gone in for casual sex and hadn't purchased condoms in months. Even if he had, he wouldn't risk her getting pregnant.

"Rafe. I need you."

The breathless rush of her voice excited him as nothing else ever had. He'd stop in a moment. He just needed one more second. She was so sweet. She was everything.

She groaned deep in her throat. He felt her breast against his chest, cupped her hips to hold her closer . . . and lost it.

He didn't recall taking her to his bed or undressing them, but if he lived to be a thousand he'd never forget the incredible heat of her—*or the unexpected barrier.*

His eyes widened. He stilled, staring down at her, wanting so much, yet knowing he couldn't have it. Groaning as if in pain, he started to pull back, but she twisted beneath him, her mouth finding his, her legs anchoring her to him.

"Rafe."

He could no more deny their need than he could deny his next breath. His mouth locked on hers: then he slid his hands beneath her hips and made them one. She closed around him like a tight, silken glove.

Guided by love, he kissed the side of her neck, her mouth, comforting her, drawing her back to passion with softly murmured words he had never used before, hadn't known he knew until this woman gave what could be given only once. Soon he felt her relax and he began to move, his body calling hers to follow. She did without hesitation, matching his in a rhythm as old as time.

He felt his body spinning, tried to stop. He had to stop, but it was too late. With a will of his own, his body sought completion, determined to bring her along.

Pleasure mounted as he surged into her, each stroke bringing him closer and closer until, with a hoarse shout, he exploded. She was there with him. Their mingled cries of satisfaction filled the room.

Something was wrong. Kristen felt tears sting the back of her eyes.

Lying beside Rafe in his bed, she might as well have tried to snuggle up to a rock. His hard body was stiff and unyielding. The beautiful emotions she'd felt earlier while they were making love evaporated.

Her arms tightened around the sheet covering her bare breasts. She hadn't been able to give him the peace he so desperately needed. Her love wasn't enough.

The bed shifted as he rolled away. She bit her lip and shut her eyes. She wouldn't cry. She'd be mature about this, even if she felt as if her heart were being wrenched from her body.

She opened her eyes to make some casual remark and gaped instead when she saw his back crisscrossed with scars. Nausea rose in her throat. She sprang upright. "Rafe!"

He whirled around, his face contorted in pain as if he were feeling each lash that marked his back anew. He shoved his arms back into the shirt he'd just taken off.

Kristen knew with chilling certainty who had done this. How could a father do that to his child? She stared in mounting horror. No wonder he hated his father so deeply.

"Not very pretty, is it?" A muscle in his bronzed jaw leaped.

Tears welled up in her eyes. "Rafe."

Her tears seemed to anger him. "I don't need your pity."

"You don't want anything from me, but you have my love just the same," she told him quietly.

He seemed to sway. The hard expression left his face, to be replaced with what was almost panic. "No, you can't love me."

Rafe needed her love, even if he didn't want it. "Too late."

The brackets at the corners of his mouth deepened. "You don't understand. I come from men who inflict pain as easily as another parent offers love. One of my earliest memories is of my father whipping me with an extension cord because I forgot to put a toy away and he'd almost tripped over it." His chest heaved with the force of his indrawn breath. "My mother believed a man should discipline his children, so there was no one except my grandmother two streets over until Lilly came, and even then there was nothing she could do."

His face became as hard as granite. "My grandfather abused my father and he continued the tradition. It stops here." He turned toward her. "I'd rather chop off my hand than harm my child. We shouldn't have made love."

Kristen swallowed her hurt. "You're nothing like your father."

Rafe didn't appear to be listening. His hands were clenched. He stared at her as if he didn't see her. "I shouldn't have let this happen. I should have stopped."

"We made love together, Rafe. I didn't want you to stop," she said. "It was beautiful."

"This shouldn't have happened," he repeated, his voice rough with strain and self-loathing. "You can't get pregnant. I won't risk harming my child."

For the first time in her life, Kristen knew what it would be like to be needed. No one else needed her the way Rafe did. "You could never be cruel or heartless. I've watched you with Adam Jr. and the students. You're kind, patient, and generous."

His laughter sent chills down her spine. "My father was the best-loved man in the church. The other boys thought I had the coolest old man around. He was the head deacon. Everybody loved him."

After he'd lived with shame and humiliation for so long, she wasn't going to change his mind easily. She'd have to show him. "Come back to bed. We'll be more careful next time."

He didn't move. "There's no future with me."

She had no future without him. "Come to bed, Rafe."

Slowly he walked to the bed and sat down. He made no move to take her into his arms. She placed her head on his chest, circled his neck with her arms, careful to keep her hands high on his back. Slowly his arms came around her, squeezing her tightly. This time she was unable to stop the flow of tears.

Kristen knew the exact second Rafe eased her away from him and left the bed Saturday morning. She had to clench her hands to keep from reaching for him. Neither one of them had slept much. Nor had they talked or made love again.

She heard the shower come on and opened her eyes. Weak light shone through the sheer blue curtains. A quick glance at her watch told her why: 6:15 a.m. She wished she knew if Rafe usually got up this early or if she had run him from his bed.

Throwing back the covers, she slid her feet over the side and got up. She found her clothes and quickly dressed. She was writing a note on the back of a bank deposit slip when he came back.

He looked tired. She searched and thankfully found a smile. "Good morning—I was leaving you a note. I have to be at work by ten."

"Do you want breakfast?"

A normal conversation when things were anything but. "I'll grab a bite later. Good-bye." Not giving herself time to falter, to beg him to hold her before she left, she hurried out of the room.

Watching her practically run from him, Rafe felt like a bastard. She didn't deserve this, but it was better if it ended quickly. Prolonging it would only make it more difficult. Deciding he'd make coffee later, he started for his office.

He was too keyed up to concentrate on finishing the keyhole desk. Paperwork wasn't much better, but at least he could erase those mistakes with a few swipes of an eraser.

At his desk, he stared at the ledger. He'd been working on it with little success when Kristen arrived last night. He flipped it closed and took it to his file cabinet to put away. That was out, too. It was too much of a reminder of Kristen.

Putting it away, he flipped though his files and pulled out the folder of a prospective client who wanted a pair of walnut display cabinets for her Fabergé collection. The price could easily run to twenty thousand dollars. Money was no object. She wanted style, elegance, and superior workmanship. That's what Rafe would give her. At least in this he knew what he was doing.

Flipping through the folder to look at a few pictures the client had given him, he turned to start back to his desk and happened to glance out the window. The folder slid from his hand. He was out the door in three long strides.

He heard Kristen's heartbroken sobs the instant he opened the office door. He couldn't get to her fast enough. She leaned weakly against the hood of her car, one arm curved around her waist.

"Baby, don't." He wrapped her in his arms, holding her tightly. "Please. Shhh." When her tears showed no sign of abating, he picked her up and took her to his office and sat down in his chair.

He felt helpless and guilty. He stroked her back with a hand that trembled, kissed the wetness from her cheeks. He had hurt her. She should never have gotten involved with him. He could have prevented this. "I'm not worth your tears."

That brought her head up. He saw the anger burning in her watery eyes and didn't blame her. He deserved her scorn.

"Do I look stupid to you?" she asked tightly.

Rafe couldn't follow the flow of conversation, but had no difficulty realizing he was tiptoeing through dangerous territory. "Of course not," he said cautiously.

"Then why would I wait all this time for a worthless man to be my lover?"

The word *lover* dried the spit in his mouth. She wasn't finished with him. "If you say anything so idiotic again, I'll get a blowtorch and weld all your hand tools into one big blob."

Staring down into her angry, tear-stained face, he didn't doubt her. She'd fight for him even if she had to fight against him to do it. "I made you cry."

She sniffed and swiped an unsteady hand across her face. "That's because you're a man. Men aren't always the most sensitive. I wanted to be held this morning and you acted as if we were strangers. You were pushing me out of your life after what we shared last night, and that hurt."

He had no defense except the one he'd kept telling himself all night as he lay awake with her in his arms. "I didn't want to hurt you."

"Loving you could never hurt. Pushing me away will," she said, her gaze locked on his. "I don't want to give up your friendship because we're lovers."

He almost winced. There was that word again, and, since Kristen had been a virgin before last night, she wasn't using the word casually. "For us there is no tomorrow, only yesterday."

Her gaze never wavered. "It can be, if you let it."

He wanted to believe it was possible, but he couldn't gamble with her happiness or the possibility of fathering a child. "We're not going to make love again until we're sure you're not pregnant. When will you know?"

She dropped her head. His thumb and finger lifted it back up. She blushed and said, "Three weeks."

Rafe breathed a little easier. She wouldn't be at her most fertile until next week. He might not have ruined her life. His hand left her chin to stroke her hair. "Just promise me one thing. Promise me you won't cry if it doesn't work out between us."

Her smile was tremulous. "I promise to try."

Despite the aching loneliness she eased within him, he set her away from him. "How about breakfast? I make a pretty good omelet."

She came off his lap and sent him a watery smile. "Thank you, but

I'd better get back. Angelique is coming over for breakfast. She'll be worried if I'm not there."

"All right." He pushed to his feet, feeling the awkwardness descend between them once again. "I'll walk you to your car."

"Unnecessary. I'll see you later." Waving her fingers, she was out the door.

Wanting to see for himself that she made it this time, he ignored her wishes and followed her outside. As he watched her drive away, he was very much aware that she could have cancelled with Angelique and stayed for breakfast. The thought made him feel guiltier.

twenty-seven

The weatherman had predicted rain for New Orleans and the thick, gray clouds overhead showed every indication that they were going to prove him right. The overcast day matched Kristen's mood exactly as she made her way from the parking lot to St. Clair's. She had made a complete and utter mess of everything. Rafe's father had a much stronger hold on him than she ever could. How had she been so naïve as to think all it would take to heal Rafe was for him to let go and admit he cared about her?

The blast of a car horn pulled her up short and she stepped back on the sidewalk. When the car passed, she continued down Royal Street, busy even at nine-thirty. Passing a coffee shop, the aroma of freshly baked beignets and strong chicory coffee filled her nostrils. Her lips pursed. She hadn't eaten and she wasn't hungry. There had been no appointment with Angelique for breakfast. It had been a pitiful excuse that a child could have seen through.

Her hand clenched on the shoulder strap of her handbag. Obviously, Rafe hadn't wanted her to stay. She'd been afraid that if she had, she'd start crying again and that time she wouldn't have been able to stop.

We won't make love again until we're sure.

She walked around a slow-moving couple and continued down the street. She'd lied about her menstrual cycle. It was due in two weeks, not three, and she was like clockwork. The thought of pregnancy hadn't entered her mind when she'd decided to go to Rafe. She hadn't thought it would go so far so fast. But when she'd kissed him, her body had spiraled out of control.

Now they both might have to pay the consequences. What if she was pregnant? Her stomach did a back flip. She wasn't sure if it was from dread or excitement.

Arriving at St. Clair's, she saw that Jacques was already there and had opened the shop a few minutes early. She hated to admit it, but she hoped that meant he might close a bit early. She wasn't sure she could cope with an endless stream of people today.

Entering, she immediately saw Jacques hanging a new picture in place of the Arthello Beck painting he'd sold the day before. "Good morning, Jacques."

"Good morning," he greeted, glancing over his shoulder. He frowned.

Kristen turned her head. She should have taken the time to find her shades. Make-up was no help for red, puffy eyes.

"You feel all right?" Jacques asked, coming to stand by her desk.

She busied herself putting away her purse. "I'm fine."

"Kristen, I was married for twenty-seven years. I know when a woman's been crying."

She blinked rapidly. Her mouth opened, but nothing came out. She reached for her purse and pulled out a tissue.

"I'd send you home if I thought you'd go." He put his hand gently on her trembling shoulder. "Let's change desks today. You can work on the inventory that just came in. You'll be closer to the storage area."

She had to swallow before she could say, "Thank you."

"Rafe impressed me as an intelligent young man," Jacques said as she rose to her feet. "Give it time."

"That's the one thing we don't have," Kristen said as she walked away.

Damien knew when he was being given the runaround. He'd handed it out enough, but this was the first time he was on the receiving end. Angelique was acquiring the annoying habit of becoming the first in a long list of unpleasant firsts.

And he was the one supposed to give her things first. What a joke!

Standing in front of her door, he jabbed her bell, and then paced. There was little assurance that she'd answer it quickly. For the past three days, she had been putting him off when he called. She was always about to see a client or go into a meeting. If he called her at home, she was busy on her dissertation.

He whirled back to the door and jabbed the bell repeatedly. "I know you're in there, Angelique."

Unfortunately, an elderly woman happened to be passing with her silky terrier. Eyeing him warily, she picked up the little dog and hugged the wall until she was well past him. Damien shoved his hand over his hair.

Another first. Scaring old ladies.

"This isn't over, Angelique." Spinning on his heels, he stalked to the elevator.

Inside, Angelique leaned her head against the door. There was a lump in her throat, a pain in her heart. This was for the best.

Damien was just angry because she'd thwarted him. A self-assured man like him wouldn't easily accept a woman gaining the upper hand or dumping him. Probably a first. That was the reason he was so persistent. There was nothing special about his interest in her. He only wanted her for sex.

He'd get tired and move on to someone else. And just the thought of it made the pain in her chest deepen.

Scrubbing her hand over her face, Angelique went back to the papers scattered on the floor and picked up the laptop. Damien was her past. This was her future.

Claudette took the phone call in her father's study. She sat in his favorite chair, where he'd wielded so much power and authority and taught her to do the same . . . no matter how distasteful. She felt closer to him here than any other place. After a rough day at work or on Sunday afternoon they'd spent long hours here, planning or just sharing the quiet comfort of the elegantly appointed, high-ceilinged room.

She'd never felt intimidated by the massive furniture or her father's sharp mind. On rare occasions they'd sit and read for pleasure while a fire roared in the hearth or rain beat steadily against the lead glass windows, as it did today. It was fitting, she thought, that she be here when she talked to the man who held the key to her future and that of Thibodeaux International.

She listened closely to everything he said, each word indelibly seared into her mind. She had been right to take this course of action. It was bold and would cost heavily, both professionally and personally, but the alternative was too dire to even think about.

Honor above all else.

Jacques glanced up when the door opened. They hadn't seen a real customer in two hours. The people who came in were trying to get out of the rain. He didn't mind. There was always the possibility that they'd see an item they liked and decide to buy.

"Damien."

Damien closed the umbrella and stuck it in the antique brass umbrella stand his mother had gotten for the gallery years ago. It came in handy on rainy days like this. "Hi, Dad. Is Kristen here?"

Jacques studied his son's tight jaw, the glint in his eyes. It looked like Damien and Angelique had taken another wrong turn. "She's in the back, but I don't think you should bother her."

"Why?" Damien snapped out.

Since his son was usually well-mannered and respectful, Jacques overlooked his brusque tone. Unrequited affection tended to put a man in a bad mood. "I think she and Rafe are having problems. She doesn't need you harassing her about Angelique."

Damien stuck his hands in his pockets. "Angelique won't see me."

Jacques's eyebrow rose. "What did you do?"

His hands whipped out. "I—" He shoved his hand over his head. "I may have become a bit concerned when she started talking about the meaning of love or something. . . ."

"Something? You weren't listening to her?" Jacques asked in disbelief.

Damien almost rolled his eyes. "Come on, Dad. I wasn't expecting it and I might have gotten a little gun-shy—then Judge Randolph showed up and things went downhill fast." Damien told his father what had happened at the restaurant. "I thought things were fine until the next day when she began avoiding me."

"Randolph gives new meaning to the words *dirty old man*," Jacques said with disgust.

Damien's eyes were like chips of black ice. "He came to see me the next day with a lot of bull about wanting to save me. I set the self-righteous bastard straight. If he ever sees Angelique again, he'd better be on his best behavior or he'll answer to me. But the way she's avoiding me, I may not see her, either."

"You think Kristen will tell you what's going on?" Jacques asked.

"I'm hoping," Damien said.

"Go on back—just be sensitive," Jacques said, taking a seat behind Kristen's desk. "There's no sense in all of us being miserable."

Damien planted his hands on the desk. "Claudette told us in an executive meeting that he's out of town on a fact-finding mission. I can't put my finger on it, but she's been different all week."

Jacques stopped stacking papers. "You don't usually discuss company business."

"Like you said, there's no sense in all of us being miserable."

"It could mean nothing," Jacques said, hoping in spite of himself, in spite of it being wrong to want another man's wife.

"Or it could mean she's finally taking a hard look at the situation." Damien straightened.

"Maybe. Maybe not." Jacques nodded his head toward the back of the shop. "Go."

Knowing that his father didn't want to discuss it anymore, Damien walked to the back. Seeing Kristen with her forehead in her palms, he knew his father was right. "Kristen."

She looked up. Her facial muscles flexed as if she were trying to smile and couldn't quite get them to cooperate.

"Is there anything I can do?"

She bit her lip, then shook her head once.

Damien would be the worst kind of bastard if he tried to get information from her when she was so upset and barely holding it together.

"I just dropped in to see Dad and I thought I'd say hello. I didn't mean to disturb you. 'Bye."

"Damien."

He turned back. "Yes?"

"Do you really care about Angelique or is it just sex?"

He started, then jerked his head toward the front of the shop. He'd never had his sexuality discussed so openly in his life. His father had been bad enough. Damien stared back at her. Kristen had always impressed him as the shy, naïve type.

She stared right back, red, puffy eyes and all. "Well?"

"I'm not sure how I feel, but I do know it's not just about sex," he said. If she asked anything else, he was out of there.

Kristen seemed to consider his words as she clutched a crumpled tissue in her hand. "Angelique didn't ask me not to tell you, but I can't betray a confidence."

Damien eased closer to the desk. He'd known something was going on. "Can you give me a hint?"

"You already know the answer. All you have to do is figure out what you're going to do about it."

"What?" He frowned. "This isn't some Oriental mysticism we're discussing."

"I can't say more."

He reached for her. "Kris—"

"Leave her alone!"

His hand still reaching for Kristen, Damien turned toward the harsh-sounding voice and saw the broad-shouldered man who had been with her at his father's house the night of the party. Damien looked into the other man's cold, black eyes and saw his life pass before him. He didn't need Kristen's soft exclamation to know that this man was the cause of her tears. Slowly he lowered his hand.

"I'm sorry, Kristen," Damien said, not because he was afraid but because he had been wrong to become upset when she had tried to help him. "I hope you'll both accept my apology."

"It's all right, Rafe." Kristen came unsteadily to her feet. "Rafe Crawford, Damien Broussard, Jacques's son. He's a friend of Angelique's."

Damien was the first to extend his hand. Rafe slowly lifted his. "Again, I'm sorry. Angelique won't see me, and I was trying to find out why."

"I told you. You have the answer," Kristen said, but her gaze kept straying to Rafe. "You'll figure it out."

"Hope so." He nodded. "Rafe. Kristen."

Rafe didn't pay any attention to Damien leaving. Kristen held his complete attention. He'd seen the good-looking man talking to her and jealousy had shot through him: then the man had shouted at her. Rafe had wanted to hit him. The only reason he didn't was fear of causing her to lose another job. Considering he was Jacques's son, that's exactly what would have happened.

"What brings you here?"

You, he wanted to say. He hadn't been able to work all day and when the rain started a little after two, he'd given up and driven to the gallery. He couldn't give her what she wanted, but at least he could show her he valued the precious gift she'd given him. He just wished he'd come sooner. She looked miserable and she hadn't stopped crying.

"I thought I'd walk around the Quarter for inspiration."

"Oh," she said, biting her lower lip. "Then you won't be staying?"

"I might. You mind if I stick around for a while?"

"No," she quickly said. "There's some mahogany and teak statues that you may find interesting. Let me show you." She took him to the glass-encased collection. "Take your time. They're really beautiful— quite spectacular."

"But they can't match you," he said, then clamped his mouth shut.

She blinked rapidly as if she were fighting tears. "Thank you."

Embarrassed by his outburst, he turned back to the carvings.

Damien returned to the front of the gallery, deep in thought. It appeared that Kristen and Rafe might work out whatever problems they were having. At least they were talking. He wished he could say the same about him and Angelique.

"She tell you?" Jacques asked.

"Not unless you consider her cryptic message that I already had the answer, telling me." He picked up the umbrella. "All I have to do is figure it out."

"You will."

"Yeah. Good-bye, Dad." Stepping outside, Damien unfolded the umbrella and started down the street, his mind going over his last conversation with Angelique. He turned on St. Peter's and headed toward the Mississippi River.

He dismissed the first thought that came to him because they had talked that through. Yet, somehow his mind always circled back to the same thing.

Letting down the umbrella, he went inside Jackson Brewery and up to Pat O'Brien's on the third floor. The combination of rain and Saturday had the famous restaurant and bar crowded, so he was pleased to be shown a small table near the window looking out over the Mississippi.

The sky was a dull gray. The kind of day he'd like to be in bed curled up with Angelique or pulling sweet cries from her body. His fingers drummed on the table. Until he figured out why she was avoiding him, he wasn't going to be able to do either.

Ordering a glass of mineral water with a twist of lime, he folded his arms and continued to stare out the window. *You have the answer.* That could mean he had already discussed it with Angelique.

He jerked upright in his chair, startling the waitress, who was about to place his drink on the table. Once again, if he had listened to his mother it would have saved him a lot of time and misery. She'd always tried to instill in his hard head that he should follow his first mind when he had tough choices in life or on an exam. "That's it."

He tossed a ten on the table and strode from the restaurant. He was going to wring Angelique's beautiful neck.

twenty-eight

Damien had calmed down considerably by the time he rang Angelique's doorbell twenty minutes later. Both his parents had preached that if he went looking for trouble, it would find him. Attacking Angelique would solve nothing. He was a lawyer. Words and reason were his forte . . . if he got the chance to use them.

He rang the doorbell again. "Angelique. I know you're in there. The doorman said he hadn't seen you come out of the building today."

Silence.

Tired of this, Damien went for the kill. "What kind of psychologist runs from her problems?"

The lock clicked almost immediately. A fuming Angelique jerked open the door. She had circles beneath her eyes and she wore her grubby clothes, which meant no bra. Damien congratulated himself on keeping his gaze locked on her very angry face.

"How dare you question my professionalism," she hissed.

"You had no difficulty questioning mine," he retorted.

Her head jerked back as if he had hit her. He used that unguarded moment to push his way inside.

She swung the door shut and turned to face him. "I'm busy, Damien."

"Hiding from me."

She crossed her arms over her unbound breasts. "You certainly think highly of yourself. You think I have nothing better to do than hide from you?"

His eyes narrowed. "That's right. I do think highly of myself and apparently you don't. You either thought I was too stupid or so weak that you had to save my career for me or that I was so self-serving and shallow that I'd be ashamed of you. Either way, that's not saying very much."

Angelique let her arms fall. "I never thought you were any of those things!"

"Yes, you did. When *you* decided it was over. How do you think that made me feel?"

Uncertainty crossed her face. "We were just dating."

"And sleeping together, or didn't that mean anything to you?" he snapped out.

Her face flushed with anger. "I don't sleep around."

"When your character is being attacked unjustly it's not a very good feeling, is it?" His mouth flattened into a narrow line.

She shoved her hand through her hair impatiently. She was losing this battle and knew it. "I apologize if I offended you. Now, if you don't mind, I have to get back to work on my dissertation."

"Mind if I read it?"

Her eyes narrowed. "No one has read it yet, not even my advisor."

"Seems to me that you should have another pair of eyes look at it." He walked over to her work area, then released the single button on his dark gray jacket and hunkered down by the papers scattered around the sofa. "I'll leave after I read it, and I won't bother you again."

That was what she wanted, for him to leave her alone, so why did her chest hurt? She walked over and gave him the thirty sheets that she had sweated bullets and spent hundreds of hours in research to write. "I was about to fix a sandwich. Yell when you finish. I'll be in the kitchen."

Damien took the papers, then sat cross-legged on the floor and began to read.

Realizing she was standing there trying to gauge his reaction, Angelique forced herself to leave and fix that sandwich she no longer wanted. Damien was out of her life, so his opinion didn't matter.

About to open the refrigerator, she closed her eyes and leaned her head against the door. She was doing it again, lying to herself when she'd made a vow long ago that she'd never do that again. She wanted Damien, and knowing she'd never be with him was killing her.

• • •

"I'm finished."

Angelique sprang up from the table and rushed back into the den. It had taken him exactly twenty-seven minutes.

One hand negligently slipped into the front pocket of his gray slacks as he stood by her sofa. "Thank you for letting me read it." He started for the door.

Angelique stared at him in disbelief, then crossed her arms stubbornly across her chest. She wasn't going to ask. She wasn't.

He reached for the doorknob. "What did you think?" she blurted, unable to help herself.

He gazed at her, his expression unreadable. "You really want my honest opinion?"

She hated it when people asked that question. She'd always been tempted to say, *No, I want a jackass's opinion, but since one's not around, you'll do.*

"Yes."

"It's biased and weighed heavily by your obvious mistrust and dislike of men."

"What!" she sputtered.

"You paint men as users and women as long-suffering weaklings who have little backbone, but somehow manage to keep home and hearth together."

"That's not—"

He talked over her. "Who do you think man, since the beginning of time, went into battle for? Why they fought vicious animals with only their bare hands or clubs? Why our forefathers suffered inhumanities and injustices that could have broken them? I'll tell you why. They did it for the families they had waiting at home, depending on them. They still do.

"Nowhere in those pages did I see men like my father who put in ten-hour days and went to school at night to make a better life for me and my mother, to make us proud of him although we already were." He walked over to her until he was towering over her. "I didn't even see your foster father, and for that you should be ashamed."

That hurt and cut to the quick. "The paper is not about good men."

"How can you be a clinical psychologist and not weigh all sides equally?" he asked. "If you look at a patient you're counseling with prejudices and preconceived notions, you'll do more harm than good. You know that."

She did. "I wouldn't do that to my patients."

"Then write your dissertation the same way . . . without prejudices or biases and not to get back at anyone." He moved in closer. "Give me the same fair consideration." His tone became low and intimate. "Don't judge me. Don't make my decisions for me. Don't lump me with the father who abandoned you, the lover who hurt you, or all the men like Randolph who made you feel less than the intelligent, beautiful woman you are." He pointed to his chest. "This is me. Look at me and see me, not them."

He turned, walked over to the door, and wrenched it open. "If I were you, I'd take another long, hard look at your dissertation and at me. You'll only have one chance." The door closed behind him.

Angelique stood there, vibrating with anger. How dare he attack her professionalism. She was good at what she did! The recovery rate in her case file was the highest at the center. She'd even heard talk that she was being considered as the director of a new satellite facility they planned to open next year. What did he know?

She went to her dissertation, picked it up, and began to read. Halfway through, she sank back into the sofa. Her mouth was tight with anger and it was directed at herself.

He was right.

She had taken out her anger and frustration on the men in her life who had abandoned or mistreated her. She was scheduled for her oral defense of her dissertation in four weeks and what she'd written wouldn't cut it. She could plow ahead or work her tail off to correct it.

She picked up the phone. "Hello. Dr. Jones. I hate to call you on a Saturday, but there's a problem with my dissertation. Do you think we could meet this afternoon or tomorrow and discuss it?" She said a little prayer and waited for his answer.

"Thank you, sir. I'll be right over."

Heading for her bedroom, she pulled off her sweatshirt. If she went down, she'd go down fighting.

"Why don't you take the rest of the day off?" Jacques asked Kristen. "It's been slow all day. Take Rafe with you. I admire anyone who enjoys art, but he's been with those statues for over an hour."

Kristen had thought the same thing. He had to be bored, but he showed no sign of leaving. Rafe, who liked his solitude and who probably had twenty things to do, was sticking around to see that she was all right. "Jacques, I can't. I got in late and I took off last Saturday."

"You work hard. I won't take no for an answer." He walked over to Rafe. "I'm giving Kristen the rest of the day off. Please see that she gets home. It's still raining outside."

Rafe, who had appeared to be studying the pattern of the hardwood floor by his feet more than the art display, lifted his head. "Yes, sir. You have your umbrella?" he asked Kristen.

She pulled it out of her purse. "I really think I should stay."

"I don't." Jacques took both their arms and led them to the door, opened it, escorted them onto the stoop under the awning, then closed the door behind them.

"Which way is your car?" Rafe asked, shifting nervously from one foot to the other.

"I'm all right, Rafe," Kristen said. "You don't have to watch over me."

He let his gaze sweep the crowded streets and sidewalks before coming back to her. "I took something from you that can't be replaced. It wouldn't have happened if I hadn't cared. If you hadn't cared. I just want you to know that it can't be the way you want, but it mattered to me. *You* matter."

He was giving all he could. She shouldn't be greedy. She raised the umbrella and handed it to him. "We never did see that movie."

"Afterwards, you can find us another restaurant," he suggested.

"I'd like that." She stepped onto the street. For the time being she'd have to accept him as a friend, not the lover she wanted—and live with the possibility that he might never be again.

• • •

Sunday found Angelique and Kristen subdued. Neither had to explain the reason why. After church, both opted to return home. Angelique to continue working on her dissertation with the suggestions her advisor had given her; Kristen to start working on the database for nineteenth-century African-American art. Each was dealing with the possibility that the man she loved might never be hers.

Kristen didn't know what to expect when she and the students arrived at Rafe's shop Monday night. She caught him watching her more than once Saturday at the movie and later at the restaurant. It was almost as if he were trying to peer into her and determine if she were pregnant. His fear that she was, was a constant source of pain for her. After speaking to him, she'd gone to her assigned work area in his shop.

"Kristen, you're working with me tonight," Rafe said, picking up the pieces to her box from the card table. "Tonight we work on installing the hinges, and they have to be done exactly right."

She followed him back to his workbench, wishing she didn't have the feeling that if they hadn't made love she'd still be working with Jim, and that guilt, not concern, drove him. She watched his strong hands, remembered them heating her body, stroking, loving. He picked up a chisel and demonstrated how to cut a series of shallow cuts for the mortises or joints. Too bad she couldn't chisel away the hard shell around his heart so he'd let himself love her.

"Your turn."

Without comment, Kristen took the chisel. It was going to be a very long week.

Saturday morning found Angelique typing furiously in her office. With Professor Jones's help, she'd been able to rethink her paper and make it more even. It wasn't the stuff that a talk show would want, but it presented a fairer picture of relationships between the sexes. She had to admit that some women, like men, were users and often had their own agenda.

She didn't even blink when she heard the doorbell. The last time she'd gotten up for a soft drink it had been close to four in the afternoon. Kristen didn't get off until five. The professor and her associates knew to call first. That left solicitors, who occasionally snuck past the doorman. She wasn't going to delude herself that it might be Damien. She'd done that too much already.

The phone rang twice. Stopped. Then rang twice again. Her foster parents' signal. Hitting "save," she was up and running to her bedroom for the phone. She snatched it up. "Hello?"

"Hi, Angelique. We've come to visit," said her mother in a voice always filled with love and happiness.

"You're here?"

"Open the door. These heels are hurting my feet."

"I'll be right there." Smiling, she went to the door. Her foster mother bought shoes for beauty and style instead of comfort. Angelique opened the door and blinked in surprise. With her foster parents were two of her foster siblings. "What are you all doing here?" she asked when they were inside.

"Visiting," answered her foster father, thin as the proverbial rail, dressed in his favorite clothes, khaki shirt and pants. "We thought we'd drive up and see how that paper is going."

"Yeah," David Hall said. "Papa Howard can't wait to wear that suit you bought him. Gia and I are working on getting him out of his old shoes into some cap-toed lace-up by Ferragamo."

Elmo Howard snorted. "Can't even pronounce the name. I'm not about to put 'em on my feet."

It was an old argument. David, trim and well-dressed, with almond-colored skin and gray eyes, managed a department store in Baton Rouge. The family teased him that the women customers made up problems so they could stop by to see him.

"Now, Papa Howard," Gia Sample said, her tone placating. "You'd look great." Petite and pretty, she had coal-black skin and hair. She was the last of the Howard "brood" and had graduated in May and now worked as a dietician in a hospital in Baton Rouge. "Mama doesn't mind."

"And she can't go twenty feet without sitting down, either," he reminded them.

Bette Howard, full-figured and proud of every ounce, wiggled her stocking-covered toes. A true Southern lady, she never stepped out of the house without being in full make-up and dressed to the hilt. Today she wore a pretty white suit. She relished David's job as much as he did. "But I sure look pretty."

"It's good to see all of you." The rest of the infamous twelve were scattered over the state. Whatever her beginnings, she had a family who loved her.

"Get dressed. We're going out to dinner," David said. "And don't take all day. Breakfast is just a faint memory."

"I'll be right out." She ran to get dressed and missed the conspiring wink between David and Mama Howard.

The five of them piled into the fifteen-year-old van. Its odometer had stopped at one hundred thousand miles when Angelique was in high school. Fortunately, Papa Howard was a shade-tree mechanic and kept the vehicle running smoothly. "What do you want to eat?" she asked, propping her arms on the back of her mother's seat as she had done so many times in the past.

"Doesn't matter," Mama Howard said. "Just so I don't have to cook it." In the passenger seat, she gazed out the widow. "They sure have some pretty houses here. Seems like, as many times as we've been here, we never get to look."

"Papa Howard can take St. Charles Avenue and we can be in the Garden District in nothing flat," David said. "Some of the most beautiful houses in the city are there."

Angelique started to protest, but then remembered that Jacques, not Damien, lived there. "Sure, why not?"

As her foster father cruised through the beautiful neighborhood, she tried to remember what Jacques's house had looked like. She had been paying more attention to Damien than where they were going.

"Look at all these cars lining the street. Someone's having a party," Gia said, scooting closer to Angelique and looking out her window. David sat behind them at the other window.

"What a hunk! Too bad he's with someone," Gia said. "Don't you think he's all that, Angelique?"

Angelique, still trying to remember Jacques's street, wasn't interested, but she looked anyway. Her eyes bugged and before she knew it her nose was pressed to the window. Damien stood on the lawn with some long-legged woman.

He turned and looked directly at her. He didn't even have the courtesy to appear embarrassed. He waved.

"Look! He's waving. My goodness! He's motioning us to stop," Gia said, excitement in her voice.

"Keep going!" Angelique's fingernails dug into the back of Mother Howard's seat.

"Where are your manners, Angelique?" her foster mother admonished. "Pull over, Elmo."

Angelique slumped in her seat.

Damien came to the passenger side of the van. He was all smiles and so handsome Angelique wanted to kiss him until neither of them could breathe, then toss him off the nearest cliff.

"Hello." He looked at her. "Hi, Angelique."

Four pairs of eyes centered on her. "You know Angelique?" Gia asked.

"We dated until she dumped me," Damien confessed with a smile.

Once again, Angelique felt the scrutiny of her family.

"You seem to have gotten over it quickly," she said, then could have bitten off her tongue.

He laughed and extended his hand to her foster mother. "Damien Broussard."

Her foster mother introduced everyone. "You have a beautiful home."

"Actually, it's my father's but I know he wouldn't mind if you'd like to come inside. He should be arriving any moment."

"No." Angelique glared at him.

"Yes," Gia said.

"There's no place to park," Angelique pointed out happily.

"I'll move the orange cones I had for another guest and you can park there." Damien picked up the three cones directly in front of his father's house and stacked them on the sidewalk. Elmo quickly pulled in.

"What a nice young man," Mama Howard said.

Gia nudged her foster sister in the side. "Are you crazy, giving up a man like that?"

"Yeah," David piped in. "He looks like he's a BMW to me."

Angelique scrunched up her face. She detested the acronym for "black man working." "I'm staying in the van."

"No, you're not. You get out of this van now," Mama Howard said from the sidewalk.

Angelique got out of the van. No one crossed her mother when she spoke in that tone or had "the look" that could pick you out from a hundred feet away in the choir stand or on a playground, and said, *Your butt is mine if you don't straighten up.*

"Don't slouch," her foster mother said, straightening the straps of her pink sundress and finger-combing her hair as if she were a little girl. Angelique thought of protesting, but Mama Howard still wore "the look."

Out of the corner of her eye, she saw Damien waiting patiently. So was the long-legged woman, who had moved to the black wrought iron gate leading up to the Georgian mansion.

"This way," Damien said.

With her foster mother holding her arm, Angelique had little choice except to follow. With each step toward the woman who had taken her place, Angelique's shoulders became a little straighter, her chin a little higher. *She* had walked away from him. No. She had *tossed* him away. As stupid as it seemed, she wasn't going to have his last memory be of her looking pitiful or being spiteful.

"You were right about my dissertation. Thank you."

He sent her a look that turned her legs to water, then he spoke to Mrs. Howard. "You and your husband raised quite a woman."

Bette Howard beamed with pride, then chuckled. "She fought us every step of the way until she was in high school."

"My parents tell me I did, too."

The long-legged, and yes, disgustingly beautiful young woman in a multicolored chiffon peasant top and light blue denim jeans opened the gate. "Hello."

Damien waited until all of them were on the walkway before he did the introduction. He made points with everyone by remembering their last names. "This is Simone Fairchild, my cousin."

"Cousin!" Angelique exclaimed.

"Thanks for the compliment," Simone said, smiling knowingly.

Angelique looked away in embarrassment; then she was shoved aside by David, who was practically drooling over Simone. So much for family loyalty.

"Let's go inside, and you can meet the rest of the guests."

twenty-nine

The rest of the guests were friends and family members. Jacques showed up while Damien was still introducing them. He didn't seem to mind that five extra people, four of them total strangers, were thrust upon him unexpectedly. He pointed out that there was enough food on the three buffet tables on the terrace and enough chairs and tables set around the pool and in the gardens beneath the trees.

As with her family and Simone, Damien mentioned in his introduction that Angelique was a candidate for her doctorate in psychology and that she had dumped him.

"Will you stop saying that," she hissed.

Elizabeth Fonteneau-Fairchild, Simone's mother, smiled indulgently. The elegant woman was the essence of wealth and social grace. Dressed in a white silk blouse with embroidered sleeves and midnight blue crepe pants, she was chic and looked comfortable. She wore one ring, her wedding ring. Since the diamond was the size of a marble, it was enough. Even beneath the shade of a magnolia, the stone winked each time she moved her hand. "My nephew has always been impertinent. Just like his mother, my sister," she said with amusement.

"I heard she could handle him, though," Angelique said. "He told me about the tennis racket incident when he forgot to call."

"Jeanne was all of five-feet-two and even then, Damien was six feet." Elizabeth's slim arms circled her stomach as she laughed. "From then on, she kept a chair by the back door so she wouldn't have to go get one. He didn't try that again, but there were other incidents."

"Like what?" Angelique asked.

Damien groaned.

Elizabeth ignored him and regaled her with stories about Damien's wild youth. Angelique was enjoying hearing them until her foster father wandered over and started telling them about *her* past.

He still had nightmares thinking about some of the headstrong things she did. For instance, the time she wanted Kentucky Fried Chicken instead of meatloaf for dinner.

Angelique groaned.

He went on to tell them that his wife had three sick children at home and made the mistake of giving Angelique two dollars and saying if she wanted chicken, to go get it. The restaurant was two miles away on a busy street near the freeway. They'd thought she was in her room until they couldn't find her for dinner. They discovered her at the restaurant, happily eating. They'd learned never to try and bluff Angelique.

Damien looked straight at her. "We have something else in common. I don't bluff, either."

"Time to eat," Jacques announced. People converged on the buffet table laden with shrimp rémoulade, blackened fish, a variety of fried seafoods, crawfish étouffée, Creole brisket of beef, bread pudding plus an assortment of fruit, cheeses, and bread.

Angelique took her plate of fried oysters and fried green tomatoes and sat at one of the long tables. Damien passed by with her foster parents and went to a smaller table near the pool. His aunt joined them. Their happy laughter drifted to her.

Angelique stabbed a crayfish viciously. For a man who was dumped, he was disgustingly happy.

It was dark when Damien and his father walked Angelique and her family to their van and waved them on their way. He hadn't missed the furtive looks Angelique kept sending his way. His plan was working out perfectly.

"Nice family," Jacques said as he walked back to his house.

"Yes," Damien agreed, opening the iron gate. "I got that impression when I called them Tuesday. Do you know how many Howards there are in the Baton Rouge phone book?"

Jacques slapped his son on the back. "You certainly are sneaky. Guess you chose the right profession."

Damien winced, then laughed. "You think?"

"You're going to a lot of trouble just to get a woman to go out with you," Jacques said, pausing on the wide front porch.

"Angelique makes life interesting. Besides, she impugned my character."

"In other words, she's a challenge you can't resist?"

"Yes." Damien opened the front door, "What makes it so great is that she can't resist me, either. It's just taking her a little longer to realize it." His eyes narrowed in determination. "But she will. I guarantee it."

Damien stared out the living room window of his apartment later that night, feeling restless and edgy. He knew the reason, but there was nothing he could do about it until Angelique learned to trust him, to trust her feelings for him. That might take a while. In the meantime, he was sleeping alone and waking up as hard as a rock.

He sipped his wine. His father was right. He was going to a great deal of trouble just for a date, but he didn't regret the elaborate planning if it brought the results he hoped for.

The doorbell rang just as the mantle clock on the marble fireplace struck eleven. He'd had late visitors before, but they usually called first. Setting the flute on the glass coffee table as he passed, he went to the door and opened it.

Angelique stalked inside, then whirled on him. She looked magnificent with fire in her eyes and he instinctively knew the perfect way for her to release all that energy. "You must think I'm an imbecile."

He closed the door and locked it. Now that she was there, he didn't plan for her to leave until morning.

Her gaze flicked to the lock and then back to him. "You set up everything." She folded her arms. "The cones set out for the van should have tipped me off sooner. Kristen wouldn't have given you their phone number. How did you find them?"

Since she wasn't throwing things, he figured he was relatively safe. "I called all the Howards until I located them."

"You mean your secretary did?"

"*I* called," he said. Somehow it had been important that he did so.

Her delicate eyebrows shot up. "People don't like being manipulated."

"What made you finally figure it out?" he asked, picking up his wine, trying to keep himself from breaking down and begging her to stay.

She took the wine from his hand and drank. "The more I thought about it, the more implausible it seemed that my family just happened to come up and they just happened to drive by Jacques's home when you happened to be outside and had a party going on."

"David called when they arrived at your apartment," he confessed, taking it as a good sign that she hadn't dashed the wine in his face.

"And your relatives. What did you tell them?"

That had been the one easy part of his scheme. "That a woman had dumped me and, if they wanted to see her, be at Dad's house Saturday afternoon."

She drained the glass, set it on the table, and went to him. "You know what that makes you?"

Maybe he could duck if she swung. "No."

"A very special man," she said, her voice trembling. "I was a fool. If you give me another chance I promise to do better this time."

His first instinct was to grab her and rush to his bed . . . if he could make it that far. "Are you going to try and save me again?"

She began unbuttoning his shirt. "You can take care of yourself."

There was something that he wanted to ask, but she began kissing his chest. His body heated; his brain shut down. He pulled her to him and devoured her lips.

He had been right. They didn't make it to the bedroom.

Angelique woke up in Damien's arms. They'd finally made it to his massive four-poster. The drapes were drawn. Moonlight splayed across their entwined, satiated bodies. She felt contented and delicious. "I guess I should go."

He rolled on top of her. "If you think you're leaving, you're crazy."

Her arms clasped him around the neck. "Kristen and I always go to church together. I need to call her."

"Later."

"Later," she repeated as his mouth and body took hers.

Kristen had been up a couple of hours when Angelique called. Hearing the happiness in her friend's voice, she bit back the need to ask her to come home because they needed to talk. "I'll see you when I see you. Good-bye."

Kristen slowly hung up the phone and went back to the bathroom and picked up the home pregnancy kit. If the advertisement was right, it could tell if you were pregnant twenty-four hours after you missed your first period.

Her period should have started this morning. It hadn't.

No matter how many times she counted and rechecked the calendar, the results were always the same. No matter how stressed she was, her menstrual cycle was like clockwork. Not even when her father died or when Adam was blinded by the carjackers or when she'd broken up with Eric had it varied.

Kristen lifted her head and stared at her pale, scared reflection in the bathroom mirror. She didn't need the test to tell her what her body had already told her. She was pregnant with Rafe's child.

Her hand curved around her stomach. Part of her wanted the baby, the other part was afraid of what it would do to Rafe. He'd blame and hate himself. With his father dying, he didn't need one more thing pushing him to the edge.

She gripped the edge of the vanity. She didn't know how she'd face him tomorrow night, but she had to. They were finishing up this week. If she could just act normally, he'd never know.

"You're not coming up," Angelique said firmly, her hands against Damien's chest.

"I won't stay long," Damien said, biting her lower lip while his body pinned hers lightly against her ten-year-old Toyota.

She shivered. Every time he'd touched her they ended up making love at his apartment. From the blunt arousal she felt against her stomach, the same thing would happen if they went to her apartment. "I'm not falling for that again. It's 6:15 pm. I should have been home hours ago."

"Thirty minutes."

Feeling herself weakening, she kissed him on the cheek and ducked under his arm. "I'll see you Wednesday at eight."

"I thought we said six," he told her with a grin.

She blew him a kiss. "Get out of here while I still have some will power left." Waving, she entered her apartment building. She'd missed almost an entire day of writing on her dissertation, but she felt energized and ready to take on the world. She punched the elevator button and stepped on.

Love did that to you, she thought. She didn't shy away from the truth. She'd done enough of that. She loved Damien and knew he cared. For now that was enough.

Passing Kristen's door, she rang the doorbell to let her know she was home. She was smiling when the door opened. It faded when she saw Kristen's drawn, tear-stained face. She entered, shoving the door closed behind her. "What is it?"

Kristen bit her lower lip. "I'm pregnant."

Angelique's eyes widened in shock. She pulled Kristen into her arms. Questions swirled around in her head. One she didn't have to ask was who the father was.

Kristen sat propped in her brass bed, drinking the tea Angelique had prepared for her. She'd told Angelique everything. "I can't tell him."

"You can't hide it forever." Angelique sat on the edge of the bed.

"It'll just be for a little while." Her delicate cup rattled against the saucer. "He's going through so much with his father."

"And being pregnant, you're not?"

Kristen drew in a shaky breath. "I have friends and family to turn to. He doesn't."

"Because he's chosen to live that way." Angelique put her hand on

Kristen's knee. "I know about shutting people out. You're miserable, but you'd rather chew your fingers off than admit it. It takes time and love to change that. Being pregnant, you don't have time."

"I have to believe it will all work out. I don't think I could stand it if it didn't," she said, her voice thin and shaky.

Resigned, Angelique took the cup and stood. "Slide under the covers and get some rest. I'll go get the laptop and work in the living room."

"You don't have to do that." Kristen scooted down in bed.

"Stop talking and go to sleep. I'll be here if you need me." Standing, Angelique started from the room.

"I'm glad you and Damien worked it out."

"Sleep." Angelique snapped off the overhead light. *Rafe, if you don't get it together, I have a nice fire-ant bed I'm going to introduce you to.*

He had finally managed to drive her away.

All night, Kristen had avoided looking at him. She made excuses to work with Jim as she'd done all week. At least he could see her eyes and assure himself that she hadn't been crying.

He woke at night, worried about her. Scared she was pregnant, and how that would affect her life. Worried that she wouldn't tell him if she was. Worried that if she was and later married, how the baby's stepfather would treat it.

The boys were all excited about finishing their boxes; Kristen hadn't said a word about hers. Maybe that was for the best. "You've all done a wonderful job. I'm proud of each of you and your plan to take shop when school starts in the fall. I know you'll do well."

The young men high-fived. Kristen's smile was so brief he wasn't sure that he hadn't imagined it. "You all right?"

"Yes," she answered. To the teenagers, she said, "Let's go. I'm sure Jacques and your families are anxious to see your boxes. Don't forget to thank Rafe."

The boys shook Rafe's hand, thanking him profusely. When he looked up, Kristen was gone.

• • •

Rafe didn't drink, but he figured that if it would dull the pain, he'd give it a try. He popped the top of the beer can and guzzled it down despite the bitter taste. Maybe if he drank enough of the stuff he'd be able to forget that he was following in his father's malicious footsteps.

Like his father had always told him, he'd ruin anything he touched. He'd tried to help Kristen, but he'd ended up bringing her nothing but pain and heartache. She'd given him so much and he had repaid her by taking something precious and irreplaceable from her.

He was his father's son. His legacy to anyone who loved him would be suffering and misery. He took another swallow and held the can to his mouth until it was empty.

He popped another tab. He didn't plan to stop until the six-pack was gone. Maybe then he wouldn't feel like ripping off his skin—anything to make the pain go away.

As his unsteady hand popped the top of the last can, Rafe discovered that no matter how much he drank, the pain was there to stay.

Maurice grumbled about the high fare from the airport when the cab dropped him in front of his home Friday evening, but he paid the driver, who unceremoniously dumped his Louis Vuitton luggage on the driveway and drove off.

"Prick." Maurice considered leaving his bags for the maid to pick up, but finally hefted the three pieces of heavy luggage. If Mia wasn't there, he'd have to deal with the uppity cook and he was feeling too good to let a confrontation with that dried-up prune ruin it.

The last two weeks had been the way he'd always dreamed of living. Wherever he'd gone, he'd been treated with respect and deference, pampered in luxury. Mentioning the Thibodeaux name had given him entree into the inner circle in every city he visited.

The only problem had been that he hadn't been able to get a little on the side. Last night Claudette had called and asked him to come home. He was almost looking forward to screwing her.

Dropping his luggage, he stuck his key in the lock and frowned when it wouldn't work. He pulled the key out just as the door opened.

"Good evening, Mr. Laurent," Mia said nervously.

Maurice got hard just looking at the luscious little maid's firm body. He'd yet to get more than a few feels from her. "Get my luggage. Where is my wife?"

"On the grounds, I think, sir."

"Leave them and come with me." Knowing she was too scared not to follow orders, he walked away. He got harder just thinking about sliding into her.

He opened the study door and glanced back. The stupid girl was wringing her hands. "Come here."

"Sir, please." Tears sparkled in her big, brown eyes.

"If you value your job, you'll come here." The crying annoyed him, but he'd have to overlook it since he needed a piece and she was handy.

When she was within arm's length, he grabbed her arms and pulled her inside the study. Then he slammed her back against the closed door.

"Please, Mr. Laurent, no!" Eyes closed, she tried to twist away.

"Shut up!" Maurice snapped. His hand closed roughly over her small breast.

"Turn her loose, Maurice."

Maurice stilled: dread made his blood run cold. He spun around. Standing behind her father's desk was Claudette, coldly furious.

thirty

❦

Seeing all his hard work and sacrifice disappearing, he started toward Claudette, hands outstretched, to lie his way out of it the way he'd always done. Two heavyset, broad-shouldered men merged out of the shadows. Maurice pulled up short. Both were dressed in black business suits, but their eyes were flat. "What's going on?"

Ignoring him, a livid Claudette came around the desk and crossed the room to Mia, who had her head down, crying. The man nearest Claudette accompanied her.

Maurice saw all his plans evaporate over a worthless woman. "It's her fault. She's been after me since I came here," he shouted. "I was just trying to teach her a lesson so she'd leave me alone."

The young woman's head came up. Her teary eyes widened as she looked at Claudette. "I didn't. I swear!"

Claudette placed a gentle hand on the woman's trembling shoulder. "I'm sorry. Has . . . has this happened before?"

Shame flushed her cheeks. She tucked her head. "He threatened to have me fired."

"She's lying!" Maurice started toward Claudette, but the burly, clean-shaven man with her blocked his path. "What are they doing here?"

Once again, Claudette ignored Maurice. Instead she spoke to the man standing close to her. "Mr. Thomas, please take Mia to the kitchen and have Bridget look after her, then ask Simon to drive her home." Claudette looked back at Mia. "I'm sorry, Mia. More than you'll ever know. You have my word that it won't happen again."

Opening the door to the study, Claudette stepped aside. "Please go with this man. I'll call you later to see how you're doing."

The young woman nodded, then allowed the man to take her arm and lead her away.

Closing the door, Claudette went behind her desk and picked up a manila folder filled with a two-inch-thick stack of papers. "This," she said to Maurice, "is a complete file on you from your birth in Akron to a middle-class, hard-working couple who kicked you out when you were seventeen for dealing drugs, to your arrest for embezzlement in Atlanta sixteen months ago."

Sweat popped out on Maurice's forehead. *Damn.* "My parents were just being hateful. I was never charged with anything. My record is clean."

Claudette threw the file on the desk in disgust. "Only because the actual embezzlement was done by an employee of the insurance firm. My information says you talked her out of implicating you, but the theft was your idea."

"That's a lie!" Maurice yelled, his mouth as dry as cotton.

"That's not what she says, is it, Mr. Lawson?"

"No, Ms. Thibodeaux, it's not," Lawson said, his soft voice a glaring contrast to his brawny build and cold eyes. "She said he promised to help secure her release, but he disappeared two weeks after she was convicted and sent to prison. She said she's been trying to contact him ever since, but he didn't show up until three weeks ago after she warned his cousin that if he didn't, he'd be sorry."

She'd threatened him, all right. He thought he had conned her into keeping her mouth shut by telling her he was working on a deal that would make them rich. Once he had the money, he'd get a high-priced attorney and get her out. She just had to give him a little time. He'd lied, of course. The door behind him opened and the other man came back and positioned himself on the other side of Claudette.

"Bodyguards? You think I'd hurt you?" Perhaps he could still talk his way out of this . . . if he could get her alone.

Claudette simply stared at him. "You lied from the start. You even charmed DeLois in Human Resources at Thibodeaux out of doing an employee or reference check on you. Your surname might be French, but you learned the language from one of your many lovers." Her voice chilled. "A trapped animal is unpredictable."

His mouth hardened. "You didn't think that when I was on top of you!"

Both men started toward him. Claudette simply raised her hand and they stopped. But if looks could kill, Maurice knew he would be knocking on the gates of hell. He loosened his tie. "I'm sorry, honey, you caught me off guard. Send these men away and we'll straighten this out."

Opening the folder, she took out a sheet of paper and placed it on the desk so he could see it. "And how do you propose we straighten out your marriage to Ann?"

Shit. He gulped.

"You married her so she couldn't testify against you—then you left the city and came here. There is no record of a divorce."

"I-I . . ."

Claudette talked over him. "Please show this person out of my house and make sure he takes nothing bought with my money."

Maurice's eyes bugged; he started backing up. "You can't do that! How am I supposed to get back to the city? What about all my clothes, my car?"

"See that he gets the essentials." Claudette settled into her father's chair. The fit was perfect.

"Think of the gossip!" Maurice warned. "I'll sell the story to every tabloid in the country," he threatened when they grabbed him by the arms and pulled him toward the door. "You'll be the butt of jokes across the country."

"But I'll be free of a leech like you." Claudette leaned back and folded her arms. "Which *you* may not be, if Ann Young has her way. Seems she won't need to testify if the police find certain incriminating evidence against you. That wasn't your first illegal operation."

"No! Stop! You can't do this!" he screamed as they pulled him out the front door. His humiliation was complete when Mia, Simon, and Bridget watched as he was stripped down to his black silk briefs, then tossed a pair of faded jeans and a grubby sweatshirt.

• • •

Kristen knew what Rafe was going to say before he opened his mouth. Her hand clenched her pen as he came through the gallery door just after they opened on Saturday morning. She could only be grateful there weren't any customers and that Jacques was in the back unpacking a shipment. "Hello, Rafe."

He stuck his hands into his pockets, then pulled them out again. "Hello—I came to see if . . . if everything is all right."

She gripped the pen and held his tortured gaze. "I'm fine."

His stance rigid, his eyes desolate, he asked, "You . . . you aren't pregnant?"

"No, I'm not." She barely managed to get the words out without sobbing.

Relief washed across his face. "I been thinking that it's probably best that we don't see each other anymore. I'll be busy and you'll be busy with your job and everything."

Her nostrils stung. She swallowed. "All right."

He nodded, looking lost and alone. "If you ever need me though, you call."

"I'll be fine." She picked up his business cards on the desk and handed them to him. "I want you to have the rest."

His large hand closed around the cards. Her heart cried out for him. "Good-bye, Kristen."

The door closed. She watched him walk away and felt as if her heart was being wrenched from her body. Tears rolled down her cheeks. Her eyes shut in pain and misery.

The door opened. Her lids snapped up. It was Claudette, not Rafe. Kristen tried to stand, but her legs wouldn't support her. She let the tears flow.

"Kristen, I'm sorry. I'm not here to cause you any problems," Claudette rushed to say. "I've come to apologize. I've spoken to Marvin, and you can have your old job at the museum back."

"What's going on here?" Jacques asked, coming from the back of the gallery.

"I came to apologize," Claudette said, standing by Kristen's chair. "I'm afraid I've made things worse."

"You mean you finally see Maurice for the user he is?" Jacques asked, but he was kneeling in front of Kristen. "Rafe?"

"Yes," Kristen said, her voice trembling as violently as her body.

"I understand," Jacques said with a wealth of meaning. "Go home and try it tomorrow."

"I can't stay here. I'm going home. To Shreveport." She took her purse from her bottom desk drawer and stood. Her teary eyes pleaded for his understanding. "I'm sorry."

Coming to his feet, Jacques waved her words aside. "I'll take you home."

Kristen shook her head. "I'll be fine. You can't close the gallery."

"I can."

"I can stay here," Claudette offered.

Both looked at her.

"You don't have to. I can manage." Kristen extended her hand to Claudette. "Thank you for coming to see me and for clearing my name with Dr. Robertson."

Claudette took her hand and held it securely. "I'm just sorry there was a need and that you had to go through this."

"If I hadn't, I wouldn't have gotten to know Rafe better." Her smile unbearably sad, she left.

"I feel responsible for her," Claudette said, watching Kristen, her head bent, walk down the street.

"You shouldn't. You were as much a victim as anyone," Jacques told her.

"I was a fool."

"You were lonely and vulnerable," Jacques said, hoping no one came into the gallery until he could tell her what was on his mind.

"Gossip is going to run rampant when this gets out." She told him everything. "The Thibodeaux name will be dragged through the mud."

"Why don't you give them something to talk about?" He took her hand, felt it jerk in his. "Have dinner with me tonight. In fact, how does your schedule look for the next twenty or thirty years?"

"What?"

"I love you," he said without hesitation. "I didn't realize it until it was too late."

Claudette's heart thumped. She was attracted to Jacques, felt comfortable with him, but was that enough to build on? "Jacques, I don't know. I haven't had much luck with men."

The gallery door opened and a couple entered. Jacques immediately went to them. "There's an emergency and I have to close." He pulled a card from his pocket and scribbled in it. "My card—and I'm offering a forty percent discount on your purchase as my way of an apology."

"Thank you, we'll certainly be back."

Jacques closed the door and flipped the "closed" sign. "Where were we?"

"No one has ever put me ahead of business," she said softly.

"That's because you hadn't met the right man," Jacques said. "James and Maurice don't count."

Shock crossed her face. "You knew about James?"

"We were at a party together a week before he died. He'd been drinking and I took him home. He told me about your marrying secretly, but he had to agree to an annulment or your parents would have filed charges against him because he was twenty-one and you were sixteen."

Stunned by the revelation, her eyes widened in disbelief.

Jacques never suspected she hadn't known. Taking her by the arm, he gently urged her to a chair in front of Kristen's desk. "He loved you, Claudette. A private detective your father hired found you the day after you eloped. James said you were the only one who ever believed in him."

"I thought he had used me." She gazed up at him with misery in her eyes. "I thought I had made another mistake with Maurice just as I had with James." She shook her head, still trying to take it all in. "How could they have done that to me? To him?"

"Your parents were very rigid in their beliefs and what they wanted for their daughter." Jacques leaned back against the corner of the desk and folded his arms. "They didn't think James was good enough. They might have been right. He tried to straighten up, but the night he was killed in the one-car accident, he'd been drinking and using drugs."

Her hands clutched in her lap. "I might have saved him."

"Or he might have taken you down with him. Your parents were only doing what they thought was best. It's tough being a parent," he said thoughtfully.

Claudette looked at him. "Damien is wonderful. I'm proud to have him working for me."

"Thank you," Jacques said. "It wasn't easy. He was rebellious as a teenager."

Her lips curved and she relaxed against the chair. "He still is."

Jacques's arms fell to his sides. "What do you mean?"

Claudette could smile about it now, although at the time she had been annoyed with Damien. "He came to me last week and told me he was dating Angelique, that she had worked her way though two years of undergrad school as an exotic dancer and if I had a problem with it, he'd see me in court if I tried to fire him."

Jacques grinned. "That's my boy. He does make me proud."

Her face softened. "He had a good example."

He caught her hand and hunkered down in front of her, saying a little prayer that he could get back up without embarrassing himself. "Does that mean you're going to go out to dinner with me tonight?"

Her hand trembled in his. It surprised her how much she wanted to go. "Jacques, I just threw my hus—Maurice out of my house, but I still feel like a married woman."

"You're not, and that's all the more reason to go out and celebrate." He kissed her hand. "We're not as young as we used to be. We wait too long and the parts might not work." .

She blushed and then laughed. "Jacques."

He picked up her other hand. "It's good hearing you laugh again."

"There hasn't been much to laugh about lately." Maurice had made her feel desire, but he had never given her laughter. She had a feeling Jacques could give her both. "I don't know."

"Stop thinking about what your father would have wanted, what people will say," he told her, a hint of frustration creeping into his voice. "Do what *you* want."

Her hands trembled even more in his. "I haven't done a very good job of that in the past."

"That's because you haven't had me," he coaxed. "What do you say we give us a try?"

Claudette stared down into his warm brown eyes. Jacques was one of the most honorable and dependable men she knew. Deceit wasn't in his nature. "If I say no, will you ask me in a couple of weeks?"

"Yes."

She smiled and felt a lightness in her heart she hadn't felt in a very long time. "Then ask me and we'll see."

Kristen ran an errand, called Angelique, then caught the 4:30 flight out of New Orleans. Even though she was routed through Houston, the taxi pulled up in front of her mother's and Jonathan's home in Shreveport shortly before seven that evening.

Picking up her small carry-on, she started up the curved driveway to the sprawling one-story ranch house nestled among towering oaks and rang the doorbell. They had wanted to give her a key, but she hadn't wanted to impose on their privacy.

Kristen rubbed her hand up and down on her white trousers. She hadn't called. She had no idea if her mother was at home or at one of her many volunteer meetings. Kristen's hand clenched, and she glanced back toward the street. The likelihood of a taxi passing was slim to none. She was about to sit in the red deacon's bench on the wide porch when she heard the lock turn.

Eleanor's eyes went from elation to concern on seeing her daughter. In less time than it took Kristen to draw in an unsteady breath, she found herself enveloped in her mother's arms, breathing the scent that was uniquely hers. She held on and let the tears flow.

"Honey, you're home now. I'm here. Whatever it is, I'm here." Somehow, Eleanor managed to get a sobbing Kristen and her luggage inside to a Queen Anne chair in the living room off the foyer. They sat in the same cushioned seat until her tears quieted.

Kristen opened her purse for a tissue and dried her cheeks. "I didn't mean to cry all over you."

"Honey, what is it?" Eleanor asked, smoothing Kristen's hair back from her face.

"I'm pregnant." The story poured out. By the time she finished, she was digging in her purse for another tissue. "I love Rafe so much, but my love only brings him pain."

Furious, Eleanor muttered under her breath about a part of Rafe's anatomy that she'd like to bring a little pain to and prevent him from fathering another child.

"Mother, please don't hate him," Kristen pleaded, then tucked her head. "It was only that one time. We both . . . it wasn't his fault. I went to his place." She finally looked up. "He believes in his father's legacy of cruelty more than he believes in us."

"Come on, let's get you in bed and I'll bring you some tea," Eleanor said. She felt happiness at the thought of Kristen having a baby and anger that the father hadn't cared enough to stand by her and share what should have been a joyous occasion.

"He's making you a tea caddy for your birthday." Kristen swallowed hard. "He made me a writing box. I forgot it. His work is beautiful."

Eleanor didn't trust herself to say anything. She helped Kristen to her feet and into the bedroom she used when she stayed with them. After putting her to bed, Eleanor went into the kitchen and picked up the phone. "Jonathan, please don't be in surgery."

He answered on the third ring. "Dr. Delacroix."

"Oh, Jonathan!" Eleanor cried, her arms circling her waist as she leaned her head against the white cabinet.

"What's the matter, Eleanor?" Jonathan asked, his usually calm and self-assured voice rising in anxiety.

"It's our baby. I just put her to bed after she cried her heart out." Eleanor reached for a napkin and dabbed the moisture from her own eyes. "She's pregnant with Rafe's baby."

"I'm on my way."

"Your patients—"

"Can be rescheduled or seen by Malcolm or Gerald," he said, referring to the two associates in his practice. "What kind of man would I be if I took care of another man's family and neglected mine?"

"I love you," she said quietly.

"Love you, too."

Eleanor hung up the phone, debating if she should call Adam and ask him to come. He and Kristen had always been close. Perhaps he could help, but she had a bad feeling that only Rafe could take away Kristen's misery. Eleanor had always liked him. She had been in the courtroom in Little Elm when he'd shown the judge the scars on his back to help Lilly win her divorce case. There was something lonely about him that pulled at you, but at the moment she wanted to make a eunuch out of him without anesthesia.

The phone rang while she was debating what to do. She quickly lifted the receiver. *Rafe, let this be you.* "Hello."

"Hello, Mother, it's Adam."

Eleanor tensed. There was no mistaking the distress in his voice. "What is it? Is Adam Jr. sick again?"

"Myron is dying and he's asking for Lilly," Adam said flatly. "She insists on going and I refuse to let her go by herself. We're waiting on the cab."

Lilly's ex-husband continued to cause problems for her family. "You're right to go with her. You want to drop Adam Jr. off here?"

"No. She needs him."

"And you," Eleanor said, understanding completely. *You needed your loved ones around you even more in a crisis.* "This won't be easy for her."

Adam snorted. "He wants her forgiveness so he can die in peace— never mind all the hell he put her through or the pain seeing him will cause. I can understand why Rafe refuses to go."

Eleanor's grip on the phone tightened. "Have you spoken with him today?"

"Lilly's tried several times but she keeps getting his machine," he told her. "We'll call when we reach Houston. We're staying at the Wyndham. There's the cab. Let Kristen know, will you? I think she and Rafe have become pretty close."

"Yes?" *What an understatement. Rafe, I could cheerfully strangle you for doing this to Kristen, for making her miserable at a time when she should be happy and celebrating.*

" 'Bye, Mother."

"Good-bye. Take care." Eleanor hung up the phone. Adam and Lilly had enough to deal with without being worried about Kristen.

The back door leading from the kitchen to the garage opened. Jonathan came in with his arms wide, reaching for her. With a muffled cry, Eleanor sought the shelter and comfort of his embrace.

thirty-one

❧

It was almost ten when Rafe returned home Saturday night. He slowed down to make the turn to his place. His thoughts were troubled. For the first time, he hadn't experienced a sense of pride and accomplishment when making a delivery. He hadn't cared about the praise or the offer of referrals or even the check he'd tucked absently in his shirt pocket. All he could think about was Kristen and the devastated look on her face when he said good-bye.

It was like a knife to his gut. She'd thank him one day, but now she had to hate him for taking her virginity and leaving her with nothing, not even a kiss good-bye.

Rafe saw the motion light had been triggered before his truck straightened on the mile-long driveway. He wasn't concerned. A small animal could activate it. As he neared his shop, he saw the beat-up station wagon. Frowning, he pulled up just as a slender young man jumped out of the front seat. He appeared to be in his early twenties and wore a black-and-white striped shirt.

"Hi, your name Rafe?"

"Yes, can I help you?"

"I got a delivery for you. Kinda hoping you'd be a little longer. She's paying me to wait as long as it takes." He opened the back door and leaned down. "Wake up and come here." He straightened and turned with a fat, black puppy and promptly handed the animal to Rafe.

Automatically, Rafe accepted the dog. His calloused hand unconsciously, gently stroked the shivering animal. "What are you doing?"

"I told you. Making a delivery." The young man grinned, patting the dog on its broad head. "She paid me twenty dollars an hour to wait.

Said she didn't want to leave him in a cage or anything." He glanced around cautiously. "You don't really have an alligator around here, do you?"

Rafe tensed. "Kristen sent you?"

"Yeah, that's her. Some babe, ain't she?"

At Rafe's hard look, the young man backed up with both hands outstretched. "Just making an observation, man. She wasn't paying attention to me or any of the guys. She was just looking for him." He pointed to the puppy. "He's pure Lab. Protective and loves water. He'll be good company for you, she said."

Even hurting, she'd thought of him. He deserved to rot in hell. "I don't want him." Rafe tried to hand the animal back.

Hands upraised, the young man took another step back. "No can do. She said you might try to give him back. He's bought and paid for. Besides, she gave me an extra fifty to make sure he stays. Wouldn't wanna upset the lady any more now, would you?"

That caught Rafe's attention more than the soft lick on his hand. "She was upset?"

"Crying like a faucet." The deliveryman opened the car door. "Women get emotional over the strangest things. I better be going." He handed Rafe a thick envelope with his free hand. "His papers, shots, diet, and all that good stuff. You'd be surprised what stupid things people feed puppies." He slipped inside the station wagon. "Any problems, our number is on the front of the envelope."

Rafe gazed at the fading taillights, then down at the dog that had gone to sleep in his arms. How had she known that he'd always wanted a dog? His father had coon dogs, but they were for hunting, not for playing with. "I can't keep you."

He'd have to take him back. He climbed into his truck.

Seventeen minutes later, Rafe rang Kristen's doorbell. The sleeping puppy in his arms didn't stir at the sound. Impatiently, he rang again. He glanced at his watch: 10:32. She had to be at home. The thought went through his mind that she might suspect it was him and just not answer. He didn't blame her.

Determined to leave the dog, he went next door to Angelique's. She could take care of the animal until morning. He wasn't becoming attached to another thing he'd have to give up. Kristen was enough.

The door opened. Angelique stood there, with Damien directly behind her. Neither appeared happy to see him. "Hi, Angelique. Kristen didn't answer. I need you to keep him until morning." He held the dog out to her.

Angelique folded her arms over her black top. "Kristen gave him to you."

"I can't keep him." Just like he couldn't keep Kristen.

"You'll have to see Kristen about that."

Regret entered his voice. "She won't answer the door."

"She isn't there to answer it."

"Where is she?" he asked, fear shooting through him as he whipped his head back around toward her door.

"Shreveport."

He whirled back around. "Shreveport? Is everything all right?"

"She just wanted to be around people who loved her unconditionally."

Rafe winced and drew the puppy closer to his chest. "When is she coming back?"

"I don't know. She quit her job."

Rafe shut his eyes. He'd done it again. Forced her to leave another job.

A gentle hand on his arm caused his eyes to snap open. "Kristen cares about you. If you care about her, you know where to find her in Shreveport."

"She's better off without me," he said, each word more painful than the last.

"Kristen doesn't think so." Angelique reached out to stroke the dozing puppy. "She didn't want you to be by yourself ever again."

It was best that he stay by himself. Kristen had learned that the hard way. "He'll be all over the shop and into everything." He tried again to give the dog to Angelique. "You keep him."

"There's a no-animal rule in my sublease," she told him, looking not the least bit unhappy about the restriction.

Rafe looked at Damien.

"Sorry, man." Damien held up both hands, palms out. "Same rule in my building."

"What am I going to do with him?" Rafe asked quietly, then looked down at the puppy.

"I'm sure you'll figure it out," Angelique said with an encouraging smile.

Looking a bit dazed, Rafe walked away.

Angelique watched Rafe walk as if every step were an effort as she felt Damien's arms go around her waist. "They're both hurting."

"You gave him something to think about." He nuzzled her ear.

"You helped." She turned in his arms, backed him inside, closed the door, and kissed him. "You've seen Mrs. King next door with her silky terrier."

He gathered her closer. "I like Kristen and want her to have what we have."

Angelique's heart hammered in her chest. "It wasn't easy."

"Someone once said nothing worthwhile ever is."

She smiled up at him, loving him more each time she saw him. "They could certainly be talking about us in some ways, but in others we don't have any problems," she said, feeling his hardness pressing against her.

"You do have that effect on me." He stared deep into her eyes. "I love you."

The room swirled. Angelique fought off the dizziness and gripped his arms. "W-what did you say?"

"I love you," he repeated softly, finding the words were as easy the second time as they had been the first. There wasn't the slightest urge to run for the door. He could spend the rest of his days with this woman and die a happy man. When it was right, it was easy. "I want to wake up with you in the morning and go to sleep at night with you in my arms."

She swallowed. Swallowed again, then drew in a deep breath. "You want us to move in together?"

"That's what married people do, isn't it?"

Tears streamed down her cheeks.

Alarm and fear gripped him. "Please don't say no! I never knew I could love as deeply and completely as I love you."

She grabbed him around the neck, squeezing him, laughing and crying. "I never thought . . . I hoped . . . I prayed . . . I love you so much."

Damien didn't mind in the least that she had a death grip on his neck. "So your answer would be . . ."

She leaned back, grinning at him. "Yes."

"Do we call your parents or my father first?"

"We can do a three-way and tell them together—then afterwards I have plans for you."

Rafe sat in his truck for a long time outside Kristen's apartment, just holding the puppy, before he settled the sleeping animal next to his thigh and started the motor. He turned onto Canal Street and headed for the freeway. He saw the sign for I-20, the way to Shreveport. Gripping the steering wheel, he kept going.

At his apartment, he found a box for the puppy, padded it with a couple of his old shirts, put the animal inside, then sat down beside the box in the kitchen. His hand was on the animal, but his mind was on Kristen.

He could give her nothing. She was better off without him. He kept telling himself that until he couldn't take it any longer.

Picking up the box, he came to his feet. "Come on, we have a trip to make."

Rafe pulled up in front of Kristen's parents' rambling, single-story house just as dawn broke. The exclusive neighborhood was quiet except for the occasional bark of a dog. Rubbing his hand over his face, Rafe cast a glance at Sleepy. He hadn't meant to name the dog—naming meant establishing a connection, and he wasn't keeping him.

He had been on the highway for almost four hours, stopping only for gas and a doggy break because if he didn't see Kristen soon he felt as if his soul would die.

When he did see her, what was he going to say? Here's your dog back? I'm rejecting him just like I rejected you? Sorry I ruined your life?

He glanced at his watch: 6 A.M. Her stepfather was a doctor. Shouldn't he be up early to get to his office or make rounds? Hoping that was the case and that they wouldn't throw him out, he got out of the truck, closing the door softly so as not to wake the puppy.

Knowing he'd choke if he thought about it, he rang the doorbell, then stuck his nervous hands in his pockets. The door opened. His hands came out of his pockets. At least her stepfather was up.

Jonathan wore a crisp white shirt, charcoal slacks, and a gray tie. From the hard glare he sent Rafe, he wasn't too pleased to see him this early in the morning, even if he *was* up. Leaving didn't cross Rafe's mind. "Good morning, Jonathan. I came to see Kristen."

Jonathan saw the haggard look on Rafe's face and decided against rearranging it. "Come in."

"Who is it, Jonathan?" Eleanor said as she came around the corner. Her surprised gaze matched her husband's when she saw Rafe. *He looked terrible.*

Rafe snatched the baseball cap from his head. "Good morning, Mrs. Delacroix. Is it all right if I see Kristen?"

Eleanor looked at her husband. A silent message passed between them. She looked back at Rafe. "Did you just arrive?"

"Yes, ma'am," he said, his gaze searching behind her.

"When was the last time you slept?" Jonathan asked as he closed the door.

Rafe shrugged. "You think she's up?"

"I'll get her," Eleanor said. "Take Rafe to the kitchen and pour some coffee in him before he falls down."

"I don't want to put you to any trouble," he said, but Eleanor had already disappeared.

"Come on, Rafe." Jonathan took him by the arm. "You'll learn as you get older that arguing with a woman is a waste of time and effort."

Rafe didn't answer, just looked in the direction Eleanor had disappeared.

• • •

"Kristen, wake up." Eleanor gently touched Kristen's shoulder. "Rafe's here."

The sleepiness in her eyes vanished. She came upright. "Rafe's here?"

"Yes. He's in the kitchen with Jonathan." Eleanor helped Kristen into her heavy silk, peach-colored robe. "He looks terrible. It's the only thing that kept Jonathan from beating him to a pulp—and my trying to help."

"I love him, Mother," Kristen said, then rushed out the door.

Seeing him sitting at the kitchen table staring morosely into his coffee cup, she pulled to a halt. She'd never wanted to see him unhappy again. "Rafe."

He jerked his head up. His eyes widened. He came out of the padded side chair so fast it toppled over. He didn't notice that, or Jonathan leaving the room with Eleanor. Rafe never slowed in his mad dash to reach Kristen. "What's the matter?" He gently palmed her cheeks, his gaze quickly running over her. "You sick?"

With her eyes red and puffy from crying, no make-up, and her hair like a bird's nest, she probably looked terrible. "I'm pregnant."

Rafe's eyes went round. The brief sparkle of happiness in his eyes died instantly. Releasing her, he stepped back. "No. No you can't be."

"I am," she said, her voice thick with unshed tears. "I haven't been to the doctor yet, but I know. I'm never late."

"But . . . but . . . you said."

"I lied. I didn't want you to feel responsible or guilty." She swallowed the lump in her throat. "You'd make a wonderful father and I love this baby."

His gaze dropped to her abdomen. He shook his head in denial. When he lifted his eyes they were bleak. "I can't be the father and husband you both deserve."

"Rafe, you are the only man who can be," Kristen told him, her heart breaking for all three of them. "I fell in love with your gentleness as much as your strength and determination to succeed."

"Can't you understand? I can't take the chance that I might be like my father or his father." He swallowed. "I'd die before I hurt you or our baby."

"Rafe, you won't," she told him, catching his trembling hands, tightening her grip when he tried to pull away. "You're so patient with Adam Jr. and the students. You'll make a terrific father and husband."

He tugged again, this time managing to free his hands. "I . . . I'll set up a fund for you and the baby. I . . . I'll have a lawyer contact you."

"Rafe, please! Don't walk away from us," she cried.

His eyes flashed. "You think I want to walk away from you, from the baby we created, from having a normal life? My first memory is of him paddling my backside with his leather belt. I kept screaming for him to stop, but he just kept on beating me all the while, telling me how worthless I was. I couldn't have been more than three." Rafe sucked in a ragged breath. "The only hugs came from my mother . . . if he wasn't around. She feared him as much as she loved him. She'd come to me after he had beat the hell out of me and tell me he didn't mean to leave welts and bruises."

"Rafe." She reached for him.

He held up his hands. "No. I'm not fit to be around you. Goodbye." He left with the sound of Kristen calling his name, her voice choked. Gritting his teeth, he kept walking.

Outside, he opened the truck door and Sleepy unfolded his fat body and wagged his tail in greeting. Rafe picked up the only link to Kristen he'd ever have. He wasn't ever coming back or seeing her again.

The cell phone on his belt loop rang. Automatically, he answered. "Yes."

"Rafe?"

The hesitancy in his stepmother's voice instantly alerted him. "Lilly, what is it?"

"Rafe, I'm at the hospital with Myron," she said, her voice unsteady. "The doctors have only given him a few hours to live. You have to come now."

He clamped his eyes shut, then opened them. "How can you ask that of me?"

"I'm not asking for him, I'm asking for you. You have to let go of the past."

His laughter was ragged. "How can I, when every breath I take reminds me of that sorry SOB."

"Rafe—"

"He took everything from me, Lilly," Rafe said, slumping down on the sidewalk by his truck. "Even my future."

"Not if you don't let him, Rafe. Fight. You've always fought. You never backed down, although there were times I wished you would have. Face Myron. Look him in the eyes, curse him if you have to, then forgive him and get on with your life."

His cheeks were wet. He didn't know if it was from tears or Sleepy's tongue. "No."

"Do you love me?"

There was never any question. "Yes."

"Then catch the night flight here. I want to know that both my sons are happy and free, and Rafe . . . Hurry."

He put his head in his hands, his back against the truck. "Not even for you, Lilly."

Through the sheers in the living room, Kristen watched Rafe. "He's hurting."

Directly behind her were Jonathan and her mother. "He's had a hard life," Jonathan said.

"With his father dying, it's only going to get worse," Eleanor said.

Kristen turned. "What?"

"They didn't expect him to last through the next twenty-four hours when I spoke to Adam yesterday. That was probably Lilly on the phone."

"Oh, no!" Kristen hurried outside and down the sidewalk. The silk robe billowed around her as she sank to her knees in front of him. "Rafe."

He looked up with hollow eyes. "I hate the bastard."

"Then tell him and get on with your life." Picking up the puppy, she stood and stretched her hand out to him. "Come on inside. We'll check the schedule and take the next flight out to Houston."

"Kristen."

"We're going," she said firmly. "No matter what. Friends help friends. Lilly needs you."

Slowly he got to his feet and took her hand.

thirty-two

While Kristen showered and dressed, Eleanor coaxed Rafe into using the guest bathroom to shower and shave, and suggested he borrow some clothes from Jonathan. She had been prepared to hate him until she'd seen the pain and anguish in his face when he looked at Kristen. He wasn't trying to run a game; he actually believed he wasn't good enough to be a father and husband.

She fed them both breakfast that neither wanted, but each managed a few bites to get the other to eat. Eleanor remember only one other time that came close to the helplessness she felt, and that had been when Adam lost his sight.

"It's time to leave for the airport," Jonathan said.

Rafe tensed. For a moment, Eleanor thought he'd bolt or refuse to go. Kristen came around the pedestal table and extended her hand. He took it and stood to his feet. "You sure you feel up to coming?"

"I'm fine." Kristen squeezed his hand. "Mother and Jonathan will take care of your puppy."

He nodded and looked at the puppy sleeping in a box in the corner. "Thank you."

"No problem." Jonathan opened the kitchen door leading to the garage.

Rafe swallowed and allowed Kristen to lead him from the room. In the back seat, he held her hand. He didn't release it until he was seated on the plane and he had to fasten his seat belt.

"I'm here, Rafe," Kristen said.

His hand flexed on the seat handle. "I don't want to go. He made my life a living hell."

Kristen circled her arm around his shoulder as best she could. "You're not going for him."

Rafe felt the airplane taxi down the runway and gripped the armrest. His stomach was in knots, and it wasn't because he was flying for the first time. He hated his father's guts. He didn't want to see him again, to remember his helplessness, remember his pain.

"I'm here. Just remember. You're not alone. I'm here," Kristen reassured.

He swallowed. He'd always been alone. His mother hadn't been able to help him feel differently, nor had his grandmother or Lilly. He'd always felt that he stood apart from everyone . . . until now.

He reached for her hand and held tight. He loved her. He could admit it to himself if never to her. If for no other reason, he'd never forgive his father for condemning him to a life without the woman he loved. Even dying, he continued to take from Rafe, and with his death he'd leave a legacy of hate and cruelty.

M.D. Anderson was a huge complex specializing in the treatment of cancer. The hall was quiet and smelled faintly of disinfectant. The nurses wore printed smocks and tired smiles. They fought a daily battle against death. Sometimes they won. Sometimes they lost.

Rafe stopped outside his father's hospital room door and leaned his head against the wall. "I can't do this."

Kristen moved as close to him as possible, trying to give him her strength. "You've spent the last twelve years proving that you can do anything you set your mind to. Don't let his cruelty defeat you. Please, Rafe."

He twisted his head to one side, saw the tears brimming in her eyes, and pulled her tightly into his arms. "When I was a kid, every time I saw him I remembered how helpless I was. I'd actually feel the belt lash across my back, the pain, and realize how much he hated me."

"Now he's the one helpless and in pain. You're the one with the power." She pushed out of his arms and palmed his face. "Don't let hate destroy your life the same way it destroyed his."

His forehead dropped against hers, then lifted. He stared deep into her eyes, then he caught her hand and pushed open the door.

Lilly was in a chair on one side of the bed, Shayla seated on the other. Standing by her side with his hand on her shoulder was an earnest-looking man in his late twenties wearing glasses. Rafe had never seen Shayla's husband, but he recognized him from his grandmother's description. He returned Rafe's nod as did Shayla, but she didn't move from the chair to greet the brother she hadn't seen or spoken to directly in seven years.

He hadn't expected the regret to hit him so deeply. Another sin to lay at his father's feet. There was no way Adam and Kristen would be this cold to each other, no matter what the circumstances.

"Rafe."

His attention switched to Lilly as she came to her feet. He didn't think he'd ever get used to the new, sophisticated Lilly. The faded dresses she'd worn while married to his father were gone, as was the sadness. Walking toward him was a beautiful, successful woman, her hair in a stylish cut, her steps assured. When she took his free hand in hers, there were no calluses from working to take care of a selfish husband and a dying mother-in-law. Lilly had watched death before.

"Thank you," Lilly said, then spoke to Kristen.

He wrapped his arm around Lilly, pulling her to him. She'd always put others before herself. His father had used her selflessness to keep her chained to him. That chain had been broken with Rafe's grandmother's death. Lilly had loved Mother Crawford more than she had loved herself, but with her death Lilly had finally been able to search for a new life. "I almost didn't come," he finally said.

"The important thing is that you're here." She released him and looked toward the bed. "The doctor said he doesn't have much time." She paused significantly. "The cancer is so far advanced they don't plan any extreme measures."

His hand flexed on Kristen's. They wouldn't try to resuscitate.

Rafe finally did what he had put off for as long as he could. He let his gaze slowly work its way from the foot to the head of the bed. He was stunned by what he saw. Gone was the giant of a man who used his strength to inflict pain and suffering on him and Lilly as the mood struck. In his place was a frail, emaciated man who was little more than ashen-brown skin and bones.

There were no monitors. No IVs. Death had already been declared the victor in this fight. Each labored breath took him closer and closer to that inevitable outcome.

Rafe waited for the hatred and the rage to come, as it always did when he saw his father. But the emotion he felt was pity. His father had turned all those who loved him against him until he had no one.

After the trial, people in Little Elm had realized what kind of man hid behind the guise of a God-fearing deacon and upstanding member of the community and shunned him. He'd left town in disgrace. Rafe would have thought he would have made at least a few friends in Houston who might come and be with him during the last hours of his life.

He turned to Lilly. "He doesn't have any friends or people from Little Elm here?"

Sadly, she shook her head. "Pastor Fowler said it's a workday. I asked Shayla and she said there was no one. He lives here, but she and Myron didn't see each other very much."

Lilly didn't have to say more. Shayla had a tendency to be selfish. She had turned her back on the very man who had always given her her way at a time when he had no one.

He was dying a lonely man.

Shayla, the one person Rafe thought his father loved, if he could love, was there out of duty. He and Lilly were there to lay the past to rest. This is what waited for a man who dispensed cruelty instead of love.

Finally releasing Kristen's hand, Rafe walked to the side of the bed and gently closed his hand over the hand that had inflicted pain and misery on him for as long as he could remember, a hand that had scarred his body. "I forgive you."

Myron's eyes opened. They were deep and dull in his shrunken face. His dry lips moved, but no sound came out. Tears welled in his eyes.

Rafe didn't know if they were from fear of dying or regret at the life he had lived. Either way, he found he could not keep from comforting the man who had given him life. He said the one word he'd sworn never to say again. "Daddy, it's all right. You don't have to be afraid. We're here."

With his gaze riveted on Rafe's, the periods between each labored breath became longer and longer until Myron's chest stilled. His eyelids drifted shut.

"Oh, Daddy!" Shayla cried, turning into her husband's arms.

Rafe rounded the bed and wrapped his arms around the both of them. He remembered the little girl who had followed him everywhere, the little girl he'd carried on his back to school when she was tired, the little girl he'd once adored.

The door opened and a nurse and a doctor came in. Rafe watched the doctor check for a pulse, listen to his father's chest with a stethoscope, then pull the sheet over his head. Rafe was surprised to feel a lump in his throat.

"I'm sorry," the doctor said, then left.

Rafe held out his hand to the man with Shayla. "Rafe Crawford."

David took his hand. "David. We're glad you could come."

"So am I. Take Shayla home," he told him. "I can come by tomorrow and we can go together to make the arrangements."

"Really?" she asked, her lashes wet. "You aren't going to walk away again?"

He realized with a start that is what he had been doing, had kept on doing in life. "No. I'll be here, and when I go back to New Orleans, we'll keep in touch."

She bit her lip. "You don't hate me anymore?"

He searched his heart. "I hated you because you had his love and I didn't. It wasn't your fault."

"But I could have helped." She wiped her face with a soggy tissue. "I was too selfish to care about anyone but me. I'm sorry, Rafe."

"We'll talk."

"Come on, Shayla," David said, leading her from the room.

Rafe went to Lilly and Kristen. "Let's get out of here."

• • •

Kristen was thoughtful as they walked down the hallway of the Wyndham Hotel to Lilly and Adam's suite. Rafe had forgiven his father, but did she dare hope that meant he was willing to give them a chance as well? She tried not to be selfish and think of herself and their baby when his father had just died, but she couldn't help it.

Lilly opened the door and they entered the suite. Adam was sitting on the sofa helping his son read a picture book. Both looked up. Adam Jr.'s black eyes lit up in his cherubic face. Shoving the book at his father, the four-year-old, thirty-five-pound dynamo raced across the room to his brother.

"Rafe!"

Rafe scooped the little boy up and held him high over his head as he'd done since he was a baby. "Hi, Hot Shot."

Kristen watched Rafe, but she also watched Lilly and Adam as Adam kissed Lilly on the cheek and drew her into his arms. She saw what Rafe didn't. Complete confidence in their faces that the man holding their child would protect and keep him safe.

Adam Jr. giggled. "I didn't know you were going to be here. I have a new word game for my computer. We can play it together."

Rafe's expression changed minutely as he lowered Adam Jr. to the ground. "I had to take care of some business."

"Don't I get a hug?" Kristen asked, leaning down with open arms to her nephew, her eyes misty. Rafe had to see that he'd make a wonderful father.

Giggling, Adam Jr. went to her. "Hi, Auntie Kristen."

When she straightened, Adam was standing by her. "Same goes for me. Where's mine?"

Fighting tears, she let him hold her. He had always been there for her, even when she wasn't sure of her place in the world. She knew she could count on her big brother. At times she had envied him his self-assurance and success, but she had never doubted his love.

He frowned down at her, then palmed her forehead. "You don't look well."

Kristen forced a smile. There was a drawback to having a neurosurgeon for a brother. "I'm just a little tired."

"Maybe you should go lie down," Rafe said, hovering over her. "I'll go downstairs and get you a room."

Adam's frown deepened as his gaze went from Kristen, who refused to look at him, to Rafe. "That won't be necessary." He pulled a room key from his pocket. "Mother called and told me you were coming. I have a room for Kristen."

"Rafe, why don't you take Kristen to her room and let her lie down," Lilly said, taking the key from her husband and giving it to Rafe. "She's probably exhausted."

"Can I go?" asked Adam Jr. hopefully.

Rafe put his hand on the little boy's shoulder. As much as he liked having his little brother around, he needed to have some time alone with Kristen. "Not this time, but I'll be back as soon as I can."

"I can go with Kristen," Adam said, his brows bunched. You could almost see the wheels turning in his brain as he tried to figure out what was going on.

"No," Lilly said, looping her arm through his. "Rafe can do it."

From the way Adam's gaze suddenly narrowed, Rafe knew if he didn't take care of Kristen he'd have hell to pay. "I'll take care of her."

"You better," Adam said and gave them the room number.

Gently leading Kristen from the room, he located her suite at the end of the hallway and let them inside. She was so quiet; he kept throwing glances at her. Maybe he shouldn't have let her come with him. If anything happened to her or the baby . . .

Through a wide doorway he saw the oversized bed that had to be custom-made. "We're almost there," he said, then urged her down on the floral print bedspread. He turned on the elongated brass lamp on the nightstand, then pulled the draperies tight, shutting out the strong afternoon sun.

Kneeling in front of her, he removed her pumps. He started to ask her if she could manage the rest, saw the moisture in her eyes, and reached for the buttons on her jacket. He had more than a few bad moments as he removed her clothes, but he finally finished, leaving her in her flesh-toned bra and a scrap of lace for panties.

His mouth was as dry as a desert. "Let's get you under the covers.

It's cold in here." He pulled the covers over her, turned off the light, and started from the room.

A whimper had him whirling and rushing back to the bed. "What is it? What's the matter?"

Kristen sat up in bed, her arms going around his neck. "Please don't go. Don't leave us."

His arms around her were no less desperate. "Oh, baby, I'm sorry."

Her body shook with the force of her tears. "Please."

"No, I mean I'm not going anyplace," he said and felt her still. With one arm remaining around her, he turned on the light again. "I was just going to find the thermostat and turn it up. I'm not leaving you or our baby."

Hope shone in her watery eyes. He kissed the tears away from her face. "In the hospital room I realized something. I'm not like my father. I might have fought against it, but I have people who care about me." He smiled wryly. "Although a few of them might want to hang me up by my thumbs for the way I treated you."

"It doesn't matter now."

"Yes, it does. I'll spend the rest of my life making it up to you." He got off the bed and went down on one knee, her hands in his.

She began to tremble.

"Kristen, I love you."

She couldn't quite draw in her breath.

"Will you marry me? I don't think I can live without you. I know I don't want to."

She could barely breathe. She didn't seem to be able to stop the flow of tears. "I was so afraid you wouldn't want us."

"You're *all* I want. I think I know the answer, but could you just say yes. Please?"

She grinned, free and deliriously happy. "Yes."

He rose and leaned over her, following her back into the wide expanse of the bed, his body covering hers. "My unspoken dream, I'll love you forever."

"I'll love you right back."

His mouth covered hers and he pulled her tight. Clothes were quickly discarded. When her hand touched his scarred back and he didn't flinch, Kristen knew that this was a new beginning for them.

The legacy of hate and cruelty was broken. In its place was one of love and undying devotion that would live on forever through their children and their children's children, to time without end, unbroken and strong.

epilogue

The most sought-after wedding consultant in New Orleans could now breathe easier. She had done it. All three couples were married.

Plucking a glass of champagne from the wrought iron table in Claudette Thibodeaux-Broussard's—a name she'd acquired only five hours ago—gazebo, the consultant took a long, well-deserved sip of King Clos du Mesnil champagne.

The garden wedding had been absolutely beautiful, as had the bride, in a tradition-breaking ivory pantsuit with a tailored half-skirt. Jacques hadn't been able to keep his eyes off her.

"Be careful," she warned two workers as they took up the fifty-by-fifty hardwood dance floor that had to be assembled that morning and taken down immediately afterwards so as not to damage the grass. Claudette was exacting about what she wanted, but the consultant preferred that to a bride who wasn't. Thank goodness Jacques's son had been the same way, since his fiancée, Dr. Angelique Fleming, was busy opening a rehab facility and he had to do most of the planning.

They'd opted for a more formal wedding at St. Louis's Cathedral. They had needed the space. Angelique had every one of her sisters and brothers as attendants. There had been a lot of crying on that afternoon and some not out of happiness. Women were actually sobbing. Damien hadn't noticed. The bride had been stunning and sophisticated in a strapless, champagne beige ball gown. Her matron of honor, Kristen Wakefield Crawford, had to have her dress let out twice.

She was pregnant with twins and glowing with happiness. People were counting on their fingers, but the happy expectant parents certainly didn't appear to care. They'd been married two months earlier in St.

Louis's as well. Rafe Crawford was certainly romantic. He'd built the arch himself under which they had exchanged their vows. The arch was now in their backyard with rose cuttings he'd taken from those he'd planted for his grandmother. He had also given his bride a magnificent walnut hope chest. He was gaining quite a reputation as a furniture maker. Kristen was gaining one in the art world, after being instrumental in placing twenty-three pieces of nineteenth-century African-American art on permanent loan at the Haywood Museum.

The consultant took another sip of champagne and lifted her glass toward the heavens. "To new beginnings and love knocking at someone's door."

Dear Readers:

Thank you so much for your support of *I Know Who Holds Tomorrow*. With your help it made bestselling lists across the country.

I sincerely hope you enjoyed *Somebody's Knocking at My Door*. It was a very difficult book to write, not only because of the extensive research, but because of the emotional pain Rafe endured as a child that continued to haunt him as an adult. Loving caregivers are a blessing that many of us take for granted. I hope we won't from this moment on.

My next release is my romance, *Someone to Love Me*. Also planned is the continuation of the Graysons of New Mexico, with Morgan Grayson's story, *You and No Other*. I'm very excited about both projects and hope you're delighted as well.

Have a wonderful, blessed life,

Francis Ray
www.francisray.com
E-mail: francisray@aol.com
or
P.O. Box 764423
Dallas, Texas 75376

READING GROUP GUIDE

1. In doing the research for this book the author spoke with several people who were physically and emotionally abused as children. Only a few were able to let go of their hatred and move on. Could you forgive and forget?

2. Angelique had a great deal to say about the double standards between men and women. Do you feel a woman can be intimate with a number of men and still be considered a "good woman"? Why or why not?

3. What do you think of Kristen's decision not to expose Maurice? Is sexual harassment still as prevalent or has all the sensitivity training helped? What would you do if you were a victim of sexual harassment? Would you tell your significant other?

4. Kristen and Jacques realized how much Rafe and Claudette needed them and were willing to keep their love a secret for fear it would end their friendship. Could you be a long-suffering, "silent" lover and put the other person's happiness ahead of your own? Why or why not?

5. Angelique's past as an exotic dancer caused problems for her and Damien. How important is background and family when you're dating? If you're thinking of getting serious? Marriage? Do you think whatever happened before you met should stay in the past?

6. Kristen, Angelique, and Claudette were greatly influenced by their first love. How about your first love? Is he/she still a part of your life or do you count your blessings that you moved on?

For more reading group suggestions, visit
www.stmartins.com

Get a
Griffin St. Martin's Griffin